my life as a

Pop album

LJ EVANS

MY LIFE AS A POP ALBUM Copyright © 2017 by LJ Evans

Published by LJ Evans Books
www.ljevansbooks.com
Cover Design © Designed by Grace
Cover Image © Alexey Rumyantsev
Editing Services Megan McKeever and Jenn Lockwood Editing Services

LCN: Publishers' Cataloging-in-Publications
Evans, L. J., 1970- author.
LJ Evans Books, [2017] | Series: My life as an album series ; v. II.
Subjects: LCSH: Brothers--Death--Fiction. | Brothers and sisters--Fiction. | Man-woman relationships-- Fiction. | Forgiveness--Fiction. | Guilt--Fiction. | Travel--Fiction. | GSAFD: Love stories. | LCGFT: Romance fiction. | BISAC: FICTION / Family Life / General. | FICTION / Family Life / Siblings. | FICTION / Friendship. | FICTION / Romance / Contemporary. | FICTION / Romance / New Adult. | FICTION / Southern. | FICTION / Small Town & Rural. | FICTION / Women.
Classification: LCC: PS3605.V3684 M916 2017 | DDC: 813/.6--dc23

ISBN 13: 9781973515746
ISBN 10: 1973515741
ASIN: B079BK5HZX

Printed in the United States of America

Playlist

Available at http://bit.ly/MlaapAlje

Featuring Ed Sheeran

1. I'm a Mess   2. Happier
3. Even My Dad Does Sometimes   4. Tenerefe Sea
5. Where We Land   6. This   7. Perfect   8. Little Bird
9. Fall   10. Kiss Me   11. Firefly   12. Photograph
13. Cold Coffee   14. One   15. Save Myself
16. How Would You Feel?   17. All of the Stars
18. Thinking Out Loud

Message from the Author

Thank you for taking the time to read my story. This book was inspired by music and love, so I hope that you are inspired by those same things as you read the words. In all my books, my characters learn how to live their lives resiliently. They find a way to get through life's challenges with grace, humility, strength, and—most importantly—LOVE.

A lot of authors at this point will give you a long list of their social media sites, places to leave reviews, and a laundry list of their other books, but the truth is, I don't want to give you those things… not yet.

I'd rather you get to reading. I'd rather you fall in love with my characters, their worlds, and the love, laughter, and *family* that is held within these "pages."

So… here it is… Mia's story of recovering from the loss of her brother and finding her own path to her future and the love waiting for her there… I'll touch base with you again AFTER you've read the story…

Happy Reading!

LJ EVANS

♫ *where music & stories collide* ♫

Sigh…okay. Some of you want all that information now, so if you do, please feel free to go to the Second Message from the Author.

 *Dedication*

To philosopher Ed Sheeran for sharing his love songs with the world and for inspiring my love story. To my hubby who understands the words that drive me and loves me anyway. To my daughter who floors me with her own creativity. To my family, readers, and other indie authors who have cheered and supported me in ways that continue to astound me. This is for all of you.

Prologue

Hello

Hello. I'm Good Girl Mia. Mia Andrea Phillips. You probably don't know me, but you might know my brother, Jake. You might know Jake because, for a short while, he was plastered all over the sports channels and magazines as the future of the NFL. That was when he was the superstar quarterback for the University of Tennessee, and before his diabetes and his bad kidneys forced him to quit.

My brother, Jake, was the first one to call me Good Girl Mia. It was his way of teasing me about never getting in trouble. And it's the truth. I am a good girl. There's nothing I can do about it. I have always been the good girl. I've been the friend, the helper, the one you could count on. The one to drive you home if you drank too much. The one to stop you from making monumental mistakes. The one who never gave her parents *any* problems because her brother and his girlfriend gave them enough.

In fact, I've been so good at helping others that I actually gave Jake a kidney. Yep. An actual body part. Unfortunately, that didn't end very well, so maybe I'm not as good at helping out as I'd like to be…

If you are a good girl also, then you know how it goes. You know that good girls never break rules and that they never, ever run off with the bad boy.

Well then, how in holy potato peels did I end up here, with a sexy-as-all-get-out musician lying naked next to me? Well...that's the real story, isn't it?

Chapter One

The Meet

I'M A MESS

"I'm a mess right now, searching for sweet surrender."
-Ed Sheeran

My best friend, neighbor, and almost sister, Cam, once told me that her life could be played out in a series of Taylor Swift songs. I understood what she meant because her life with Jake was like all the old Taylor songs. Angst and heartache and yearning.

After I had graduated from the University of Tennessee and moved back home to run the family business, my life became a series of Ed Sheeran songs. "I'm a Mess" seemed to resonate with me at first because I felt like I was just going through the motions while secretly looking for a sweet surrender. And I definitely couldn't figure out how everything was all going to work out.

I guess that wasn't completely true as I did have one thing going right for me and that was working at my daddy's car dealership. The one he planned on handing over to me in the fall. Contrary to most people's opinion of me, I liked running the dealership. I loved the vague idea that we might be starting a tradition where someday I would pass the dealership on to my kids. Not that there was any chance in the near future of me having children.

Because, let's face it, my personal life was the part of my life in all sorts of disarray. You'd never know that by looking at me. I prided myself on the fact that very few people knew about the emotional turmoil that rolled like waves through me on an almost daily basis. My mama once told me that if you went into someone's house and the place was nice and tidy but the cupboards were a disaster, that it said something about them. I knew exactly what she meant because that described me to a T. Neat and tidy outside, chaos on the inside.

My life wasn't going to get any easier that July because that's when *HE* entered my world, flipping it on its axis even more.

That day, it was hotter than blue blazes with the humidity like a wall you could almost see if you squinted hard enough, and I contemplated lying down on the tile showroom floor to cool off like our dog, Sparky. Instead, I lifted up every last hair on my head and stood under the air conditioning vent trying to dry the sweat off my neck.

And, of course, it was then, when I had my hair, bangs and all, swept up like a Conehead, that he sauntered into our dealership. While I was a sweaty puddle, he looked like a Jamie McGuire book boyfriend come to life.

He was lean and muscular in a blue t-shirt and just-tight-enough ripped jeans that accentuated every sculpted line. Lines of gorgeous muscles that belonged in an underwear ad. He was tall, but not too tall, around about six feet, and had sexy, bed-tousled looking brown hair that highlighted his pale gray eyes. Eyes that were the color of the winter skies right before a tornado. I was a sucker for a boy with tattoos even if I thought I'd never date someone who had them. And this piece of gorgeousness had them.

There were words wrapped around each wrist and some sort of bird on his neck. None of it was easy to make out over a distance, but that made me think about how, if I was close enough, I could brush aside those curling ends and investigate more. I suddenly wanted to do that very much. Every fiber in my body was aching to drop my grossly sweaty hair and sweep up his, just so I could get a good look at him and his tattoos while inhaling his scent.

Of course, this had me rolling my eyes inwardly at myself. And it was then that I remembered how ridiculous I must look with no hair and a sweaty grimace. So, I slowly, ever so slowly, let my dark hair drop down, wishing I wasn't as absurd as I looked.

On most days, I was proud of my hair. I'd just spent thirty minutes in normal Tennessee two o'clock humidity, however. So I was pretty sure it was flat where I didn't want it to be and curling funny where it shouldn't. But better down than cupped in my hand like a swim cap.

"Ms. Phillips?" he asked in a voice that was lyrically smooth, like a chord from an Ed Sheeran love song. He sounded just like he looked: sultry and intoxicating. The Good Girl Mia side of me was screaming to back away from the boy.

"Yes?" I was surprised to hear my own voice sound so normal while looking at this stunning human being. I've read a lot. I mean hundreds upon hundreds of books, and this guy could certainly be on any cover and attract sales like flies attract fish.

He proved that even more when he smiled, and the smile took over his entire face. It was a smile that showed off the cleft in his chin and eyes that sparkled like rain hitting those clouds inside them.

"Really?" he asked while his smile spread more.

"Um. Yes, why?" I asked.

He threw a thumb back over his shoulder. "Those folks back there said I should talk to the owner. They sent me to pick up the car for the charity auction at the Abbott farm tonight."

I didn't know what to address first. That he didn't believe I was the owner, which—to be fair—was a completely normal mistake as I was only twenty-two, or the fact that he was supposedly picking up Jake's cherried-out Camaro. The Camaro that my family and Cam had agreed to auction off for the American Diabetes Association.

I wasn't expecting a dark-haired bad boy to be picking up Jake's Camaro. I was surprised that Daddy or Cam would let anyone drive it. They were having a hard enough time giving it away. But then, I guess it shouldn't really be a surprise as none of us wanted to drive it. It was still too emotional for both our families. It had sat in the dealership's showroom since his death. The mechanics kept it running, but that was it.

"Who exactly told you that you were to pick it up?" I asked, making a beeline for the management offices in the back with him tagging along behind me.

"Blake. Well, I guess it was Cam. But Blake said to take her orders as if they were his own. I kind of think it's really the other way around with those two sometimes." He winked at me. "Do you know them?"

Again, I didn't know what to respond to first. The wink that left my still upside-down heart pattering like a kitten who'd just chased a bug, or the absolute nonsense he'd asked about me knowing Blake and Cam.

"She's pretty much my sister," I told him flatly as we reached the office. And she pretty much was. We'd grown up next door, and our families shared everything, including Sunday dinners. And if Jake had been alive, she would have married him and made the sister thing legit. Instead, she was with Blake who was also from our town but lived in Nashville now as an entertainment lawyer.

I pulled out my iPhone from the desk drawer and texted Cam.

ME: There's some moron here who says you told him to come get Jake's car?

I waved the book boyfriend into a chair, buzzed the intercom, and asked Mary Beth for an iced tea. "Would you like anything?" I asked the man.

"Sure, iced tea sounds great."

My phone buzzed back.

CAM: LOL So you've met Blake's pride and joy?

I stared at the text like it should make sense. She hadn't really answered.

Mary Beth, who'd worked for my daddy for almost as long as I'd been alive, brought in two sweet teas. She fluffed her hair that was ratted tall like she still belonged to the eighties while she took in the BB—the book boyfriend—in front of her.

"Thanks, Mary Beth."

"That's such a southern name." The BB's grin returned with the cleft in his chin stretching in a way that made it seem like it was smiling too. "I'm really glad I came to Tennessee."

He took a big gulp of the sweet tea and choked almost as if he'd slammed back a shot of whiskey. "Holy shit, that's sweeter than cotton candy."

Mary Beth smiled politely at him. "Thank you." Then she turned to me. "Anything else you need?"

Mary Beth seemed to think that any time the parts manager, a mechanic, or one of the male salesmen came into the office, she had to chaperone me like a debutant. It was both pleasant and smothering at the same time.

"I think we're good. Thanks. I'll buzz if I need anything," I said as I texted Cam back.

ME: You're telling me the moron is allowed to drive Jake's prize possession?

I took a sip of the tea and turned to find the keys of the Camaro on the wall behind me. When I turned back to the BB, he was watching me carefully, and I literally fought the urge to wipe at my eyes and fix my hair. I'd never been a girl overly concerned with the way I looked. I didn't go overkill with the makeup. I fixed my hair in the morning and typically forgot about it until it went up into a messy bun at the end of the day. But this man, this BB, made me want to appear as good as any book girlfriend could look.

My phone buzzed.

CAM: Maybe you're right. Can you bring it? And bring the pride and joy back with you. Blake will never let me live it down if he gets lost.

I sighed. "They've had a change of heart. I'll give you a ride."

"What? They don't want me to pick it up or the car isn't being donated?"

"Don't take it personally. The car. It's just… special," I said with a pang of emotion in my voice that I hadn't expressed aloud in a long time.

"But the dealership is donating it anyway?"

"No. My family is donating it."

He grinned. "Oh. I see."

"I doubt it."

I finished my sweet tea quickly. I suddenly needed to get all of this over with. The car and the BB would both be deposited safely, and I could go home where, hopefully, they would both stop pulling at the scabs inside me.

"I've been asked to give you a ride back out to the ranch. Seems there is some fear of you getting lost," I told him.

The BB chuckled. "Damn Blake. He never lets anything slide, does he?"

The BB's laugh made my insides go squishy again. I suddenly resented it. I didn't want this temptation to Mary coming into my life and stirring up the pot. I had enough on my plate with taking over the dealership, starting my MBA classes in the fall, and trying to recover from a broken heart. I didn't need him here making me feel anything. Especially not the desperate longing that hit me when I watched him.

"Let's go, Lost Boy," I said as I grabbed my purse, my phone, and the Camaro keys. I stopped by Mary Beth's desk.

"I'm off. I'll be at the Abbott's ranch if you need me for anything." I looked over at the sales folks that were waiting in the air-conditioned room for a new customer that wasn't going to show in the summer heat. "I guess I'll have to leave Denise in charge for now. She's the only one that can sign contracts while Ben is on vacation."

Mary Beth patted my shoulder. "Don't you worry, sugar. We'll keep this place rolling. Remember, we're closing early, anyway. Everyone in town will be at Jake's fundraiser."

I swallowed back the lump in my throat, nodded, and walked out of the showroom with the BB following me.

Chapter Two

The Camaro

HAPPIER

"Promise that I'll not take it personal baby
If you're moving on with someone new,
Cause baby you look happier, you do."
-Ed Sheeran

As I rounded the corner of the building, I stopped suddenly at the sight of Jake's Camaro. It wasn't like I hadn't expected it. I'd come out to drive it for goodness' sake, but it was still hard to see.

Daddy had had the body department take it out and detail it. It looked sparkling red in the shimmery sunshine. It was so Jake that it was hard to even look at, let alone drive. Jake had loved this car. Even more, he'd loved Cam sitting next to him in it.

"You okay?" The BB seemed to sense that he had stepped into the middle of something but wasn't quite sure what.

I nodded, unlocked the door, and slid into the driver's seat. I reached across and unlocked the passenger side, and the BB got in as I adjusted the seat. Daddy was pretty much the only one to drive it after Jake, and they'd been close to the same height at a lean, mean six feet two inches or so. My short frame made it a stretch even with the seat as close to the dash as I could get it. The truth was, sixties muscle cars weren't made for short girls.

I adjusted the mirrors and then finally, unable to delay it anymore, turned the ignition. It roared to life and instantly brought back memories of me in the treehouse with a flashlight and the sound of Jake coming home from the lake. You could hear the car all the way down the street, typically, with the music blaring. And yet, our neighbors had never complained. No one had ever told my parents that he drove too fast or had his music too loud. They all looked the other way. I guess that was mostly due to his superstar status in town.

"You sure you're okay?" the BB asked.

"Stop asking that," I said with a huff that I didn't really mean. It was bad enough that I had to drive Jake's car. I didn't need some perceptive hunk delving into my emotions.

"Okay," he said with a grin that said he found me slightly humorous, and I didn't know if I hated that or liked that.

I pulled out of the lot and headed down the street, making the turns automatically till we got out to the pastures and farms. We passed the turnoff for the lake, and I couldn't help but let my head be drawn that way ever so slightly; wondering if Jake was watching over us all from his place by the tree with branches like a goalpost that he and Cam had loved.

"So, you know Cam well then?" he probed further.

"We grew up together," I said, not wanting to be rude, but definitely not wanting to talk.

"You know Blake, too?"

I just nodded.

"Don't feel like you have to elaborate or anything," the BB said.

I didn't want to elaborate, but I could also sense my Southern manners kicking in. It wasn't polite to let your guest do all the talking. Not that he was really my guest. I hadn't invited him to Jake's fundraiser, but if Blake and Cam had, then it was pretty much the same thing.

I sighed. "I'm sorry. I'm just a little emotional today. This was Jake's car."

I could feel the BB's eyes boring into me, but I didn't look over. "Jake, as in the guy the fundraiser is named after?"

I just nodded.

He seemed to be putting it all together, which meant I didn't have to spell it out for him. "You're his sister?"

I nodded again. I am his sister, but it still felt like it should be said in the past tense. I was his sister. He's dead. God, I couldn't believe I had tears in my eyes. What in bejesus was wrong with me? I hadn't cried over Jake in a long time, and especially not openly in front of another human being.

"Wow. I'm sorry. That sucks," he said.

As we neared the ranch, I tried to get my emotions back under control by turning the attention back to him.

"And who are you exactly?"

"I was hoping you'd ask," he said with that infectious, knowing smirk that simultaneously made me want to wipe it off and join along. "I'm Derek Waters. Musician. Songwriter. My band is playing tonight."

Of course this beautiful BB would be a musician, I thought to myself with a whole pile of sarcasm. Cam had said he was one of Blake's protégés so I should have put two and two together instead of being stunned brain-dead by his gorgeousness. Blake did specialize in writing contracts for up-and-coming musicians after all.

"I can't believe they were going to let you drive Jake's car," I groused before I could help myself. Then I flushed in embarrassment because that was definitely not something a polite Southern girl was supposed to say.

To my surprise, he laughed at me. A big laugh that seemed to come from his belly and had me glancing in that direction, taking in how awfully good he looked in those snug jeans of his. This made me want to rip my eyes off and stuff them away where they couldn't do any more damage.

I pulled into Blake's grandparents' farm and was taken aback by the volume of trucks and cars. A massive tent had been put up near the barn, and people were busy hanging twinkle lights and setting up tables with flowers.

Somewhere in the middle of all that would be Cam, going a mile a minute even though she was eight months pregnant. It hadn't been a planned pregnancy. She and Blake weren't even married yet. Like all things Cam, stuff happened before she thought about it. She appeared to be taking it in stride, which seemed so not the Cam that Jake and I had grown up with that it made me sad once more.

Old Cam would have been kicking walls at the idea of carrying anyone's baby, and especially the idea of carrying anyone's but Jake's.

"Shall I go see where they want the car parked?" the BB asked, and I realized that I needed to start thinking of him by his real name, Derek.

"That would be great," I said.

He jumped out of the car, and I literally sighed with relief. I thanked God that I could go back to being my normal self instead of the drooling Neanderthal girl I seemed to have become around him.

Blake found me sitting in the car. He leaned his shaggy, blonde-haired head into the window to give me a half hug. "Hey, Mia! Why don't you get out, and I'll drive the car over to where we want it set up?"

"You don't trust me?" I asked, teasing.

"She seems completely trustworthy to me," Derek said, coming up behind Blake.

I couldn't help the visible eye-roll. Blake saw it and grinned his joyful smile that was never far from his face. I could tell why Blake and Derek got along. They both seemed like generally happy guys. I wondered what it must be like to be that happy all the time.

Blake turned to Derek and waved his finger at him. "No."

Derek grinned. "I didn't—"

"No!" Blake cut him off.

"Hey!" I protested because I was a good driver. I was as careful driving as I was with almost everything in my life.

Blake took me in and then started backpedaling, "That's not what I meant. Honest."

Evans

I realized I was missing something, but I wasn't sure I wanted to know what it was. Not with Derek belly laughing again. It made my stomach flop like when you flipped backwards over the top of the monkey bars for the first time.

I got out of Jake's car, grabbed my bag, and headed for the tent. "I'll leave you two children to whatever it is you're doing. I'm assuming Cam's inside?"

I didn't wait for a response. I could still hear Derek laughing, and it sounded like Blake punched his shoulder, but I didn't bother to look back. I was glad to be leaving gorgeous with gorgeous behind me.

In the tent, I found Cam going a mile a minute like I had expected, which was still good to see because for a while after Jake had died, she'd come to a full stop like she never had in her whole life. Now, with Blake and the baby, she was almost back to normal, except that it was a different normal.

Her dark hair, with its chestnut highlights, was shorter than it used to be when we were growing up, but she still had it in a ponytail in acknowledgement of the heat. She was in a t-shirt dress which, again, was so anti the old Cam that it was hard to take in. It was probably much more comfortable than jeans due to the little round ball sticking out of her middle, though.

"Cam!" I said and hugged her. She hugged me back, and this stupid, emotional me got teary-eyed, causing Cam to notice.

"Hey, kiddo!" She pulled back, taking me in. "What's wrong?"

I waved her off. "Nothing."

"Did the moron upset you?"

"No. No. I think it was just driving the Camaro."

As I said it, Blake drove it up onto the grass near the tent, and the beefy engine got to us both. "He really loved that car," Cam said quietly.

We both stared for a moment, taking it in. Cam had ridden in the car way more than I had. She'd been Jake's sidekick and soulmate from the time she was born, and even my birth, two years after her, had never come in between them.

Blake exited the car, smiled at her, and then went off in a different direction once Cam had smiled back. It made me wonder, like I had a million times before, what Jake would think of Cam and Blake. Would he be like Ed Sheeran in "Happier"? Would he be happier to see her with someone new rather than with no one? I thought he would like to see her being taken care of and with someone that knew them as well as Blake had. I thought he would like to see her able to smile once more, but I also thought he'd hate the idea of her in anyone's arms.

Cam was never one for tears, and even though the Camaro had momentarily gotten to her, she'd already turned back into her normal, bossy self which was good because it kept her from punching something instead. She handed me a box of mason jars filled with candles.

"Here, they go on all the tables, according to the event planner."

"Okay, but I have to leave soon to get ready. I'm sweaty as sin," I told her.

"You'll just get sweaty all over again. We've got the misters and fans set up, but today had to be one of the muggiest days of July, didn't it?"

17

"Are you wearing that dress?" I asked her.

"You don't think it works?" Cam gave me her mischievous smile that used to mean she was plotting against Jake, but now was aimed at me.

"Yes! You look beautiful. I'm just trying to decide what I should wear."

"I'm just teasing. I have a purple dress in the house."

She was referring to Blake's grandparents' house here at the ranch. She and Blake were staying with them for all the fundraiser shenanigans. Honestly, though, they stayed here a lot when they visited from Nashville. Blake's grandparents had more rooms. Plus, I think it was easier for Cam to be here than at our house or her house where everything reminded her of Jake. Or, really, of her and Jake—the one being they used to be.

I took the box as instructed and placed the jars on the tables near the flowers that were already wilting in the heat. When I'd made it about halfway through, I was surprised to find the box lifted out of my hands.

I turned to find Derek smiling at me again. "Let me help."

"Don't you need to be practicing or something?" I asked with a wave to the stage because the last thing I needed was this BB by my side again.

"Won't make any difference this late in the game. We'll either suck or be a hit," he said. He gave a self-deprecating shrug accompanied by yet another sexy smile.

For some reason, this time the smile reminded me just a little of Hayden's smile when he wanted something. And I was trying to forget all of Hayden Hollister's smiles, even though they lived with me most nights. This had me narrowing my eyes at Derek in a way that probably wasn't fair to him but I was sure was well deserved anyway.

"I'm sure you have something better to do than help me put out mason jars, unless I'm not trusted to do that either."

"I'd trust you to do anything you wanted to my… tables," he said. My stomach did that monkey bar flip again because he was definitely flirting with me. It had taken me awhile to really figure it out for sure because I wasn't used to guys flirting with me.

Well, that wasn't exactly true. I was used to slimy guys hitting on my size E's and talking to them more than my face, but gorgeous BB musicians weren't normally the kind to do anything with me, much less flirt.

I tried to grab the box back, but he easily shifted it away from me and moved to the next table where he handed me a jar. There wasn't much I could do unless I wanted to make a huge scene, so I just took the jar and placed it on the table. Thankfully, we were done in no time.

"What are you doing now?" Derek asked as he twirled the empty box in his hands. He seemed wound tight with inner energy. It was like Cam and Jake, and even Blake. But never me. I was a read-a-book-and-bake-cookies kind of girl, not a run-until-I-broke kind of girl.

"Going home to shower and change," I said with a shrug.

His grinned widened, if possible, cleft stretching even more, and then he said, "You can't say things like that to me."

He gave me a once-over, and I suddenly hated my dark pantsuit with a passion, even though just that morning I'd loved it as much as I'd loved Hayden. As president of our business fraternity, Hayden had been all about business fashion, setting the tone with his custom-made suits.

I was just about to say something sarcastic back to his sexy innuendo when the box he was spinning flew out of his hands, and the corner hit me in my right breast before falling to the ground.

"Holy profanity!" I gasped, covering my injured part with my hand.

"Shit!" he said at the same time. He reached out to touch me and then stopped, realizing where I was hurt.

"I'm..." He didn't even know what to say as he stared at my hand and the breast it was covering.

Blake and Cam took that unfortunate moment to come up to us, with me clutching my boob, and Derek acting like he had permanently maimed me.

Blake put his arm around Derek's shoulders. "I thought I made myself clear on this matter."

Blake was smiling, but there was a tone to his voice that was deadly serious.

Cam took it all in.

"No way in hell, Derek. She's off limits," Cam said. Suddenly, I got what it was all about earlier with Derek and Blake.

I was used to Cam protecting me. She'd been my shield when it came to boys ever since I'd entered high school and Jake had gone off to college. The only boy to date me then had gone through her, which was no easy feat. But I wasn't a fourteen-year-old virgin anymore, and their protectiveness was just humiliating.

"You guys are embarrassing," I said.

Cam looked dubiously at my hand on my breast. I removed it even though it was still smarting. "It was an accident."

Everyone stood there for a moment, Blake sending "back off" vibes to Derek, me still mortified, and Cam looking like she was ready to start a fight, baby bump and all.

"You guys are awful. Anyone able to give me a ride back to town?" I asked, changing the subject.

"I have to go back to the hotel and get ready too. You can ride with me," Derek said. The three of us groaned.

"It's just a ride," Derek said with a smirk that really suggested it might be something else entirely. It seemed that he was egging Blake and Cam on because it wasn't like he was going to attack my sweaty, suit-clad body in the back seat of whatever vehicle he owned.

"You have the rental here?" Blake asked.

"Shit, no. Owen dropped me off at the dealership on his way back to the hotel."

Blake sighed. "Take my truck."

Blake fished the keys out of his jeans pocket and flung them at Derek, who caught them deftly. I would have dropped them. I was not anywhere near the athlete that Cam and Jake had been. Jake had gotten his football scholarship to UTK, and Cam had won a diving medal at the World Championships before she'd been recruited by Virginia Tech, whereas I could barely stand on a treadmill without falling over.

Cam's eyes narrowed at Derek as he swung the keys in a circle around his slender fingers. "She's my sister, dipshit, got it?"

Derek looked all innocent, but his eyes were flashing a challenge that said otherwise. It made me tingle all over in a way that was not normal for me. Because, butterbeer, the thought of him treating me in a non-sisterlike fashion was enough to add another layer of sweat to my already sweaty body.

"God, Cam, I'm not twelve," I said before turning to Derek. "I'd appreciate the ride."

Derek and I walked away, but I could feel Blake and Cam's eyes on us all the way to the truck. The passenger door was closest to us, and Derek grabbed the handle and opened it for me. "Thanks," I said with a gulp. It felt too date-like for me to be comfortable with, even though I knew we weren't going on a date. The furthest thing from it.

He climbed into the driver's side, and we took off out of the ranch. I slyly tried to take him in as he drove. He had to be a little older than me. Maybe twenty-four to my twenty-two? But he had a youthfulness to him that made him seem younger. Maybe it was the sense of carefreeness about him. Even before Jake, I hadn't had a carefree bone in my body. But now…now that I was all that Mama and Daddy had left, I took even fewer risks, which meant literally none.

He turned and caught me staring. He lifted an eyebrow and grinned. "They told me no."

I flushed and looked out the window. "As if."

"I haven't heard anyone use that term since the eighties," he chuckled at me again.

"You weren't alive in the eighties."

"Well, I've seen a lot of eighties films."

"They are the best," I said with a sigh.

"Yep."

I turned toward him. "You really think that, or are you just appeasing me?"

"Two things I never joke about: music and movies."

"Those are the only two things?"

"I'm sure there are a few more things, but I can't think of any at the moment."

At least not any he wanted to share, because I swear I saw the first look of seriousness flash over his face. But it was gone as quickly as it had come.

"I get the music, but why movies?"

"Well, my brother is Dylan Waters," he said, as if that was supposed to answer my question.

"Am I supposed to know who that is?"

Surprise washed over his face. "Director. Producer. *The Spy Network*?"

He named a movie that had taken the world by storm last year. It was liked by fans and critics, and it had won a bunch of Oscars. I hadn't seen it because I'd been busy with senior year and Hayden, or rather, busy with not having Hayden. Instead, I'd been busy writing love letters to someone who hadn't chosen me, and burying my head in books as a way of avoiding my reality.

"I heard it was good," I said with a shrug.

He laughed again. "You haven't seen it?"

I just shook my head.

"I think you've surprised me at least twenty times since I've met you." This time, there was no smile to accompany the words. Instead, there was that quiet, thoughtful look on his face once more.

"Turn left here," I said as we approached town. We drove down the street in silence. "It's the one on the right with the green truck."

He pulled into the driveway behind Daddy's truck, and I felt like I was fifteen and my only high school boyfriend was bringing me home. As if I should be expecting something but wasn't sure if I wanted it or not. He turned to me. "Do you need a ride back out to the ranch?"

"Nah, I'll go with my parents."

I reached for the handle and was surprised as all get out when he stopped me. When his hand hit my bare wrist, heat seeped from his fingers into my skin like honey into a biscuit. And just like him, that feeling was smooth, silky, and dangerous. Yet it was also soothing, somehow. Like comfort food with a kick.

I thought maybe I needed to stick my head in an ice chest if I was getting this discombobulated over one touch from a boy band star. I looked down at his hand, and he pulled back as if he was as shocked as I was that he'd stopped me.

"I'll see you tonight," he said.

It was one of those sexy, more-of-a-statement-than-a-question kind of things that made me swallow hard and look away. All I could do was nod at him and then climb out of the truck, hoping that I hadn't left my pride on the seat along with the sweat stains.

I couldn't help but look back and saw him wave as he pulled out of the driveway. Suddenly, I was dreading tonight on a whole new level. And maybe that was good because it would distract me enough that I wouldn't break down. I'd be able to be the quiet, supportive Mia everyone had come to count on

Chapter Three

The Fundraiser

EVEN MY DAD DOES SOMETIMES

"So don't wipe your eyes.
Tears remind you you're alive…
But just for tonight, hold on."
-Ed Sheeran

When I entered the house, the aroma of chocolate and cinnamon hit me. It was the smell of Mama's favorite cookies. She tended to bake when she was anxious or upset. It was something we often did together, coming up with weird and delicious new concoctions. So, with the fundraiser tonight, it was no surprise to find her cleaning bowls while warm cookies rested on a plate. I took one and then gave her a hug.

"Was that Blake's truck?" Mama asked.

"Yeah. His new one-hit wonder gave me a ride back after I took the Camaro out to the ranch," I told her carefully.

I saw Mama's breath catch. Even though there was no way she wanted me to know it, getting rid of the Camaro had probably been hardest on her. It wasn't that it was any easier having it sit at the dealership where it reminded us all of the person who would never drive it again. But I also don't think any of us knew how to handle the thought of giving it away to some stranger.

Maybe this would help her be ready to tackle Jake's room. Four years later, it still looked like he and Cam were going to come back from college and take up residence in the place they'd spent their whole lives.

Truth was, my heart broke a little thinking of poor Mama having to continually say goodbye to her baby boy. It made the guilt swarm over me like mosquitos at the lake at dusk. It made me wish again that I could trade places with my brother. The superstar with so much potential versus the girl that was pretty much invisible.

Because I couldn't make that wish come true, I did what I always did and tried to make Mama feel better with another squeeze. It was a poor substitute for her lost son, but it was all I was able to do.

"It'll be okay," I told her. The words felt false even to me. It wasn't that I didn't want things to be okay. I desperately wanted them to be okay, but I had no faith yet it would happen. Sometimes I wondered how Mama didn't hate me when I'd failed her and Daddy and Jake and Cam.

"You smell sweaty," she said, hugging me tighter. That brought me back to that beautiful BB, Derek, and I was suddenly all mortification. Smelling sweaty in the presence of such gorgeousness was god-awful. Especially when his gorgeousness hadn't smelled sweaty at all. He'd smelled like… I don't know…woods, and life, and something I couldn't name yet.

"Ew. Thanks a lot. I've been around a cute guy, and my mama tells me just how awful I look."

I immediately wanted to take the words back when Mama turned fast to look me in the eye. "You? Around a cute guy? Where is my Mia and what have you done with her?"

I grimaced because wasn't that the truth. Good Girl Mia was never around hot musicians. No one at home knew that I'd, once upon a time, been around a golden boy who'd left me for someone else. That humiliation I kept all to myself.

"I'm going to take a shower and get rid of the sweat," I told her, but really I was hoping I could get rid of my mixed-up thoughts.

I heard Mama chuckle as I left, and that helped because I'd made her laugh, and sometimes I thought she had forgotten how.

When I was safely ensconced in the shower, I let myself cry a little. Not enough to leave me with puffy, red eyes, but enough to relieve some emotions so that I would be able to hold myself together at the fundraiser where it was going to be a true test. I tried to remind myself that philosopher Ed was right, that even daddies cried sometimes, and that it was okay. I just couldn't let anyone else see. And tonight, I definitely had to hold it together.

♫ ♫ ♫

By the time I stepped out of Daddy's truck, I had my shield back on. I was going to be able to hold up Mama and Cam without collapsing myself. Because the whole car thing was going to chip off another piece of their souls. So, I had to stay strong.

I hit the grass and wobbled. I wanted to bang my head against a wall again. What had possessed me to wear the one pair of sparkly stilettos that I owned? Then I did an inner eye-roll because I couldn't hide from myself the truth as to why I was wearing these stupid heels. I'd had a stupid musician on my stupid brain when I'd picked out my stupid outfit.

Daddy came around the truck with Mama's hand in his, and he offered me his elbow, which I happily took. He made my heart jump with pleasure when he looked down and said, "You sure look pretty tonight, baby girl."

Daddy wasn't one for a whole lot of compliments. Never had been. It wasn't like we didn't know he loved us and was proud of us. I mean, how couldn't he be proud of Jake's superstar status? And it wasn't like he'd just turn the reins of the dealership over to just anyone, daughter or not, so I knew he was proud of me too. But his compliments came in extremely small doses, so I savored them when I got them.

Daddy's words reminded me that I wasn't just in stupid stilettos, but I was also in a dark green minidress that I hadn't worn in over a year. Not that I had a whole lot of choices in my wardrobe. I had business clothes, and college slacker clothes, and not much else.

But this dress was a huge mistake, and not just because it was short and showed more of my E-sized boobs than I was normally comfortable showing. It was a huge mistake because it was the dress I'd worn on my semi-date with Hayden. The date that had ended in me losing my virginity. It was pretty pathetic that I'd been at the end of my junior year of college when I'd finally lost it, but my high school boyfriend and I hadn't lasted past his graduating. Truth be told, while Tim Martin had been a good kisser, nothing had made me want to get butt naked with him and do the deed.

Hayden had though. He'd been the first boy to make me feel the zap. That zap of kinetic energy that travels all the way through you. He was a golden boy. One hundred percent golden with golden hair, golden eyes, golden skin, and a golden life. He wasn't quite a player, but he had two of us girls on his string—hook, line, and sinker. I'd been the loser. I'd been the fish thrown back in the water for later, and it had broken my heart.

Now here I was, wearing this stupid dress on yet another emotional night where another gorgeous guy had sort of paid attention to me and was probably capable of breaking me in more ways than I'd been broken before. Well, maybe not. Giving a kidney and having it kill someone could really do a number on you.

As I didn't have much in my closet that didn't rattle your eyes with a cry of "business," it had been this or a little black dress I had to wear a strapless bra with. Take it from me, size E breasts and strapless bras just really aren't made for each other. They're more like lemon and milk.

I tried to shake myself out of my reflective musing as we walked into the big tent and were greeted by a rep from the American Diabetes Association.

"Mr. and Mrs. Phillips, thank you so much for holding this fundraiser tonight. I'm sure your son, Jake, would be very proud to be a part of it."

Jake would have been proud. He would have been smiling his godlike smile because he'd always loved being the center of attention. Thrived on it. He'd been raised as the center of everyone's attention. Our parents. Cam's parents. Cam herself. Our town. He'd even been the focus of the whole country for the two seasons he'd played for UTK, his smile plastered across the television screens.

Mama looked away and tried not to cry, and I immediately wanted to strangle the guy's throat. It wasn't his fault though. Who would know that, four years in, the loss of Jake was still a burning volcano in all our lives?

"You're welcome. We wanted to do this. Cam wanted to do this. If it helps anyone else…" Daddy choked up and then got hold of himself. "If it helps even one person, it's worth it."

Thank God that Cam and Blake came in then and saved us all from breaking into an embarrassing round of tears and if only's. Saved me from blurting out just how sorry I was that I couldn't have been enough to save him. It allowed me to readjust my shield so that it would stay in place.

Blake had Cam's arm through his, and she was glowing in the way that only Cam could ever glow. Like all the flames from the candles on the tables were magically being drawn to her. That glow made it nearly impossible to look anywhere else. Blake certainly couldn't. Course, it probably helped that the baby kicking inside her was his.

Her purple chiffon accentuated her tall, slender frame that, even with the baby bump, was still so athletic she probably could have beat Jake in a race at the lake. Her wavy chestnut locks were drawn up in a half-do that her best friend, Wynn, had taught her and I how to do when we were nothing more than tweens trying to be cool. Wynn herself would probably be wearing it when she showed up later.

Tonight, I hadn't worn our traditional half-do. I'd still been as hot as a used tea bag when I'd gotten out of the shower, and I'd known our Tennessee summer would continue to blast its heat and humidity at us, so I'd opted for a French twist that was already trying to escape. But it would keep my hair off my neck and out of my face for the majority of the night. The huge disadvantage was that I now had nothing to hide behind. I'd have to be really good at the mask that I wore.

I did pretty good holding it together. Even after dinner and the speeches that Cam led, I kept myself poised, ready to catch Mama or Cam if they faltered. Cam surprised me by being able to speak about Jake in a way that she never had been able to at his funeral. One look at Blake, smiling encouragingly at her, told me all I needed to know. That was the one thing that was different and better about Cam now. She was so much calmer with Blake than she had ever been with Jake.

I think, with Jake, she'd always been on high alert. He'd had so many people pulling at him that she'd always felt the need to draw him back to her. To keep him focused on the two halves that they were together. With Blake, she seemed content. Like she was still going the speed-of-light pace she always had, but now she had Blake moving equally fast alongside her.

Sure, Blake had his own little group of people pulling at him, but he wasn't the star. Instead, he signed the stars to contracts, which brought me back to Blake's protégé: the one onstage.

It was clear Derek shined in a way that wasn't far off from the way Cam and Jake had. There's always this aura that bubbles around dynamic people that invisibles like me don't ever quite get, but can see and stare at in awe anyway. Derek was like that, especially onstage. Moving as if the stage was somehow part of his being. Guitar and microphone and him blending into something that was almost magical.

I was surprised by his band. I guess I'd expected some wannabe pop band, but instead it was rich with blues and grit. It made me think of the old-time jazz and blues singers that my best friend, Harry Winston, and I used to listen to on vinyl records at his grandma's house.

Derek sang one song in particular that hit my heart like a hammer to brick. It was full of deeply felt words about humanity being a collage of mistakes made beautiful. I was a book girl, and words were like a drug to me. They could bring me under with a well-positioned adjective. His song was like that, drawing me under.

I didn't even realize how focused on Derek I had become until Cam sank down next to me and said, "He definitely didn't get hit with the ugly stick."

"Hmm?" I drew my eyes from the band and Derek to Cam to see she was quite enjoying my momentary lapse. I tried to throw her off the scent with a guffaw, but, like any sister, she knew me too well.

Instead of teasing me like I expected, she took a direction I didn't quite follow. "You remember Seth?"

Who wouldn't remember the blue-eyed, Cuban hottie? He'd taken up kingship in our high school my freshman year and trailed Cam like she was the only thing holding him above water.

"You remember the line of women he left behind?" I got it then. She was warning me off Derek, like Cam had always warned me off boys that she didn't think were good enough for me.

"Do I have stupid written on my face?" I asked.

"Well…"

I punched her in the shoulder gently, and she punched me back. It hurt, but I knew better than to hit Cam and not expect return fire.

"If you weren't pregnant, I'd kick you," I told her.

She just chuckled, and we turned back to the stage to where Derek was crooning. His gritty voice wafted over me like the scent of warm bread, sending chills down my spine.

Unfortunately, he caught me looking at him, and that sexy smile came over his face, stretching his cleft and making me feel like I was flipping over those darn monkey bars all over again. I should have been kicking myself instead of trying to kick Cam. Because nothing good could come from a girl like me thinking a book boyfriend like him was stunning. Hadn't I already learned that painful lesson?

"Did I tell you I saw him?" Cam asked, and I'd been so entranced in Derek's beauty and my own brooding that it took me a moment to realize that she was referring, once again, to Seth Carmen who'd hit her at her junior prom and gone scurrying back to New York when Jake had punched him back.

"You did?"

She nodded. "Blake and I were in L.A. for Derek's contract signing last month, and we got invited to this huge shindig at his brother's house. His brother's some bigwig director. Anywho, when I walked in, there was Seth's waterfall."

"The one he made at his grandparents' house?"

"Yep, and then there he was too. It was kind of surreal."

"How was he?"

"Sober, calm. He seemed grown-up. He had a girl with him that appeared to be keeping him on his toes, and all I can say is, good for her."

"So, Derek's brother bought the waterfall?" I was trying to put the puzzle pieces of Derek together. He'd told me just how famous his brother was, but I hadn't equated it to the kind of famous that puts showy art in their houses. Derek didn't come off as anything more than a struggling musician.

"He bought it for a million and a half dollars," Cam said with an awe that rarely comes from Cam.

"Get out of town? Really?"

"Yep. That's according to Keith, who works for Derek's brother now and was there with some stunning man on his arm."

"No way!" I breathed out.

"Yep."

"Well, good for Keith."

While I had to admit that it seemed strange to think of Seth, the moody bad boy we'd known, as a famous, calm grown-up, it didn't seem as strange to think of Keith with a boyfriend.

And holy banana slugs, thinking of sexy men made my eyes flirt back to the sensual crooner onstage before I could help it. Derek reminded me a lot more of my brother Jake's charisma than Seth's prowling panther. Derek seemed more… eagle than cat.

That man's eyes drifted continually to our table, and every time they did, I felt like my whole world stopped. Cam insinuated that he was a player from a family of money, and he'd seemed smooth and confident earlier, but here he was making me feel like I was the center of his focus. Of course, that was probably just my imagination. Hayden had said I was good at imagining things that weren't there.

Maybe all the women in the audience felt that Derek was focused on them. Maybe that was his charm. Maybe he was a magical boy-nymph, drawing women with his songs like sea nymphs drew sailors.

"Jake would've beat the crap out of him just for looking at you," Cam said wistfully. She'd done really well all night, but now I caught a glimpse of the hole Jake had left in her heart that would never fully disappear.

"Nah, he would have let you do that for him."

Across the dance floor, I saw Blake find Cam with his eyes. He lit up like a truck at the lake at midnight when he saw her, and she responded with a smile that was full wattage Cam that no one could resist. I felt happy for her, which made me all teary again. God. It would be good to have this blasphemous night behind us.

Blake waved her over.

She sighed. "I guess it's time to announce the winners of the silent auctions. I'm kind of dreading it."

I knew what she meant.

I squeezed her hand as she darted from the chair and flew toward Blake on feet that would never stop.

Derek's song ended, and he announced that he was turning the mic over to Cam. After the auction, another band that Blake had ties to was taking over. Something with more country twang than Derek's group. Something that fit into the Tennessee lifestyle just a hair better.

Derek and his band still got a hearty round of applause as they left the stage. I couldn't help my eyes as they followed him into the crowd, with my heart pounding like that kitten chasing the bug again and my brain yelling at me to cease and desist.

Chapter Four

The Dance

TENEREFE SEA
"You got the kind of look in your eyes,
As if no one knows anything but us.
And all of the voices surrounding us here,
Just fade out when you take a breath."
-Ed Sheeran

I found my way to the drink table, and for the first time since college, I was thirsty for something stronger than water. There was no way that I was letting myself put anything with alcohol near my face, though. Not when I was barely holding my front in place like a placard advertiser. It was bad enough that I was an emotional drunk on a good day. No, there would be no drinks for me tonight.

Like some echolocation device set to a Derek setting, I felt him before I heard him. I seemed to ping like crazy whenever he was nearby. Was that a good thing? Absolutely not. I might as well just rebreak my own heart before he had the chance.

I turned toward him anyway because I couldn't seem to stop myself. He was sweaty from the heat, and the lights and his effort. He'd been all in, going at it like there might not be a chance to play again, and I liked that. I liked that he'd lost himself in it like I could lose myself in a good book.

"You look beautiful." He said it with a hint of something in his eyes that made me realize that I was the mouse and he was the bat in our echolocation scenario, and not the other way around. Did eagles use echolocation? Because Derek was definitely more eagle than bat.

I handed him a water, and he took it with thanks. I watched as he uncapped it and downed the whole thing in one big swallow, his Adam's apple bobbing up and down in a neck that looked like it would be perfect to first kiss and then snuggle into.

Get a grip, I scolded myself and purposely turned away from this sensual man so that I could watch Cam announce the winners of the auction items.

"Your band is good," I told him without looking at him. He was watching me, though. I could feel his gaze taking in every inch of me. I shifted uncomfortably, my heels sinking in the grass, and as I swayed, he caught my elbow to steady me.

That smooth-as-honey connection slid back between us at his touch. I swallowed hard and mumbled something that might have been thanks but sounded like the frogs at the lake. I drew my arm away once I'd regained my balance.

"You sound surprised," he said with a hint of that laughter that had been in his tone all afternoon.

I shrugged. "I guess I didn't know what to expect."

"Come on, tell me the truth. You thought I was gonna go all boy band up there, didn't you?" He was laughing at me, and himself, and I couldn't help but turn and smile back at him.

When I did, his gray eyes were flashing thunderclouds at me. Not storms of anger, but storms of a different kind.

Storms I knew I couldn't even come halfway close to matching. I'd be a disappointment in that area.

Derek sighed a self-deprecating sigh. "It's okay. Everyone thinks the same thing. They see my pretty boy image and just assume I'm part of some boy band. Not that there's anything wrong with boy bands. They have their place and their fans. I'm just saying, I'm not really that kind of musician."

"Then why don't you change your image?" I asked him without looking at him.

"So tell me, how would you make me over?" And I didn't have a choice but to take him in because he was daring me to do it. I flushed a thousand shades of red while I glanced at his chiseled muscles and suggestive smile.

He saw my flush and winked. I wanted to say something mocking, but, as always, I wasn't good when put on the spot like that. "I wouldn't know where to begin," was all I could come up with.

"I could think of a few places…" He started to step closer but was interrupted in his path to me by his name being called, leaving me feeling equal parts relieved and regretful.

He jerked out of his slow seduction mode and looked up with a confident grin that I hadn't seen on anyone since Jake used to wear it.

"What did you win?" I asked, because I clearly hadn't been paying attention to anything that Cam was saying.

"I only bid on the Camaro," he replied.

"Wh-what?" My breath caught in my throat.

"I couldn't let something with so much love and emotion behind it go to just anyone, could I?" Then he left my side to go and collect his prize.

Onstage, Cam hugged Derek and handed him a set of keys as my brain tried to catch up. Derek had bought Jake's Camaro. It was no longer Jake's. It was now Derek's. And somehow, instead of being sad or upset, as I might have been, I was suddenly glad. Because if Jake had sold it to anyone, he would have wanted some confident, godlike creature just like him to own it. And didn't that just fit?

There was a round of applause, and Cam was done with the mic. The new band came on, so I made my way deeper into the tent to mingle with Wynn and her husband, and our neighbors and families. People who had lived the Jake drama with us. People who understood the true importance he'd had in all our lives.

It wasn't even fifteen minutes later that my echolocation senses went off again, and I turned from visiting with Blake's grandparents to find Derek at my side once more. He'd taken a shower, who knew where, and changed from his sweaty band clothes into more tight jeans and a button down. His brown hair was wet and curling below his ears, and he smelled like soap and… something close to wood varnish with a hint of lemon and honey. It was a masculine and heady scent in the heat of the tent.

"I was hoping you'd dance with me." He gave me a hopeful smile that didn't quite fit the image that I'd built up in my head of his sexy arrogance.

There was a slow song playing. I wasn't sure that I could handle being touched by him. Just his hand on my arm twice had almost been enough to make my knees give out. What would it be like to have my whole body pressed up against his? My soft curves to his hard muscle. It made me shiver internally.

"Sure," I heard myself say, but I swear that was the exact opposite of what my brain was screaming. Good Girl Mia wanted me to run far, far away. He reached out a hand. I looked down at it hesitantly before I put my own inside it and melted all over again.

He drew me with him until we'd just barely reached the dance floor before turning and pulling me up against him. He still had my hand entwined in his own, but it was now pulled up tight against his chest. His other hand made its way to my waist and gently pulled me closer than I'd originally placed us.

He sighed. "I almost thought you'd tell me no."

He smiled down at me impishly, but his eyes weren't dancing with the same humor as before. Instead, they had that stormy look that made me imagine how deep a color they would be when he was in the middle of a passionate… I shook myself out of that thought before I could let it go nowhere good.

I tore my eyes from his to look around his shoulder, because even in my heels, there was no way I was tall enough to see over his shoulder. My parents were talking to the Swaynes at a table near the back. They were smiling and laughing, and I loved seeing them that way. It'd been a long four years for them. Parents should never have to bury a child. Guilt tore through me. It was good at hitting me when I least expected. Tonight, remembering Jake, it wasn't so unexpected.

I switched my attention back to Derek rather than the guilt.

"Why wouldn't I dance with you?" I asked.

"Let's just say I get the feeling that you don't approve of me." He was still smiling. Did he ever stop? He was more like Blake than my brother in that way. I could hear the smile in his voice even if I wouldn't look up at those really sexy lips and the chin that called to me to run my fingertip over it.

"I don't disapprove of you." Cam may not lie, but I was good at it. I had learned to do it to protect those I loved from myself.

He didn't respond but twirled me out and around, and then back, this time even closer to his body than before. Through my thin green dress, I could feel every inch of him. I tried to put a little space between us, but his hand at my waist didn't loosen. Instead, it tightened.

I wasn't used to being treated like this. As if he truly wanted my body tucked up against his. I mean, don't get me wrong, as I said, my PlayBabe channel curves had guys ogling me, but the response was usually something crass about me, my boobs, and their penises. With Derek, it felt like he wanted to absorb me. All of me.

Then again, maybe not. Hayden's words made me doubt myself. I'd imagined a lot of things before and been wrong.

The song ended, and Derek didn't let go. I finally looked up into his eyes, and they were dark with desire that I knew I wasn't just imagining, because his look was followed by words that matched. "I really like your hair that way. But all I can think of is how it would look if I pulled it down."

"Tenerefe Sea" reverberated through my head. Ed's voice singing about all the voices fading away as he breathed out how lovely she looked, because the look in Derek's eyes made me feel just like Ed's words, like no one knew anything but us.

"I hear, Mr. Waters, that you are quite practiced at saying those kinds of things." I was hoping my voice was steady and light, but I knew it sounded breathless because, let's face it, I loved books and songs and all the well-rehearsed one liners. Didn't I have a dog-eared note in my wallet to prove it?

He smiled. "I have had practice."

I dragged myself away and he let me, but he didn't let my hand go. I looked down at it expectantly. "Where are you going?" he said with a grin as the next song started. Faster. More country rock than seduction.

"You want to dance again?" I was surprised.

He twirled me in response, and to my utter astonishment, started a country line dance that just about blew me away. Sure, I lived in Tennessee, and there were plenty of guys who could keep up with the girls in a line dance, but I wasn't expecting it from a Hollywood playboy.

God help me, I let myself be pulled in by it. The look. The happiness. The unexpectedness of it all. How could I help it? Somehow, in the process, my heart had lightened just a little, and so I let him keep me with him for another three songs because it had been so long since my heart had been lightened.

When the band started to wrap up, we had danced so much that I was sweaty and hot again. And he was sweaty and hot again. As Cam had pointed out, a shower in our July Tennessee heat didn't last long.

We made our way back to the drinks. This time, he reached for a beer and handed me one. I shook my head and just grabbed a water bottle. Still no room in the tent for drunk Mia.

I fiddled with my cap, trying to find something to say to this BB who had just danced more songs with me than anyone since high school.

"So, you leave tomorrow?" was all I could come up with.

"Not tomorrow. Tomorrow the guys and I are going caving over in McMinnville."

"Like spelunking?"

He chuckled, and I looked up to see his gray eyes full of mischief again, seduction gone. Or on pause. God, I hated myself for wanting it only to be on pause. "Yes, but no one really calls it that anymore."

I couldn't help but think that that was too bad. Spelunking was a super cool word.

"Are there even caves in Tennessee?"

His smile broadened. "Quite famous ones. Cumberland Caverns."

I just stared. How did I not know that?

"Would you like to go with us?" he asked.

I stopped, water bottle halfway to my mouth. "Crawling in a cave?"

"The advantage is that it's a permanently air-conditioned room down there, plus you get to see some amazing formations," he said.

"Is this a thing you do often?"

"Almost every stop on our tour this summer was designed with a cave in mind."

I expected him to laugh, but then I realized he was serious.

"Really?" I said.

"Absolutely."

"I don't know what to say to that."

He just grinned his crazy grin. "So, you wanna come?"

Tomorrow was Saturday. It was our busiest day at the dealership. There was no way that I could run off and go cave diving with some gorgeous musician. Besides, that would be incredibly stupid of me. There was no way Good Girl Mia would continue to allow me to be anywhere near Dangerous Derek after the pull he'd had on me tonight.

"Can't. Tomorrow is our busiest day."

"At the dealership?"

I nodded.

"You need the day off tomorrow, baby girl?" Daddy's voice startled me. I didn't know how long he'd been standing behind us. I turned pink. What had he heard?

I shook my head no, but it was as if Daddy hadn't seen it. "I wanted to go in tomorrow anyway. I need to talk with Denise about some of the recent sales."

"It's okay, Daddy. I told Joe I'd be there to help him straighten out that mess in the parts department."

"You haven't had a day off since you graduated. Go. Have fun. Enjoy something new," Daddy said. He patted me and then wandered away as if he'd settled it all.

I shifted uncomfortably. What on earth to do now? If I tried to get out of it, Derek would know it was because of him. I was no good at making people feel bad. At least, not in my personal life. At work, that was a totally different story. I could lay down the law there and not give a hoot.

However, this was also an outdoorsy thing, and me and the outdoors didn't typically end well. Jake and Cam had been all about the outdoors, but not me. The first and only time my daddy took me fishing, I'd burst into tears when he tried to get me to string the worm on the hook, because I'd felt so bad for the little creature. I sobbed, and Cam looked at me like I was some foreign body. Jake smirked.

I sobbed so hard that Daddy finally gave in and took the worm off the hook, and I buried it in the ground, hoping it would regenerate like Doctor Who. Then we took Jake and Cam's bikes out of the truck and left them to their fishing. Daddy took me home to Mama where she helped me bake cookies, which was way more my thing.

If Derek noticed my indecision, he didn't let it stop him. Instead, he dove in headfirst where Daddy had left off. "I'll pick you up at eight, then?"

"A.M.?" I wasn't really any more of a morning person than I was an outdoors person.

"Yes, baby, eight a.m. It's a bit of a drive, and we want to be there early."

My heart stopped. He was teasing me, calling me a cry baby. But I couldn't help my mind from wondering what it would be like if he was calling me baby for a whole other reason. So, instead of fighting it all, I found myself giving in.

"Seems like I don't have a choice."

"You always have a choice. But I can guarantee you'll regret it if you tell me no."

"I think I'll regret it if I tell you yes."

The crowd had pretty much dissipated. Derek followed me as I went to find Cam and Blake. Blake was pulling things from her hands as she started to clean up. Cam on overdrive. "Stop. That's what we paid the clean up crew to do."

"It's just—"

He kissed her mid-sentence. And she stilled. It was amazing to watch the effect he had on her. "No. Let them do it," he insisted, and she acquiesced. I was stunned. Cam had let Blake win. Cam never let anyone win. Not even Jake.

She saw me with Derek hovering nearby and frowned. A frown that was then echoed by Blake. I just ignored their frowns and squeezed her goodnight. "Love you, Cam."

"Love you too, kiddo," she said back with a smile that was as close to teary as you would see Cam get.

Blake kissed me on the cheek and said goodnight before dragging Cam off toward the house before she could find something else to dive into. His hand was wrapped through hers, pinkies entwined. My heart swelled with happiness for her, and yet filled with a sudden longing for me that my broken heart echoed.

Mama and Daddy joined me, and we headed toward the cars with beautiful Derek matching our strides. "You won the Camaro?" Mama asked Derek with a little waver to her voice.

"Yes, ma'am," Derek said. He was serious with her, not the flirty charmer he'd been with me. "I promise to take good care of her," he added, but he wasn't looking at the Camaro. He was looking at me, and it made my longing body respond like yeast to sugar.

"You taking it to McMinnville tomorrow?" Daddy asked.

"No, we've got the SUV we rented."

"What's this?" Mama asked.

"Mia's going caving with Derek tomorrow," Daddy said nonchalantly.

Mama looked like a squirrel caught stealing from the bird feeder, frozen in place. "Caving? Is that dangerous?"

"It's very safe. And we won't do the expert treks with Mia. We'll keep her to the less advanced stuff."

"Who's we?" Mama asked.

"Mama!" I said, humiliated at her giving him the third degree as if I was fifteen instead of twenty-two. Even though I understood that she worried about me differently now than she had at fifteen.

Daddy pulled Mama to him and kissed her temple. "People do it all the time. They have guides and safety equipment. It'll be good for Mia to experience something of the real outdoors."

He smiled cheekily at me, like I was five and crying over the worm on the fishing hook. I stuck my tongue out at him.

"She's feistier than she looks. Make sure she doesn't leave you at the bottom of a pit," my daddy teased.

"Is that how it is?" Derek asked with that impish smile again.

"You're all awful," I said and moved as fast as I could in my ridiculous heels toward Daddy's truck. At the last minute, my stupid manners kicked in and made me turn back to look at Derek, "Thanks for inviting me. See you at eight."

Then I dove into the truck before I had to see his face or hear a response.

Chapter Five

Caving

WHERE WE LAND
"Do I love you?
Do I hate you?
I can't make up my mind."
-Ed Sheeran

Like I said, me and mornings aren't really friends. And the morning after the fundraiser, I was especially groggy. It was close to midnight when we'd gotten home, and on top of that, I'd spent several more hours researching spelunking. Caving, shmaving, I liked the word spelunking, thank you very much.

What I'd found online had been both interesting and terrifying. I'd never been in small spaces like they showed. Some people didn't do well in them, so I was hoping that I wouldn't freak out and embarrass myself. Leave it to Mia to do something like that. Like crying over the worm and trying to bury it.

Plus, I had nothing to wear because all the gear they'd shown seemed specially designed. It had said it would be cool and you should be comfortable, so I figured I'd do best with layers. That morning, I put on workout gear with a t-shirt and windbreaker over it along with a pair of Doc Martens that I'd dug out of my closet from when they were the thing to wear with dresses. When I looked in the mirror, I knew I looked absurd. But it was all I had.

I pulled my long hair into a low ponytail assuming we'd have some ugly helmet to wear, and hoped that I didn't look completely like the loser I felt like.

I slipped quietly onto the porch with a mug of coffee and a power bar. Mama and Daddy hadn't emerged from their room. Thankfully, that meant no more embarrassing moments with them acting like I hadn't had a good time in years.

Maybe they weren't that far off.

Even my relationship with Hayden had been more serious, painful drama than good times. I'd found Hayden in my first business class my freshman year at UTK. He was dynamic, like all the dynamic people that I'd been around my whole life, and I couldn't help but be pulled into his orbit.

He'd smiled at me, and I thought it meant something. I thought that maybe he was smiling at me the way Jake used to smile at Cam long before he realized that she was the only one for him. So, I tagged along after Hayden, doing everything he wanted, in hopes that he'd see how much he needed me like Jake and Cam had needed each other.

For a while, I thought we'd be together forever. We'd even shared a few tangled, drunken college kisses. Then Marcie invaded our friendship. Beauty Queen Marcie who was her own dystopian universe come to wreck mine.

Even after he'd chosen Marcie, I stood by him. My only role model had been Cam standing by Jake through his swarm of high school girlfriends. I listened to Hayden gripe about Marcie, feeling like I understood him better than she did. I would say all the right words, hoping someday he'd finally believe that we were destined to be together.

And for one night, when he'd broken up with Marcie for the millionth time, we'd been as close as two people can get. Then, the next week, he'd gone back to Marcie again, and I broke for half a second and told him I loved him. He responded by telling me that he loved me too. But that he also loved Marcie and that he needed Marcie. That her world fit into his world better. Which really just meant her powerful, wealthy family fit with his powerful, wealthy family. It didn't really mean she knew him.

I told him that too. He responded by telling me I was good at imagining things. That it was one of the things he loved most about me: my innocent, colorful way of looking at the world. But he still went back to Marcie. And I still had a broken heart. Embarrassingly, I hadn't walked away. Instead, I'd written love letters that he'd responded to with an apology note that only made me feel like he'd wake up some day and realize that I was the one that fit his life and not Marcie.

My brain was there, on Hayden and Marcie as it hadn't been much of yesterday, when a dark SUV pulled into the driveway. Instead of being late, like I really expected an overly confident musician to be, he was ten minutes early.

It gave me another piece of the Derek puzzle that I was collecting. As if he was a mass of cardboard waiting to be put together into a complete picture of an eagle with a guitar slung from its wings.

I kicked myself. Hayden was right: I had an overactive imagination. It was a side effect of reading so much. Truth was, the world wasn't always the way I pictured it. I definitely needed to keep that in mind today with this tempting male body in my view.

Derek emerged from the SUV with a jauntiness that all confident men seemed to have. Jake had had it. Hayden had it. Why couldn't I find some mousy guy who wouldn't break my heart? Because looking at this BB in his ongoing series of tight jeans, tight t-shirts, and hiking boots was enough to break my heart right there before I even let him near the shreds of mine that remained.

"Hey," he said with that carefree smile that made me long to feel as happy as he appeared.

"Morning." I looked down at my clothes, self-conscious. "Is this going to be okay?"

Stupid. I realized my mistake as soon as he began slowly taking in every inch of me in my workout gear. Workout gear that showed my curves in a way I wasn't comfortable showing outside the gym.

"You look really good," he said in that sexy-as-hell voice that caught my breath. "Do you have some waterproof gear in that bag?"

He referred to the backpack at my feet that I'd scrounged from our supply closet. It looked like it had once been pink, but was now a motley gray, and someone, probably Cam, had duct taped every inch of it. I just didn't have anything else that would bear the brunt of hiking in a cave without being ruined.

"I have a change of clothes, a flashlight, and a couple protein bars," I offered with a shrug.

"Don't worry. I think we can manage to scrape some things together for you between me and the boys."

"I'm sorry," I said.

He frowned. "Why would you be sorry? I kind of figured you wouldn't have much. The boys and I don't mind."

He came up to the steps and grabbed the dirty backpack.

"This thing looks like it's been through the ringer."

"That would be Cam, not me. I'm more of a read-it-in-a-book versus do-it kind of girl," I said and then flushed as he raised his eyebrows at my words. What I wanted to do was thunk my head against the porch pillar. God, I was such a bumbling idiot around him.

"But doing it is much more fun," he whispered to me with a glimmer in his eyes.

Warning bells went off all over my body. If Mama had come out on the porch at that moment and forbade me from going, I would have scurried inside like the fifteen-year-old I suddenly felt like.

He grabbed my hand loosely, almost like Blake had Cam's last night, and my heart zinged while my body reacted like it had every time he touched me.

Focus Mia, I told myself. *Get your head out of the clouds.*

He opened the front passenger door for me, and I looked inside. Three large men were scrunched into the backseat of the SUV like raccoons in a garbage can.

I backed up. "I can take the back seat. I'm used to being in the middle. I'm pretty small."

Once again, my words came out all wrong, and I turned pink again. I was like a high schooler who'd just learned how to use a double entendre. He chuckled behind me, but let go of my hand only enough to help me into the raised SUV.

"No way. I wouldn't trust them anywhere near you," he said.

I wasn't quite sure what to do with that statement. Was he being Blake-like protective, or was he saying he didn't want them near me because he wanted me? Like last night, I wasn't used to being treated this way, and I wasn't quite sure I could trust my own instincts.

Derek hopped into the driver's seat and turned to me with happy eyes. "Guys, this is Mia. Mia, that's Lonnie, Owen, and Mitch. Rob, our drummer, couldn't make it today."

Of course, there wouldn't have been room for him in the SUV even if he wanted to come, which made me feel bad all over again. "Is that because of me?"

"Oh no, he got in trouble with the missus and is spending the day groveling on the phone and sending flowers," the red-haired lumberjack in the back guffawed. He leaned toward me with a grin almost as infectious as Derek's. "I'm Lonnie, by the way."

"He's married?" I couldn't help the surprise that jumped out before I could use my manners to hold it back.

"Stupid ass," said the tattooed man in the middle with a shaved head and skin so dark and rich that it made me think of Mama's chocolate crinkles. He was a little smaller than the other two, but not by much, which probably accounted for him being unhappily in the middle.

"Owen's just jealous that Rob bagged Trista before he could, so don't listen to anything he says," chimed in the third man, Mitch. He was built like a professional wrestler and looked the most ridiculous of all of them shoved by the window. His hair was spiked and blue which somehow made the wrestler image even more probable.

Derek backed out of the drive and started down the road.

"So, Mia, Derek says your brother owned that beauty of a car he bought last night. What the hell would make a guy give up a car like that?" Lonnie asked, and my heart snagged on a branch at his words.

"Dude," Derek said with a warning glance in the rear-view mirror.

"It's okay," I said. "He used to own it. But he died."

Silence, followed by scuffling in the backseat, and I could see the other two men hitting Lonnie on the shoulder and the back of the head like a group of teenage boys fighting over the last MoonPie.

I couldn't help but smile, and when I looked back toward the front, Derek caught my eye with his, and my breath hitched at the concern that seemed to reside there. Egads, I was in trouble with this man. Where was Ginny Weasley's wand and an obliviate spell when I needed one?

"Shit. Sorry," Lonnie said, but it was muffled in his attempt to ward off the others' pummeling fists.

"I can't take you boys anywhere. Maybe I should drop you back off at the hotel, and Mia and I will hit the caverns on our own."

Sudden stillness in the backseat. "You'd like that wouldn't you? Mia all on your own in the caves. No way, man, you got yourself into this. We all get to help her now, and she'll see that you may be the front man for this traveling circus, but you're in no way the best of the troupe," Owen teased.

It had been a long time since I'd been surrounded by boys. When I hung out with Cam in high school, it had been Cam, Wynn, and me and a whole boat full of them. Cam attracted boys the way roadkill attracts maggots. Not the most attractive image, but true. The guys were always all over her. Not that she cared. She only had eyes for Jake, but I think that just made it even more of a challenge for the boys. Not that she realized that either.

I kind of missed the relaxed atmosphere that normally surrounded a group of boys. My first best friend had been a boy, Harry, and I missed him. We'd become fast friends in elementary school when we'd both reached for the last Laura Numeroff book on the shelf, and we'd remained that way till his family moved to California after eighth grade. We stayed in touch, though. In fact, I was going to see him in a few weeks for his wedding. Maybe. If I could get up the courage to attend by myself even though I'd RSVP'd as Mia plus one because I was still a hopeful idiot.

Anyway, the truth was that boys were easier to get along with. They didn't judge you as much. They just said what they thought most of the time, and if you accidentally burped or farted, they thought it was funny instead of embarrassing.

As we turned down the highway to McMinnville, I listened happily as this boy scout troop joshed and slammed each other, and my heart lightened again ever so slightly. Guilt and heartache stepping aside enough to let me breathe for just a few minutes.

My lighter heart gave way to nervousness when we pulled into the lot at the caverns. The place itself was rather unassuming, just a little ranch house in the middle of some trees. But I knew I'd be underground before long. Really far below ground, and that was enough to make my caffeinated stomach flip uncomfortably.

The guys unwrapped themselves from the backseat and pulled out equipment from the back. Backpacks, helmets with funky lights, and gear that seemed more appropriate to fishermen on *Deadliest Catch* than a dark cavern.

Mitch took off to the office to let them know we were there.

"I think they'll have a helmet you can use, but let's piece together some other gear," Derek said as he searched through everyone else's packs. No one seemed to mind his invasion.

Before I knew it, I had on a vinyl jacket and some wader-like pants. Everything was so large that it needed to be rolled and tucked with these wide rubber bands that had magically appeared from somewhere. Finally, Derek slung a flashlight around my neck.

Once, when I was little, the firefighters had come to our school and I'd been selected to put on the fireman's gear. I felt like that all over again, and I knew I looked even more ludicrous than I had when Derek had shown up at the house.

Derek took a step back, and the corners of his mouth quirked ever so slightly. "I'm ridiculous," I said with a sigh.

"No," he said, but he was trying not to laugh.

"Is this some sort of spelunking hazing or something? Are you guys really going to wear this stuff too?" I asked.

"Caving. And we don't do hazing," he said.

Lonnie came around the SUV, and sure enough, he had on similar gear. "Aww. Don't you look adorable."

"Oh my God," I sat down on the bumper, "I can't do this."

Derek hit Lonnie on the shoulder. A shoulder that must have been getting sore after all the hits it had taken on the drive over. "Don't listen to this stupid shit."

Mitch came back with a helmet and a bunch of papers. Apparently, you had to sign your life away and say that you wouldn't hold the caverns responsible if you died, or passed out, or were in any other way injured on the journey. My nervousness increased to an entirely new level because, let's face it, me dying in a cave was not an option Daddy had considered when he'd pushed me into this.

I watched as Derek drew on his own waders over his jeans. That action stopped my nervous brain cold because he was so unforgivably sexy even in a stupid fisherman outfit.

Once everyone had on these absurd outfits, they loaded the backpacks onto their shoulders, and Derek held out a hand. "Phillips, you gonna do this?"

Somehow, he had finally figured out that I was legitimately freaked out about this. I shrugged, grabbed the dirty pink backpack and the helmet Mitch had given me, but ignored his hand.

"I'm here. Might as well."

He smiled encouragingly in response, those stormy eyes taking me in as if I was a horse about ready to bolt. Which wasn't that far from the truth.

We met our guide, and he briefed us on the do's and don'ts of spelunking. It seemed like we were going to be doing some crawling and ladder climbing. There was also a good chance we'd hit some mud after the summer storm that had blown through last week, so it was a good thing we were layered up. The guide promised it would all be worth it though. I was going to reserve my opinion until the end.

Then we went in.

And I didn't have a chance to be nervous any longer, because I was immediately challenged by the space and the darkness. I didn't even have one panic attack. Instead, I found it an interesting conundrum. How could I wedge myself through the tight darkness to the other side where I could hear Derek's voice cheering me on? "You're almost there, Phillips. You got this."

Every time I got to the other side, the guys would always high five me and act like I'd just solved world hunger or something equally as important. It perked my spirit up in a way that it hadn't been in forever. Since before Jake.

"Come on, Phillips, couple more tunnels before the big show." Derek pulled at me.

I'm not sure why I went from Mia to Phillips in the cave. Maybe it was so the guys would treat me as one of the guys. Or maybe, like Cam's and Jake's coaches, it was a way of getting me to focus. I could see that Derek was coaching me through it, making sure I didn't freak out. And it did help.

After an hour or so in, we stepped out of a dark tunnel into this huge cavern with gypsum crystals, stalactites, stalagmites, and rock formations that I'd vaguely known existed but never really thought about seeing in real life. It was like being flown to another country.

There was even a waterfall inside the rocks. It was breathtaking — cool and peaceful, like I wished my life could be instead of the mess I thought it was. I held my breath at the same time as I felt my heart expand, or maybe that was just my world.

I kind of felt like this whole cave was me. Like, on the outside, I looked just like a regular old hillside, but on the inside, I was a series of stunning waterfalls and gorgeous formations that hadn't been seen by the majority of the world. I felt like most people would just drive by, not knowing what really lay underneath.

"Crazy, huh?" Derek said, and for once, my echolocation hadn't worked because I hadn't known he'd come up next to me.

I just nodded.

"It's always a good reminder to me that there's way more under the surface of everything. People. Nature. Even music. It's layer upon layer that gets put together into something whole that people judge for the whole, but may be way more if you take it apart and examine all the pieces." He spoke quietly and seriously, almost as if he was in a church.

It was like he'd mirrored my own thoughts. I looked up at him. It was lighter in this part of the caverns, and while the shadows played on his face, I could still see those stormy eyes looking down on me like I was the music he wanted to see the layers of, and it both scared me and excited me. This gorgeous BB looking at me like that. Like maybe I could be my own fairytale.

I tried to remind myself that my books and fairytales were what had already gotten my heart broken once, and turned back to the next crevice.

After we'd spent about four hours underground, we came out dirty, tired, but happy into the main cavern. Where, to my utter amazement, there was a ginormous chandelier and a stage. All set up over three hundred feet under the ground!

"What?" I breathed out.

Derek laughed at my amazement and gave me a shove with his shoulder. "Never heard of the Bluegrass Underground either, I take it."

I just shook my head. How did I not know this existed in Tennessee just a mere hour or so away from home? It was like I had been living under a rock. Not this rock, but a real rock where only grubs showed up.

"PBS puts on concerts here about once a month. What I wouldn't give to play in this space..." he said almost wistfully, letting me see again, briefly, that there was more to this beautiful man than just a carefree attitude.

Scarily, that attracted me almost as much as his laugh and his smile.

We walked back the half mile to the main building, and thankfully, there was a restroom where I could change and wash my hands and face. The bulk of the dirt was on the outerwear I'd borrowed from the guys, but my Doc Martens were probably history.

I slid into my jean shorts and t-shirt along with flip flops. My hair was stuck to my head from the helmet, but I coaxed it back to life enough to look like a regular ponytail instead of a smooshed raisin.

When I came out, Derek was leaned up against a fence, waiting for me. The boys were nowhere to be seen.

"You cleaned up fast," he said. He was eyeing me again in that way that made my toes want to curl up in their flip flops. "I like your shirt." It sounded way more seductive than it should have.

I looked down and realized that I was wearing my faded "Mischief Managed" t-shirt. Harry Potter and I have always had a fabulous relationship. But it was his tone that had the red hitting my cheeks like a snowstorm hits the mountains.

"I think I'd like to know exactly what kind of mischief Mia Phillips is capable of getting into."

I crossed my arms over my huge chest and looked away. "I don't think I get you," was all I could respond because I really didn't.

He pushed himself off the fence and came closer. All my insides were screaming to run the other way. Back to the cool caverns and the place where he was calling me Phillips, and I could just concentrate on getting through a tight space to the other side.

"What don't you get?" He reached out and tugged at the edges of my ponytail, dragging it forward and twirling his fingers into it. I looked down at those slender musician fingers and swallowed hard.

"I can't be your normal target," I breathed out.

"Target?" A frown covered his sensual face in a way that seemed almost foreign to him. His hand froze, still tangled in my hair.

"You know. The long line of women that you've clearly got trailing after you."

He laughed, his cleft stretching in that way that made me hunger to touch it with my finger or my lips. I wondered how he could possibly be so happy so often. "Where We Land" threw lyrics in my direction because I found myself wanting him to tell me his secrets. I wanted to see what caused those brief moments of thoughtfulness I'd glimpsed. But I also wanted to let the good times flood into my life, led by this happy, sexy man, and I wasn't sure if I loved that or hated that. I couldn't make up my mind. I definitely knew I was afraid to free fall because where would I land if I let him take me into his spiral?

"Did Blake tell you that? He's such a schmuck. He knows that isn't true," Derek said, but he was still smiling so I didn't know if I could take him seriously or not.

"Cam told me. And Cam always tells the truth." I pulled back and pushed his hand away from my hair and my face so that I could try to think clearly again.

"Cam?" He frowned again. "I've only met Cam a couple times, and I swear to God I can't think of any woman that would have been around when she was there."

"Okay, so why would Blake tell her you were a player?"

Realization seemed to hit him like a pebble on the water, and he chuckled again. I didn't think there was anything funny about it. I guess only a guy would think that being a player was cool and not the turnoff it would be to a notoriously serious girl like me.

Derek realized I wasn't seeing the humor, and his laughter disappeared. "It's a joke," he started. "My dad lives at the PlayBabe Mansion, so Blake calls me a player, or playbabe, or playdude or whatever he thinks will get under my skin the most."

I realized he meant *the* actual PlayBabe Mansion, owned by Hugo Brantly. The guy whose magazine had made Playboy and Penthouse look like Christian magazines.

I just stared because, like he'd done multiple times since I met him, he made it impossible for me to figure out what to respond to first. There were probably a dozen follow up questions I could have asked, but it was hard to unravel them all. Instead, I felt both frustrated and oddly relieved.

I was saved from responding by my phone vibrating. As if she'd realized we were talking about her, the text was from Cam.

CAM: *Jesus! Blake just told me that you went caving with the moron. Please tell me you are alive and well.*

I stepped away from Derek.

"Mia," he started to protest, but at the same time, the boys came storming out of the restrooms. They were flinging water at each other and laughing like ten-year-olds instead of the twenty-somethings they must have been.

I put more space between myself and Derek as I texted back.

ME: *I'm alive. It was actually pretty amazing. Mia dirty in a cave. You would have been shocked.*

My phone pinged almost instantly.

CAM: *I sent that two hours ago! I was almost ready to call your mama.*

I'd turned off my phone in the caverns. No signal anyway, and I'd just turned it on as I'd come back out of the bathroom so that I could post pictures on Instagram. Poor Cam. She rarely worried. Especially not enough to call Mama because she knew Mama already worried too much.

ME: Sorry. Was deep underground.

She came back with:

CAM: Seriously, who are you and what have you done with Mia?

I smiled because Mama had said the same thing last night, and I looked up at Derek as I realized that Serious Mia was out of her normal shell because of Dangerous Derek. He was watching me again. I could tell he wanted to finish our conversation, but I wasn't ready for any of it.

"I'm starving, man," Mitch said as he flung an arm around Derek's neck. I wished I could be so casual with anyone. It wasn't a normal move for me, no matter if it was someone I'd known my whole life or not. Jake used to fling his arm around me and rub the top of my head just to torment me. Brothers. God, I missed him still.

"Let's head back into McMinnville. I read, somewhere, about a good pizza joint they have," Lonnie suggested.

"You up for pizza?" Derek asked.

"What idiot would say no to pizza?" I replied, and all the boys hooted their approval.

Derek eased up next to me as we walked into the parking lot. "Everything okay?" he asked, referring to my buzzing phone.

I nodded. "Cam was worried once she found out I was with you."

"Goddamn, Blake!" Derek swore. "If he wasn't already on my team, I'd swear he had it out for me."

I smirked. "Maybe he just doesn't like you enough to see his sister-in-law with you."

"Who? Me? Everybody likes me." His tone was teasing, but his eyes were serious and stormy.

We got back in the SUV, and even though I offered again to climb in the back, no one would let me. I sighed. At least they'd been taught some manners. Not everyone had. How many times had I squished into the back of Hayden's tiny sports car while his friends rode up front?

I texted Cam.

ME: On the way to pizza with the moron and his gang. Did Blake really tell you he had a string of girls? He insists it's a joke. That Blake is teasing because his dad lives at the PlayBabe Mansion. Don't ask. I didn't.

We'd driven back into town and parked before my phone buzzed again.

CAM: Seriously. Who is this? The Mia I know is not interested in scary sexy musicians, doesn't go caving, and doesn't hang out with a gang of boys.

This was followed by her next response.

CAM: Blake's laughing at me. He says Derek's dad does live in that disgusting mansion and that's why he harasses Derek. He hasn't seen Derek with any particular girl, but he does know that the girls love him. I'm seriously putting the man in time out.

A minute later.

CAM: Mia. This is Blake. Cam is now in time out.

Buzz.

CAM: Mia

Buzz.

CAM: Cam will not be getting her phone back for a while. Do NOT do anything stupid with the band boy. Come home. Do I need to come get you?

I couldn't help it. I chuckled to myself at the thought of Cam and Blake fighting over her phone. It made the guilt-filled knot that had formed over my shredded heart lighten a little more.

Derek held the door open for me and leaned in as I went by. "By the way, that smile is completely my kind of target."

And just that quickly, my smile was swept away as I came to a standstill inside the door. There was nothing for me to imagine in those words. They were straight up.

Derek grabbed my hand and gently pulled me toward the table that his juvenile friends had commandeered. I was completely at a loss for any good words. Did I love it? Did I hate it? I couldn't make up my mind.

Chapter Six

The Offer

THIS

"This is the start of something beautiful.
This is the start of something new."
-Ed Sheeran

It was nearing eight o'clock by the time we'd dropped the guys off at the hotel, and Derek headed back out toward my house. My stomach and face hurt from laughing. I hadn't laughed so much in… maybe ever. Laughter wasn't really what I was known for. I was known for getting jobs done, helping people, reading, and just keeping everybody on the right track. It was what made me good at running the business. It was what I was most comfortable with.

Before I was ready, Derek turned onto my street and parked in front of my house. Unfortunately, I had been right. This gorgeous, sexy BB had stormed into my world, and now, after I'd spent less than twenty-four hours near him, I was already going to miss him. *Thank God he's leaving*, my head said, but my heart and body protested.

With manners that I would have doubted when I'd met him at the dealership, but which he'd continued to show, he opened my door and held out his hand to help me down. He didn't let go of my hand as he walked me to the porch.

Pitter patter went my weak heart.

Mama had turned on the porch light, but it wasn't quite fully dark yet in our summer in Tennessee. It felt strange and date-like to be going up the steps with him. It hadn't been a date, had it?

Derek saw our porch swing and grinned. "I love everything about Tennessee. Porch swings, sweet tea, and beautiful women."

I bumped him playfully with my shoulder, and he tugged me toward the swing. He sat, pulling me down next to him and sending the swing into a dizzying rock.

"Whoa," he grinned, eyes flashing that Puck-ish look of happiness that was like a kid with a new toy.

The swing slowed, and I pulled away a little, uncomfortable on the swing with him so close and us alone in the semi-darkness.

"I had a good time today," he said.

"Me too," I said, and it was truthfully the best day in a really long time. So long that it was hard to remember back to another day where I'd felt like this.

"I'm not ready to say goodbye to you yet," he told me, and my heart skipped a beat just like the heroines in all those romance novels I'd stuck my head in to escape reality.

"I'm sure we'll see each other again sometime. After all, Blake is pretty much family now," I reminded him.

"Yes, but I'd like to see you again tomorrow."

Once I realized he wasn't kidding, I had to look away because, boiling butterbeer, his eyes were that stormy gray that made me think of passionate skies and passionate kisses that he hadn't given me, but I could imagine would be more like broiling butter than silky honey. Or… maybe both, and that just made me shiver to my core.

"I think that's pretty much impossible seeing as you leave for Oklahoma tomorrow," I said a little breathlessly. The guys had talked about it nonstop at the pizza place.

"Come with me. With us."

I snorted because, really, what person in the world spends less than twenty-four hours with someone and then asks them to tag along on a three-week journey across the country? No one. Not even in stupid fairytale romance novels. Okay, maybe in one or two, but that wasn't my life at all.

"Mia," he said as he pulled my hand back into his and twisted it up so that my fingers were trapped against his chest. "It surprises the hell out of me that I'm saying it, but I'm completely serious. Come with me."

"You're crazy."

"Yes."

"I can't. I have a dealership to run, remember?"

"At twenty-two?"

"How do you know how old I am?"

"I'm good at asking questions of the right people. But you're avoiding the question," he said.

"I don't think there really was a question."

"Come with me."

"No."

"Well, here's the problem. I just bought this really cool muscle car, and I have to get it back to the West Coast."

My heart tugged as he talked about Jake's Camaro even though I was really glad he bought it.

"So?"

"Well, my manager is pissed as hell. Doesn't want me driving all the way because he says I'll be too tired for the shows."

"You have five members in your band."

"Ah, yes, but they also take turns driving the bus. Besides, would you really want me to trust them with the Camaro?"

He looked down at me with eyes that promised me something if I'd only take a leap. But Good Girl Mia didn't take leaps. This Mia stayed and ran the dealership so her daddy could semi-retire. This Mia studied in advance for her master's program that started in the fall. This Mia protected a broken heart by living the life that was expected of her.

"Don't be ridiculous. I run a car dealership; I don't go spelunking—"

"—caving."

"—spelunking with a band on a tour across the country."

"Not your thing, huh?" he said, but I could tell he didn't believe me. I almost expected him to throw out, "Methinks the lady doth protest too much," or something equally senseless.

"It's not me at all." I tried to sound firm, but I knew I was failing.

"But you had fun today."

"Sure."

"And you kind of like the boys."

"They're pretty irresistible." I smiled.

"And me, am I pretty irresistible?" he asked with that seductive smile. I had to look away before I gave in to something so crazy that everyone would really think I had lost my head. Because, let's face it, the happiness, the joy, the lightness of today had been fairly intoxicating. It was a drug that was hard for even me to resist.

"That's debatable."

I pulled my hand away and rose from the swing. He needed to leave right now before he said something else that would make me forget all my best laid plans.

He must have sensed my change in mood, but he didn't get up off the swing yet. He took me in again with eyes that seemed to read through my soul.

"This looks more like the real Mia than the pantsuit you wore yesterday."

"You don't know anything about me."

"You know you want to come. Think of all the hidden waterfalls we can find together. It's just three weeks. An adventure. How long has it been since you've had an adventure?"

Never! my heart called out. I'd only read about adventures that others took. I crossed my arms over my chest, smooshing their preposterous size into nothingness, trying to protect myself from Derek and his unspoken promises.

"Thank you for taking me today. I'll never forget it, but my adventure stops here," I said, trying to keep my voice from shaking.

He got up slowly, and I felt like the eagle was circling the mouse as he made his way to me. I wanted him to kiss me, just so I could say that one of the best twenty-four hours of my life had ended in a kiss that made me dissolve into nothingness.

But he didn't. Instead, he unlocked my arms from my chest and pointed to my t-shirt. "I think you want more than you let yourself have."

Stupid "Mischief Managed" t-shirt! I could have responded that didn't everyone want a little magic and adventure? But reality isn't a novel. My world was anything but.

"I hope you have a really good time," I told him firmly.

He lifted his hand and wrapped his fingers into my tangled ponytail. "I'd have more fun with you."

Guilt hit me because I was a sucker for it. You'd think I had grown up Catholic. This strange, sexy man couldn't push me over the edge, though. When I didn't respond, he sighed again, like I'd disappointed him, and that almost got me more than the guilt. I didn't want to disappoint this beautiful man. I wanted to read the tattoos on his wrists, and kiss the bird on his neck, and…

I shook my head.

He pulled away with regret in his eyes. "Well, we aren't leaving until around ten tomorrow. If you change your mind, you know where to find me. My manager would thank you. He'd probably even pay you."

He moved toward the steps while still eyeing me, as if I'd change my mind and run after him. He got to the bottom of the steps, shook his head ever so slightly, and then continued out to the SUV.

He looked back over the hood and said, "You're breaking my heart, Miss Mia. I'm gonna have to write a song about you."

I eye-rolled him—because who says stuff like that?—and then waved goodbye before going inside so that I wouldn't have to watch him drive away. I heard him honk the horn in one last pitiful effort to make me think about him, which truly wasn't hard. Getting my heart to stop racing, that was hard. Getting my mind back to the dealership, and my master's classes, and my reality, that was hard.

Inside, Mama and Daddy were cuddled up next to each other on the couch, some ancient rerun on the TV. They sat up as I came in. That made me realize why I couldn't run away with a sexy musician: because there were only three of us in the room instead of four.

"How was it?" Daddy asked while Mama looked me over for bruises and scrapes, even though she tried not to let it show.

"Honestly? It was amazing!" I said and sat down on the loveseat, throwing off my flip flops, and curling my feet up under me like I was ten years old.

"Really?" Daddy and Mama both seemed surprised.

"It was so beautiful. And quiet. And… God, there was this gorgeous waterfall right inside the mountain."

"You didn't freak out at the tight spaces?" Daddy asked with shock.

"Thanks a lot, Daddy."

"Well…"

"I know, I know," I said. "I'm not normally an outdoor kind of girl."

Which is true.

"You're definitely not a dirt kind of girl," Mama said.

Daddy ignored her and asked, "Was it difficult?"

"There were some really tiny spots, and ladders, and a bit of rock climbing, but I think they took me on an easy course."

"Who woulda thunk our little Mia would be a cave diver?" Daddy said with a grin.

"So, he headed back to the hotel? When does he leave?" Mama asked with something in her voice that made me think she heard some of our conversation on the porch.

"Tomorrow."

Silence. I could have left it at that, but I didn't.

"He wanted me to go with them. Help drive the Camaro back to the West Coast and go caving with them while they're on their three-week tour."

More silence.

"Of course, I told him no."

I couldn't meet their eyes as I plucked at the fuzz on the quilt that lay on the couch. Why had I even told them all that? I definitely didn't want to go, did I? On a rock tour? With a steamy hot musician who spoke words that my pieced-together heart would have a hard time resisting?

"You should do it," Daddy spoke quietly.

"What?" Mama and I both said at the same time.

"Mia. You should do this."

Silence from both Mama and me.

"You have Harry's wedding in a couple weeks, right? You were going out to San Francisco anyway. This would just get you going sooner."

I had the best of intentions to go to Harry's traditional Indian wedding. He was getting married to the girl his family had picked out for him. Personally, I wasn't sure I could ever agree to an arranged marriage after seeing the love Jake and Cam had for each other. If you saw them, you'd get it. You'd want that deep, universe-twirling connection that they had for yourself. They were perfectly fitted together. I guess I wanted to hold out for that. I had hoped I had a chance at it with Hayden.

Harry had called a couple times this month to make sure I was coming to the wedding, but the truth was I hadn't made the flight arrangements yet. I wasn't sure what held me back. It was probably related to the mess I was inside these days. Going to a wedding when I felt lonely and heart-broken wasn't really that appealing.

"You should do this," Daddy repeated when I still hadn't said anything.

"You really think I should go across the country with a group of guys we hardly know, spelunking?" I said it in a joking tone, but when I looked up, I could see he really was serious. Mama was serious too, but she looked like she was about to cry. She didn't like to cry in front of me anymore though, so she got up and headed for the stairs.

Daddy and I were silent again after she left.

"She just needs time."

"I understand," I answered.

"No, I don't think you really do. Not because you don't want to, but because losing a child isn't something you can comprehend if you aren't a parent. Your mama lost her baby boy…" Daddy had to pause to get himself together before he continued. "And the thought of losing both her children…It's just too much to bear some days. But that doesn't mean we can keep you here wrapped in Bubble Wrap."

"It's ridiculous, anyway. I have a lot to do at the dealership, and my classes start soon."

"Not till the end of August. Sounds like you'd be done with this by then."

"You're really telling me I should go?"

"Yes."

"Why?"

"For so many reasons, baby girl. But the best one I can give you is because life is too short not to."

We just let it set. I didn't commit to anything, either going or not. I couldn't. Instead, I got up and hugged him and headed for the stairs with the dirty backpack and ruined Doc Martens. "I'll think about it."

"You wouldn't even have brought it up if you didn't already want to go," Daddy said behind me.

I turned and our eyes met. Daddy knew me better than I guessed, even though he'd never know the real reasons I had to say no to this. Not the easy ones, like the fact that I was scared as hell of being broken even more by a gorgeous musician, but the more serious ones, like I hadn't done my penance yet.

I turned away and headed up the stairs to my room. I grabbed my stuff to shower in the bathroom that I used to have to fight Jake over. For a guy's guy, he could take an absurd amount of time getting ready. Especially in high school when he'd been dressing to impress the ladies.

I slipped into a pair of leggings and a t-shirt that were my normal bedtime apparel and left my hair down wet. It would be an unruly mess tomorrow, but I'd deal with it then. I was exhausted, both emotionally and physically.

When I got into my room, Mama was sitting on my bed, holding my orange and white stuffed cat that I'd had since Jake had won it for me at a school carnival. It was matted and worn, and the neck stuffing didn't hold the head up, but I hadn't been able to get rid of it. Instead, it had sat on my bedside table for the last few years.

I threw my dirty clothes in the hamper and turned back to her. She patted the bed, and I curled up beside her.

"I'm sorry I left," she said.

"It's okay."

"No, it's not, but sometimes it's hard for me to look past everything we've lost to everything we still have."

My eyes flooded with tears. I wouldn't cry, though. I wouldn't make Mama feel worse than she already did. I wouldn't, so I looked down and picked at my comforter like I'd picked at the quilt.

"Life as Jake's sibling wasn't easy, and I'm afraid that life without Jake isn't any easier for you," Mama said, grabbing my hand and running her fingers over the back of it as if she was trying to scrub away all our pain.

"Mama—"

"You should go," she said as if she had to get it out before she changed her mind. "You never do anything for you. For fun. Without a purpose. The dealership will still be here when you get back. So, go do this. Be free. Worry about just you for a while. I'm not sure you've ever been able to just worry about you."

Both my parents had surprised me with their insight into me tonight, making me realize that the front that I wore so well wasn't always as good as I thought. Or maybe that's just parents for you; they can see past the surface hill to the waterfall underneath.

"But do me a favor?" she asked, and I risked looking up at her face because that was what she wanted, and she moved her hand to my face where she rubbed my cheek softly. "Keep me posted, so I don't worry."

I just nodded. Because if I spoke, I'd be awash with the tears that I was hiding.

"You're a good girl, Mia," she said, rising from the bed. Didn't I know that? Wasn't that really the whole thing in a nutshell? Good Girl Mia knew she shouldn't go anywhere near Dangerous Derek and three weeks of adventure. Yet somehow, the Good Girl was losing tonight to some strange rebellious Mia who wanted something more for herself than she was allowed to want.

I just nodded.

"Now go live a little." She kissed me on my head like she had when I was a tween, and then left, her own tears barely in check.

When she had gone, I could let my own roll down my cheeks because I hurt for her and Daddy, and for Jake and Cam. And all the things they didn't have because my stupid kidney had failed them.

Jake and Cam had finally gotten together her senior year of high school when Jake had come home to get his diabetes and his kidneys in order. Everyone had been worried, but they'd gone off to Virginia Tech in a world of their own, only to have to come home with him on a dialysis machine, waiting for a kidney. Mine had been a match. So we'd begged the doctors to let me give it to him, even though they thought I was too young. Maybe I had been. Maybe my kidney wasn't ready to be yanked out and put into his body, because it had killed him instead of saving him.

I wiped furiously at my tears. I definitely didn't deserve to go on an adventure, and my heart probably wouldn't be able to take another twisted break. Yet, I also knew that the feeling I'd had today—not just the lightness, but the sense of normalcy—was pulling me in like an anglerfish luring in its prey.

Before I could overanalyze it all, I picked up my phone and texted Cam.

ME: *Do you happen to have the moron's phone number?*

My phone buzzed in response.

CAM: *Cam is still missing her phone. This is Blake. Why do you need the number?*

I typed back.

ME: *I can't talk to you about this. Can you please give*

Cam her phone?

Buzz.

CAM: You okay, kiddo?

That was definitely Cam.

ME: Yes. I just need the moron's phone number.

CAM: Do I need to send Blake over to kill him?

I was ready to type out the whole thing to her, and then I realized that I didn't want Cam to tell me her opinion. I didn't want to know if she thought I should stay or should go. Cam always had a way of swaying me to her thinking. I needed to do this on my own.

ME: No! I just need to give him an answer to a question he asked, and I didn't think to get the number.

She sent the number over via Blake, I was sure.

CAM: Love you.

ME: Love you too! I'll text you tomorrow. Night. Give my love to Blake.

Then, I turned off my light and crawled into bed. I stared at my phone and the number they'd given me for probably twenty minutes. As soon as I sent the text, I wouldn't be able to stop whatever happened. It would be out of my control, and I really wasn't so great with things like that these days.

I scrolled through my Ed music and hit "This," Ed's voice echoing my own confusion. Would this be the start of something beautiful and new? Or would Derek be the one to make me lose it all? Was I ready to throw away all my good intentions for this? The possibility of a promise of a "this." A possibility that I knew I hadn't imagined, because Derek was very clear and vocal in his intentions, but I also knew that the "this" that he promised was temporary. Three weeks of temporary.

Maybe that was all that I needed, though. Three weeks to get my head back on straight and maybe forget about the boy who'd broken my heart. Maybe. Because three weeks with Derek, who already made me feel desirable and wanted and…free, might be able to make those wounds feel not so fresh. Then I could come back and settle down under the weight of the guilt that would never leave me, without the broken heart to also go with it.

With fingers that shook, I typed.

ME: Hey, Derek, this is Mia. Mia Phillips. I got your number from Blake, I hope that's okay. Anyway. If your offer still stands, I think I'd like to come with you guys on your spelunking adventure.

Then I held my breath, waiting. I could see the dots come up almost instantaneously that said he was typing back a response. I wasn't sure if I hoped he'd send a laughing emoji that said he'd just been kidding, or if he'd be glad.

DEREK: Thank God! You just saved me an entirely too embarrassing scenario tomorrow where I planned to show up on your doorstep and beg like you've never seen anyone beg before.

ME: Now you'll think I'm easy.

I hit send before I could take it back. I clunked my phone against my forehead. God. Easy? Really?

DEREK: You cannot say things like that to me when I'm in the dark in bed.

ME: Don't be gross.

DEREK: I can promise, there's nothing gross about it.

ME: I'm regretting I said yes already.

DEREK: No, you're not.

ME: I seriously do not know what to say to you sometimes.

DEREK: I leave you speechless. That's good to know.

ME: I wish there was an eye-roll emoji.

DEREK: Can we pick you up at ten?

ME: Does that really mean ten, or ten to ten like today? I have to pack for three weeks.

DEREK: No pantsuits!!!

ME: What if that's all I have in my closet?

DEREK: Then I'll have to burn them. In a great big bonfire offering to the pantsuit god.

I caught myself before I responded that then I wouldn't have anything to wear, because who knew where he'd take that conversation. My lack of response brought another text from him.

DEREK: I'll see you at ten.

ME: Okay.

DEREK: Sweet dreams, Mia.

ME: Good night, moron.

Then my phone stopped buzzing. I placed it on my chest, which was heaving in a way that was so unusual for me. That I'd only really felt one other time: the time Hayden had texted and asked me to go out on a date with him. Well, it was really to attend this big charity thing with him on his dad's behalf. We were going to stay in a nice hotel in the city, and he'd broken up, yet again, with Marcie just the week before. I'd known that it was my chance. My chance to be something more to Hayden Hollister than his vice president in our business fraternity.

I'd bought my green dress and been as excited as a dog in a sprinkler. He'd picked me up with his golden smile, and driven me to a golden hotel, and we'd had a golden time. I'd ended up in his bed after too much wine that I didn't even like but that he drank by the bottleful.

When we got back to our reality, I found out that, while I'd been dreaming of our new life together, he'd gone and gotten back together with the beauty queen.

So, that whole adventure hadn't ended very well, just like I had lots of doubts about this adventure ending well. But I thought that if I knew going into it all, that it was just a three week thing, that I would be okay. That I'd just try, for once in my godforsaken life, to just live in the moment. To just be a twenty-something girl on a crazy adventure with a group of boys who had nothing but pleasure in mind.

It was hopeless to try to sleep. I switched on my bedside light, grabbed a notebook from my pile of unused journals, and started to make a list of things to bring with me.

Chapter Seven

Stop One

PERFECT

"Baby I'm dancing in the dark,
with you between my arms.
Barefoot on the grass,
Listening to our favorite song."
-Ed Sheeran

True to his word, Derek showed up at ten. I am not sure who was more of a basket case, my mama or me. I'd already waffled between not going and going about a hundred times since getting up after a restless night.

I had two bags packed. A medium sized suitcase that was really only half full because I didn't have very much that was not business clothes. I was either going to have to do laundry every third day or find some more clothes to wear. Next to that was my smaller bag which held my laptop and a handful of books. Because I wasn't going anywhere without some books. Sure, I had hundreds more on my Kindle app, but there were some books I didn't go far from in my life.

Derek pulled up in the Camaro. My heart fell to the pit of my stomach like stones in the lake, and when I looked at Mama, I could see that she was battling all of her emotions as well. Daddy reached out, grabbed her hand, and squeezed before tucking her close up against him.

I wasn't supposed to be causing them pain. That was the deal I'd made with myself, and yet, there I was getting into Jake's car and driving away with a boy who wasn't Jake at the helm. So that I could be free. I didn't deserve it. I swallowed hard.

But now that they wanted me to do this, not going would make them feel equally bad. There was no way out of the emotions I was causing my parents. Guilt hit me hard, as it always did. It was part of the reason I was running away. Because, let's face it, that's what I was doing. Running.

Daddy handed me a wad of cash, and when I protested, he said he was going to put even more into my account and that I should just think of it as a signing bonus. I told him he was crazy, but I didn't turn it down. Daddy didn't usually hand out money like it was free samples any more than he handed out compliments.

Derek jogged up to the steps in his usual uniform of tight, ripped jeans and another tight t-shirt. God, he really was like a Jamie McGuire book boyfriend. My heart pounded crazily, and I couldn't help a weak smile.

He smiled back, gray eyes flashing.

"Mr. and Mrs. Phillips, good to see you again," he said, shaking their hands. I could have sworn he grew up in the South instead of Hollywood because everybody knows that Californians don't know squat about manners.

Daddy held on tight to Derek's hand. "You'll take good care of our Mia on this crazy trip."

"Yes, sir. I'll look after her better than my guitar, and I promise that's saying a lot."

"I'm not a musical instrument," I said with a huff. He turned those devilish eyes on me, and I knew that if we weren't in front of my parents, he probably would have made it into a sexual innuendo. My heart pounded. Was I really going to do this?

I went to pick up my suitcase, but Derek beat me to it, brushing my hand away, and I couldn't help but rub the spot where our hands had met. Melting away already. And I was going to spend three weeks in a car with this guy? What on Earth was I doing?

"Wow, it doesn't feel like there's anything in here," he whispered to me with a sly wink, and I turned a thousand shades of red.

I turned away from him to my parents. I squeezed Daddy, and he held tight, patting my back and saying, "Have fun, baby girl."

When I went to Mama, she was already in tears. "Mama," I started and was about to say that I would stay, but she cut me off.

"No, no. I'm just being a silly ol' lady. I love you." She hugged me tight. "You enjoy yourself, but don't get mad at me if I text a lot."

"I hope you do," I told her, hugging back as hard as I could.

Derek had my stuff stowed in the back of the car, and I picked up my slouchy bag with the books inside. I gave my parents another quick hug and then stepped off the porch to where Derek already had the door of the Camaro open.

"Make sure you check the oil and water. Jake's... the Camaro can be temperamental when it gets hot," Daddy warned.

"I promise. I really will take good care of them both," Derek said just as he had before. He sank into the driver's seat. We pulled out, and he honked.

I turned back and waved at them on the steps, wrapped around each other. They looked so alone. God.

We drove in silence for a few minutes while I collected myself. Trying hard not to cry. Trying hard not to demand that he turn around. Then, I realized we didn't have the boys with us. And really, he was driving after he'd told me that was why he needed me to tag along in the first place. I said as much to him.

"The boys headed out in the bus when I came to get you. They're just a little ahead of us. We'll hook up with them for lunch. And I'm driving today, but you're driving tomorrow before we get to our gig."

More silence. It should have been awkward, but it wasn't. Maybe he understood that I needed to get myself back into a place where I could behave normally. In any event, he waited quietly for me.

He fiddled with the radio, going from one country station to the next.

"You're not going to find much more than country in this part of Tennessee," I told him.

"What would you listen to if you had a choice?"

"Ed Sheeran."

He sighed. "That's so not what I expected of you."

"What? He's an amazing writer."

"I don't dispute that. But I've come to expect the unexpected from you, and Ed is a little too mainstream these days."

I didn't know what to think about that. That he thought I was unexpected. I felt I had lived my life in one big expectation box. But I could also sense that this was somehow important to him. Probably because his life was music.

"My friend Harry and I used to listen to blues and jazz and ragtime tunes on vinyl. That kind of stuck with me." I shrugged.

"That's much better." He grinned.

I took off my flip flops and curled myself up into the seat of the Camaro. Old muscle cars always had plenty of room in their seats for tiny people like me to curl up. It was an advantage. The disadvantage being that old cars were always loud. Traveling for three weeks in the Camaro wasn't going to be a picnic.

I looked over and caught him taking me in before his eyes flitted back to the highway and the long stretch of nothing ahead of us.

"You look good like that," he said with a tone in his voice that made my body turn hot and zingy.

I ignored his comment. I was just in another pair of jean shorts and a t-shirt, hair in another ponytail. I knew I looked tired as sin after two nights of pretty much no sleep. And let's not forget that the emotions of the last couple days had been high. Dark eye rings had greeted me in the mirror this morning.

My phone buzzed.

CAM: Please tell me your mama is wrong!

ME: If you mean, am I currently in the passenger seat of Jake's Camaro driving to Oklahoma with the moron? Then I'm afraid she's right.

CAM: Blake's literally going to kill him.

ME: It's not like that.

CAM: Ooookaayyy.

ME: Seriously.

CAM: I'm not your mama. Don't lie.

ME: Okay. It's not like that, Cami.

CAM: Ugh. Don't Cami me.

I couldn't help but smile.

CAM: Why are you doing this?

I thought about how I could best respond to that question. I wasn't a hundred percent sure I could answer it, even to myself. Especially when no one in my family even knew about Hayden's existence. I looked over at Derek—heartbreakingly gorgeous Derek—and the closest thing I could think was because I didn't think I could not do it. So, I typed that. Her response came quick.

CAM: I'm worried about you, kiddo.

ME: Don't. It's gonna be okay.

CAM: Hmm. Well, at least have fun. But don't do

anything I would do. Do only what sensible Mia would tell crazy Cam to do.

It made me smile again.

ME: I promise.

I wasn't sure I was telling the truth, though. Because I wasn't sure I could promise her that I would be my normal Mia self. Normal Mia wouldn't even be in the car.

I put the phone down. Derek was still glancing between me and the road. I hadn't had to look up to know that. I'd felt it the whole time I'd been texting Cam. That intensity he gave off was wafting over me like the echolocation it was.

"Cam?" he asked. I guess that's pretty much the only person he'd seen me text. In truth, I didn't text many people more than her. Wynn. Harry occasionally. My mama. Cam's mama.

"Yes. I'd be careful the next time you see Blake; he might be carrying a gun."

Derek laughed that belly laugh that made his chin stretch and drew my eyes to his chest and the way it heaved under the muscles. He looked too good to be real. The fact that I was the girl sitting next to him in his car seemed dreamlike.

"She's not your sister, but it's like she is. Tell me how that works," he said.

Surprisingly, I wanted to. I didn't tell many people Jake and Cam's story. Our families' story. In our town, you didn't need to tell it because it was a legend. In college, I'd wanted to not talk about it. I'd wanted to just be Mia and not "Jake's little sister, Mia" because I'd thought it would make the guilt go away. But it never had.

So, I found myself telling Derek the whole story. I told him how we had all grown up together in our houses with the shared yard and tree house. I told him that our families were so close that it was like one family with two sets of parents. I told him how Jake and Cam had grown up in each other's pockets, and that when you saw them together, it was like they were one person instead of two. Like they were only whole when they were together. And when they were apart, they were still people, but missing something.

I told him about Jake's time at UTK and how he'd had to give football up. I told him how Jake had followed Cam to Virginia, and how they'd lost it all to Jake's disease. And I told him, which I *never* told anyone, about how when Jake needed a kidney, and I was a match, that I couldn't imagine saying no to him—to Jake *and* Cam—because they deserved to be a whole person instead of the painful halves they would be if he didn't survive. So, I gave them a kidney, but he hadn't survived anyway… and, well… enough said.

When I was done talking, I looked out the window at the flat ground and grass flying by the Camaro. I wasn't sure why I had wanted to tell him all of that when I'd kept it to myself for so long. For some reason, I'd wanted this BB to know my story. The story of a girl who gave up a body part to save a brother who everyone wanted to survive more than the girl herself. And how that hadn't worked out.

"Wow," he said after a few minutes of silence. It was as if he'd really taken the time to absorb my story. Like he seemed to absorb me every time he touched me. Even though I heard him, I didn't turn from the view outside. I wasn't sure what I'd see in those expressive eyes of his, and I really wasn't sure I could handle whatever was there.

I felt his hand grasping for mine, and it wasn't till then that I realized I was clutching the edge of the seat so tightly it could have torn. He forced my fingers open and clasped them in his own. "Mia?"

I looked down at our joined fingers before I finally had the courage to look up at his face. There were no smiles there now. God, I felt like such a depressing twit. One of the things that had attracted me the most about him was all those enormous smiles, and less than an hour on the road with him, and I'd wiped it away.

"You know it isn't your fault, right?" he asked with a frown.

"What?"

"Jake rejecting your kidney. That had nothing to do with you."

"Oh, I know that," I said, but then I looked down from his eyes to his hand. I did know that. I mean, I did. Then, some days the guilt overwhelmed me. I'd thought so many times that if he'd gotten a different kidney, the story would have had a different ending.

He squeezed my hand. "I'm not sure you do."

I pulled away and lied the lie I always did. "Seriously. It's not a big deal. We've all kind of moved on. But you asked, so I told you."

"I did ask," he said. "But I also know what it's like to live with guilt."

His eyes were on the road, and he wasn't smiling, but I also couldn't really imagine the happy Derek I'd seen over the last couple days being weighed down with the guilt inside me. Even though I'd glimpsed a quiet side to him here and there. The guilt that weighed me down was like a whole train, and he didn't seem to be carrying that much baggage.

Silence filled the car for a little while again while some newbie country singer sang something that was more pop than country.

"I'm really glad I bought the car," he said, and I couldn't help but be drawn to his face again. I saw a gravity there that really kind of wrecked my heart all over again because I knew he didn't mean because he liked sixties muscle cars. He meant he was glad because now my family had someone keeping it safe that understood what was beneath the red paint and beefy motor.

Suddenly, all of it was a little too much for me: this crazy, journey, the responsibility, the serious look on Derek's face. So, I did what I always did when the world was too much, and that was to pull out my book.

"What are you doing?" he asked.

"I was going to read. There's nothing else to do."

He put a hand to his chest. "Ouch. Nothing else to do."

I ignored him and looked down at the book, only to be drawn back to his face by his question.

"What's it about?"

"Um. It's *Pride and Prejudice*."

"And?"

I wasn't quite sure that he wasn't joking. "You know. It's *Pride and Prejudice*. By Jane Austen."

"Oookaay?"

"You've got to be kidding me. You don't even know who Jane Austen is, do you?" Holy bejesus, what was I doing in a car with some guy who didn't even know one of the most famous writers of all time?!

"I know who Jane Austen is. The writer chick from the eighteen hundreds. I just haven't read anything of hers."

"Do you even know how to read?"

"Ouch again."

"Okay, musician boy. Who's your favorite author?"

"Current or classical?"

I shrugged.

"Well, my man Will had a lot to say in iambic pentameter, which was pretty much music in those days, so he's gotta be up there."

"That doesn't say anything. I mean, anyone can throw Shakespeare out there and sound impressive."

"I'm trying to be impressive, then?" he asked with a twinkle back in his eye that made him hard to resist, but which I was also relieved to see after the seriousness of before. It also made me realize that he'd done it on purpose. The shift in conversation to shift the mood.

"I didn't exactly say that."

"You did," he smirked. "If I'm trying to be impressive, I see that I'll have to say someone more current but noteworthy. Hmm. How about Robert Ludlum? No. He's still dead. Plus that's really a spy novel, which doesn't seem like your kind of thing."

"Excuse me?"

"Well..." He twirled a hand toward my *Pride and Prejudice.*

"So, girls who read Jane Austen are only into romance novels and erotica?"

He swerved, and I clutched the door handle. "Jesus!" I breathed out.

"I swear to God, you're going to be the death of me. You can't say things like that and expect me not to react."

"What?" I frowned, trying to think about what I had said.

He burst out laughing. "Erotica. Do you really read that?"

I could feel the red creep into my face because I hadn't really thought about it when I said it. "I read everything."

His eyes met mine, and the car swerved again, and I had to put a hand out toward the wheel before he quickly straightened it out.

"Is *Pride and Prejudice* erotica?"

My turn to laugh. "God no."

"Thank God."

"Why would it matter?"

"I don't think I could drive knowing that you were reading porn," he said with a look on his face that made me turn pink all over again.

"Erotica isn't porn."

"Isn't it?" He met my eyes with his own, flashing something at me. Something that made me all fuzzy inside.

Three weeks, I told myself. *Holy button holes!* I was going to be spending three weeks with this.

He was right after all. Erotica was probably pretty close to what was in those PlayBabe magazines. But I hadn't read PlayBabe even though I'd protested that I read everything.

I shrugged in half-agreement. "Maybe. But Jane Austen is definitely not that. Her work first came out in serials in the English newspapers, so definitely not gonna be erotica."

He reached over and turned off the pop station that was supposed to be country. "What are you doing?" I asked.

"Read it out loud. At least we'll both have something to do rather than listen to that shit."

And that's what I did until we stopped for lunch. Read Jane Austen aloud in my dead brother's Camaro with a sexy musician behind the wheel while I was curled up in my shorts and another Harry Potter t-shirt. It should have felt like I was on an alien planet, but instead, it felt like I was home.

♪ ♪ ♪

At lunch, we met up with the rest of the band. They were driving the tour bus, which was just an oversized motor home with the name of their band, Watery Reflection, painted on the side. But who was I to tell them that it wasn't a real tour bus?

They all greeted me like I was already a member of their group with hugs and jokes that put me immediately at ease. I hadn't been sure what they would think of me tagging along. I got to meet Rob Colt, their drummer, for the first time. He was a lean machine of a man with naturally white-blonde hair. He seemed like he couldn't sit still and was bouncing a knee in the booth as if he needed to be somewhere else. Plus, the guys were still harassing him about his wife, Trista.

"Is she meeting us in Oklahoma City?" Owen asked.

"Yeah, but she isn't ready to divorce me yet, so you can't have her," Rob threw back.

"You'll screw up bad enough eventually," Owen said with a grin.

I was having a hard time imagining this bantering was serious, but they had said yesterday that Owen had a thing for Rob's wife, so who knew.

"So, Mia, Derek hasn't scared you away yet?" Rob asked, turning to me as he shoved his club sandwich into his mouth.

"Is he supposed to be scary?" I asked.

The boys all laughed.

"You'll see. Don't let that jovial clown nature of his trip you up. Underneath, he's all emotional drama," Mitch said, and Derek threw a french fry at him.

He was grinning at them, but I wondered. He seemed generally happy. Almost insanely so, but he'd also gotten fairly serious with me, including that vague reference to understanding guilt.

"Dude, you know that isn't even true. He just writes that sappy shit so the ladies will throw their panties at him," Lonnie responded.

"You guys are not helping my cause at all," Derek said with a sad shake of his head.

"Were we supposed to help you? You should have sent out a text," Owen joked. "I already sent one to Mia warning her off."

Derek punched him in the shoulder and then turned to me. "Whatever you do, *do not*, and I repeat *do not*, give your phone number to any of these bozos."

"Well, we'll need to text her while you're driving. You know, safety first," Mitch chimed in.

"She can just answer my phone for me," Derek said. Was he really worried about the band having my number?

"Are you sure? Maybe some panty-throwing lover girl will be texting you." Lonnie laughed.

"I do not give my number to any panty-throwing girls," Derek said firmly and then all but pushed Owen out of the booth to stand up. "We gotta hit the road, folks. We've got a few more hours till we hit Fort Smith."

Fort Smith was where we were stopping for the night. I guess the boys weren't the type to do eleven-hour days in the car, which made me wonder why I really needed to be along for the ride, but at this point it was too late to question it. Truth was, I didn't want to go back. Not yet. I had given myself three weeks to live a different life. To be somebody other than just Good Girl Mia.

Back at Jake's Camaro, I said I'd drive, but Derek said no way, he wanted to hear more about Elizabeth Bennet. I just shrugged, curled up in the passenger seat, and kept reading.

We got to Fort Smith in the early afternoon. It was a decent size town, on the Arkansas River, but didn't seem to have much in the way of hotels. Derek said we were staying at a Courtyard, which suited me just fine. We'd spent the night at plenty of them when we'd traveled for Jake and Cam's sports events over the years. They were predictable.

When we got to the hotel, I grabbed my own bags, and Derek tried to protest, but I just stuck my tongue out and moved away. He wasn't happy about it, but after I'd stuck my tongue out, he didn't fight me. Instead, he stared at my lips. I breathed deeply and headed toward the entrance.

When we got to the check-in counter, it finally hit me that I didn't have a reservation. Not one that I knew of, anyway. Derek just walked up, handed his credit card over, and the guy said he had two adjoining rooms ready for us. He handed Derek two keys, and then we rolled away while the other band members got checked in.

"Did you change your reservation for me?" I asked as we waited by the elevator.

"Well, technically my manager did, but yes." He shrugged.

"I can pay for my own room. I can pay my own way through all of this," I told him.

"You're helping me out. I told you my manager would pay you. It isn't a paycheck or anything. Is room and board gonna be okay?"

"You're kidding, right? I get to go on this crazy adventure with… your band, plus you're putting me up? I really think I'm the one who should be paying you."

As soon as the words were out, I wanted to thunk my *Pride and Prejudice* against my forehead because Derek got that sexy grin on his face again. Before he could say anything, though, I just waved my finger at him.

"Don't even. I have to be really careful what I say around you." But I had a smile on my face too.

"I've been telling you that!" he laughed.

We got to the hotel room doors, and he handed me one of the keys.

"We're gonna go down the street for food later. You're coming, right?"

In so many ways, I wanted to say no. That I'd just spent an entire exhausting day in the car trying to ignore how strong his magnetic pull was on me. Plus, there was my two nights of no sleep. I wanted to say that I needed to rest if I was going to drive the Camaro tomorrow, but his eyes and his smile were really too darn irresistible. Yikes! I was so in trouble.

"Sure, just knock on the door when you're ready to go." I smiled weakly and then headed into my room.

I could hear him through the adjoining door, banging around and starting the shower. I jumped in the shower too and tried to scrub away the tiredness. I looked in the mirror and decided that I needed to do something to make myself look better than I felt, so I straightened my long locks, which I didn't do very often, and actually put on a light coat of makeup. When I went to my suitcase, I wasn't sure what to put on. Should I just put on more shorts and a t-shirt?

I knocked on the adjoining door. Derek opened it so fast that it almost felt like he'd been on the other side, waiting. He just stared at me. It was suddenly awkward for the first time. Almost like he didn't know who I was.

"Um. Sorry to bother you. Was wondering where we were going. Are my shorts and flip flops going to be okay?"

He just stared some more.

"Hello?"

"Jesus Christ!" He ran a hand through his hair and closed his eyes.

"Okay. Sorry I bothered you." I turned to close the door, but he grabbed my arm quick as a lightning bolt through a southern storm.

"God, sorry, stop. Don't fly away." It was all mumbled. "Give me a sec to catch my breath."

I looked around him into his room. Was he working out? Was there another girl there? Ugh. What the hell was I doing?

"You seriously have no idea?" he asked, and he moved till he was a breath away from me. The smell of him, that smell that was almost like honey and wood polish, wafted over me, making it hard to breathe.

I was looking at his chest. Really, that's where my eyes naturally went when we stood next to each other. He tipped my chin up at him, and those gray eyes met mine in a way that wedged my toes into the hotel carpet.

"Miss Mia, my god, you stop my heart."

I closed my eyes and laughed, trying to shake the nickname that had flown from his mouth. Trying to shake my reaction to his blurt.

"Stop it," I breathed out because his intensity was too much.

He seemed to sense that he'd overwhelmed me, and he lightened the mood instead of persisting.

"You're wearing a towel, Miss Mia. A damn towel!" he chuckled.

I looked down in disbelief. Holy potato peels! I'd gone to his hotel room in a towel! Idiot, idiot, idiot! I was surprised he didn't think I was throwing myself at him like that long line of girls that people mentioned but he denied having. My body wanted me to throw myself at him. God, it did. But Good Girl Mia wasn't that far gone. She was still there putting up the good fight. I blushed a deep red.

"Ugh. I'm so sorry, what a dork!"

I backed away again, and he let me go, but he followed me into my room.

"How do you keep doing that?" he asked as I backed away toward the closet and my suitcase.

"What?" I asked, rifling through the handful of clothes there.

"Surprising the shit out of me!"

I looked up at him, and he was grinning again. Thank God. "If it makes you feel any better, you keep surprising me too. Or maybe it's more like I can't believe the imprecated malarkey I do around you."

"Did you just say imprecated and malarkey?"

I had. Because who didn't love a good word whether it was an old-time word or not? "Yes. Do my big words make you uncomfortable, pretty boy?"

He chuckled and moved toward me again so that I was now stuck up against the door of the closet. "You'd have to do a helluva lot more than that to make me uncomfortable."

He caught a strand of my hair in his fingers and slowly began to twirl it. Straightened, my hair was mid-back in length, but he took that one strand and curled it until he had it wrapped so much that his finger could rest against my cheek.

"I'd like to see that," he said with a voice so deep and sexy that I swear my body was instantly a pot of mush.

"See what?"

"You. Trying to make me uncomfortable."

We stood there. His hand on my cheek, and me unable to move because of my imprisoned hair. Little did he know that while I'd read a lot about things that I could do that might make him uncomfortable, there was no way I'd ever be able to actually do anything like that. There was no way my brain would ever shut off long enough for that to happen.

Even right then, when I wanted so badly for him to kiss me, I couldn't overcome all the walls, and barriers, and warning signs in my brain to take action on it. I waited to see if he'd make the move I couldn't. I was a mixture of disappointment and relief again when, instead of easing toward me, he let go and backed away.

From my suitcase, he pulled a summer dress. I only had a couple, but I'd thrown them in because they weren't business apparel. The one he chose was so girly that it was almost too embarrassing to wear. It was all flowers and lace, but made of cool cotton which you needed in the summer in the South.

"Wear this," he said. He put it in my hands and backed away. He sat down on the bed. He was waiting for me. I wasn't sure I could move. I looked down at the material in my hands and down to my curled toes before I took a deep, calming breath and headed into the bathroom where I put on the dress and stared at the flushed, straight-haired girl in the mirror. I didn't even look like me to myself.

He knocked on the door of the bathroom. "You ready? The boys are getting hungry, and believe me, you don't want to see Mitch when his blood sugar is low."

I opened the door in response. He took me in again, head to toe, and whistled. "Damn, Miss Mia. Just damn."

I smiled, because who couldn't smile at that? Some gorgeous BB talking to you in that way, with a nickname he had now called you three times in the span of five minutes. A nickname that sounded so sweet that it could make its own sweet tea. No one could resist that for long. No one.

I slipped on my flip flops again, grabbed my bag, and met him at the door. We walked to the elevators in silence.

Down in the lobby, the boys did their own whistling, and Owen tried to put his arm around my shoulders, but Derek shoved him off. They all laughed and catcalled, but it only made me smile more. Derek didn't grab my hand, but that was okay. It was like I was Phillips again and not Miss Mia.

We walked down a few blocks to Wishbone's Music and Chicken Joint. It sounded so authentically southern that I thought that was why Derek had picked it, but when we got there, I saw that they advertised live music on certain nights, so maybe he had played there before.

Tonight, there was no live music. Instead, tonight was karaoke night.

Need I say more? Because karaoke, alcohol, and southern food are a combination made to be together, like chips and salsa. There were just a few things I was good at in life. The ones most people knew about were baking, reading, and being the serious girl. The one thing not many people knew about me was that I was also good at karaoke.

In college, our business fraternity had a monthly karaoke night, and there was no way in any universe that I was going to embarrass myself in front of Hayden. So, I'd done a lot of practicing. I'd even taken a choir class just so that I wouldn't sound like an idiot.

In any event, all it took was one single alcoholic beverage and a karaoke machine, and I was all over it. Derek leaned back in his chair, long legs splayed out in front of him, hands behind his head, and grinned like he'd won the lottery as I sang Sandra Dee onstage. Because if you do karaoke, then *Grease* music is a must.

Owen and Mitch joined me with more drinks in hand, and we picked some crazier and crazier songs to sing. I was smiling again. Smiling like I hadn't until this gorgeous man and his boys had entered my life only three days ago. Derek didn't sing, which surprised me. But he watched. And the more he watched, the more I wanted to sing for him.

Eventually, the boys picked some hair band song that I knew I could not—would not do—so I made my way back to the table and sank down into the chair next to Derek. I gulped down some water, hoping that emotional Mia, who usually came out to play when I drank, would stay away. Honestly, the way Derek was smiling at me was daring her to come out. So, I put my head down on my arms on the table and closed my eyes. Suddenly, I was exhausted again.

Derek put a hand on my hair and ruffled it in a way Jake would do, but also in a way that wasn't brotherly at all, and my eyes flashed opened again to meet his. "Miss Mia, you're something else." He stared at me for a long moment. "And you're wiped. Let's leave these boys here and head back."

My stomach fell at the look in his eyes and his words that matched, but I just nodded.

"Hey assholes, we're leaving," he shouted at them over their raucous singing. "See you at nine tomorrow. Don't be late, Phillips here doesn't like it!"

They all just gave him a one-fingered wave from the stage. I grabbed my bag, and we headed out into the night air that had cooled ever so slightly but still managed to feel like a shower curtain was wrapped around you. Derek grabbed my hand, and we headed off. I was distracted by the hand holding, by the feeling of him so close as we walked, by the smell of him.

Finally, I looked up and saw scenery that I hadn't seen before. "I think we went the wrong way."

He frowned. "No."

I pulled away to turn and look back the way we'd just come. "I think so. The hotel is that way."

"Nah," he said as he grabbed my hand again, and we kept walking even though I was ninety percent sure I was right. Pretty soon we hit a park by the river which had definitely not been on our way to the restaurant from the hotel.

I started laughing. "You don't have a clue where we're at."

He looked like he wanted to deny it, but then he grinned and shrugged. "Seriously. No internal compass."

"So, Blake teasing you about getting lost was true."

"Hey, I've only gotten lost one time with him."

I busted out laughing. He put his hand to his heart again. "You keep wounding me, Miss Mia."

Then, he reached for me, wrapped his arm around my waist, and pulled me onto the grass off the sidewalk. We started dancing in the moonlight under the stars by the river. There was no music, but Derek seemed to hear his own in his head. And I swear I could hear Ed Sheeran in mine. Ed was telling me how he found a girl, beautiful and sweet. How he was dancing in the dark, with her between his arms, barefoot on the grass, listening to his favorite song, and how he thought she looked perfect tonight.

Derek twirled me and then pulled me up close to him. "What am I going to do with you, Miss Mia?"

It was the most romantic moment I'd ever had in my whole life. My body was softening into his while I waited for him to kiss me. I'd wanted him to kiss me for what felt like a century already.

I was pretty sure that if he kissed me now, with a couple drinks in me, I'd be in his bed like I'd been in Hayden's bed after a few drinks. Without the willpower to say no. With normal Mia sleeping under the intoxication's power.

Derek hadn't batted an eye at letting me know he wanted me, and I suspected that I hadn't been invited just to drive the Camaro. But I wasn't sure I could handle sleeping with him yet. Even though, it felt like it was inevitable. Even though I wanted these three weeks of freedom and passion so badly I could taste it.

I wasn't ready, yet, to sleep with him and have him regret it so much that he wanted to leave but couldn't because I was tagging along with him and not the other way around. So, instead of waiting for him to kiss me, I pulled him back toward the street.

"Take me back to the hotel so I can get some rest, otherwise I'll crash Jake's car, and Daddy will never forgive me," I told him.

"Except it's my car now, and I'd forgive you anything."

That hit me in the gut all over again, like he was so good at doing, because no one had ever said that to me. *Ever*. That they forgave me. Or would forgive me. How could they when I couldn't even forgive myself?

Because this Dangerous Derek was already so good at reading me, he sensed my seriousness like he had multiple times already and backed off again. "Come on, Miss Mia. Let's get you back to the hotel. I promise I won't tell the boys you got us lost."

I punched him on the shoulder, and we walked back the way we'd come.

Chapter Eight

Stop Two

LITTLE BIRD

"And I'll owe it all to you.

My little bird."

-Ed Sheeran

We weren't on the road until nine-thirty. I guess the rest of the band wasn't as punctual as Derek, and this seemed to drive him crazy while we waited for them in the lobby. While he paced, I had time to dart out and pick up Starbucks for us all after making Derek tell me their favorites.

The boys were happy as clams with the drinks and told Derek I was a keeper. Which made me flush and him grin like there was actually something going on between us more than heavy flirting and wishes that hadn't become reality.

Sitting in the driver's seat of the Camaro made me think of Jake again. It was easier when Derek drove to think of it as his car, but in the driver's seat, it became Jake's all over again.

I took a deep breath, put in the address of the hotel in Oklahoma City on my iPhone, and plugged it in to the stereo system that Daddy had had installed.

To get my mind off Jake, I teased Derek, "So, there's this thing called Google Maps, and it's surprisingly good at keeping you from getting lost. You don't need an internal compass anymore. Just so you know."

He grinned at me. "Smart-ass."

He reached for my bag and started digging in it.

"Excuse me." I said.

He looked up. "Yeah?"

"Um. What are you doing in my bag?"

"Is that a problem for you?" He grinned again once he realized that it was. "Sorry. Years with the boys. We don't have any personal boundaries."

He didn't stop looking in my bag, however, until he came out with my copy of *Pride and Prejudice* and waved it at me. "My turn to read."

It was surprising that I didn't keel over dead right there, because this gorgeous man was going to read to me from my favorite book? In that sexy-as-sin voice? I guess fairytales do come true.

I had to turn my focus to the road and our journey so that I didn't faint and crash. Thankfully, it was only going to be a couple hours to the next hotel as the band had a practice session that afternoon at The Criterion where they were going to play the following night.

I'd done some research once I'd figured out their schedule. The Criterion was a Live Nation partner, and they had some pretty big bands come through. It made me realize, for the first time, that Derek and his band were really on the uptick. They'd been signed. I mean, I knew Blake had written the contract, but somehow it hadn't really hit home to me that this group of almost adolescents was really going to be famous soon.

They were good. I'd heard them at the fundraiser, but again, I don't know, it just hadn't really penetrated my thick skull. Maybe it was because when he was hitting on little ol' me, from a little town in the middle of nowhere with nothing but size E's to show the world, it didn't seem like it was something someone super famous would do.

In order to ignore all my doubts, I turned my brain back to Derek as he read from my favorite book.

Once we got close to Oklahoma City, Google Maps did a marvelous job navigating us through the maze of streets, even though Derek kept telling the voice that she was sending us on a wild goose chase. I was smiling by the time we reached the hotel. When he went to put my book back in my bag, a scrap of paper fell out. I saw it with a patter of my heart that wiped my smile away.

Derek, being the no-privacy guy I had found him to be, read it aloud. "I'm sorry we weren't what you imagined us to be. But I want to say thank you. Because you still care when it seems like no one else does, you comfort when it's needed most, and you love even when it hurts." He stared at it for a moment. "What's this?"

I shrugged because I couldn't breathe. I wasn't sure I could still drive into the parking garage.

"Is this a book quote?"

I shook my head ever so slightly, but I couldn't answer. I was frozen on the inside. Those words had been all that had held my shredded heart together for a long time. It was Hayden's apology note. The one he wrote when I said I loved him, and he chose Marcie instead. It was the note he wrote after I sent him a pile of love letters, and he continued to call because he said he needed a friend. It was the note that made me hold on so tightly to the possibility of him coming back to me. Like Jake and Cam had always found their way back to each other. But he hadn't come back.

I pulled the car into a slot in the parking lot of the hotel. We didn't get out. We sat there as Derek continued to look down at the paper.

"Did some guy write this for you?" he asked, and it was obvious that a guy had. Hayden's handwriting was such a typical male scribble.

The question really was, did *just some guy* write me that? Some guy? Was that all he was? Just some guy I'd loved? Just some guy I'd lost my virginity to? Just some guy who couldn't love me enough to choose me first? Just some guy who'd left my already guilt-knotted heart with a new ice-picked hole in it?

"What kind of asshole would write something like that?" Derek asked, bringing me back to him and away from Hayden.

"He's not…" I started to defend him, protective of my first love.

"Mia, you don't encourage someone to love you when you know you're going to hurt them. That's not love, that's some egotistical jerk playing games." Somewhere deep inside me, a tiny voice spoke up asking if maybe Derek was right. Because Hayden had known how I felt and hadn't stopped calling me. Hadn't stopped even though he was with someone else.

God, it stung. All the words coming from this beautiful man's mouth. The one who should, in all rights, be breaking hearts just like that. A jerk playing a game. But Derek hadn't done that. Not yet. So far, he'd only been up front, and real, and honest.

"It wasn't like that," I still protested and tried to grab the paper from his hand, but he didn't let me. Instead, he tore it up into little shreds that made my heart feel like shards of glass being pounded by manic feet.

I should have been furious, watching as Derek shredded the words I'd carried around for almost a year and a half. Somehow, I wasn't. Because that tiny voice was still beating out a tune about it maybe being true. That all this time I'd been thinking that Hayden just needed someone to stick around and believe in him, when really, maybe he just got off on the fact that I was always waiting in his shadow.

It made me realize that I'd been weak. And stupid. It was embarrassing beyond belief that I would have been that naïve. That needy. That I had been following him around like a stupid puppy following its master.

"Mia?"

I couldn't look at him. I knew I'd turned a thousand shades of red. He tried to grab my chin and turn it to him, but I couldn't let him. I just held on tight to the steering wheel and parked in the lot at the Renaissance Hotel as my stupidity and emotions overwhelmed me. I didn't want to see what he was feeling in those expressive eyes. Pity? Shock at my inanity? Disgust? God, please don't let it be disgust.

"Little Bird, please look at me."

This new nickname hit my stomach like a tornado hits a barn, but I still couldn't look at him. I pushed his hand away as he tried to undo mine from the steering wheel.

"I think it's beautiful that you gave your heart to him," he said quietly. My throat closed up. A sound came out that was a clog of emotion and tears. I wouldn't cry, though. I was good at not crying.

Somehow, I choked out, "Stupid, not beautiful."

"It's not stupid to love someone."

"It is when you know they'll never reciprocate it."

"That's just my point. How were you to know that he would never love you back when he said this kind of shit to you?"

"Actions speak louder than words," I said. Didn't I know that? Hadn't I seen it my whole life with Cam and Jake? Jake may have denied loving her when they were younger, but it was obvious every time they were together and he couldn't keep his eyes off her. She drew him. He drew her. They were fireflies colliding in a night sky. Beautiful and brilliant. I didn't think Hayden had ever looked at me like that. Why hadn't I seen it before?

"I hate that saying," he said to me. "It isn't true. Sometimes words have a much more lasting impact on you than anything anyone ever does."

I was shocked. Because words had been my life, and I couldn't believe there was anyone else out there besides Harry Winston who could ever believe that words could change you. That they could change you for the good or the bad.

We sat there in silence.

"Little Bird, please look at me." This time when he tugged gently at my chin, I let him turn my face to his, but I was still not brave enough to look up. To meet those eyes which had to be saying "this chick is lame" even as he was trying to comfort me.

I could feel him taking in every inch of my face, and he moved his thumb so that it ran along the very edge of my lip, and my body instantly went into honey butter mode. He leaned toward me and whispered quietly, "He didn't deserve someone as loving and loyal as you."

Finally, I risked looking up at him and couldn't suppress the intake of breath at what I saw in his eyes. It was admiration at a minimum. Maybe something more. Something I was a little terrified to name.

"I'm going to kiss you," he told me as his lips inched toward mine. It was as if he was afraid I'd fly away if he did it without warning me. That I really would be that little bird.

When I didn't pull away or protest, he closed the tiny space that was left between us and touched his lips to mine in a kiss that was so light and so reverent that it started to break my walls, leaving behind solitary blocks and tiny little crumbs that would not likely be able to be put back together again anytime soon.

It wasn't that there wasn't passion in that kiss, because purple biscuits, my toes were curling in my flip flops again. But this kiss wasn't about sex. He was trying to send me a message. A message that I wasn't sure I was ready to hear yet. About me and wishes and fairytales.

Just as the kiss started to turn into something that had me twisting my fingers into his soft t-shirt and pulling him toward me, there was a knock on the glass.

We both jumped back and looked up to see Lonnie grinning like a crazy lumberjack at us. "Hello little children, am I interrupting?"

"You're such an idiot," Derek said, shoving the door open so quick and hard that the handle hit Lonnie in the crotch and he doubled over, groaning. Derek jumped out of the car, still ranting about him being a dumbass and a big baby.

I brushed my fingers over my lips before getting out as well, and when I turned, Derek was watching me over the roof of the car with his gray eyes still storm clouds that I wanted to lose myself in. He was waiting for me to fly away. But I didn't want to fly anywhere. Rather, I wanted to go around the car and ease myself into his side and take his hand in mine. I couldn't, though. My brain wouldn't let me. My walls that were becoming pieces were still there, preventing me from making a physical step like that.

Instead, I opened the trunk and took my bag out. Derek came over and insisted on grabbing it, even though he had his own, and we walked into the lobby of the hotel to check in.

We had adjoining rooms again. It was strange. Like Derek and his manager had specifically asked for them. It made my heart pitter-patter in that way that was very hazardous to my health while I struggled to be sensible. To keep my imagination from leaping places it shouldn't go.

When the knock on the adjoining door came a few minutes later, I answered it with equal amounts of trepidation and hope. Derek was leaning against the doorframe, ever present jeans and t-shirt angled tight against his body. He wasn't smiling, though. He was serious.

Good job, Mia, my brain pounded out, *see what happens when you let your heart take over? Cheerful men become serious zombies.*

"I have to get over to the venue to rehearse. We're already later than we expected, and George is going nuts," Derek said as if it was an apology. I wasn't sure what for. His manager had already called a dozen times while we were on the road.

"Are you going to get lost? Maybe I should Google it for you," I tried to tease. He didn't bite.

"We aren't done with our conversation," he said.

I turned away, but he followed and had me by the arm, turning me back around, before I could take more than five steps. Then he was kissing me again. And this kiss wasn't reverent. Or maybe just not as reverent, because it was also demanding and feverish, and it made my body ache. Ache in places I'd never ached before. Never ever. My fingers tightened into balls in his t-shirt again.

His lips left mine, and I opened my eyes to see a smile on his face. Relief flooded me. Serious Derek had gone away again. "I really, really want to stay and finish this conversation."

God, his tone was back too, the playful lightheartedness making me ache almost as much as his kiss had.

"Just go," I said.

"Do you want to come?"

I shook my head. I didn't. I needed some space. I needed to figure out what my warring body and brain were going to do with all the new information it had gathered that day.

"I don't know how late we'll be." He was apologizing again. "Knowing George, he'll have us try a dozen different things before he's satisfied that the set is right."

"Don't apologize. This is what you're here for."

"I know. It's what I wanted. It's what we planned." His hand brushed through his locks. "God, I just didn't plan on also wanting to be here with you."

My heart leapt at his words. Words that wiped clean the ones I'd been carrying around for eighteen months and that had been torn to pieces in the Camaro.

"Moron." I pushed away, trying to lighten the mood. Trying to summon my inner Cam who was so good at being flippant and sassy. "Go do your gig. I'm fine. I'll see you when I see you."

He stepped back with the grin back on his face. When he got to the adjoining door, he pointed at it. "I'm leaving this open."

Oh my God. Was that a statement or a promise? My heart skipped wildly. I just nodded and made a shooing motion with my hands. He started to leave but then took two rapid strides back to me, kissed me quick, and then walked away without looking back. I heard his hotel door slam shut.

I sank down on the bed. My heart hammered in my chest. My lips felt happy. I think I was smiling. A smile I didn't know I could still use. For once, I didn't want the guilt and the doubts to overwhelm my happiness, and I knew if I just sat in the silence, it would overtake me until I was barely able to breathe.

So instead, I reached for my phone. I couldn't text Mama, because she would just worry. And Cam would want to bust something.

I texted Wynn.

ME: I think I'm falling for a sexy musician.

Moments later.

WYNN: Cam told me you'd gone insane and are on some tour across country with the band guy from the fundraiser. Where are you?

ME: Oklahoma City. At the Renaissance Hotel. And tomorrow I'll be at The Criterion watching him play. And the day after that I'll be spelunking with him at Alabaster Caverns.

WYNN: Is this really Mia? Or has somebody stolen her phone?

I didn't know if I should now be offended or relieved that so many people didn't believe that this adventure was something I would normally do. I guess I really hadn't done anything in my life that would shock anyone. The only noteworthy thing I had done was give a kidney when I wasn't even eighteen. And look how that had ended.

ME: It's me. What do I do?

WYNN: The word spelunking kinda gave you away actually. Do you really want my opinion? I can tell you what Cam would say, don't give him one chance to look at anyone else. Do anything and everything to demand he looks at you.

ME: You're funny. If I wanted to know what Cam would do, I would be texting Cam. Besides, we all know what she would do. Bust everything until he didn't have a choice but to look at her.

WYNN: LOL. Are you really falling for him or just lusting want-to—have-sex after him?

I wanted to text that I just wanted to have sex with him. Even though that was not something Wynn would ever expect to hear from me. I wanted to say that I was just in this for three weeks of escape. But only a day into this adventure, I was suddenly unsure I could do that.

ME: ????

WYNN: Well, I'll just say one thing then. GO FOR IT!

ME: Would you?

WYNN: Doesn't matter. Just do it. *Wink emoji*

After we'd said goodbye, I lay thinking again which was never a good thing. I knew I'd go stir-crazy if I stayed in the hotel room staring at the walls.

I decided I would go do laundry. I'd already burned through a stack of my clothes; there wasn't a lot more in the suitcase.

Just as I was getting ready to leave, Mama texted to ask if we'd arrived. My stomach turned unpleasantly because I hadn't texted her, and I'd made her worry. I apologized for not letting her know that we were at the hotel. I told her that I was going out to do laundry. Mama surprised me by texting back that I should just go shopping instead. She told me she knew Daddy had put money in my account, and that I should go splurge.

It seemed so not Mama. Neither her nor Daddy were big spend thrifts. They were save-now-for-later kind of people. Not that we'd really been denied anything growing up. It was just that they saw the need to put aside for the future.

I did need clothes, though. Something different from my usual business apparel or my teenage leftovers. Even though I knew it was yet another thing I'd feel guilty about later, I Googled the nearest shopping mall and found one not too far where I could get regular clothes and some caving gear.

I didn't want to take Jake's—Derek's—Camaro without his permission, so I took a Lyft. I hadn't spent the day shopping by myself, ever. I'd always had Wynn, or Cam, or some member of my fraternity with me.

In this case, I had no one to run opinions against. That was also kind of good. I had to rely on my own opinion. I had to decide what I liked and didn't like. I picked up some more summer dresses and a pair of skinny jeans that didn't make my curved hips and small legs look too out of proportion. And a couple blousy tank tops that I could wear to the clubs the band would be playing at and not feel like a leper. I got a pair of wedge sandals to go with it all and felt almost like a normal twenty-two-year-old. Almost.

Then, I hit the sporting goods store. Once there, I had to ask for help, and one of the salesmen was really nice. He asked where I was going caving and what I liked about it. I had to be honest that I was new to it all, but my friends were more experienced. When I was done getting a neoprene backpack, elbow and shin pads, a helmet, and some slick gear, I felt almost like I knew what I was doing.

The guy wrote his number on the receipt.

I just stared at it as I walked out. That had never happened to me before. I'd been way more talkative with him than I normally was. For once, I almost felt like maybe I could be the firefly Cam had always been. That maybe, just maybe, I'd be able to shine in the brilliant sky, instead of fade into invisibility like normal.

That just made the guilt hit me as it always did hardest when I started to feel too good. Because I didn't deserve to shine. I definitely didn't deserve to shine brighter than Jake or Cam. I wanted him back so he could shine with her.

By the time I got back to the hotel, my mood had sobered back up. It was almost eight o'clock. I wasn't really hungry, and even though my body was begging for sleep, my brain wouldn't rest.

Derek was obviously not back yet. I changed into my leggings and t-shirt, shut off the light, and climbed into bed. Then I did what I normally did to escape my brain and the world, which was to immerse myself in a new book. I opened the Kindle app on my phone and read the newest Jessica Park novel until my eyes drooped shut of their own accord.

I don't know how long I'd been asleep when something woke me. Maybe it was the hotel's air conditioning kicking in or laughter in the hallway. I glanced at the clock to see it was midnight.

I rolled over and screamed as a dark shadow moved at the edge of the room.

Just as I'd screamed, I realized it was Derek. He was leaning on the adjoining doorway, staring at me. Maybe my echolocation device had woken me up instead of a noise.

I sat up. "You scared me to death."

He didn't move. "I'm sorry. I was trying not to wake you."

His voice was gravelly. Tired. I realized that not only had he read the whole time in the car, but then he'd sang all afternoon. I hoped he wasn't going to be hoarse for the show.

"You sound tired," I said quietly.

"Beyond belief."

What my body wanted to do was scoot over, and pull the sheet back, and invite him into my bed. Not for sex. I mean, that would have been awesome too, but just so that he could rest and I could make sure he did. But even though my boundaries had started to crumble, there was no way I was capable of inviting a guy into my bed of my own accord.

He seemed to be waiting for my invitation. Or for something. I wasn't sure.

"You should get some rest," was all I could offer out in a breathy voice that sounded way sexier than I could have made it if I'd tried.

"I'm not sure I'm going to be able to do that with you in here and me in there." He shoved his hands into his jeans pockets.

My breath hitched. I nodded in agreement. Because I wasn't sure I'd go back to sleep knowing he was in the next room either. With the door open. With the possibilities swirling between us like mist that might turn to rain.

He eased toward me and the bed, not backing down as he had the day before from my uncertainty. He looked down at me. "I'm really tired, Little Bird."

Finally, I couldn't not offer it up, because really, it would be rude to deny the man his rest, right? So, I pulled back the covers, scooted backwards, and offered up the space where I had just been.

He yanked his t-shirt over his head, and I stared in wonder at abs so beautifully contoured that I was sure he'd already been an underwear model. He stared at me as I stared at him. I wasn't entirely sure that I wasn't drooling. Embarrassingly. Then, he popped open his jeans and slid them down over lean hips and a rear end that would have looked brilliant in a football uniform.

I gulped air.

He slid into the covers, still watching me. We both lay down, staring at each other, eyes open, with a good twelve inches between us. He yawned. "This is not at all how I envisioned our first night in the same bed going," he mumbled, eyes drooping.

"You envisioned us in bed together?" I asked quietly, and his eyes flashed back open.

"God, Little Bird, since the moment I saw you in that hideous pantsuit at the dealership."

I smacked him, hand to bare chest, and he caught it up against him, eyes already shutting again. "But I'm no good tonight. Completely wiped."

"Go to sleep, moron," I said quietly.

He already was, with my hand still wrapped in his, held tightly against his chest. I stared for a long time, wondering again what the words wrapped around his wrists said, but it was too dark to see. I wanted to reach out and kiss them. And kiss the small tattoo on his neck. Instead, I found my own eyes drooping closed just as his had done.

I felt more relaxed than I had in so very long. Like I had come home. Or maybe like he had come home after a long haul. Like a sailor on a journey coming home to port. Ed was singing about a little bird in my head. Singing about coming inside and lying down with him, and staying there to kiss and read the truth in his lips. About holding each other, but also about not diving in too soon because that would only lead to heartache.

And for the first time in a long time, I was still smiling when I entered my dreams.

Chapter Nine

The Criterion

FALL

"And I will fall for you.
If I fall for you,
Would you fall too?"
-Ed Sheeran

A phone was ringing. I smacked at mine on the bedside table, but it did nothing to stop the song that I couldn't quite place, but sounded oddly like Ed's "Little Bird." Definitely not my blues ringtone. I hated mornings. I wasn't kidding. Really hated them.

When I moved and kicked another body, I squeaked in shock before the night came rushing back into my head. I rolled over to find Derek there, eyes still shut against the daylight that filtered in through the dark hotel curtains.

The noise was coming from his phone tucked in his jeans on the other side of the bed. How it didn't wake him up was beyond me. I leaned over him and searched the floor, eventually coming up with his phone and hitting the home button to stop the sound. When I went to pull away, his arm snaked around me and kept me there. Half on top of him.

I looked down to find his groggy eyes open, and his impish smile stretching his cleft. I couldn't resist any longer;

my finger touched it before I could stop, like I'd been dying to do since the first day I'd met him. He caught my finger and pulled it to his mouth where he first nibbled on it and then sucked on it gently.

Oh my God, I was just a rolling blob of bubbling butter. I was toast. He moved from my finger to my wrist, kissing, nibbling, sucking, his eyes watching me the whole time. Curious. Waiting for me to fly, or stop him, or… I don't know. Maybe he wanted me to surprise him. Shock him. I couldn't. Not even when I was trying to be this Other Mia. There was only so much unexpected in my repertoire, whether he liked that or not.

"You look good in the morning, Little Bird." His voice was scratchy and sexy as hell.

"You're beautiful," is what slipped out of me. I immediately wanted to thunk myself. Ridiculous. I wanted to wave my wand and make it go away.

He smiled. "I am, aren't I?"

I went to pull away, but he caught me tighter around the waist and moved his lips to my inner elbow. Who would have thought that my inner elbow could be an erogenous zone? Not me, but my body was quickly liquefying. Pretty soon he'd have to have someone come scoop me into a bowl to move me.

His phone started again. This time I knew it was "Little Bird." I wondered how long it had been his ringtone. He groaned and reached for the phone I'd placed on the side table, but his other arm still held me tightly against him. He wasn't letting me fly. Not yet. I wasn't ready to move, because I'd only be able to pour myself onto the floor.

"What?" he groused. "Shit. It is?" He pulled the phone away to look at it, and I realized he was probably late. We hadn't set any alarms. Daylight was obvious through the curtain strands. How late was it? I couldn't check. I was wrapped in a grip so tight that I thought I'd be a permanent member of his chest at any moment.

"Damn. Give me five." He clicked off with another groan.

"You're late?"

He nodded, but his eyes had returned to mine, searching them for something, and I still wasn't sure what he hoped to find.

"I'm sorry."

"You do that a lot," he said, still taking me in.

"What?"

"Apologize for things that are out of your control. You have nothing to apologize for. I should have set the alarm."

"You were too tired to remember."

"Mia."

"Yes?"

"Just kiss me."

I stared at him for a moment, and then I did. I kissed him! Good Girl Mia kissed him first. True, he'd asked for it, but my lips met his, not the other way around. I wanted to applaud, but as soon as my lips hit his, his hand went to the back of my head and pulled me even closer. His tongue that had turned my insides to liquid butter moved inside my mouth in a way that made me crumble all over again.

My hands went to his hair and his face of their own accord while his hands snuck under my t-shirt to graze the bottom of my braless breast. My breath faltered, and my eyes flew back open to meet his.

He pulled back ever so slightly, removing his tongue from my mouth but leaving his hands where they twirled against the tender skin on the curve of my breast near my side.

"God… you kill me," he said, and I could feel how much he wanted me. The push against his briefs that made my whole body tingle.

"I think it's been five minutes," I told him.

"Who cares?"

"George."

A pounding on his door from the other room made him grimace. "That's probably Lonnie. He's the only one stupid enough to come get me."

Sure enough, we heard Lonnie's laughing voice on the other side. "Derek, man, you gotta come on. George is about ready to piss his pants."

"I'm coming!" Derek yelled back, but he hadn't moved. He hadn't loosened his hold on my waist.

"You don't look like you're coming," I said and then instantly regretted it when his smile turned all sexy Puck again.

"I could very easily be coming. But it wouldn't be right or fair to either of us."

I tugged myself away, and he let me go with a sigh.

He raised himself out of the bed, tugging on his jeans, and I got a good look at the tattoo on the back of his neck. It was an eagle. Not huge, but with wings spread out, one pointing toward his ear, the other toward his shoulder blade. It was intricately made, even though it was only a couple inches long. An eagle. Just like I'd thought he was at the fundraiser. An eagle swooping down to capture me, the mouse. I wanted to touch it, but he'd already moved away.

"Shut the door behind me," he said, and I wasn't sure if it was to keep Lonnie out or to keep himself from returning to me. Or maybe to keep me out. I laughed inwardly, the smile reaching my face, and he groaned again.

He came back and kissed me quick like he had the night before, and then slipped out the door without looking back. I got up on shaky legs and shut and bolted the door just as I heard him let Lonnie in on the other side.

"Dude, you're never late. You better get your ass in the shower before George bans Phillips from traveling with us," I heard Lonnie's loud mouth boom out.

"Like to see him try," was Derek's muffled response, and then the shower kicked in.

I looked down at the clock, surprised to see it was ten o'clock. We'd slept so soundly. I texted a good morning to Mama so she wouldn't worry, then headed to the shower myself. When I came out, I had two texts. A return from Mama, and one from Derek saying they'd be at the venue until the show, but that he'd leave tickets and a backstage pass for me at the ticket window. He said to come early.

That meant I still had at least a seven-hour window to myself. I wasn't used to time alone with nothing to do. Mostly because I never let myself have it. It was too painful.

My phone buzzed.

WYNN: How was the sex?

ME: Nonexistent.

WYNN: Oh no! I'm sorry.

ME: But the kissing was hot. And we still slept together.

WYNN: Ooooh. You little slut you. Cam is going to have your hide.

I was smiling again.

ME: What Cam doesn't know won't hurt her.

WYNN: You think you can keep this from her? She's going crazy with the baby so close and being on bed rest.

ME: What?

And there was the guilt, hitting like a snake bite. Why was Cam on bed rest? When had this happened? I'd only been gone two nights.

WYNN: You didn't know?

ME: No!!!! I'm calling her now.

WYNN: Okay. She'll probably be pissed that I spilled the beans, but then she's always known not to trust me with a secret. LOL. Love you.

ME: Love you too.

I hit Cam's picture in my favorites.

"Hey, you delinquent, you," Cam answered.

"What the hell is going on?" I demanded.

"Three days with a musician and you're already swearing. Come home so I can have your mama wash your mouth out with soap." There was laughter in her voice, and that made me feel slightly better.

"Seriously, Cam, what's up?" I said.

"God. It's nothing. They just don't like how fast all those stupid fake contractions are coming, or maybe they were real contractions too? I don't know. They want me off my feet for a few days."

"Like how long?"

"Hopefully not long, I'm already going crazy. You know Blake, if I even try to set a toenail on the floor, he's manhandling me back to bed. He literally carried me to the bathroom last night before I punched him in the gut."

"You did not."

"I did too. I can pee by myself, thank you very much."

"But other than that, you and the baby are okay?"

"Yeah. They just don't want me to go into labor six weeks early. They're trying to get me to go another couple weeks."

All I could think was that it was just like Cam to not wait the full term on anything. She wasn't good at waiting. I was surprised as all get out that she'd agreed to Blake's wish to not know the sex of the baby.

"I'm going to come home."

"Don't you dare, I'm not even home. I'm back in Nashville."

"Then I'll come to Nashville."

"If you show up here, I'll lock you out."

And Cam would. You never went against a determined Cam, because you always lost. I wasn't sure how Blake did it because he seemed to win more than his fair share against her.

"Are you having fun?" The laughter was back in her voice.

"We haven't done any spelunking again, yet. That's tomorrow."

"Is that what the kids are calling it nowadays?" More laughter.

I flushed even though she couldn't see me. "It's not like that."

She laughed harder. "Like I said, you can tell your mama that, kiddo, but you can't keep the truth from me."

Jake used to call me kiddo. Cam had too, but not as often as she did now with Jake gone. Sometimes I wondered if his soul had embedded itself into her when he'd died. After all, he hadn't been able to live without her in life, why would death be any different? There was still so much of him that seemed to surround her.

"Seriously," I finally responded.

"Has he kissed you?"

Silence.

"Details!"

"It was nice."

"Nice!!! Jesus. I'm sending Blake after him. A hot guy like that shouldn't be kissing *nice*." She sounded thoroughly insulted on my behalf, and I had to laugh.

"God. You're awful. It was way more than nice, okay? It was… earth-shattering."

"Now that's better." Cam was smug.

"I'm hanging up now."

"No! Don't go! I'm bored to tears. Tell me something else. What's the rest of the band like?"

I spent the next hour talking to her about the band, and karaoke, and how Derek and I had gotten lost. How he was reading to me as I drove, and how I felt more comfortable with him than I had with anyone in forever. Maybe ever. She listened, which wasn't something Old Cam had been good at, but New Cam worked hard to do.

After that, she had to pee, and I had to attend to the gnawing hunger that was chewing its way through my stomach. So, I went down to the café and found a sandwich and wandered out to a park down the street to do some reading.

Instead of reading, I found myself looking at the pictures I'd taken and posted over the last couple days. I'd posted pictures of the caving trip, and the karaoke bar, and the scenery.

I scrolled back slowly through my pictures—years' worth—until I got to the one that always made me stop. It was of Jake and Cam. He'd pulled her up against him, with his chin leaning on her head and her arms wrapped around him. Her eyes were closed with a peaceful smile on her face. They had fit perfectly together. As if God had molded them as one cookie before dividing it down the middle and sending it to Earth.

I loved and hated this picture because it made me wish all over again that I could have taken Jake's place. He had so much to live for. So many people who were looking to him. I hadn't even had a best friend past eighth grade once Harry had moved away. I had just floated around at the edge of Cam's world.

When I'd met Hayden, I'd wanted so badly to be the other half of his cookie like Cam had been Jake's. I'd wanted to fit in his world and in his arms like God had made me just for him. But I hadn't. Not even when he told me things I knew he never told Marcie about his dad and the App World that his dad ran and that he wanted so badly to take over.

I guess God, or destiny, or whatever is out there knew best, because the truth was that even if Hayden had chosen me, it wouldn't have worked. I wouldn't have been able to go with him. I had a family that I couldn't leave. I had a dealership to run so Daddy and Cam's daddy could retire. I wasn't just taking it over because I felt responsible. I liked the dealership. I liked the people, and the community, and how we could help people get the vehicles they needed in their lives. So maybe destiny had made Hayden choose Marcie so that I wouldn't be tempted to leave behind the things that I needed more than belonging to someone as their other half.

My alarm went off, reminding me that I needed to go get ready for the show. But I wasn't smiling anymore. I was wondering again how in all that is holy I had ended up on a spelunking adventure with a musician who promised me nothing but kisses and charm.

I couldn't quite shake my morose mood as I showered and straightened my hair again and then put on a new black A-line tank and my new jeans, which I knew I'd regret in the heat, but went with the tank so nicely. I finished it off with my new patterned wedges and looked in the mirror on the closet. I was amazed at how normal I looked. How twenty-something. Instead of the old-before-my-time look that usually accompanied my reflection.

I was still Mia. But Mia with an edge that had never existed. Cam would be proud. Wynn would be shocked. Jake and Mama would have told me to go change. And Hayden? I didn't know what Hayden would have thought. Did it matter?

Just as I was getting ready to leave, I got a text from Derek.

DEREK: Hey Miss Mia, have you left yet?

ME: No. Was almost ready.

DEREK: Can you do me a huge favor?

ME: Ummmmmm…

DEREK: Get your mind out of the gutter, Phillips.

I laughed. It felt good after the melancholy I'd felt all afternoon.

DEREK: Can you pick up our food order at Aristotle's? It's next to The Criterion. I'm sure your Google Map thingy will tell you where. No food here, and Mitch is already whining about his blood sugar.

ME: Sure, no problem.

DEREK: *Sorry to make you run errands. That isn't why you're here.*

ME: *Who's apologizing now?*

DEREK: *Hurry! I need to see you.*

I didn't respond. I couldn't. When was the last time anyone had "needed" to see me? Never—that's the honest to God truth. My parents didn't count. Parents needing to see you was completely different because that was normal and expected. This… this need… I realized I didn't even require fancy words to make me turn to mush in the mush pot. Just those five simple words, "I need to see you."

I took a Lyft to the restaurant, and a guy at the counter had to help me to the car with the boxes of pizza and pasta. It was a crazy amount of food for the five guys, which begged the question of who else was with them backstage?

Thank God the Lyft driver knew his way around the venue and could drop me off at the back entrance after Derek cleared it with security.

Mitch and Lonnie met me at the back door. Mitch came out first and dead stopped, making Lonnie run into him like a cartoon character, which made me smile.

Mitch whistled.

"Holy crap, Phillips, you look good."

"Dude." Lonnie pushed him aside and took me in. Neither of their appraisals made me tingle. Only one person could do that these days it seemed. Instead, it just made me happy. My heart lifting again from my funk like it always did around this band of crazies.

The Lyft driver opened his trunk, and the guys helped me with the food. The three of us headed into the backstage area where we were overtaken by people hustling about as if the earth could be saved by their movements. I clutched my bag and the two boxes of pizzas as I tried to keep up in my new wedges.

We got to a staging area, and the other guys were there, but not Derek. We set up the food, and not only the band, but all the stagehands dove into it like it was their first meal in months.

"Where's Derek?" I finally asked Owen as he handed me a plate with a slice of pepperoni and olive pizza on it, remembering from our time in McMinnville what I liked.

"He went up to get your ticket and VIP pass so you wouldn't have to go fight for it."

That made me all squishy inside. That Derek was looking out for me. I had just taken a bite of the pizza when I first sensed him. He'd stopped on seeing me, just like Mitch had, but he just stared. No whistle. No comment. No one else had seen him yet. He was still quite a few feet away. He inched his finger at me, asking me to go over there. I tried to swallow the bite I had taken as I slowly made my way to him.

When I reached him, he took me in all over again.

Finally, after what felt like forever, he said "This is a good look on you." His mischievous smile with the stretched cleft appeared on his face.

"Oh, come on, you know you like the pantsuit better," I tried to tease.

He grabbed my hand and pulled me up close to him so that my entire body was tucked up against his front.

"I'd say my body disagrees." His voice was husky and sexy, and I could feel his body part that disagreed pushing against his jeans and my tank.

He kissed my temple, and I melted into him. He took the VIP pass he had in his hand and placed it over my head, caressing my neck as he moved the long length of my hair out of his way.

"So much skin, Little Bird, and not enough time."

And he was right. Not enough time to recover from being a puddle of goo. Behind us, Rob yelled out, "Derek, man, you better come get some chow before Mitch devours it all."

I heard Mitch mumble something about blood sugar and everyone was hooting. It wasn't serious—the blood sugar thing. It wasn't Jake. It was just a joke because the man was always starving, but it tugged at me anyway when they teased about it.

Derek entwined his long, musician fingers with mine, and we walked back toward the table and the gang eating there. Rob shoved a plate covered with pasta at Derek, and we found a spot on a set of amps to sit. We ate quietly while the buzz around us continued in the normal playful manner that surrounded the guys whenever they were together.

Pretty soon, a tall, model-like redhead showed up. She was in a black dress that showed off long everything. Long legs, long arms, long neck, and a barely curved body that I'd always envied, because when it comes to bodies, the grass is truly always greener on the other side. She embedded herself on Rob's arm.

"That's Rob's wife, Trista," Derek said when he noticed me watching her.

"Did Owen really have a thing for her?" I asked because even as I watched, Owen was off flirting relentlessly with some female stagehand.

Derek shrugged. "I think all the boys liked Trista."

I looked at him. "Even you?" I asked. He shook his head slowly, watching me.

"No. She's not my type."

"Tall, beautiful, redheads? Come on," I said, putting my plate down and eyeing him like a teacher eyes a kid out of his seat.

He put down his own plate, grabbed my wrist, and pulled me onto his lap. I let him as I tried to ignore the panic that fluttered into my heart.

"Haven't you figured it out yet?" His voice was still husky. I worried it was from too much reading and singing, but it only made my heart beat faster.

I couldn't respond, so I just shook my head.

"I think you've been my only type my entire life."

I couldn't help it, but I eye-rolled. Because, really? I'd known the guy less than a week and he was trying to give me a line like that? About the rest of our lives? Who talks like that? Especially on a three week joy ride?

"Did you just eye-roll me?" he teased. I went to push myself off of him, but he held on even tighter. "If I didn't have a gig right now, I'd be able to show you just what I meant."

I eye-rolled again. Cam would be singing my praises if she were here. He took several strands of my hair in his finger and twirled them up till they were near my mouth, like he had the other day. It was sexy as all get out and made sure I couldn't go anywhere unless I wanted to come away with a bald spot.

His finger teased the corner of my lips. He leaned in as if he was going to kiss me in front of the band and the rest of the world that seemed to be backstage, but then George showed up at his side.

George frowned at me. I could already tell he didn't like me. I wasn't good with people not liking me.

But I also quickly realized that George was a sleazy car salesman. I knew sleazy car salesmen. After all, I'd been around them my whole life. We tried to avoid that type at my daddy's dealership like bats avoided the sun. George's slicked dark hair and stupid goatee were supposed to seem hip, I supposed, but to me it just made him seem like he wanted to be the rock star but hadn't made the cut.

"Derek, you wanted to run through that song one more time before the show started, right?"

"George, you haven't met Miss Mia. Mia, George. George, Mia," Derek said, while keeping his finger entwined in my hair, although it was no longer teasing my lips.

I stuck out my hand. George looked down at it, hesitated, and then shook it. "Mia. Good to finally meet you. You sure have this man all turned upside down."

"George," Derek warned.

George ignored him. "He hasn't been quite himself since he met you."

"I'd say the same thing about me. I really should be home running the car dealership instead of spelunking with a musician," I told him with an attempt at a friendly smile.

He eyeballed me. "You run a car dealership?" The doubt running through his voice angered me. After all, I was just a twenty-two-year-old girl with size-E boobs. What would I know about a business, right?

"We pulled in about forty-five million dollars in sales last year. Number one dealership in the non-Nashville area. We're pretty proud of that," I told him. He eyed me again, still doubtful.

Screw him. Screw all men like him. I felt my temper rise. I pulled myself from Derek's lap, hair screaming before he let go.

"I'll just see you after the show. Good luck!" I started to walk away, but Derek caught my hand in his.

He turned to George. "I'll be out in five," he said to his manager, then waited while George glared at me one more time before huffing away.

Derek turned to me. "Don't."

"Don't what?"

"Don't let him make you feel inadequate."

I just stared at this beautiful BB that had entered my life like a star falling from the sky. How could he possibly know that George had made me feel that way?

"He's just anxious that things will change. But he also knows I sound better than I have in months. That's because I finally have someone to sing for."

"Wh-what?"

He looked at me like he was surprised that I was surprised at his words. He sighed and pulled me close again.

"I physically want to damage this bastard who wrote you that letter. You, Little Bird, have given this old soul something to sing about at last."

I stared into his gorgeous stormy eyes. "I don't ever know how to respond to you."

"Just kiss me for good luck, then."

I stared at his eyes, and then his mouth, then looked around at the crowd that was trying hard not to watch us backstage. He tugged my chin toward him. "Miss Mia, kiss me."

So, I did. And he reached into my heart and pulled out several pieces, putting them in his back pocket with the extra guitar picks he carried there. The walls of Mia that were crumbling were being sorted and stored into his possession. I didn't know how to recover from that.

It certainly wasn't what I'd wanted for this three week adventure. Was it?

He pulled away, that playful smile on his face, and started to walk toward the curtain, but only got about five strides in before he came back. He kissed me quick in that way I was rapidly getting accustomed to him doing and then disappeared onto the stage.

I stood there, staring at the empty space, as the people around me ebbed and flowed.

Eventually, Rob took mercy on me and brought Trista over. "Phillips, this is my wife, Trista."

"At least for today I'm his wife," Trista said with a bright smile that let me know she was both teasing and sending him a message.

"This is why I love her. Keeps me on my toes."

"And honest," she retorted.

"Truer words could not be spoken. Mia hasn't been around all this before. She's green as a new blade of grass, make sure she doesn't get trampled?" Rob asked before he kissed his wife's cheek and then departed.

"Come on, I'll show you to our seats," Trista offered, and I followed in her wake, because really, that's what it felt like. Like I was following a supermodel as part of her posse.

We had seats just to the right of the stage, in an area corded off from the regular crowd. I guess my VIP pass was really a VIP pass. I'd never had that before. Even as Jake's little sister, we'd still been stuck in the regular bleacher section. Trista turned to me as soon as we sat down.

"Tell me, how exactly have you snagged our unproclaimed bachelor?" She wasn't asking in a spiteful or snotty way like I half expected. Instead, it was as if she really was curious, like Jake and Cam would be curious about any person who'd entered my world. Slightly protective.

"I'm not sure you'd call him snagged," I said with a weak smile.

"Then you don't know Derek."

"That's true. I really don't," I said, even though I felt like I did know Derek, but not in the way she was talking about.

"Derek has never, ever, and I mean ever, brought a girl backstage. Nor has he ever, after the show, taken any of the girls who have presented themselves to his hotel room."

I wasn't really surprised by this now. It was what he'd protested that first day at the caves, and had now been validated by his band, and yet it was still strange to me.

"Why is that?" I asked.

Trista shrugged. "I think it has a lot to do with his dad, but you'd have to ask him."

"Because he lived at the PlayBabe Mansion?"

Trista smiled. "Not just his dad. Derek and his brother, Dylan, lived there too. I think their mom was actually a 'Babe' or something. They all worked for Hugo."

I just stared at her. She laughed.

"See, story he needs to tell."

This gave me more pieces of the Derek puzzle that I was collecting. I thought about it while the first band was up — some country blues band that wasn't bad, but I couldn't concentrate on. They were local to Oklahoma City. They weren't registering to me because they didn't matter... I wouldn't see them again.

Once Derek came onstage, my brain went blank in a different way. I'd heard him at the fundraiser. Throaty and sexy, playing music that had made me tingle and reminded me of Otis Redding and all the greats. Reminded me of "Fall" and "Thinking Out Loud" by Ed. But, to be fair, I'd had a lot going on at the fundraiser. I'd had a lot of emotions going through me. I'd been worried about Cam and my parents. Even then, he'd drawn me. It was what had started the whole player conversation with Cam. Now I knew that he was literally a PlayBabe offshoot. Weird. Strange.

Tonight, with my focus solely on him, it was different. The surprising thing about Derek onstage at this show was all the different instruments he played. He hadn't done that the night of the fundraiser. Here, he played dueling keyboards with Mitch and a wood flute that reminded me of Peter Pan. In one song, he pounded some kind of African drum, alternating beats with Rob on the regular drum set in a way that had my veins throbbing. He was extremely talented, in more than just a singer / songwriter way.

I still noticed his smooth movements and the way he drew the eyes in the room, including mine. The whole crowd, men and women alike, were drawn to him. Even when he'd pop back to Rob, drumming away, or stand next to Lonnie as they jammed together, the eyes of everyone were really on him. There was something dynamic and beautiful about him, like watching an eagle soar through the sky. You couldn't really look anywhere else, even though the snowy mountains might be just as compelling. It was the eagle you watched.

The thrilling part? He still watched me. Like he had at the fundraiser. And the scary thing? The audience noticed. Especially the girls sexed out in the front row, hoping he'd call one of them backstage. They noticed him watching me and stared daggers the way lascivious fangirls do. The way hopeful hunters do. I hated it, but loved it. Good Girl Mia wanted to run and hide because she never wanted to be the center of attention with people hating her.

Adventurous Mia, New Mia, kind of wanted to shove it in their faces but didn't know how.

Trista, on the other hand, just stared back and eventually flipped a couple of the tramps off and told the muscled security guards to make sure they didn't make it anywhere near backstage. People listened to Trista. She was the kind of person that anyone listened to.

Toward the end of the concert, before the encore that would be demanded, Trista grabbed my arm and hauled me backstage again as the tramps in the front row screamed obscenities that even Cam would have blushed at.

"We'll miss the final song," I said.

"Believe me, you don't want to be out there when they're done," she said in a tone that reminded me of Cam watching out for me all over again.

"Why?"

"Those tramps in the front row? They'll be obnoxious. It gets crazy when they are all vying to be *seen* by the band. Better to know what happens but not have to watch it."

We sat on a couch in the dressing room while we waited for the guys.

"How do you do it?" I asked, truly curious.

"Well, I'm not a band wife. I don't tag along to every event."

"Isn't that hard when they are on the road?"

"Yeah, but I don't get all of him that way, anyway. He's thinking music the whole time, or doing that stupid caving. You do know they cave, right?"

I blushed. "Yes. I kind of like it."

"Really?"

I nodded and she laughed.

"Well, no wonder you've snagged him."

"What do you do then?" I asked, even though I'd heard something about modeling.

"I'm a hand and foot model." That surprised me because she could be a whole-body model in my opinion. She seemed to read my mind. "Modeling is exhausting. Plus, I like to eat. Anyway, the hand and foot thing pays well, and then I have an organic makeup company on the side."

"On the side?" I looked at her, flabbergasted.

"Well, it's just an itty-bitty start-up, but it's coming along."

"Wow."

"Thanks." She smiled almost shyly.

The band came in. They were sweaty and smiling, hyped up but exhausted too. The energy in the room could have reached the ceiling. Derek pulled off his shirt just as our eyes met, and he smiled that smile that was quickly becoming a necessity of mine just as the view of his six pack abs made my heartbeat increase to the fluttering of a hummingbird.

He reached for a clean t-shirt and pulled it on before loping over to me and squashing down beside me on the couch. "So, how'd it go?"

I stared. "You know you were fabulous."

He grinned. "I was?"

I hit him on the shoulder, and on my way back, he grabbed my hand and entwined our fingers again. George entered. I found I didn't really like George. His energy was so not Derek that I wondered how they had even been put together.

"Derek, there are some radio folks outside that want an interview." He stated it like Derek didn't have a choice.

Derek groaned, kissed the back of my hand, and said he'd be back in a bit. The rest of the band and the crew all packed up while Derek was gone. I tried to help, but no one would let me. Trista waited for Rob, and then they took off back to the hotel.

Pretty soon, it became obvious that the other guys were just waiting because of me. Derek hadn't said if he wanted me to stay or if I should just go back to the hotel. It felt awkward.

"You guys don't have to wait with me, you must be really exhausted," I told them. I grabbed my bag and stood. "In fact, I probably shouldn't wait either, right?"

"If you leave, Derek will go fuckin' crazy. You should definitely stay," Mitch said.

"Okay." I sat back down. "But you guys go. Really. I'll be fine."

They seemed hesitant.

"Oh my God, I'm not fifteen. Go. I'll be fine."

"Okay, okay," Lonnie said with his goofy smile, and the boys all shuffled off while I waited.

At first, I flipped through my Instagram account again, posting some pictures of the venue. But I didn't want to hit the pictures that would tear at my heart, so I flipped over to another site. Tiredness washed over me, and I found my eyes drooping. It was almost one o'clock. I fought it, but fell asleep on the couch in the dressing room.

A gentle stroking on my hair woke me. I looked up into Derek's face. He wasn't smiling. "I couldn't find you," he said throatily.

"Sorry."

"Goddamn it, stop apologizing." It wasn't said in anger, but it was probably the most frustrated I'd seen him, ever.

"Habit."

He stared at me in the semi-darkness. "We'll break it. Just like we broke the pantsuits."

I expected his tease to be accompanied by his gorgeous smile, but it wasn't. He was serious. It wasn't his normal mode; the happy guy seemed his norm. But I was finding this solemn side came out with more ease than I'd expected at first.

He pulled me to my feet, hand going to my hair.

"I saw your fan club tonight."

He watched my lips.

I cleared my throat.

"Trista says you never…"

"I don't believe in having sex just to have sex."

My turn to stare, because what? What twenty-something guy didn't want sex without strings? Wasn't that what had started this whole three week journey? Him wanting to sleep with me? I knew he wanted me. He'd pretty much said that. But I could also hear Hayden again, telling me that my imagination stopped me from seeing reality. My holes in my heart started to bleed a little.

"I don't know what to say to that," was all I could say.

This did bring a smile to his face. Not his huge one. Not the one that stretched his cleft into its own smiley face, but one that did lighten his mood.

"I have a solution for that," he said with so much innuendo that I was right back to not having to doubt. He did want me.

He proved it by kissing me. A slow kiss that burned from my toenails, slowly up my legs to the pit of my belly, and up until it reached my heart where it caused melting to occur all over again.

I tangled my fingers in those slightly too long locks of dark chocolate and opened my mouth and soul to him as he took them both with his tongue and his musician fingers and his smile. We were lost in a moment of heat until the lights went out on us.

I felt his smile on my lips. "I think they're kicking us out. Has Miss Mia ever been kicked out of anywhere?"

I shook my head because I couldn't talk. He grabbed my hand and then his guitar case, and the scent that always surrounded him wafted up from it.

"What is that smell?"

"What smell?"

I pointed to the guitar case. He pulled it up and took a whiff. "I don't smell anything."

"It smells like wood wax, or honey and musk, or…"

"Ah. The guitar oil."

Guitar oil. That was a puzzle piece that finally clicked into place. He smelled like guitar oil. How very, very à propos. And sexy. Guitar oil and him would be embedded into my brain until… well, forever.

We made our way outside, and the muggy air hit us like a fry basket. We looked around. "How are we getting back?" I asked.

Derek looked as if the same thought had suddenly hit him. "I guess we're walking."

I looked down at my wedges.

"Butterbeer," I said just as he said, "Shit."

He laughed at me, "Butterbeer?"

I shrugged. "There are a lot more interesting words in the world than cuss words."

He kissed me as if that was the best response he'd ever heard.

"I'll call a taxi," he said.

By the time we got back to the hotel, it was close to two. I was dead on my feet, and I knew he must be twice as tired. We were supposed to leave at seven a.m. It was a two and a half hour drive to Alabaster Caverns, and they only allowed the wild caving the guys wanted to do from eight until three, so we had to be there early if they wanted to spend a good chunk of the day underground.

I went to my door, and Derek didn't even ask, he just came with me and followed me into my room, stripping down to his skivvies at my bedside while I watched. He beckoned to me, and I stood motionless. Because hadn't he just said he didn't believe in sex just for sex? We stared at each other until he must have realized that I was incapable of moving to him.

He slowly approached me, watching to see if I'd fly. I was getting good at not flying away scared, but flying to him was still harder. "Little Bird, there is no way in hell I'm making love to you tonight, so don't give me that look like I'm about to steal from the cookie jar."

He grinned, but it was a tired grin.

He tugged at the hem of my tank. "Don't get me wrong. I want to make love to you. But when we make love, I want it to be an all-night adventure. If not an all-day and all-night adventure. I want to hear you moan many, many times."

I was so confused. Sex? Not sex? Where did I fit? His fingers, skimming my stomach as he pulled at my top, did nothing to help my confusion.

I let him lift my shirt over my head, wrapping it behind me so that he could pull me toward him with it. I was captured by my own shirt. He kissed me tenderly on the lips.

"And tonight, I can barely think, let alone have the self-control to make you moan as many times as you deserve."

My body was a puddle of mush and my brain went right along with it.

"For tonight, you're just going to have to put up with me spooning you in a desperate attempt to believe that we'll have our moment sometime very soon."

Shirt gone, he tugged at the button on my jeans and then kissed my belly button and my thigh as he slid the jeans off my frozen body. Because I was still very much frozen, even if I felt like a puddle of simmering butter inside.

My jeans got stuck on my wedges, and he gently lifted my foot and removed each of those before pulling off my pants. I balanced on his shoulders as he helped me lose the jeans that I never knew I hated until they were in the way of my body touching his.

When I had nothing left but my bra and undies, he stood and took my hand and led me to the bed. He lifted the covers, and I climbed in. And true to his word, he crawled in behind me, arm draped over my waist, legs tucked up against mine, and I felt that feeling again. That somehow, I had come home. To a place I hadn't known that I'd wanted, and yet was somehow never going to be able to leave again.

The truth hit me so hard that I couldn't breathe.

The truth was that I was going to fall for him, and I wondered, would fall too? Would we learn to speak our own language with kisses on cheeks? Or would I be left having fallen off the edge, alone, again?

Chapter Ten

Getting Stuck

KISS ME

"Kiss me like you wanna be loved"

-Ed Sheeran

It was only four hours later when the alarm went off. I groaned because—have I mentioned?—I *hate* mornings! Derek kissed me on the neck, and all of a sudden, mornings didn't seem quite so bad. Then he bounded out of bed with more energy than anyone who had only four hours of sleep had the right to have, and mornings seemed all wrong again.

"Up and at 'em, Miss Mia," he said, and I threw the pillow at him.

"I'm getting the feeling you aren't a morning person." He grinned, and I looked at his too perfect body through half-closed eyes.

When I still didn't budge, he grabbed a leg and pulled me off the bed, where he caught me before I fell to the floor. "Cracker Jacks!" I screamed.

He laughed. I smacked him in the chest.

"Go shower," he said and then kissed me before propelling me towards my bathroom.

"I'll be back in a jiff," he said as he headed toward his door.

"Did you just say jiff?"

He smiled and waggled his brows.

"You're not the only one who can use interesting language."

I couldn't help but laugh. He came back, kissed me quick, and then let himself through our shared door while I made my way to the bathroom in a daze of sleepiness and longing.

I groaned at myself in the mirror when I saw my makeup from last night was smudged and gross. "Good look, Mia," I said with disgust.

I was in and out of the shower as quickly as I could. I pulled on my jean shorts and a t-shirt, knowing I'd have to change into my new spelunking apparel when we got to the caverns but not willing to layer up yet in the heat in the Camaro. I left my waves to dry on their own, lifting them into a messy bun because they were going to be a wreck after the helmet anyway.

When I came out, Derek was sitting there with his bags and my bags packed. I looked at the closet. Only swinging, empty hangers left.

"Did you pack my suitcase?"

It was a stupid question, because of course he had, but I was a little taken aback.

"Is this a problem too?" He smiled up at me.

"Do you have any sense of privacy?"

"You just spent the night naked up against me and now you want privacy?"

"Um. We weren't naked."

Derek chuckled.

"Okay, Miss Mia. Whatever makes you feel better."

His nicknames for me rolled round like a carousel. Which one would I get at the next stop?

"How do you know what makes me feel better?" I tossed back.

He crossed to me and tugged at the curls in my messy bun but didn't pull it out, even though I could tell he wanted to. "I can think of a lot of things that would make you feel better, but for now, words will have to do."

I was a puddle of confused goo again because words were so much better than most things people did. And he always came at me hot and heavy, but his words from last night also rattled around in my brain. The words about not having sex just for sex.

"Come on, Miss Mia. We have to hit the road. Big caving day ahead of us."

We were in the Camaro and on the road before seven. I was driving. I wasn't sure it was smart, because I didn't necessarily trust myself on four hours of sleep, but Derek promised he'd keep me awake by reading and fueling me with Starbucks.

And he was right. He did.

About an hour in, he put the book down and dug through my bag again. "Anything I can help you find?" I asked.

"It's not that I'm not enjoying Elizabeth and Mr. Darcy, because I am quite enjoying their banter, but I'm tired. I need something spicier to keep me awake."

"And you think you'll find spicier in my bag?" I didn't know whether to be complimented or insulted.

"You did mention something about erotica the other day."

Like the tween I often felt like around him, I flushed. I couldn't help it. This made his smile widen even further, in that way that sunk into my gut.

"No erotica in there," I replied, eyes on the road.

"How about on your Kindle?"

I swallowed. No way in all the shades of Hades was he reading erotica to me while I drove.

"No."

"Liar."

I shrugged. My phone with its Kindle app was plugged in so we could use Google Maps, so I wasn't worried.

"Okay. Twenty questions then," he said in his typical chipper fashion.

"You have way more energy than me this morning, maybe you should be driving."

"No. My turn tomorrow."

"Fine," I agreed with a huff.

"You want to go first, or shall I?" He asked it so seductively that I knew I was in a lot of trouble. Over my head in trouble. Ready to just drown in the lake after jumping off the forbidden cliff trouble.

"You," I whispered out.

"Who was your first kiss?"

My fear eased a little. That was easy. "Tim Martin. He was a junior. I was a freshman. He was friends with Cam and picked me up as a side benefit."

"A side benefit?"

"Is that question two?"

"No, that's a clarifying question, it doesn't count."

"It's a question," I insisted.

"Fine, it'll be question two. Explain."

"Everyone loved Cam. Everyone wanted Cam. She was madly in love with my brother, though, so no one stood a chance. In enters me and her best friend, Wynn. Good alternatives."

"I cannot believe you just classified yourself as an alternative," he said.

I shrugged again. It didn't make it not true even if he didn't like it.

"My turn," I said. He didn't look like he wanted to move on from the first conversation, but he waited for me to ask my question anyway. "Did you really live in the PlayBabe Mansion?"

His turn to groan. "Yes."

"And?"

"Is that a second question?" he teased.

"Clarifying one, but okay, yes."

"And it sucked."

"That was not my question."

"You didn't really ask a specific question." He smirked knowingly.

"How did you end up living at the PlayBabe Mansion? Is that better?"

"Yes, but it's question three."

I stuck my tongue out at him, and he reached out to rub my lips when I darted it back inside my mouth. I swallowed hard and concentrated on the road ahead of us.

"My dad ran the PlayBabe Casino in the Bahamas until it closed. Hugo brought him back to the states, and Dad became his right-hand man at the house." Derek shrugged. "It was easier for him if we all lived there because he could have my parents at his beck and call whenever he wanted."

"So, your mom lived there too?"

"Just so we're clear, that's number four."

I just nodded.

"I'll even save you a question. She wasn't a 'Babe.' She wasn't one of Hugo's 'girlfriends.' She met my dad at the casino, stupidly let him knock her up and marry her, and then followed him to the mansion. She helped out at the house, mostly organizing events. We were, not quite alternatives, but at least side benefits."

I wasn't sure how to respond, so I didn't. There seemed a lot I could ask about why he thought it was stupid that they'd gotten together, and about whether he liked living there, but I couldn't figure out which one to ask, so he moved on.

"My turn," he said and then grinned, which should have warned me that I wouldn't like the next question. "Oral or regular?"

I choked. "Excuse me?"

He laughed. "You have a dirty mind, Miss Mia."

Good Girl Mia groaned, but Other Mia wished she had a witty comeback. "What in Merlin's beard did you mean?"

He chuckled at my non-cuss word.

"I meant oral reading or regular silent reading, of course, whatever did you think?" He was laughing at me. I knew it, but I also knew he'd done it on purpose to see my reaction. He still wanted me to surprise him.

"Oral isn't all it's cracked up to be," I told him with my own smile.

"Explain."

I smirked. "Just so we're clear, this is number four."

He nodded in agreement, smile widening in that way I liked.

"Okay. But don't judge," I said.

"No promises."

I looked at him as he shrugged. "I did meet you in a pantsuit."

I eye-rolled him, then we were silent for a moment until he prodded. "I believe you were going to explain how oral isn't all it's cracked up to be."

I sighed, gulped, and continued.

"I had a roommate who liked to tell me every detail about her sex life. I mean. *Every. Detail.*"

"Your own live erotica."

I ignored his dig. "She'd be telling me all about how her boyfriend had come in her mouth, and all I could think was, 'Ew, that's kind of gross,' because, let's just be honest, that body part is what you pee with and other stuff coming out of it isn't exactly chocolate cake so, really, who would think oral sex is hot?"

I couldn't look at him after all of that. I'd just said things to him that I had never said to anyone. Things I'd barely been able to register in my own brain, let alone speak out loud to another human being. A sexy human being to boot. One that I was really thinking about having hot sex with on a daily basis.

He didn't laugh, but when he spoke, I could hear the laugh in his voice anyway. "I don't think you've been doing it right."

"What? Sex?"

"Oral sex, specifically, but maybe sex all together."

I couldn't help yet another shrug. Because he may not have been wrong. Plus, just to be clear, I hadn't done any oral sex. The one time, I'd had regular plain old missionary-style sex; it hadn't been all that earth shattering. Not the way people in books explained it, at least. And the guy I'd had sex with had returned to his ex-girlfriend, so there was a good chance that I had been doing it all wrong.

"By the way, that's number five," was his response.

"I didn't ask anything."

"You asked a clarifying question, and you seemed to have set the ground rules that clarifying questions count as a question."

"You're impossible," I grumbled.

"But gorgeous."

"I'm debating the gorgeousness as we speak."

I was surprised I wasn't more uncomfortable. Good Girl Mia usually shied away from any talk of sex with anyone. Safety discussing sex was only found in books. Definitely never live and in person.

"Are you going next or me?" he asked.

"I'm not sure I want to play anymore."

"Fine, my turn then. How many times have you had oral sex?"

I blushed again because, God, he just kept pushing at the edges of me. I didn't know if it was because he liked it when I was uncomfortable, or if he thought there was more to me than what I shared on the outside. Either way, admitting some of this stuff out loud was going to be embarrassing. And as I freely admitted to myself now, I wanted to have sex with this gorgeous guy, but I was worried that if I admitted how little I'd had sex, maybe it would turn him off.

"Miss Mia?"

"You first."

"Are you asking me how many times I've had oral sex?"

I nodded.

"As question number six?"

I nodded again.

"Given oral sex or received?"

God, I didn't want to go there, did I? Did I really want to know how many people he'd touched and who'd touched him? Was that going to make me feel more comfortable with my own limited experiences once he had me undressed in his bed? No. No. And Jiminy Cricket, no.

"Never mind. Scratch it. I don't want to know."

"It still counts as being asked."

"Not if I don't make you answer it," I griped back.

"But I wanted to answer it," he said with that sexy tone back in his voice that made me want to stare at him instead of the road. My fingers tightened on the wheel.

His phone rang. Thank God, I'd been saved by the phone. He answered it with a sigh, "What do you want, dipshit?" It had to be Lonnie. Lonnie was the one he called names the most. I thought it was because they had been friends the longest.

"He wants to know if we want to stop for food at the diner five miles ahead, or if we just want to wait 'til we get to the caverns and make something in the bus?"

"You have food on the bus?" I asked, surprised, and he held up seven fingers to mean that I had just asked question number seven. I shook my head in disgust.

"I'm easy," I responded and then blushed and thunked my head momentarily on the steering wheel as he laughed out loud at yet another double entendre that I'd let slip.

"Let's just make something at the caverns. We'll be there in about twenty, anyway," he said into the phone. Pause. "Sounds good."

He turned to me. "You are a mystery, Miss Mia."

"Hardly."

"Very much so."

He didn't ask me any more questions, though as we wound our way to the caverns using the Google Map lady to guide us. "I think I could fall in love with this lady," he said when she got us to the caverns without any mishaps.

"She's too old for you, moron."

He laughed.

At Alabaster Caverns, we made grilled cheese sandwiches in the bus, and the guys clowned around as always. I changed in the tiny bathroom while the guys changed anywhere they saw fit, and I had to look away.

Derek was impressed with the gear I had bought. "You're really invested in this now, aren't you?"

I rolled my eyes. "Well, I didn't want to continue with the hazing suit."

He pulled me to him and kissed me. Just a quick kiss, but it still curled my toes in my new boots. "Wh-what was that for?"

He smiled. "Because you're cute when you eye-roll."

I couldn't help it, really. The second eye-roll just happened as part of my everyday existence, but it got me another kiss.

"Are you kids ready?" Lonnie asked with his loopy smile. It was just Lonnie, Owen, Mitch and us again. No Rob. He'd stayed in Oklahoma City with Trista. He'd meet up with us in Denver.

We put on our packs. Derek helped me fill mine with the important gear and lights, then we headed out with the permits that Owen had gone and obtained for us. We were "wild caving," which meant we were on our own. I wasn't nearly as nervous as I had been in Tennessee, but I still had some butterflies. I was trusting a group of nothing more than adolescents to take me in a cave through tight spaces, rock climbs, and dark tunnels. I could hear Mama in my head screaming, "Run, Forest, home!"

I didn't think of my solo kidney often. Other than a side thought when I was feeling guilty over Jake or when I went for my annual checkup to make sure nothing was out of whack internally because of it. But I also realized that rock climbing probably wasn't something that would be on my doctor's approved activities list.

When we got to the cave entrance, Derek double-checked my lights and equipment, as if sensing that I was nervous. "You got this, Phillips?" he asked in his serious coach voice.

It was cute. Still all sexy BB and yet also cute. I smiled at him. "Yep, Coach Waters, sir," I teased, and he smiled that smile that made my heart ache.

"Did you warn her about the bats?" Lonnie asked.

"Stop teasing me, lumberjack," I couldn't help but quip back, but all the boys stared at me, including my gorgeous BB.

"Wait, there are really bats?" I asked, a little breathless.

Derek nodded. "Yep. In fact, they don't even let anyone cave in here for part of the year while they hibernate."

"Stop teasing me," I said, but I had a sinking feeling they weren't.

"You got this. They hardly ever bother the humans. They're more afraid of us than the other way around," Derek said.

"Um… Somehow I doubt that," I said.

They didn't let me think about it. Instead, we were in the caves and moving before I could say or think much more. Because, really, it was the thinking that usually got me into trouble.

I soon lost myself inside the peaceful darkness like I had in McMinnville. The cool, quiet air. The beauty of the formations standing as they had for centuries. The challenge of the spaces. It was something that even Good Girl Mia didn't seem to mind, because she was quiet in my brain the whole way. Or maybe Other, Adventurous Mia was taking over more than ever.

At one point, I could hear the bats. Little shuffling noises that were high above me and made my heart skip a beat, but I just reminded myself that they didn't eat humans. At least, not that I knew about. I continued on into the next chamber where there was no sound again.

About an hour and a half in, we went through a really tight spot. We had to climb up a little and then squeeze through a crevice to the other side. I hadn't had any problems with the tight spaces the other day, or so far today. I hadn't panicked or embarrassed myself yet, which I considered pretty good, but then, about halfway through the crevice, I got stuck. Backpack and E-boobs… um, not always a great combination in the middle of a cave.

The more I struggled to get through, the more I seemed to jam myself in.

Owen was behind me. I could hear him in the crack not too far away. Mitch and Lonnie had gone ahead, followed by Derek, then me. Owen was the caboose as he had the most experience.

I tried not to panic, but a well of fear curled up from my stomach to attack my heart. I felt a rush of blood come and leave my face. Nausea hit me.

I knew Owen was nearby, and that Derek was only a few inches away, just outside the fissure, waiting. I wasn't alone. But I was stuck. Butterbeer!

"Hey, Phillips, what's the hold up?" Derek called back. He didn't sound concerned yet.

Breathe, Mia, breathe, I told myself, and I took a huge breath in and out to try to calm the racing in my heart and to relieve the twirling in my stomach.

Owen reached me. "Hey," he said calmly and quietly.

"Hey to you, too," I said, but my voice was shaky.

"Mia?" Derek's voice was concerned now because I hadn't answered. No Phillips this time.

"I'm stuck," I called back.

"Stuck?" Derek asked, and there was laughter in his tone as well as relief.

"Yes, moron, stuck."

"Like your foot?"

I looked at Owen and rolled my eyes in the greenish twinge of our cave lights. I could vaguely see his distorted smile that returned mine. If I was a more fearful girl, I'd say it looked manic and crazy, like I was going to get eaten for dinner, but really, it was just the lighting, my overactive imagination, and my panic speaking.

"Um. No. Not my foot," I called to Derek, but Owen started chuckling because he realized quick enough that it was my boobs and backpack that had wedged me in.

"What—" Derek started and then stopped as he realized just what I was talking about even without seeing me. He burst out laughing. I was so going to smack him when I reached him. "Just push them in, Phillips. It's just fatty tissue."

I thunked my head against the cave wall. "How would you like your balls squeezed between a rock and a hard place?" I shouted back at him.

"Totally different animal. I'm going to have to give you some anatomy lessons."

Even though I was stuck, embarrassed, and annoyed, that still hit me in the loins like a forbidden kiss. Holy potato peels, I had it bad for this boy.

"Let me see if I can push on—" Owen started.

"No!" I cut him off.

Owen laughed. "Your pack, Phillips. Just going to push on your backpack. I kind of want to keep my hands attached to my body, and Derek would cut them off, along with my balls if I touched anything else."

Owen pushed on the pack, and it budged a little.

"Owen, you there?" Derek called out.

"Yep, I'm here."

"What's the situation?"

Owen laughed hard. "She's stuck. Like she said."

"Have her take the pack off," Derek suggested.

"Really, asshole?" he called back at the BB. To me, he said, "I'm going to push the pack, can you get your hands up and kind of… well… um."

"Squeeze my boobs?" I helped him out.

He nodded, but I swear he flushed in the stupid cave lights.

He pushed the pack, I smooshed by boobs as best I could from the angle I was at, and eventually, I felt my body inch to the side. With that, I could slide my shoulders from the backpack and then ease forward, dragging the pack behind me.

I made it through the crevice to the other side, and there was Derek, grinning in the stupid weird glow of our lights. He pulled me to him and hugged me, but I smacked him in the chest. "Just fatty tissue, huh?"

I tried to pull away, but he pulled me tighter, wrapping a muscled arm around my shoulders, tugging me close so he could whisper in my ear, "I can massage them later for you."

And I was a puddle of goo again.

Owen came through the crevice behind me. "I guess we have to recalibrate our tunnel runs for our new proportions." He was chuckling. I glared at Owen as both he and Derek rumbled with laughter again. Mitch and Lonnie, who'd gone ahead, finally came back to us.

"What's the hold up?" they asked.

"Phillips got stuck," Derek said with his happy grin. I hit him again. "What? You did."

"You guys have no sense of privacy."

"Awww. Did you really get stuck? Or did you have to take a piss?" Lonnie asked with a smile.

I know I turned a million shades of pink, but at least the lighting was poor, and I was pretty sure I could play it off. "No, dummy, I got my pack stuck."

"And that's not all," Derek laughed.

"You are so dead, mister," I mumbled and tried to huff my way over to Mitch, but he grabbed my wrist and held me back.

The boys were laughing and moving off toward the other side of the little opening. "Are you sure you're okay?" Derek asked, and this time his voice was quiet and concerned, and his eyes looked stormy black in the half-light.

"Yes. Sore. But fine."

"You sure?"

"Yes, moron, let's go." I let him lead me, hand still grasped around my wrist, through the rest of the caverns. He stayed closer to me now, wouldn't leave me as far back as he had in the past. That was fine, even though I didn't get stuck again.

It was late afternoon by the time we emerged on the other side, the hazy sunshine making me squint. I was filthy, but happy and tired. Probably more tired than I'd been in ages. I hadn't had much sleep the last couple nights, and then the climbing, hiking, and crawling on top of it.

We took a selfie at the exit. Dirty and happy. I posted it on Instagram and then sent it to Mama and Cam just so they would believe me.

We made our way down to the park's restrooms, hosed off outside, and then went in. I showered, and was out in my t-shirt and shorts again, in no time. I made my way over to the motor home that the boys liked to call their tour bus.

"Anybody home?" I called out.

I was pulled farther into the bus, toward the little back bedroom, by a hand that I was coming to know as well as my own. Then I was being kissed. Hard, passionately. His hand, when it touched my breast, was gentle, but it still hurt. My boobs were really sore. My breath hitched of its own accord, and Derek pulled back.

"You really aren't okay?" Concern glittered in his stormy gray eyes.

"I'm just tender. No biggie," I said with a shrug. "They'll be fine by tomorrow."

"Really?"

"Yes."

He didn't look like he believed me.

"When are we heading out?" I asked.

He gave me a puzzled look, and then realization dawned on his face, which made me nervous again. "Shit, we made reservations to spend the night here."

"Here? As in, at the caverns, here?"

"Yes. In the bus, here."

I stared at him.

"You want me to spend the night here in the bus with you and your three overgrown teenage boys?"

"Wow, that sounds really bad when you put it that way," he said.

"You're awful."

"We have the big bed to ourselves." He waggled his eyebrows at me and pulled me down so that I was sitting on his lap on said big bed, which was really the size of maybe a full mattress. I'd hardly call it big.

"You're gross," I responded.

"You don't really think that," he said as he proceeded to kiss my neck that was exposed by my messy bun.

I got another good look at the eagle on his neck this way, and this time I got to run a finger along it. Spontaneously, I leaned in to kiss the tattoo. It wasn't something I would normally do, but it just felt right. To touch this beautiful mark on this beautiful man.

He pulled my fingers to his lips and kissed them, our eyes meeting, and I doubted I'd ever be able to fully meet the desire that I saw there. I was terribly afraid I'd disappoint him.

The door of the bus crashed open, the boys wrestling and shoving at each other as they entered. It was nonstop guy energy with them.

"Knock, knock, lovebirds. Better put your clothes back on," Lonnie teased. He could clearly see us down the narrow hall, and it was quite obvious that we had clothes on but—you know—guy humor.

Derek sighed. "Someday, I'll have you to myself when I'm not exhausted beyond belief."

This time I knew it was a promise. I shivered.

He pulled me with him toward the kitchen.

That night, we barbecued hamburgers outside, ate s'mores, and the boys brought out their guitars and instruments to sing to the stars that were glittering down on us. People from other campsites were drawn by the music, and the guys put on an impromptu show. They didn't just sing their own songs, they took requests, and almost always could play what was asked.

The guys pulled out a whole crate of instruments from the bus and let the kids from other campsites play. Derek moved through them, showing them how to play and keep beat. He was incredibly patient with all of them. It made my heart pitter in a different way than I had become accustomed to it beating around him, because it was yet another unexpected action from this sexy man.

After the kids had all picked something and knew how to use it, Derek chose his harmonica and started in on some old-time camp songs, ones that I'm sure Cam and Jake knew from all their time out at the campsites and bonfires, but that I only vaguely recollected. I watched as everyone came to life with their music, enthralled by the deep voice of the man that I was coming to adore more than I knew was smart.

I had to remind myself it was just three weeks. No matter what Derek said about sex not just being sex for him. Because at the end of three weeks, I had a life and a family to return to that no amount of sex or lightheartedness would let me leave.

I leaned back and watched the stars move. No moon tonight. Just stars. In the distance, bats screeched. It didn't even freak me out. Echolocation seemed like a good thing to me now.

I must have fallen asleep, because the next thing I knew, Derek was waking me with a stroke of his calloused fingers on my cheek. I smiled up at him. I was tired and sleepy, but also happy. Happiness was what the three weeks were about, I reminded myself. Happiness, along with relief. Escape.

"Let's hit the sack," he said with a devilish smile.

I just nodded and let him draw me into the bus. We took the "big" bed, but I slept in my leggings and t-shirt. Derek still stripped down to his underwear, and he still pulled me close with my back up against his chest like he didn't want to let me fly away. Which was fine by me. I didn't want to go anywhere.

And I fell asleep happy.

♪ ♪ ♪

Somebody was snoring. I'm not sure I really ever fell deeply asleep knowing I was in the same vehicle with a group of overgrown adolescents. Thank God the snoring didn't come from Derek, otherwise I might have had to disown him.

As I came fully awake, Ed's song, "Kiss Me," that I knew almost as well as the lines of *Pride and Prejudice*, filtered through my brain. I could hear Ed's crooning, "Settle down with me... Your heart's against my chest, your lips pressed to my neck. I'm falling for your eyes, but they don't know me yet."

I wasn't sure if Derek knew me yet. I wasn't sure I knew him... But I felt like he knew me better in a handful of days than Hayden had known me after four years. That was something I hadn't expected.

It was early, but misty morning light was streaming in the motor home windows that nobody had bothered to shut the night before because these overgrown toddlers were so completely lacking in any need for privacy.

Derek's hand was laying on my chest, and I finally got a chance to look at the words tattooed on his wrist. It read, "To err is human," and when I carefully turned it to read the other side, I expected to see the normal, "To forgive, divine." That was the famous Alexander Pope quote, after all. But instead, it read, "To forgive, sanity." To err is human; to forgive, sanity.

The fact that Derek—laughing, happy Derek—had to have the reminder of forgiveness being the road to sanity tattooed on his wrist made my walls and heart crumble another piece more. It told me something about that serious side of him that peeked out randomly, like a weed forcing itself into the rose garden.

I was desperate now to see the other wrist. I twisted, not even thinking about waking him up; the other wrist was on the pillow behind me. The words were tiny and double-wrapped like a double-corded leather band. It read, "Humanity is a collage of mistakes made beautiful."

They were the words from his song, "Humanity." It was the song that had snagged at my heart at the fundraiser, and then, again, the night before last at The Criterion. The song was about how we were all interdependent, and how we needed each other not just to survive, but to grow and love and be forgiven for our mistakes. Who was Derek asking forgiveness from? Or what was he trying to forgive? I didn't know in that moment. I wasn't sure I could bear to know.

"Question number eight, Little Bird?" he said huskily. His sleep-filled voice tickled my ear and melted me as he always did with a simple touch or word. Words. I loved words as much as I hated mornings.

I turned so that I was looking at him.

"I'm not sure which one to ask," I whispered as the boys snored in the background.

"You're wondering about the tats."

"Yes."

"And now you wonder what's burning up my soul? What acts of horrors I'm asking for forgiveness for or trying to forgive?"

"Am I that easy to read?"

He grinned at me, lazy. "Yes and no. That was question nine."

"What? No. I didn't even ask eight."

"Am I that easy to read? I believe that's a question."

I put my fingers up. "You got this many then. Phillips? What's the hold up? Are you sure you're okay? Maybe something about, are you sore? That would be seven, eight, nine, and maybe even ten if we are counting those kinds of questions."

He chuckled quietly. "I only have ten more, then?"

"Nine now."

He kissed me, tugging at my bottom lip and invading my mouth with his tongue in a way that made me groan quietly. His hand wandered up my t-shirt to where I was still wearing my sports bra. I was in a motor home full of maledict boys and wasn't going to be flitzing about without a bra.

I drew back and watched him as he watched my lips.

"How many guys have you slept with, Little Bird?"

He was avoiding talk about the tattoos, but I let it go, unsure if I could take what he had to say with my own wounds barely scabbed over most days.

Plus, hadn't I known that particular question was going to come out of his lack-of-privacy-loving lips as soon as he started talking erotica and oral sex with me? And yet, I wasn't sure I could answer him. Embarrassed. Not embarrassed. I didn't know what to feel.

"Do you mean like we've been sleeping together, or do you mean had sex with?"

"That's your ten." He grinned at me, and I eye-rolled him, which earned me a quick kiss. "You know what I mean," he told me. "Full on naked, body part inside body part sex."

I couldn't help the blush, and I put my fingers up like I was counting to give myself time. Like it was hard to think about the right number. I could see his eyes get dark and stormy over the tips of my fingers, like he wasn't happy. Finally, I showed him one finger. He looked down at it for a second before realization kicked in. He reached over and bit my finger, keeping it in his mouth and turning my whole body to a quivering mush pot.

"You are going to be the death of me," he said, like he had so many times already. But he said it with a huge smile.

Then he kissed me again. Hard, demanding, like he wasn't going to stop, ever. And I kissed him back. Hard, demanding, like I'd always wanted to kiss a boy. With feelings blossoming deep inside me as the walls crumbled and Good Girl Mia hid behind the curtains.

He rested his forehead on mine. "It's good that I'll only have to kill one man. I might have been labeled a serial killer if your fingers had kept going."

I laughed. A light laugh. Like my heart was actually light. Just as that thought hit me, the thought of being light and happy, the guilt came rolling back over me. Because that was my life. I couldn't escape the guilt for long. It always hit me hardest when I'd been avoiding it the most.

I rotated in Derek's arms so I wouldn't be tempted to kiss him any more and looked up at the ceiling of the motor home. Derek let me, but I could feel him watching me as well.

"Question number twelve, moron?" I asked him as I felt his gaze along my face.

"I'm not sure which one to ask," he teased, lightly prodding me back out from wherever I'd gone.

I wanted to grin again, but I was still overwhelmed with the guilt. Trying to battle it aside, but I couldn't. Because I knew that if my stupid body hadn't failed, Jake and Cam could still be like this. Arm in arm. Flirting. Kissing. Teasing. That Jake would be living out his dreams. It wasn't fair that he was gone and I was here running around the country avoiding my reality.

Derek seemed to sense the shift in me, like he had so easily been able to do since first meeting me. "Johnny Cash may have had addiction issues, but he was also a pretty smart man."

"Yeah?" I said without turning to look at him while I tried to calm the remorse and panic in my heart.

"One of my all-time favorites of his goes something like this, 'Close the door on the past. You don't try to forget the mistakes, but you don't dwell on them either. You don't let them have any of your energy, or any of your time, or any of your space.' Seems like you give your past doors and mistakes way too much time and energy and space."

"You don't know me at all."

"Really? That's your comeback?"

"Is that thirteen?"

He started tickling me in the ribs. I am very ticklish. So I was instantly kicking, and laughing, and trying hard not to scream in the middle of a motor home with three other boys trying to sleep, but he was relentless. I couldn't help but squeal.

"Kiddies. You've woken us all up with your shenanigans," Lonnie said from the makeshift doorway in the motor home.

Derek looked over me to him with a smirk. "Payback for your waking us up with your lumberjack snore."

I laughed because Derek had picked up on my nickname for Lonnie the day before. Lonnie would always be a lumberjack to me. Lonnie, ever the guy, burped and then farted in the doorway.

"Classy, man, classy." Derek shook his head. "Ladies present, jackass."

"Nah, Phillips is just one of the boys now," he said and continued to burp his way down the hall.

Derek rested his head on my chest.

"I apologize deeply for his grossness," he said into my boobs which, I realized, were still a little sore from their escapades yesterday. Too bad it hadn't been from all-night sex. Wait. Had I just thought that? Where was my Good Girl Mia filter?

She'd come and gone this morning. I kind of liked her gone.

Chapter Eleven

The Find

FIREFLY

"Teach my skin those new tricks. Warm me up with your lips."
-Ed Sheeran

We were on the road after a chaotic morning in which the boys each took turns ribbing each other as if it was a celebrity roast. It was an almost eight-hour journey to Denver, but the band seemed ready to do it in one day so that they would have most of the next day to relax. It made me wonder if Derek had pushed this agenda.

The thought of Derek having almost a whole day to relax made my stomach flop in anticipation, the kind of stomach flop that comes before a roller coaster ride. Excited and yet full of dread at the same time. Fear and desire rolled into one.

True to his word, Derek took his turn behind the wheel. I went back to reading *Pride and Prejudice* because I wanted to avoid the last seven questions. He let me because I think he was avoiding them now, too.

We'd passed Freedom and turned onto US-64 when a repeated sound made my heart twirl for a different reason. I stopped reading and put my head toward the glove box. There it was again. A soft mewing.

"Oh my God, pull over!" I shouted, panicked.

"What?" he asked with concern but was quickly doing what I asked.

I jumped out of the car, slammed open the hood, and stared into the engine compartment with horror. Derek joined me.

"Shit!" he said and ran back to the trunk.

I was already pulling the little body out from where it shivered, hiding. A tiny little kitten, barely old enough to have its eyes open. A little orange-and-white striped tabby that reminded me of my old stuffed animal that Jake had given me. Except this one was covered in blood from where only part of a tail remained. I was instantly crying and holding it to me as it mewed pitifully.

Derek was back with a t-shirt. "Here, wrap it in this. Try to put pressure on the tail."

The kitten mewled at me. A sad mew full of pain. I wanted to throw up, but I did what Derek said, and then hurried back into the Camaro. I handed my phone to him.

"Ask Siri for the closest vet," I told him.

He did. It was still about twenty minutes out, at a little hole-in-the-wall town, but it would have to do.

I cuddled the kitten who was mewing the whole time while Derek drove like a madman. Like I imagined Blake might drive when Cam went into labor. Like I imagined Jake had driven that prom night when Seth had hit Cam, and he'd come to rescue her.

I was out of the car and through the door of the vet clinic before Derek had even stopped the engine.

"We need help," I told the receptionist.

She saw my bundle and the blood and took off to the back. A young female vet and a vet tech came running. "What happened?"

"We heard her mewing as we were driving. Looks like she lost part of a tail," Derek said, coming in behind me.

"Okay, we got this," the vet said, taking the t-shirt-wrapped bundle and rushing into the back.

The receptionist approached. "Why don't you go wash up. Bathroom's over there. When you come back, we'll fill out the paperwork."

I walked in a daze to the door marked bathroom. Derek followed me into the one-person room. I let him. I washed up, and he helped with the blood that lined my neck and face like I'd been slit open by a vampire.

"I'll go get you a new shirt from the car," he said gently. I just nodded.

He came back with my "Mischief Managed" t-shirt. I pulled my bloody one off, tossing it into the trash. The blood had soaked through. I pulled more paper towels out, and Derek gently helped scrub off the blood from my still tender breasts. Then he helped me tug the clean shirt over my head as if I was two and couldn't do it myself.

I was usually tougher than this. I didn't usually lose it in front of other people. I didn't show that kind of emotion. Good Girl Mia was not the drama queen. I was good at hiding everything I personally felt. But for some reason, that helpless little tyke, all bloody and crying, tore at me. It had me shaking and tearing up in a way that felt foreign to me.

Out in the waiting area, the receptionist handed us both waters and a clipboard of paperwork. We quickly realized that it was all geared as if the cat was our own. "Excuse me," Derek said. "The cat. Well…it's not ours."

"What?" The lady looked up, surprised.

"We were camping last night at Alabaster Caverns. We don't know who the kitten belongs to," he explained.

"Oh! Poor thing. Probably a stray. I'm surprised it didn't get eaten by the bats."

My stomach turned, remembering the screeching that had filled the stars last night. I could feel the color fade from my face. I swayed; Derek caught me and held me up against his side as if that's where I'd always belonged.

"In that case, we'll take it in as abandoned," the lady said.

"What will happen to it?" I breathed out.

"We have some funds and an arrangement with the animal shelter. It'll be looked after, and hopefully someone will take it in."

I stared at her, her words swirling in my brain. Abandoned. Hopefully someone would take it in. And so uncharacteristically Mia, I started sobbing. Derek pulled me into his chest, and I cried there as if I was truly that toddler he was treating me like.

"Maybe we could keep it? Would we be able to take it with us after it gets fixed up?" he asked the lady over my head.

"I don't know what the recovery will be like. If you'd like to wait and talk with the vet, I'll let her know."

I could feel Derek nod. "We'll be outside for a few minutes," he told her.

He tugged my hand and pulled me outside, then leaned up against the wall of the clinic and held me tight up against him while I tried to get a hold of myself.

"I'm sorry," I breathed as I calmed.

"There you go again," he said, looking down at me with a tender smile. I just stared at him through eyes that I knew must be puffy and red. "Apologizing for things out of your control."

"Sobbing like a two-year-old is not out of my control," I told him, voice shaking.

"Well, to be fair, that was a pretty traumatic experience. Hell, I thought I was going to bust into waterworks."

"But you didn't," I said with a lot of self-condemnation.

"Why are you beating yourself up over a few tears?" He seemed genuinely puzzled.

"I'm usually much better at holding myself together, that's all." I tried to pull away.

He looked around and saw a diner across the street. "Stay. I'm going to go tell them where we'll be and leave my cell number."

He went into the clinic and was back at my side before I could think seriously about darting away. Plus, where would I go?

We took in the "Seat yourself" sign and found a booth in the corner where he squeezed in next to me. The waitress came over, and Derek ordered coffee and toast for us. I didn't want anything, but I just let him do his thing while I continued to count backwards by threes from 1,552 in my head and focused on anything but my tears, the cat, and abandonment.

He grabbed my hand and twisted his long fingers amongst my own. His "to err" tattoo snaked around my wrist, making me think of all the errors in my own life.

"Little Bird?"

"Hmm?"

"I think you've had to be strong a lot in your life," he said quietly with no laughter in sight.

I wanted to thunk my head against the table because I was so awfully good at taking this gorgeous, laughing BB and making his serious side peek through. I didn't want him to be me. I didn't want him serious and thoughtful. I wanted him laughing, and teasing, and full of joy.

I tried to shake myself out of my funk as the waitress set down the two coffees and a plate of toast with honey and jam.

"It's a gift," I said lightly.

"Don't do that," he growled.

I looked up, surprised. His eyes were dark storm clouds again, but not full of passion. This time, just anger was there.

"Wh-what?"

"Try to brush it aside and be light and happy. Is that what you do for your family? Are you the one that makes everyone else feel better? Is that how you survived Jake?"

I didn't want to hear him talk about Jake. Or my family. Not when I was barely getting my shield back up. "Don't go there," I said with my own growl.

"Yes, damn it, I am going there. Doesn't anyone ever ask you how you feel about it all?"

"Of course they do. I got sent to a shrink when he died. And this isn't about Jake!"

"Okay. They sent you to a shrink, but when you came home, did anyone ever say to you, are you okay?"

"Yes!"

"Did they ask you how you felt about giving him a kidney and then having him die with your kidney inside him?"

My whole body felt like it was being ripped in half. How could he ask me that? How could he dare? This was nothing like him asking me about Hayden. No one had a right to ask me about Jake. It was my own little burden. The burden I deserved to carry. My kidney killed him.

"Stop it," I said with anger, but also fear. Fear that he'd prod at a scab that I didn't know if I could handle being scratched at today. Not today, when I'd already lost it over a helpless kitten.

"No, I won't. I want to know, Little Bird. How did that make you feel?"

"You don't have a right to ask me that." I could no longer meet his gray eyes when they stormed at me more, so I looked down to the table, my hands wrapped around the coffee cup.

"I don't? Not even after you've been giving me, piece by piece, a bit of your heart that you've had hidden for so long?"

My eyes jumped to his face again. How did he know? How? I hadn't even really known it myself.

"Mia. Little Bird, please. Just tell me. What has it been like going through this so alone?"

"I haven't been alone. I've had Mama, and Daddy, and Cam and her parents. And Wynn. For Pete's sake, there's a whole godforsaken town of people that lost Jake and have been there for me."

"No, Little Bird, they haven't been. They've all grieved and waited for you to pick up the pieces."

"That's a bunch of malarkey!"

"You aren't? Picking up the pieces? You're not trying to be the one to run the dealership because your dad wanted Jake to? You're not the one trying to take care of Cam in her pregnancy because Jake would be busting something if he knew? You're not the one making sure your mama smiles every day even when she only has one child living?"

"Stop it!" I put my hands to my ears and closed my eyes like I was five and Jake was teasing me with worms they'd caught and were going to string up on hooks again.

Derek gently pulled my hands into his and then tipped my chin so that he could scour my face with his eyes. I could feel the heat of them even as I kept mine screwed tightly shut.

"God, you're so damn beautifully heartbreaking," he said gently.

Tears. More god-awful tears. They squeezed out from underneath my lashes and down my cheeks because I wasn't used to anyone examining me this closely. No one wanted to examine me this closely. They wanted me to be okay because they had enough on their plates dealing with their own sorrow and anger and hurt. Or if they were Hayden, they just had their own dreams in their eyeline.

Derek pulled me up against him again, and I found myself sobbing into his shoulder once more. Crying like I hadn't cried since Jake died. Like no one had seen me cry because I'd done it alone in my room, knowing I didn't have a right to cry in front of any of them.

"Little Bird, I asked you once if you knew it wasn't your fault that Jake died, and I guess I know my answer now. You don't, do you?"

I curled my fingers into his shirt. I so wanted him to stop, and yet, at the same time, I didn't. I wanted to feel healed. I didn't want to just have a scab covering my wound. I wanted the wound to be gone. Maybe have it leave a scar, but a scar that would have the skin knitted together again into one piece instead of the torn, ragged edges that were still there.

Eventually, I pulled away again and reached for a napkin to wipe my face. "I'm sorry," I said again. It was a bad habit. He was right. But I was sorry.

"If you ever say you're sorry to me again, I'm going to have to find a lake to toss you in," he said, and this time, he grabbed my chin and shoved his lips against mine. They were hard and unyielding, demanding that I listen to him and what he was trying to tell me with his body and his words.

I responded. With hurt and anger and sadness, but at the same time, with a deep longing. Longing to have someone up close to me who had nothing but me and my well-being in his mind. Someone who didn't care about Jake's or Mama's or Daddy's well-being. Someone who was willing to put me first. I'd never had that. Never. I'd always been second, or third, or last.

His cell phone rang, and he removed his lips from mine but didn't let me go. He still held me tight up against his chest as he answered it.

It was the vet. They'd finished and wanted to talk with us.

Derek left some cash on the table, and we walked across the street, fingers tangled in a way that allowed me to run my fingers over his guitar callouses. I wasn't sure what to do with this gorgeous BB. I wasn't sure at all, but I thought I might want to keep him. And I knew that was a dangerous thing to want, because reality would invade our lives soon enough. In less than sixteen days. And as I'd found out the hard way, reality wasn't forgiving at all.

The vet said the kitten should recover completely with no long-term repercussions. Some cats couldn't pee correctly after losing a tail, but because this one still had about a quarter of her tail left, she thought the kitten would be just fine. They wanted to keep her at least overnight. She was probably only about three weeks old. Probably should still be nursing on the mama. They wanted to make sure she'd eat from a bottle.

"Were you thinking of keeping her?" the vet asked.

We looked at each other. We hadn't discussed the kitten again since we'd left. "Yes," Derek said without removing his eyes from my tearstained face. "I think we would very much like to keep her."

I was back to the puddle of honey butter. Because I was pretty sure he wasn't talking about just the kitten.

"Okay, then. Why don't you come by in the morning, and we'll see if she's ready to check out?"

"I have to be in Denver tomorrow for a gig," he told the vet.

"That's a long haul." She smiled because Derek had that effect on people. He was smooth and charming. Sexy and disarming.

"How early can we pick her up?" he asked.

"Normally we don't open till eight, but I'll meet you here at seven?" she offered.

"Thank you. That would be great," he responded with full-on charm in his smile. "Is there a place we can stay tonight?"

"We have a couple little places. Probably not what you're used to, but they're clean. I'd recommend the Wooly Bison, just down the street."

"Thanks. And please call and let us know if anything changes," Derek said.

We left with my heart still feeling raw and bloodied, but somehow ,also hopeful.

He opened the Camaro passenger door for me and then got in the driver's seat. Sure enough, just down the street was a quaint sign for the Wooly Bison. I wasn't sure I wanted to stay at a place called the wooly anything, but I guess that old saying, beggars can't be choosers, was true.

Derek checked us in as he always did, holding both our bags and not letting me help, and we went to a tiny room with a wrought iron bed, and old, but clean, wallpaper and carpeting. It wasn't a place I'd recommend as a vacation hot spot, but I also didn't feel like I'd go to sleep and wake up with bug bites scattered across my body.

Derek called Mitch and let him know what was up. I called Mama and Cam to give them an update and see how Cam was feeling. I chuckled for the first time in hours because Cam on bed rest was not a happy Cam. She said Blake's grandmama had brought her a whole kit of cross-stitch items to help keep her busy. Cross-stitch! Because, really, who would ever think that Cam would do something as domesticated as cross-stitch?!

When I got off the phone, Derek was watching me. I had sunk down in the wingback chair that was by the window, the sheer curtains diffusing the bright Oklahoma sunshine into a dreamlike world.

He was sitting on the bed that was covered in a beautiful quilt that someone obviously handmade, because you don't get that kind of quality in a manufactured environment. I focused on the quilt because it was too hard to focus on him. It made it hurt to even breathe.

"Miss Mia," he said quietly.

"Hmm?"

"I need you to come here."

His voice was so deep and sexy that it made my whole body tingle, even across the room. For the first time since the hotel room in Oklahoma City, my body froze. Because... well, because I knew what he wanted. We were alone. We had the rest of the day and night until we had to go anywhere. We had nothing scheduled. No plans.

Except, I thought that Derek definitely had plans.

I swallowed, unable to get up from the chair, frozen as I was.

"Miss Mia," he said, but there was a demand to his tone that made me want to respond. Like a good girl would, to any demand. A command was meant to be obeyed, right? But I also knew what was going to happen once I obeyed this command, and I was still slightly afraid of his reaction if we did this thing right now.

He crooked his finger at me. Another command. I swallowed and forced my frozen body to my feet and moved, with a huge effort, from the chair to the bed. I stood in front of him.

He sighed and grinned as if I'd just given him a Christmas present. He placed his beautiful hands on my waist, and his fingers curled under my t-shirt to touch my bare skin in a languid swirl that quickly turned the frozen chunk inside me into a puddle of mush.

He looked up at me, which wasn't a very big distance because he was tall, even though he was sitting, and I was short, even though I was standing.

"You're so beautiful it hurts," he told me sexily.

Which, really, was my line in my head for him. "Right back at ya," I said.

"But I don't think anyone has ever told you that," he said, and my heart hurt again, but for another reason. It was an ache for something I felt like I'd missed.

"So, Little Bird, I'm going to keep saying it to you until you know it's true and not just a line I'm using to get you into this bed with me."

"You're a moron," I said, trying to make light of it, but he knew me better by now. He knew that, really, I didn't know what else to say to him.

He tugged at the hem of my shirt and pulled it up where I reached for it and pulled it over my own head so that I was standing in front of him in my bra and jean shorts. I fought the urge to cover myself, and instead, placed my hands on his shoulders as he pulled me closer in between his legs.

He leaned forward and kissed my stomach and inched up to kiss the space between my breasts as he reached around me and undid the clasp of my bra. When it was gone, he took my right breast into his mouth and sucked. And I moaned. My first moan of the day.

As he progressed his way across my body, the moans came one after another. Each time he touched a new part of me with his lips, and his tongue, and his very able fingers, my body and my voice responded equally.

I was his butter to mold into whatever shape he wanted, like those butter sculptures you see at state fairs. His to create into whatever he so desired.

When my clothes were gone—all of them—he picked me up and laid me down on the bed while he disrobed. I wondered if he wanted me to return the favor of kissing every part of him like he'd kissed every part of me. I was really ridiculously new to all of this. He didn't know that yet.

Then I told my brain to shut up as he joined me with a wicked smile that stretched his cleft and had me reaching for it with my finger.

"Miss Mia, have you ever come on a man's hands?"

It was hard to respond. Because my breathing was already out of control. "Is that number thirteen or fourteen?" I teased.

"It can be one hundred if you'd like. I just want to know, has anyone ever given you that type of pleasure?"

His eyes were stormy. So, god-blessedly stormy. I felt like I might lose myself in just his eyes, and I wasn't sure what would happen to me if I lost myself in the rest of him, but for once, I didn't care. I wanted to lose myself. I didn't want to be Good Girl Mia, or any kind of Mia.

"Mia?"

"No," I croaked out.

So he proceeded to show me, with his long musician fingers, and his kisses on my lips, and on my throat, and on my body, just what it was like to come on a man's hands. Slow, and hard, and oh my god, so achingly beautiful. I was gasping, and moaning, and tugging at his shoulders, wanting even more of him and the peace he brought me. Because it was utter peace. More than in the quiet of the caverns. More than in the pages of a book.

He was smiling as he felt my body shake and shiver into him. A smile that was so damn cocky, and yet so damn loving at the same moment that I felt any last wall I had crumble away, leaving me as bare and open in my soul as I was right now in my body.

"I want to show you just how non-yucky oral sex can be, Little Bird, but I'm going to have to save that for later tonight, because right now, if I don't put myself inside you, I might just explode," he said with another cocky smile.

He reached for his jeans on the floor and pulled out a condom, and I eye-rolled. He kissed me quick. A kiss for an eye-roll.

"Why are you eye-rolling me?" he chuckled.

"Do you really carry condoms in your pocket?"

His smile was wiped away, and he looked at me with all seriousness. "Only since I met you," he said huskily.

He hovered above me and looked into my eyes which were, oddly, still open. I wanted to see him and everything he was doing to me and everything that I was doing to his body. With Hayden, I'd had my eyes closed the majority of the time, afraid. Afraid of losing my virginity and afraid of losing him. I'd just been afraid.

Now, with Derek, I wasn't afraid. I was longing. I was aching. I was hoping. He seemed to see that in me because he was so slow when he entered me, and so slow in every move he made until we were both moaning together, and I felt like every part of me was now entwined with every part of him. He fit inside me like that perfect puzzle piece should, even though it hurt briefly because I'd only done this once before.

Then we went beautifully over the edge together until there was nothing but us, and our hopes, and our torn souls reaching for each other.

It was life altering. The books were right. Hayden had been wrong. All wrong. There was nothing about this time that was like that time with Hayden, when he took, and I gave, and nothing was left after. Now, I felt like we both took, and we both gave, and what was left was more than what we had started with.

I lay curled up against him, head on his shoulder, and I felt myself smile for the first time that day. A real smile. A smile I still was getting accustomed to because it had never been a regular part of me. I don't think my whole life had seen me smile like this.

He kissed my forehead and pulled me closer against him.

"Thank you," he whispered.

"Umm. I think that should be my line," I giggled. Mental head thunk because it was me, giggling.

He chuckled. "I knew you'd been doing it wrong."

"Or at least he was." I smiled against his chest and was rewarded with another deep rumble from deep inside him.

"Thank God," he sighed out. "Now I get to be the best sex you've ever had."

"Conceited much?"

"Your words, not mine."

I slapped him playfully and went to pull away, but he tugged me back up tight against him. "I'm not done with you yet."

It was meant to be sexy. And holy potato peels, it was, but it also triggered memories of the only other time I'd done this and the guy had left me the following week.

"Why not?" I asked into his chest.

"Why not what? And does that count as your thirteen?"

"I think I'm only at ten," I told him.

"Are you sure?"

"Pretty sure."

"I'm pretty sure that I can make you ask a very different question," he said as his hands started to twirl at my hip and then in between my thighs. And he was right. My why went straight out of my head, and all I could think was please, please Lord, will you take me again?

And he did.

Over. And over. And over. As the light faded and the sky darkened. I'm sure the stars were out there twinkling, but I never saw them. I didn't care if I ever saw them again. I only cared about seeing the storm in his gray eyes as he reached for me, and I reached back.

Because Ed is so right in "Firefly." It was all about teaching my skin new tricks and warming me up with his lips. Our hearts together. Our lips and faces and cheeks meeting in a wild beat. Making sure I held on tight as Derek quietly sewed my broken heart back together.

# Chapter Twelve

Together

PHOTOGRAPH

"Loving can heal. Loving can mend your soul."
-Ed Sheeran

Music woke me up. "Little Bird" was playing, and I slammed the home button with as much might as I could, and next to me, Derek chuckled.

"You really don't like mornings."

What could I say? I didn't, but waking up next to him, the feel of his body next to mine…somehow that made it okay. I couldn't help but smile at him and then reached over to kiss him. I kissed him, not like a good girl, but just like me. Like I wanted to kiss the guy who fixed my heart that I had thought was broken beyond repair. I kissed him like I wanted to give him something.

He smiled against my lips and reached down to touch my nether regions, and I couldn't help but flinch because I was painfully, wonderfully tender down there.

"Are you sore?" he asked with a cocky smile.

"Duh," I said back with an eye-roll that earned me a quick kiss.

"But it's a good sore, right?" He was still laughing at me.

"You're a moron," I said. I went to get out of bed, but he pulled me to him and tickled me until I went limp in his arms, staring up at the face that was so gorgeous it could stop a zillion hearts.

"So, the oral sex? Ew or not ew?" He was still enjoying himself way too much for my liking. I flushed a thousand shades of red because thinking about what he'd done to me and what I'd done to him in the darkness of the hotel room was much more than even this Mia could handle in the morning light.

I pushed my forehead into his chest. I didn't want to respond. "I think you've reached your twenty-question limit."

"I'm assuming that's a 'not ew' then." I smacked him, face still hidden.

He kissed the back of my head and then bounced out of bed with so much impossible energy that I couldn't help but be reminded of Cam. And Jake. But mostly Cam. Today, the thought of them didn't force the guilt to bubble up. Instead, I got to keep it hidden away.

"Let's go, hot shot," he said, tugging at my foot while tickling the bottom, which had me bolting upright to remove my foot from his grasp.

"You're awful," I told him.

"Liar." Then he disappeared into the bathroom, showing me his naked parts that made my very sore body hum with delight anyway.

♫ ♫ ♫

True to her word, the vet showed up early. She gave us a checklist of things to watch for, a handful of bottles to feed the kitten with, and a list of other supplies that we would need. Then, we were on the road.

It wasn't even eight by the time we headed the Camaro toward the highway and Denver. It was going to be a long haul. Plus, Derek had rehearsal that afternoon. Thank God their show wasn't until the following day, but it was still going to be exhausting.

I had the kitten bundled in my lap while Derek drove. I looked over at him. We hadn't really slept much in the last couple days. Hardly at all on this trip. "I should drive," I told him. "You have to have your energy for tonight."

"We'll switch halfway, and I'll try to nap," he said with a smile that made my heart and body zing.

Then we rode in silence. Happy, peaceful silence.

I felt content. A feeling that I didn't know if I'd ever had.

"What are we going to name her?" I pondered aloud.

"Jane," he said.

"Jane?"

"After Jane Austen, of course."

"That's so bland though," I told him, unsatisfied.

"Calling a kitten Elizabeth seems too much."

"Definitely not Elizabeth!" I agreed. "We'll have to think about it."

"You may have to think about it, but she'll always be Jane to me," he smirked.

I cuddled the kitten as it slept, and somewhere along the way, I fell asleep too, because I came awake as the car stopped in a Target parking lot.

"I'm sor—" I started to say, but then stopped. Derek grinned at me.

"Good thing you stopped. Was going to have to find a lake to toss you into."

"What are we doing?"

He pointed to the store. "Supplies for Jane and supplies for us."

"Supplies?"

"We did use all my condoms, and I have a feeling we are going to need some more." He grinned that devilish grin.

"Who says?" I couldn't help but tease back.

"Best sex you've ever had, and now you tell me you're done." He shook his head in mock exasperation.

"It's kind of hard to say it's the best when there was only that one other experience to compare it to," I said without thinking.

He was halfway out the door, but slid back into his seat to look at me. The shock on his face got me more than anything. I busied myself with Jane the Kitten.

"You're joking, right?"

I felt the heat creep into my skin. I shrugged. What was there to say? I shouldn't have said anything.

"Who was this complete jackass? And why on earth were you still carrying a torch for him?"

I wanted to be defensive. I wanted to be mad. I couldn't, though, because I knew he was right. "Hayden. His name was Hayden."

"Well," he tilted my chin toward him, "Hayden was not only an insensitive ass, but the biggest fool on the planet, because you are the most delightful creature this side of paradise."

"You sound like such a suck-up."

"Do I?" He sounded surprised.

"Yes. No one says that kind of stuff. No one that really means it anyway."

"But I do," he said, and kissed me so that my toes curled and my aching body ached in a different way.

He pulled away. "Sorry, no time for you to ravish me here. Things to buy. Miles to travel."

I ignored all the questions swirling at the back door of my brain. Instead, I went inside with this energetic man where we bought the kitten supplies, a kitten carrier, food for us to eat on the road, and the supplies he'd already mentioned which I tried not to look at while the clerk rang us up. Then, we were back in the Camaro, with me driving.

♫ ♫ ♫

It was four-thirty by the time we pulled into Denver. George and the guys had been texting and calling for the last hour. They were stressed because some of the equipment wasn't working right, and the venue was having sound issues.

I drove Derek straight to the club. He looked tired as he came around to the driver's side to kiss me through the open window after buckling Jane's carrier into the passenger seat. He had napped for an hour or so, but it wasn't enough.

"You're tired. I feel like that's my fault," I said, being careful to avoid the word sorry.

"I believe that I started everything yesterday," he said.

"True, but—"

"No buts. Go to the hotel, take a long, hot bath. Ease those sore loins," he teased. "Although, I'll probably be late and too tired to ravish you. Damn. That really sucks."

I pushed his hand off the window. "Go! George already hates me."

"Does that bother you?"

"Of course it does. Who wants anyone hating them?"

"Miss Mia." He tried to reach back in, but I put the car in reverse and backed away.

"Have fun!" I said and then drove away from him.

The hotel wasn't far, and thankfully, it was pet friendly. I checked in and had to have a bellhop help me with the luggage plus all the kitty supplies. I felt like Mama, traveling with the entire family when we went on road trips for Jake's or Cam's sports.

In the room, I made sure Jane was locked up tight in her new carrier and then did exactly like Derek suggested; I took a bath. It made me sleepy, but it eased my sore muscles. I got out and looked at my body in the mirror. It was far from fat. It was just round... curvy. Suddenly, that didn't seem all bad. Derek seemed to like it.

Even as sleepy as I was, my brain wouldn't quite leave me alone in the quiet of the room with just the sound of the air conditioning unit clicking on and off.

I felt like I'd been on this trip for much longer than six days. It was as if I'd lived more since knowing Derek than I had my whole life. But it also wasn't my reality. It wasn't what I would be returning to in another fifteen days.

I'd wanted my heart to feel lighter. And it did. I'd wanted to escape briefly. And I had. I wanted to forget Hayden. And he was not much more than a bad memory of things I shouldn't have done.

I'd also known, from the moment Derek had walked into the dealership, that he could unravel me. Like a ball of Christmas garland that had been flung in a box for someone else to deal with the next year. And he had done that too. Unraveled me.

I just didn't know what would be left when it was all done. Would there be a Mia that could return to her old world and pick up where she left off? Because I didn't have a choice. You don't move away from parents who have lost everything because of you.

Really, I didn't want to move away from them or my life in Tennessee. I just wanted to feel...I don't know...not broken...not defective. And after this trip, I thought I might be trading one scab for a different one.

Eventually, the tiredness forced me to sleep, and I only woke up as Derek was climbing into the bed with me. Scary that I hadn't even heard the door.

"How's our baby?" he asked through a voice that was so tired I wanted to cry.

"Good. She ate, pooped, slept, just like a real baby," I whispered. "Go to sleep."

Derek kissed my neck, drew me up close to his body, and slept.

The next four days were a blur. We didn't even have a chance to use the new box of condoms we'd bought. Derek was at the venue all day, singing all night, and I was taking care of the kitten. The day after Denver, we were supposed to go spelunking, but I didn't want to leave the kitten for that long, so I stayed in the motor home while the boys went.

When Derek came back, he wasn't happy that I hadn't gone with them and said something about needing to find a babysitter for our child. I didn't know how to react to that as I often didn't know how to respond to him. Our child. It seemed crazy to even say those words out loud.

Because a child wasn't the anticipated outcome from a three-week escapade. A child couldn't be divided in two when we both went back to our real worlds. I could feel the emotion Derek was pouring into me. Even though I didn't know why, I could see that he didn't just think of this as sex, but I also didn't know what he expected to happen when the trip came to its natural conclusion.

After the spelunking, we drove to Vegas, where I had never been. Derek insisted that I get the full experience, so he drove me down Las Vegas Boulevard, and I stared in wonder at the lights, and sounds, and energy that seemed to hum through the entire place. Like the electricity that lit the lights was also lighting up the people. As if they were all automatons.

We stayed at the Hard Rock Hotel and Casino, where the band would also be playing. Our suite was huge and impressive, but was tucked away so that you couldn't see the lights from the strip. This was both disappointing and a relief because all that false energy made me feel as if I were in a different dimension even more than this whole trip had me feel.

That night, the Vegas girls at the show were more trashy than any of the fangirls at any of the other stops. They looked like hookers ready to be paid. I hated it when people put down girls for the way they dressed, but even I couldn't defend them.

As we left the theater, Derek was mobbed by a crowd that was aggressively vying for his attention. The crowd tore me from his grip, and I got shoved against a wall with a bang that twisted my ankle in the wedges I'd worn and shook my whole body. I could hear him call my name, and I saw him forcibly thrust some of the tramps aside to get back to me. When he reached me, he picked me up, and I wrapped my legs around him. He pushed his way through the crowd as casino security finally showed up and escorted us to the elevator.

I was still shaking when the doors of the elevator shut us in, and I suddenly realized why Trista didn't always travel with the band. This was insane. I forced him to put me down, and I wanted to wince as my ankle gave, but I also didn't want him to worry.

"Are you okay?" His voice was gruff, angry, but I knew it wasn't at me. He was eyeing me like Mama had when I'd come home from caving with him.

"Yes," I said, not wanting him to know how shaky the whole experience had left me. My ankle would be fine by the morning.

I was thoroughly relieved when we got to our own room. "Why was it so bad tonight?" I asked.

"It's gotten worse ever since they released the single," he said.

"What?" I asked.

He looked at me with an almost embarrassed grin that only came out when he talked about his success. "'Humanity.' They released it just before I played at Jake's fundraiser, and it's climbing the charts. That's why it's been getting crazier at each stop."

Which it had been, but I had just assumed it was because they were playing bigger venues.

Derek sank into the couch, pulling me with him. He looked worn out; more worn out than he had the entire time I'd known him. "Let's go to bed," I said.

"I just need to sit here for a few minutes," he responded, but his eyes were already drooping.

"You'll fall asleep here."

"Hmm?"

And he was out. He didn't even budge when I pulled away from him. I brought out a blanket from the bedroom and covered him up, and for the first night in many, I went to bed by myself.

At first, I couldn't sleep. I was thinking about how crazy it had been downstairs, and how different Derek and my real worlds were, and how much his world was going to continue to grow and expand and change. I also tossed and turned because I was aching to find a body next to mine that I'd grown accustomed to having tucked up against me. In only a handful of nights, he'd changed me so that I wasn't sure I'd ever be able to sleep on my own in the same way again.

Eventually, my own exhaustion took over and slumber-land claimed me.

♫ ♫ ♫

I woke to fingers on my cheek, and when I opened my still-tired eyes, Derek was smiling at me as he sat next to me on the bed. "You let me fall asleep on the couch, naughty girl."

"I'm not exactly big enough to forcibly move you," I retorted.

"I'm sure there are things you could have done that would have motivated me." His sexy tone was back, and that made my heart perk up.

I brushed my fingers over his cleft, and he bit my finger, sucking it in that way that made my whole body quiver. "I'm glad you're feeling better," I said with my own smile.

"No, no, you cannot lure me into your bed now. Too late." He pulled away.

"What?" I asked as my heart broke a little.

"Home, Miss Mia. We get to go home today."

"To Tennessee?"

His surprise registered at the same time my surprise did, because we had different homes. Homes that weren't anywhere near each other and hadn't even come into discussion, even if they'd been on my mind. We hadn't had those kinds of discussions. Instead, we'd played twenty questions about sex and love lives.

"L.A. home," he said thoughtfully.

"Umm. I'm not going to stay at the PlayBabe Mansion," I told him with a scowl.

He scowled back. "God, I should hope not. Hugo would try to get you into his bed as soon as he saw you."

"Ew!"

"I agree, ew!" He laughed at my shudder.

He had his hand moving gently down my leg, sexy as all get out, my body burning to be with his, as we hadn't been able to be together since the Wooly Bison. When he got to my foot, he started tickling, and I bucked and laughed and gasped into a sitting position, curling my feet up protectively under my body.

"It lives!" he cried with a triumphant smile.

"You're awful," I said.

"Awfully good!"

"Awfully conceited!"

"Awfully hungry!"

"Awfully ridiculous!"

"Come on, Little Bird, please get up so that we can finish our drive today. We get two days at home before we have to leave again."

I couldn't resist his beg. He wanted this. He needed this. I got out of bed, got ready, and tucked our little kitten and luggage back into the Camaro so we could drive all the way to L.A. in one long swoop.

♫ ♫ ♫

Derek was driving when we entered the L.A. basin. Even with the Google Map lady, I would have been overwhelmed. Derek didn't need a compass here; it was his home. It drew me back a little more from the bubble we'd been in where there was just me and Derek and whatever this was between us. Even the band hadn't invaded in on us in any tangible way, but now we were entering his real world.

And that made me nervous.

We hit some curving roads that led out of the noise and traffic and pulled up to a set of huge wrought iron gates with a security guard. My stomach flipped in an entirely different way than Derek made my stomach flip.

The guard smiled when he saw it was Derek and waved us through. I turned in my seat to watch the gates roll shut behind us. When I turned back around, I was floored by the enormous mansion in front of me. It's not like we don't have mansions in Tennessee. We have plenty, but I'd never personally known anyone that lived in one. Even Blake, with all his success, lived in a Victorian in the old part of Nashville.

"Is this your home?" I asked with a gasp.

He looked at it as if it was the first time he'd noticed it.

"Well, it's really Dylan's. I live in the guesthouse out back," he said flippantly.

"I don't know what to say to this," I said as my heart pitter-pattered.

He shrugged. "It's not a big deal."

"Holy guacamole, Derek, you live in a palace!"

He laughed. "So, I impressed you?

"I'm not sure impressed is the right word. Terrified?"

We pulled up in front of a set of mammoth granite steps that someone had beautifully polished. Probably a servant. Derek had servants! Panic surged through me.

Derek leaned over and grabbed my chin and said, "Little Bird," and I stopped and looked at him, trying to push aside the waves of nausea. "It's my brother's house. Not mine."

"But it's home," I said weakly.

He shrugged again. "It has been."

He kissed me, bringing me back to him. To us. To the feeling that reached my toes every time he touched me.

"Better?" He grinned.

I smiled back because it was. I just had to focus on Derek and not all the rest for now. I nodded.

We grabbed Jane and our bags and headed up those shiny steps. The first thing I noticed when we walked in was Seth's waterfall, the one Cam had told me she'd seen here. There it was, in all its enormity, somehow fitting inside this mansion and making you feel like you were going on a trip to paradise.

"Holy guacamole," I said for the second time in almost as many minutes.

"That's my brother's wife, Bianca. She's pretty showy."

"Is that my long-lost, good-for-nothing baby brother?" a booming voice gushed from a hallway. It was nothing like Derek's smooth voice. This one was all conceited command.

In came who I presumed to be Dylan Waters. He was blonder and taller than Derek. They almost had nothing in common. Except the cleft. That and maybe the charisma that dripped off them both. You knew that Dylan would own whatever set he walked onto. He was a man in charge. He was "*the* man."

Derek dropped his bags and they hugged, not the typical half hug that men do but a real hug, full of real love and affection. It surprised me again. I guess it shouldn't have. Derek was a man who seemed to feel everything deeply. It was probably what made him a great songwriter.

"George says you've been pulling all kinds of shit on the tour," Dylan said when they stepped back.

Then it clicked, the puzzle piece that was George. George was Dylan's friend, acquaintance, whatever. He wasn't Derek's choice. He'd taken what was given to him.

"He's just pissed that I haven't let him dictate my every move," Derek said with a goofy grin that seemed so different from his confident charm. All of a sudden, he was the little brother. He was the shadow in the superstar's wake. Maybe Derek and I had more in common than I had ever thought possible for a nobody from nowhere and a sexy musician.

Derek stepped back and found my fingers, pulling me forward. "Dylan, Mia. Mia, Dylan." He was beaming, happy. He wanted us to love each other. I wanted to be loved. Good Girl Mia only wants to be liked, after all, but the way Dylan appraised me, I wasn't sure if I was going to make his cut.

He shook my hand and smiled at me, but the smile didn't reach his eyes the way his brother's did. Instead, his eyes were analyzing, judging. Maybe it was something about being a director and having to analyze the actions of every scene being built in front of him, but I could see that Dylan wasn't a man to easily approve of anything.

"I've heard a lot about you, Mia."

I couldn't help but flush. "Hopefully all good."

"I hear you haven't seen *The Spy Network*," he said as if he was deeply offended, but he was watching me like a hawk. Derek was the eagle. Dylan the hawk. I knew I liked the eagle better.

My face burned more, and I punched Derek in the shoulder, but he just laughed at me and wrapped me under his arm, tugging me next to his body where I fit. I wondered if his brother thought I was yet another fangirl thriving on his brother's success.

"It's true. I'm more of a book girl," I finally responded.

"Well, thank God, because I get so fucking tired of this guy trying to bully us all into reading whatever he's decided he's liked. Please, for the love of God, talk books with him," Dylan joshed us both and winked as if we'd used "books" as a pseudonym for "sex."

And hey, that was okay because I'd found that if you did both right, they were similar. Both full of beautiful words and beautiful emotions. The fact that Derek really did like books was not lost on me.

"Uncle Derek!" a high-pitched squeal interrupted us as a tiny blonde bombshell thrust herself into Derek's arms, causing him to lose his grip on me.

"Mags!" Derek said, hugging the little body tightly to him. The way I loved to be hugged. Where there was no space and no hope for escape.

The blonde-headed body squirmed in his arms. "What have you brought me?"

He looked chagrinned. "Um."

"You didn't bring me *anything*?!" she demanded as she pushed against him until he had to put her down, where she promptly stomped her foot and crossed her arms across her tiny chest.

"Well, I've kind of been busy, little tyke."

She took me and the carrier I was holding in with a frown.

"Who's the bimbo and what does she have?"

"Maggie!" Dylan and Derek both said at the same time as if it was supposed to be a scold, but they were both laughing. I didn't know if I should be insulted by this little girl who couldn't be more than four, or if I should be insulted by their laughing at me.

"Mags, this is my girlfriend, Mia, and this is our little kitten, Jane."

Then I was frozen again. Because he just called me his girlfriend. Was that what he thought I was? I mean, we had been sleeping together—literally and bodily—for a little over a week, but I hadn't really thought he'd labeled us. Because he knew as well as I did that we only had three weeks together, didn't he?

"That's a stupid name," Maggie said.

"Maggie!" her dad said again, but this time there was actually a warning in the tone.

"Can I see it?" she asked.

"Yes, but she's been injured, so you'll have to be really gentle," Derek told her. I set the carrier down and opened the door. Jane would usually come out and investigate of her own accord. She was curious, which was probably what had gotten her into trouble with the engine of the Camaro in the first place.

Today, she just hung out in the carrier. Maggie spread herself out on her belly on the granite floor and looked inside. "Why isn't she coming out?"

"She's a little overwhelmed by all this," Derek said, but his eyes met mine with a smile that tugged at my heart again because I felt like he was talking about me as much as Jane. He knew me. How he knew me so well after so little time together was a mystery. But he did. He may not know that it was his label that had pushed me over the edge, but he'd known when I'd gone over and was trying to catch me before I fell too far.

"Can I pet her?"

"I'd just let her get used to you at first. We're going to bring her out to the guesthouse, and you can visit her there."

"How long are you here for?" Dylan asked.

"Three days. Well, two more after today," Derek responded.

"Good. Bianca's gone tonight, but she'll be back tomorrow. We can have a family dinner."

Derek groaned.

"You're hardly ever here any more. We miss you."

"You mean you miss having someone to rib," Derek said with a smile.

"Well, what the hell else are little brother's for?" Dylan teased back. "Come on, Maggie, I'm sure Betty is already freaking out because she can't find you."

The little girl scrambled up off the floor and put her tiny hand in her father's. They ambled off down the corridor, and I watched them with awe. They were matching, overpowering dynamos. Even the four-year-old demanded more attention than I'd ever demanded in my whole life.

Derek grabbed Jane's carrier, closing the door, and then grabbed my hand and his bag and tugged me toward the back of the house. I barely had time to grasp my own bag and follow.

We walked through several rooms that were ready to receive the Queen of England before we got to a wall of glass. Outside the smudge-less panes was a manicured yard filled with a pool designed for nirvana. In our part of Tennessee, most of the pools were utilitarian. They were built to swim and escape the heat in.

This pool was the kind you made movies about. The kind that filled romance novels. The kind that made me want to run screaming back to Tennessee because I knew I'd never belong here.

We made our way around the shimmering water and through a literal jungle until we found another house. A whole house! One story, but still a house. In the backyard! Derek opened the door and set down the bags. He turned to me, pulled everything from my hands, and then pulled me up close to his chest.

He looked down at me with that serious expression. The one that didn't last long but always made me sorry if I was the one that brought it to the surface.

"Miss Mia, stop thinking," he told me.

"I'm not." I tried to look away, but he captured my chin and drew my face up. His hand caressed the edge of my lips.

"You are. Don't."

Then he was kissing me. Kissing me hard and full of passion. Like he had at the Wooly Bison. Like he hadn't been able to in the four days since then. For a while, I forgot the world again and concentrated on the space where we made memories for ourselves that would always remain, even if our hearts would eventually be broken.

It was "Photograph" playing in my head as he led me to his room. The room that was a glimpse of something that didn't seem to be him at all. That must have been decorated by Bianca, because the room was beige and impersonal, and Derek was neither of those things. He was vivid colors and all humanity wrapped in a beautiful collage like his song said.

I didn't care what the room looked like as we shed our clothes and found ourselves in each other's skin. As I found my way back around his abs and his body that continued to floor me with its gorgeousness. As he found his way back around my body that I seemed to appreciate more because he found it exciting.

I realized, as we made love in a room that was his but not his, that Ed's words were true. Loving could heal. Loving could mend your soul. And it was the only thing we could take with us when we died. Like Jake had taken Cam's love with him. And if I ended up hurt, well, that would be okay, because even though the wounds would bleed, the words that we sang together with our skin touching, those words would stay inside the pages that were left behind.

Chapter Thirteen

A Relationship

COLD COFFEE

"Tell me how to fall in love the way you want me to."
-Ed Sheeran

When I woke the next morning, it was to an empty bed. I immediately hated that. Hated that I wasn't wrapped in arms that were tattooed for forgiveness. Hated that I wasn't next to a body that made mine feel safe and wanted. Hated mornings.

I heard clanking coming from what I assumed to be a kitchen. I heard sizzling and smelled coffee. It was almost enough to make me want to get out of bed. But not quite enough.

A few minutes later, Derek appeared in the bedroom doorway with only a pair of jeans on.

He grinned at me and said, for not the first time, but like it continued to amaze him, "You really hate mornings."

"I'm slowly learning to appreciate the possibilities that morning can bring," I said as I hugged the pillow and watched him.

"Breakfast is ready."

"Not tempting enough."

"Are you sure?"

"Pretty darn sure."

"Hmm." He eased toward me. "What can I tempt my Little Bird with?"

I curled my toes up protectively because he had a bad habit of tickling me or pulling me out of bed when he wanted me to get up. For the first time in days, we didn't have to be anywhere, and I was kind of liking the idea of staying right where I was. All day. Maybe I could tempt him instead.

When he got close enough, I grabbed a loop on his jeans. "I think you have this whole day off idea wrong," I said quietly, and my free hand brushed across his skin.

"Mia." He sounded like his brother talking to Maggie yesterday, with a warning tone in his voice.

"Days off are meant to be spent in bed," I said.

He groaned as my hand made another pass. Then he was on top of me, pinning me to the bed like a coyote pins his prey. Except I didn't feel like prey.

"You, Miss Mia, are going to be the death of me," he said huskily.

"At least it will be a pleasant death," I said with my own sassy grin.

"Breakfast is going to get cold. And I cooked. For you," he said, but he said it in between kisses on my lips, and on my neck, and then lower to my breast that he uncovered from the t-shirt I'd thrown on last night.

"Some things are better than breakfast," I told him.

♫ ♫ ♫

Later, we found cold coffee and cold pancakes in the kitchen. I sat on the counter while he heated things back up in the microwave, grumbling about it all being ruined now.

I wasn't the kind of girl who usually sat on counters, but it seemed… decadent. Like I was going to be tossed out at any minute. Good Girl Mia hated it, but she was losing out more and more to this Other Mia who tried new things… like adventures with sexy musicians.

Derek placed my plate next to me, and I caught his hand. I kissed the palm. "Thank you for making me breakfast," I said.

He looked down at his hand where I'd kissed it, then he looked up at me. His gray eyes turned to thunderclouds again. He pushed his body in between my legs, and I wrapped my legs around him, pulling him close, and laying my head on his shoulder. I smiled against his chest. Happy. That happy feeling continued to shock me to the core whenever I felt it with him and not the guilt that usually came with it. As if I'd discovered the last unknown frontier.

"Are you smiling?" he asked with a smile in his own voice.

I just nodded.

"God." He hugged me tight to him, and I think we would have found our way into each other's skin again if a knock on the door hadn't been followed by a little four-year-old's voice demanding entry.

We pulled apart just as Maggie and a woman who reminded me of a young Carol Burnett rounded the corner. I slid down from the counter, tugging at the hem of my t-shirt while Derek adjusted his jeans. The Carol doppelgänger's eyes widened, and she quickly averted them.

Maggie, however, came right up to Derek and hugged his leg. "Uncle Derek, where is your kitty?"

"Last we saw, she was cuddled on her blanket in the bedroom," he said, ruffling her hair in a way that made me think of Jake ruffling mine.

Maggie took off toward the bedroom, and I hoped nothing in there would give us away. "Hi, Betty," Derek said to the woman who was awkwardly moving toward the living space.

She just waved.

"Do you want some coffee?" he asked with a smile and a wink at me that Betty couldn't see.

"No, thank you. Do you want us to come back later?"

"Nah, we were just having breakfast," he said, and he tugged at my hair, wrapping it around his finger till the finger met my lip in that way that made me feel safe, and claimed, and so many other different and complicated emotions.

"I'm going to go take a shower," I said, grabbing a plain pancake off the plate and making to leave, but he hadn't let go of my hair yet.

"What happened to staying in bed on our day off?" he whispered quietly, all smiling BB.

"Seems like you have company."

He kissed me and let me go, and we both made our way to the bedroom, but I left him and Maggie to play with Jane the Kitten while I found myself in the luxury of his bathroom. It was five-star hotel type luxury with scents, and shampoos, and soaps that my mama would never in a million years have spent money on.

Which reminded me, with a wave of guilt, that I hadn't texted Mama in almost a day. I sent her a quick good morning and then texted Cam to ask about her and the baby before losing myself in the scents and heat of the scalding shower.

When I came out, Betty and Maggie were gone, and Derek was nowhere to be found. I texted him. No response. Then, I heard laughter and splashing coming from outside.

I found him in the pool. Maggie was riding a huge swan monstrosity while he pulled her through the water. She was definitely in charge, telling him exactly where to go, and he laughingly obeyed, serf to her medieval princess. I sat in my summer dress on a chaise lounge, watching them. Betty joined me.

"Hi, I'm Mia," I said with a smile.

"Betty. Sorry about earlier." She flushed and looked away.

I matched her flush with one of my own and waved her off.

"It's just...well...Derek's never had someone here before. I didn't know," she said as she watched Derek. If she wasn't at least twenty years older than him, I might have been suspicious that she had a crush on him. But I think it was just Derek's way of charming everyone, old and young alike. You wanted to like him as soon as you met him.

What caught me in her response, though, was that she said he'd never had anyone at the guesthouse. That seemed almost impossible. "Never?" I questioned.

She just shook her head.

"Miss Mia, come join us!" Derek yelled from the pool.

I shook my head with a smile and waved my Kindle at him. I'd sit and read to give him time with his niece. His beautiful niece who certainly didn't need to be told that she was beautiful. She already knew it. How are some people born with that knowledge?

They swam for an hour or more, and then we all made our way into the big house into a kitchen the size of my family's entire house in Tennessee, where a chef had lunch ready on a buffet table. I was floored again. Derek didn't even blink an eye. This was his normal life.

It made me feel far away from him again. Our realities spiraling one more twirl out from the core that was us. Soon, the gap would be impossible to cross. As if he sensed my thoughts, he grabbed my hand at the table and leaned over to kiss my cheek. "Breathe, Miss Mia, it's just lunch."

It wasn't, though. It was a whole lifestyle that I didn't know how to live in. I would never have expected this from Derek. He was so casual and down-to-earth. He was at home making grilled cheese in a motor home and eating fried chicken in a karaoke dive bar. Even though I hadn't expected this, this life also seemed to fit him. The rich kid in a world of money and power. It was only surprising that he didn't seem the least bit entitled because of it all.

After lunch, Betty bundled Maggie off to a nap that I seriously doubted would really happen, but it allowed Derek and I to make our way back to the guesthouse that he called home, but didn't really seem like a home. Instead, it felt like a resort you would visit for a few days before you returned to reality. I guess that was it. This was my resort.

My three week vacation. But my reality waited for me at the end of this journey.

I knew that Derek hadn't realized that yet. He'd called me his girlfriend after all. That wasn't something you usually did if it was all going to be over in a handful of days.

I wandered the room. There were a few pictures scattered around the side tables, beautifully manicured pictures of Maggie, Dylan, Derek, and a blonde that screamed Hollywood, and who I assumed must be Bianca. There were no pictures of Derek as a little boy or his parents. Those were the kinds of pictures that were plastered around our house in Tennessee like sprinkles on cupcakes. Our pictures were full of life. Prom pictures and graduation pictures. Plenty of football and dive pictures. Pictures of all of us on vacation at the beach or picnicking at the lake.

Here, there were only these posed pictures. An image of the family that had been manufactured for the world to see.

As I roamed the room, I picked up random instruments that were also scattered about. The instruments were the only thing in the guesthouse that did seem to fit Derek, especially after all the ones I'd seen him play on the road.

While I rambled about, Derek lounged on the couch, his guitar in his lap, plucking strings.

"Question twenty, Little Bird?" he asked.

"How am I at twenty?" I turned and crossed my arms over my chest, taking in his glorious lankiness.

"We lost count, I know, but I'm sure you're at least at twenty. Maybe more."

I paused. I really wanted to ask about the pictures and his childhood, but instead I went for something safer.

"You have a lot of instruments."

He shrugged. "I majored in compositional music at UCLA."

My mouth dropped. This was a perfect example of how a three week journey didn't make us boyfriend and girlfriend. A real girlfriend would have known this.

"You went to college?" I breathed out.

"Wounding me, Miss Mia, wounding me," he chuckled with his lips twitching in a way that said he was enjoying shocking me. "I just finished my master's program in May."

He still had his gaze fixed on me as he hit notes on his guitar. I couldn't take the heat of his stare. It was like he absorbed some piece of me every time he concentrated on me that long. I turned, frazzled, because his confession about college had made me realize that there was still so much more about him that I wanted to know, but I wasn't sure if the remaining time together would be enough to find it all out.

I set down the strange pipelike instrument I'd held onto, placing it next to one of the fake pictures that could have come pre-purchased in the frame.

"That wasn't the question you really wanted to ask," Derek prompted me.

I debated whether to ask the questions whirling in my brain, because saying, "Hey, these pictures look pretty fake," wasn't exactly something Old Mia would ever say. So I settled for something close.

"Where's your childhood?" I waved my hand abstractly at all the pictures.

"Not here." He smiled, but there was a shuttered look that came into his eyes, one that I was unaccustomed to seeing in a man who had always been an open book.

"Well, I know you didn't grow up here, but don't you have any pictures?"

"I'm sure Hugo does."

I stared at him, speechless for the second time in almost as many minutes.

"Hugo? Hugo Brantly has your childhood pictures?"

He shrugged as if it was no big deal.

He started a new melody on the guitar, one I hadn't heard before. It was aching and lovely. I realized that this was Derek's way of changing the subject. He didn't want to talk about Hugo and the PlayBabe Mansion. He was good at avoiding talking about himself and the things that haunted him, but I knew him well enough now to know that this was one of his ghosts, because he'd been serious and not smiling.

"That's new," I said as I sat down next to him, curling my feet up under me on the couch.

"It's called the 'Wooly Bison'."

I slugged his shoulder. It did remind me of our time at the Wooly Bison, though. Of the first time we'd made love as the shimmery Oklahoma sunshine filtered into our hotel room. It was amazing how he could speak to me without words, whether that was through his music, or his fingers, or his eyes. He watched me as he played. No words, just chords.

"I like you like this," he said huskily.

I looked down at myself, in my sundress with bare feet curled under me. "Like what?"

"Relaxed. Happy."

I flushed. He put down the guitar and eased a finger over my flushed cheeks. "I like you here. As my girlfriend."

I tried not to panic. I knew that this was the time to say something. To speak up about the label he'd given me and the few days we had left together. But just like he didn't want to talk about his childhood, I didn't want to talk about the future. For once, I just wanted to continue to live in the moment. It was why I'd come with him on this journey to begin with, to escape my reality.

It would come back to bite us. I knew it would, but as he continued to touch me, my brain shut off and my body took over. And then we were gone for a while again. Lost in each other, and our skin, in a way that I never knew I could be lost. Lost in a way that I couldn't have imagined even two weeks ago when I thought I was missing Hayden and was full of guilt over my dead brother.

♫ ♫ ♫

Family dinner at the Waters household was nothing like my family dinners in Tennessee. First of all, it didn't even start until nearly eight o'clock. In Tennessee, we ate with the senior citizens at five or, at the latest, six. Plus, this wasn't really a family dinner to me at all because Maggie had dinner on her own and was in bed with the nanny watching over her. Our family dinners would never have happened without all the kids scattered around the table. To me, that's what made it a family.

I was nervous as I met Bianca for the first time because I hadn't changed out of my simple sundress while she looked like she'd just stepped out of a fashion magazine. She wasn't nice and self-deprecating like Trista the Model had been. No, Bianca was a Hollywood wife. She was one hundred percent blonde, and perfect, and entitled.

As we gathered into one of the richly furnished rooms that she called a family room, she made a slight attempt to visit with me before realizing that we had nothing in common. I ran a car dealership in the backwoods. She kept her husband's entire life running while he made A-list movies.

The doorbell rang, and we were soon joined by George and a man that looked like a run-down version of Dylan. He had gray hair that you could tell used to be blonde, and a cleft chin like the boys, so it was obvious this was their dad. That's where the similarity to either of the brothers really ended though.

"Derek!" he boomed in a voice that was scratchy from too many years of smoking.

Derek didn't hug him like he had Dylan. In fact, he barely acknowledged him from across the room. "Dad."

Derek's father made his way to us. "George here has been telling me how your songs are finally taking off. Took long enough," he growled.

When he got close, I could smell the alcohol on him. It was so strong it was almost as if it had embedded itself into his skin permanently. A cologne that didn't need to be reapplied.

I held a finger to my nose so I wouldn't gag. Derek frowned at my movement while Derek's dad eyed me. It was not unlike the way Dylan had eyed me, but you could tell that the older man came up with a different assessment. "Hey, honey, I'm Doug. Who might you be?"

The sordidness in his tone took me aback. I couldn't believe that there was any way that this man could actually be Derek's father, and I wasn't sure how to respond to him. Derek tugged at my hand, interlacing our fingers, and when I looked up at him, I saw Derek in a way that I'd never seen him before. Barely veiled contempt and anger clouded his face that was normally so happy. Even the seriousness I'd seen had nothing on this look.

My heart broke in a whole new way because I could tell that the forgiveness Derek had had tattooed on his wrists was tied to this man and his childhood. The childhood without pictures. The childhood he didn't want to talk about.

"Dad, this is my girlfriend, Mia." His voice was cold as he said it, and I didn't take it personally because his whole body was coiled tight as he addressed this man. I inwardly cringed at allowing him to continue to use the girlfriend term. But like before, now wasn't the time to stop him.

"Mia, huh? That's a good name." Doug eyed me up and down again, taking in my size E's in a way that no father should. Definitely not the way a father should look at his son's proclaimed girlfriend. I stepped closer to Derek.

I felt Derek lean forward to say something that wouldn't have been good at all, but we were interrupted by a southern accent attached to a dark-haired man. "Mia Phillips! As I live and breathe!"

Then, I was being enveloped in a hug from Keith. Long forgotten Keith that Cam had just mentioned seeing at this very mansion. He seemed tall and happy. Derek pulled at my hand again as Keith let me go.

"Keith!" I said with a smile.

"I swear I can't leave you for two seconds without you running in to someone else you know," a deep voice said next to him. The man who came up to Keith had graying hair that belied his age. He was handsome and self-assured with an expensive suit that clung to his body. A suit that was mirrored by the one that Keith had on, even though they were different shades. They both spoke of money and success in a way that only custom suits could. I knew that for a fact after having seen all of Hayden's tailored suits in his closet.

"Mia, this is my boyfriend, Locke," Keith said, his smile full of so much love that it made me forget all about Derek's slimy dad.

"Nice to meet you," I smiled. Derek seemed to relax just a touch, and my stomach couldn't help but do a little flip of relief.

"How do you know Mia?" Derek asked.

"We grew up in the same town," Keith responded with a smile.

"You grew up in Tennessee?" Derek was surprised.

"Yep! Sure did. I think I was the one that kept Mia here supplied in ice cream after she'd had her surgery," Keith said before regretting it just like anyone from our town ever did when they talked about Jake and that time. It was like they couldn't help themselves, because they forgot he was gone and then hated themselves when they remembered it all over again.

"Keith was really more of Cam's friend than mine," I told Derek with a smile.

"That hurts." Keith pretended to pout.

I laughed. "It's true, though. Who ordered you to bring me my ice cream?"

Keith smiled knowingly. "Well… that would be Cam. But who can ever say no to that woman? How is she? How's the baby?"

"They put her on bedrest," I said.

Keith chuckled. "Oh my God. I feel sorry for Blake and everyone else that comes into her eyesight."

"I know, right? Blake's grandma tried to get her to start cross-stitching."

Keith laughed so hard that he had to lean into his boyfriend. It was good to see him so happy.

"So you work for Dylan?" I asked.

Keith nodded, leaned in and whispered, "I'm only here tonight because Bianca wanted someone to make sure Dad got here safely. Sometimes it feels like I work for Bianca more than Dylan."

Derek overheard and laughed the first real laugh since his dad had walked in, and that made me like Keith more than I ever had.

Bianca announced that dinner was ready, and we made our way into a huge dining room that looked like it should be in Buckingham Palace instead of a Hollywood mansion. We were spread out around the long table like polka dots on a dress.

I was near Keith, his boyfriend Locke, and Derek's dad. Derek was down with Bianca, George, and Dylan. It seemed like it was a statement that Bianca had made on purpose, separating real family from the "others."

Derek frowned as we sat down but didn't say anything. He seemed somehow out of his normal element in this place with these people. He would never have let any of the band keep us apart at a table. No matter what, I wasn't going to cause a scene when he was obviously already feeling uncomfortable.

Bianca asked casually if Keith was picking up the new art piece for Dylan's offices tomorrow, and Keith nodded. "Thank God. I don't have to make up an excuse to check on Seth then," Locke said, brushing a hand through his graying hair.

"Is this Seth Carmen you're talking about?" I asked.

"Yep, you should see the work he does now, Mia. It's really incredible," Keith told me.

"Last I remember of Seth Carmen was Jake punching him in the face," I said.

Keith turned somber. "Yeah. He was pretty screwed up back then. But we all have our demons we have to confront and bury before we find the path to real life."

His words hit me hard in the chest because weren't they true? We all had demons. Every last one of us. Mine were giving my brother a kidney and then having him die from it, and chasing a boy who did nothing but break my heart. But that didn't mean that I couldn't find a path to a real life. Whatever that would be. For the second time since Derek and I had gotten together, another tiny piece of hope niggled into my heart.

"Do you want to go with me tomorrow and check out his work?" Keith asked.

Derek was going to be at the recording studio for most of the day as they tried to finish up a couple extra songs for the bonus album, and I had planned on hanging by the pool with my Kindle. I shrugged. "Sure. Text me the details," I said, and we exchanged numbers.

"Dylan's offices are okay," Doug commented as he finished yet another scotch. His words were slurred, but you could tell he wanted to be the focus of everyone's attention. "But they're nothing like Hugo's."

None of us knew how to respond to his comment.

"In fact, this whole spread that Dylan has set up," Doug waved a drunken hand around the room, "it's okay, but when you're back at the mansion, that's where the glamour is really at."

Derek had turned toward our end of the table as soon as his dad had started talking. He was listening carefully. I cringed as Doug, who was sitting on my other side, took me in again. "I can see why Derek picked you. You'd fit right in at the mansion. Why don't you come by? I'll introduce you to folks who could make you over into a real somebody."

Derek threw down his napkin, rose, and made his way over to us. "Mia already is a somebody, Dad." The scorn in his voice was clear.

"What? Do you model?" Doug asked, surprised, taking in my no-makeup face and my wavy hair that I'd brushed into a simple braid.

"No," I breathed out.

"But you want to, right?"

I shook my head in the negative, but he guffawed in disbelief. "Hugo would love you. Eat you up like sugar cubes. You really picked a good one, Derek-my-boy."

"Mia isn't going anywhere near the mansion." Derek's voice was firm.

"Aw, ain't that cute, son. But you really should let the girl decide. I bet she'd love to have a piece of the ol' Brantly pie."

I shivered in disgust, not only at the thought of being a Brantly Babe but at the tone in Doug's voice.

"You should come with me. You'll see just how fuckin' amazing it is," Doug slurred, and he leaned toward me as if he might kiss me.

I backed up in my chair at the same time that Derek jerked me out of it.

"That place is nothing more than a legitimized whorehouse. And as I said, Mia isn't going anywhere near it."

Derek was pulling me forcibly toward the door. I didn't resist. I was shocked not only by the whole scene Doug had made but also by the angry hulk that had taken over the gentle man that I adored. He was seriously snarling with the anger coming off him in waves.

"Derek, don't go," Bianca cried out from the other side just as Dylan rose from his seat to protest as well.

"Derek!"

"I told you *family* dinner was a bad idea, Dylan. Next time, listen to me." The sarcasm in his voice was eating at me. I wanted to cry. Cry for my happy, sexy BB. That this was his family. That this was his life.

Derek slammed the French door behind us. I looked back to make sure it hadn't shattered with the force he'd used and then tried to keep up with his long strides as he pulled me along with him.

Once we made it to the guesthouse, he let me go and stormed into the kitchen where he grabbed his own highball glass and filled it with amber liquid. He swallowed it in one gulp before pouring himself a second which he drank slower. He hadn't turned on a light besides the kitchen stove we'd left on earlier, so his face was shadowed, and he wouldn't look at me as he inhaled the alcohol and breathed heavily. I just stared. I knew that he knew I was watching him. Just like my echolocation always knew when he was watching me.

"Spit it out, Phillips," he said. That broke me a little more because it was so cold and impersonal. I was back to Phillips, Little Bird nowhere in sight. Not even a Miss Mia.

"I don't know what to say." I spoke quietly, not teasing at all this time. Instead, there was nothing but sorrow in my voice.

I guess I probably should have been angry that he was acting this way. That he was shutting me out and calling me Phillips instead of opening up to me, but I couldn't be. Because this wasn't Derek. This wasn't the man I knew. Instead, I just wanted to wipe it all away.

He downed his drink, poured a third, and then made his way to the couch, where he sank down, head resting on the back, legs spread out in front of him. I made my way to him slowly, unsure of how to approach this Derek I had never seen before.

241

I sat down, freeing myself of my shoes and pulling my knees up to my chest. My bare toes barely cleared his thighs. I wrapped my arms around my legs and put my head on my knees so that I could watch him. It was not unlike how we had sat a few hours ago, when he'd ignored talking about his past and I'd ignored talking about our future, before we lost ourselves in each other. Now, the emotion wafting through the air couldn't be overlooked.

His eyes were closed as a full range of expressions poured over his face, from anger to disgust to unhappiness before settling into the worst of them all, sadness.

"I want to say I'm sorry, but I'm afraid I'll be tossed in the pool instead of a lake." I tried to lighten the mood as he was so good at lightening my mood when I went down the dark paths inside my brain.

"Apologizing for things you can't control is no way to live," he said, but he didn't open his eyes, and it wasn't accompanied by his cleft-tugging smile. It was said from some pit inside him.

I reached down to where his wrist lay on his leg, the hand not wrapped around the glass of whiskey. I pulled it to me and rubbed my finger gently over the tattoo that said, "To err is human; to forgive, sanity." I thought I finally had a glimpse of what he was trying to forgive and to forget.

"Do you want to talk about it?" I asked quietly.

This got him to open his eyes. He turned his head on the back of the couch, eyes meeting mine in the dim light from the kitchen stove.

"No."

"It would probably help," I told him.

He pulled one of the strands of my hair loose from my braid and twirled it up to my lip, caressing the corner. "I don't want to give that dipshit or my past any more energy or time or space."

Johnny Cash coming back to us. I nodded, and I removed the glass from his other hand, brought that wrist to my lips, and kissed the double-wrapped tattoo there. I was a chicken because I didn't want him to give that past any energy either. I was afraid that if I knew his story, it might make me feel more for him than I was already feeling. And I didn't know if I could handle being broken by his words about the past that was haunting him.

It wasn't the right thing. It was going to come back and implode on us both, eventually, but that wouldn't be tonight.

So instead, I did what I could so that he would give us all of his energy and time and space. I slowly unwound my feet from my hands and eased myself onto his lap, a move that, even five days ago, would have been impossible for me. I pushed my hands under his t-shirt, grazing his sculpted abs and tugging until he had to move, so that the t-shirt could disappear somewhere behind the couch. I started kissing him, starting at his neck with the eagle spread out and down to his shoulders and his chest.

When I looked back up at his face, he wasn't scowling anymore. Instead, the storm in his eyes was for the reasons I loved. That made my breath hitch because I had wanted so much for him to look at me just like that, and I was happy that I could bring him back to this moment.

"You are so damn beautiful, Little Bird."

I smiled back at him because he'd said Little Bird again and not Phillips. Then we were both adrift once more in the energy and space that belonged to just the two of us. Like Ed shared with his own "Cold Coffee," a place where we could stay forever or even just for now. Where I could give a loving hand and help him fall asleep.

hapter Fourteen

Studios

ONE

"Take my hand and my heart and soul,
I will only have these eyes for you."

-Ed Sheeran

The next morning, when I woke with my alarm, it was again to an empty bed. I was just getting to the point where I only resented mornings a little, instead of outright hating them, but waking to an empty bed made me hate them all over again.

It wasn't like I hadn't known that Derek was leaving early. He'd told me that Rob was picking him up at the crack of dawn so they could finish off those last few tracks, but actually waking up without him tucked up against me was like having someone throw a bucket of ice on me.

I growled at the light but got up to feed Jane the Kitten who was happily adjusting to life in the guesthouse. She'd found a place at the foot of our bed that was hers. During the day, she found the sunshine and a whole boatload of things to play with that gave me a heart attack.

After taking care of Jane, I buried myself under the water and scented soaps in the bathroom before dressing in jeans and one of the blousy tanks I had bought in Oklahoma City, which seemed an entire lifetime ago now.

I had just emerged from the bathroom when I got a text from Keith who said he'd be at the house in fifteen minutes. I texted Cam and told her I was going with Keith to see Seth's studio, and she told me to hold onto my panties and make sure that I didn't tell Derek that I was going to see a hot Cuban guy.

That made me smile. I was still smiling when I made my way quietly through the big house toward the front door only to have Dylan's booming voice halt me.

"Mia!" he called, and I turned, hiding my nervousness behind the mask that I had perfected. I hid my emotions from my family. I hid them from all sorts of people at the dealership. So I was fairly certain I could hide my emotions from this one director.

"Hey," I said with a forced smile.

"I heard you're going with Keith to pick up Bianca's latest artwork," he said with his hands in his trousers as he rocked on his feet. It shocked me, but he was the one who actually looked nervous. This threw me off my game slightly.

"Yes. I hope that's okay?"

"What? Oh, yeah. No problem," he said, still rocking.

I waited. He rocked. "Is there something I can do for you?" I asked. I wanted to head-thunk Good Girl Mia against the door, but it was too late, it was already out.

He looked as astonished as I felt. "No... I just wanted to apologize for our dad."

"You don't have anything to apologize for."

"I do. He's an asshole. And he made Derek's life hell at the mansion. I shouldn't have invited him."

I didn't know what to say to that.

"You…" he hesitated. "Please don't take this wrong, but you kind of remind me of the girls there. That's why I was surprised to see you with Derek. He doesn't normally like anything that reminds him of that time."

I turned a thousand shades of red and crossed my arms over my too big breasts. God, why couldn't I have had a nice set of B boobs like Cam? Now I was being compared to a "PlayBabe" or Hugo Brantly's girlfriends, neither of which was something to write home about. I guess that's what I got for running away with a sexy musician.

Dylan looked at my flushed face and grimaced. "I'm sorry. That was rude."

I looked away, still not sure what to say. I wasn't sure what he really wanted from me.

"I'm not saying any of this right. I love Derek. He's not just my kid brother, he's my best friend. I don't want to see him hurt. I just wanted to make sure you weren't…" His words faded away.

"A whore? A stripper? Someone hanging onto his coat tails, waiting for his fame to kick in?" I was suddenly as angry as a queen bee whose hive had been attacked, because, let's face it, Dylan's own wife fit that image way more than I did.

Dylan's turn to flush bright red. "Shit, I'm sorry."

He brushed his hand through his blonde hair. "That sounded awful."

"It did," I agreed.

"You just came out of nowhere."

I couldn't disagree with that, because I had. But it went both ways. Derek had come out of nowhere into my life too. He'd entered it with his crazy energy and happiness that you couldn't resist. He'd entered it like the eagle he was, swooping down to capture the mouse.

Then, I realized that I couldn't be mad at this big brother standing up for the little brother. It was exactly what Cam and Jake would do for me. I swallowed hard the anger as guilt overwhelmed me instead, and I was there in the guilt when his next question hit me.

"Do you love him?"

My brain literally froze at the question. Did I love Derek? Before I realized it, my head was nodding. I felt the nod just as Dylan saw it, but my brain and heart were still trying to catch up with what my body already knew. Oh my God. I was in love with Derek.

Cheese and crackers. I'd been worried about his girlfriend label when I should have been worried about the fact that I was in love with him. That my stupid heart had gone in the most stupid direction ever. I'd fallen in love again. When it was only going to hurt all over.

Dylan didn't realize the turmoil he'd just thrown me into. He'd seen my nod, and that was all he cared about.

"Okay then," he said as he turned and disappeared into the depths of his house, leaving me to wonder what in bejesus had just happened.

I hadn't recovered. I was still in the shock of my own revelation when the doorbell rang, and then the door opened to reveal Keith. He was happy, jiggling keys to a sports car that sat in the driveway behind him and seemed to fit his new L.A. image as much as his boyfriend had. It was like he was more at home here in his own skin than he had been back in Tennessee in his cowboy boots.

"Ready?" he asked, and I could only nod again because I wasn't ready.

I was nowhere near ready to be in love again. To be in love with a sexy musician whose life was even further apart from my reality than Hayden's had ever been.

Thank God it took longer than I expected to drive down the coast to Seth's studio, because I had a chance to get myself together. Keith didn't seem to notice my preoccupation. He rambled away as he drove about the Waters boys and how he loved working for Dylan. He talked about meeting Locke through Seth's art. He talked about how he and Seth were now good friends, and how they were helping each other through AA.

This statement surprised me enough to bring me back to the car ride and Keith, putting aside my epiphany until I had some time alone to examine it.

The fact that Keith was in AA was startling, but not Seth. Seth had needed AA back when he was sixteen, going off the rails and pushing girls off cliffs. But Keith's openness about it all as we drove in the summer sunshine allowed me to focus on him as he continued his onslaught of Hollywood insider information.

I concentrated on the sunshine along the coast, which was cool, and dry, and so very different from our humid air back home. Even though it was beautiful, with the ocean mist and spray, I suddenly missed the heaviness that filled our Tennessee air, wrapping itself around you so snuggly that there was no mistaking that you were home. I missed home. Unfortunately, that brought me back to loving Derek.

Because I also felt at home when I was with Derek. And Derek and Tennessee were not anywhere near synonymous. Derek and Tennessee were antonyms. Words that would never fit together.

Keith must have noticed that my brain kept disappearing, because he got quiet as we got closer to Seth's. Seth's studio was at his house that sat directly on the beach. It was a beautiful Nantucket ranch that, while not huge, was stunning. It was yet another surprise in a day of surprises. The house didn't seem like something a moody, junk artist should own.

"This is Seth's place?"

Keith laughed at my astonishment. "It is. Believe me, he's so tame now that you won't even recognize him."

But I did. He greeted us at the door, and when Seth Carmen smiled, you couldn't not recognize him. The panther-like quality of him that made you want to run away or just lay down and give in. Except that I didn't want anything to do with him when I had my own amazing eagle waiting for me back up the coast. The one I apparently loved!

Seth was still all hot Cuban, though. Plus, he had his own book-worthy image going on in his jeans and gray t-shirt with bare feet. The beach and this life seemed to suit him just as Keith's sports car and boyfriend seemed to fit him.

Seth offered us sweet tea and something called *ajiaco* that was a stew that he said he made himself. I wasn't quite sure I believed that. We sat out on the patio at a table made of stone and iron that I'd never seen the likes of before, and which I did believe he could have made.

"How's Cam?" Seth asked through hooded eyes, making small talk. Something he'd never been good at back when he was a teen in Tennessee.

"She's good."

"And the baby?"

"She's on bedrest. Baby wants to come out early."

Seth smirked. "Serves her right. Hope the little shitter gives her a run for her money."

I smiled back, because it was so something Seth would say, and so something appropriate for Cam.

"Speaking of on the run, have you heard from PJ?" Keith asked.

Seth's smile was wiped away, and in its place, a glower that seemed appropriately Seth again. "No."

"She'll be back. She loves you man."

"If I don't lose it and drag her back first," Seth responded. Keith looked unfazed, and I realized that Seth was still Seth.

Keith had said love, and that had my brain reeling again so much that when Seth collected the bowls and cups and moved them back into the house, I didn't even offer to help.

Instead, I followed the man who seemed so nothing like the sixteen-year-old, motorcycle-riding schmuck that I used to know that it pulled me back to the moment I was in once more. Seth was still silent and brooding. You could still feel the simmer of intensity and anger broiling under the surface of him, but it didn't seem like he took it out any longer in alcohol and motorcycles and fists.

Seth led us into his studio to get the piece for Bianca, and then my brain shut off for a completely different reason. I was stunned by the art in the room. Art that was full of color and light and beauty. It made me realize that somehow Seth was trying to find a way of putting his past behind him so that it wouldn't take up any time or energy or space. Johnny Cash would have been proud of him. Seth and Johnny were more alike than Derek and Johnny. Seth was the addict after all.

One piece in his studio caught my eye more than any other. It was a chair made of wrought iron, the legs grooved and broken and put back together with silver and gold welding in a way that somehow made me think of wounds on a heart, as if the scars were embedded there permanently. Over the top of it was draped a piece of purple satin that shimmered and glistened like diamonds. I ran my hand over the silk, then drew back in astonishment as I realized that the satin wasn't cloth at all, but unbending steel.

"This is exquisite," I told Seth.

He stared at it, not smiling. He didn't agree, he just nodded, like it hurt him to admit it.

"Here's Bianca's piece." Seth turned to the corner where a twisted tree stood. The pot it was in was made out of shards of stained glass soldered together. The leaves were made out of iron and steel, and from the branches, hung tiny snow globes filled with an array of different objects.

Keith and I both stared at it. It was amazing. All of his art was amazing.

"You're really good at this," I finally said.

He looked at me as if he'd forgotten I was there. His arms were crossed against his chest, feet wide.

"It's a living," he shrugged off the compliment.

"Says the man making millions at his art," Keith said.

"Shut up, asshole," Seth groused. That did seem more like him. Keeping people in their place.

Keith and Seth finagled the tree into the back of the sports car, and I helped buckle it in so that it wouldn't topple over and break.

"Locke said he already got the check, right?" Keith asked, and Seth nodded. A man of few words.

"You gonna be okay?" Keith asked.

"You really need to go to hell. And tell Locke he doesn't need to send you to fuckin' check up on me," Seth bit back.

Keith laughed, and I smiled at Seth's surliness.

I said goodbye and thanked him for the stew. Seth nodded one more time. "Tell Cam…" he paused. "Let her know how happy I am for her."

It was said in a quiet, deep tone that would have given me shivers if I wasn't used to a certain sexy musician's voice giving me shivers.

"Will do." I got in the car and then looked back, "Good luck, Seth."

He nodded one last time, then we drove away.

"Who's PJ?" I asked as Keith and I made our way back up the coast.

"The love of his life. She's breaking him into tiny shards because she took off across the country."

This stabbed at me because, in just about a week, Derek and I would be almost as far apart. After I'd just realized I loved him.

"I can't imagine Seth being broken by anything," I said just to stop my own tortured thoughts.

"You'd be wrong. He's the most broken man I know. But, like Seth himself says, you can take broken and make it into art, so hopefully he won't stay broken for long."

I looked at Keith, expecting a smirk, but there was none there. He was serious. Seth Carmen, hard-ass, had really been broken by a girl and was trying to put himself back together. It was enough to make me think of all the ways people can be broken by the ones they love most. And quietly hoped that somehow Derek and I wouldn't end in the same broken shards that I expected we would once our realities hit us.

♩ ♩ ♩

Keith took me to Dylan's office on the studio lot. I stared like the greenhorn country bumpkin I was. The energy, and backdrops, and people reminded me a little of the electricity of Vegas, and yet, it seemed somehow one more layer of false. Like these were even stronger automatons going at it. I wondered if anyone who lived in these bright cities ever felt real life hitting them in the face.

We took Seth's tree to Dylan's office where his assistant drooled over it and Keith, as if Keith wasn't gay and she wasn't fifty. I wondered if Bianca had arranged for the fifty-year-old just like she arranged for the older nanny. What did that say about her and Dylan?

By the time we got back to the mansion, it was almost seven. Keith dropped me at the front door, waved, and tooted the horn before driving off. I was grateful when I made my way through the big house without seeing anyone.

I wasn't sure what I was going to do when I saw Derek. I'd been trying to figure out how to tell him I couldn't be his girlfriend, and now it was even more complicated by the fact that I loved him.

But I also knew I couldn't stay in his world, girlfriend or not. Not only because it didn't fit me, but because I belonged with my family in Tennessee, helping to heal a family that had lost its gravitational force.

That's where my brain was when I walked into the guesthouse, but it went out the door when I saw Derek.

He paused midstride as I entered, as if he had been pacing, his hair stuck up at odd angles like he'd been passing his hand through it repeatedly. He looked like he'd lost everything, and my heart crumbled into itself.

"Jesus Christ! Thank God!" he said, walking toward me and wrapping me into that chest-welding hug that I loved. When he did, I realized that his whole body was trembling. He was shaking like a dog caught in a thunderstorm.

"Derek, what's wrong?" I asked, pulling back to look up at his face. His eyes were closed. Dark lashes hiding his stormy eyes.

"Where have you been?" he asked huskily.

"With Keith. I left you a note."

"Here?"

"Yes, on the counter."

I turned him to look at the counter in the kitchen where a pink sticky note sat by the cordless phone.

"Why the hell didn't you text me?" he asked. I could sense him calming down some, but there was still no sign of happy Derek. That Derek seemed to have been swallowed whole.

"I didn't want to bug you while you were recording."

"Shit, that's not bugging me, Mia, that's letting me know you're okay. I've been texting you for hours."

I grabbed my phone out of my bag and realized it was dead. I had forgotten to plug it in last night after we'd gotten back from the fiasco with Derek's dad and we'd lost ourselves in each other.

He saw the dark phone face and glowered, pulling it out of my hands to plug it in at the counter.

"What could have happened to me?" I asked, frowning as I watched him sulk and stalk in a way that fitted Seth way more than my happy musician.

"In L.A.? All kinds of fucking stuff."

"Why are you cussing at me?" I was confused.

He approached me cautiously and reached for my fingers.

"I thought you left," he breathed out, and then he pulled me into his arms again. One hand at the back of my head, the other around my waist, holding me to him.

"Left?"

"You know. Left me. Went back to Tennessee."

It was the perfect opportunity to remind him that we had only a week left together, and that I would eventually be going back to Tennessee. But I couldn't. Not then. Not when the sorrow in his voice was enough to drown a whole city. Not when he looked like his whole world had already collapsed.

I didn't because I could see now the broken part of Derek, just like Keith had shown me the broken part of Seth. These beautiful men that looked like they were strong and whole and confident. Yet inside, they were a series of crumbling walls, just like me. Derek was just like me. It made my love for him swell even as it made me hurt, because I was afraid that we were both going to end up even more broken when this was all done.

I quietly said, "Moron," and then led him to the couch. We sat with me tucked up against him and him holding me like he wasn't going to let me escape. The truth was I didn't want to escape. Not yet. Maybe not ever, even though I couldn't see another path for us.

After sitting like that for a few minutes, being reassured by each other's presence, I finally pushed past the chicken Mia I had been and found the courage to ask him. "What happened to you?"

He knew what had happened to me with Jake and Hayden, but I didn't know what had broken this man who had repaired and then stolen my heart with the ease of a cleft-stretching smile. And I thought maybe he needed me to know his story as much as I had needed him to know mine.

At first he didn't respond, so I tried to prompt him with the little that I knew. "Dylan said the mansion was hell. What did he mean?"

Derek frowned. "When did Dylan say that?"

"This morning." I wanted to add that he'd also accused me of being a PlayBabe looking for an easy target in an up-and-coming musician, but I wouldn't drive that wedge between Derek and his big brother.

"Why would he say that?"

I shrugged. "He was trying to apologize for your dad, I think." Which was the truth. Just not all of it.

He cursed under his breath and pulled me onto his lap like I had been the night before. His fingers swirled under my tank along the edge of my jeans.

"I think I like your dresses better," he said with a smirk that seemed more like the Derek I knew.

"You're avoiding my question."

"You've been out of questions for a while. We need a new payment plan if you are going to insist on more," he teased, lighter, coming back from the depths he'd been in.

"You accused me of trying to be strong for everyone else. Of not showing my emotions. You said I tried to make everyone else feel better. Yet, you do the same thing."

"My brother is alive."

"But your mom's not, right?"

His eyes clouded over, and the swirl of his fingers slowed.

"No. She's not."

"What happened?"

"Overdose."

"God. I'm s—" I stopped myself, and he didn't even smirk. Instead, he just kept going like now that he'd started, he wanted to say it.

"It was a relief actually. When she died."

He looked at me, expecting me to be shocked, as if he thought what he'd said was going to cause me to walk away. It wasn't. It wasn't that I wasn't shocked that he was relieved his mom had overdosed; it was that I wouldn't show it. Not now, not when he needed me not to. When I didn't respond, he continued.

"She'd been sick for a long time. AIDS."

"That must have been awful. How old were you?" I finally asked.

"Fifteen."

I didn't say anything. I just waited. Waited for him to come to me. Waited for him to continue to tell me what he needed to say.

"Dylan was already at college. He's eight years older than me, so he'd already escaped."

"Escaped?"

"The mansion. Dad. The women. The drugs."

My eyes widened.

He chuckled, but it wasn't his lighthearted chuckle. "Not that Dylan ever cared about any of that. He loved the attention he got at the mansion. He was a domineering asshole even then, and the younger babes really dug him."

"I can see that," I responded dryly. But he had changed directions from his mom to Dylan, so I refocused him. "What happened with your mom?"

He ran his hand through his hair again and closed his eyes, as if to shield himself, or maybe me, from what he was going to say. "I went to check on her when I got home from school. They'd moved her, the week before, to this piece-of-shit room in the servant's quarters so she'd be closer to the in-home care nurse they'd hired. When I got there, she was already gone. The needle still fucking in her arm."

He swallowed and opened his eyes to find mine.

"I should have been sad or mad that she'd killed herself. But all I could do was thank God that she was dead."

"You shouldn't feel guilty for not wanting her to suffer," I said because I realized that was the guilt he'd told me about on our first day in the Camaro together.

"I was glad because I didn't have to deal with it anymore," he said.

"That's normal."

"Is it?" He looked at me and shrugged, and I knew he didn't quite believe it, just like I didn't quite believe that I wasn't responsible for Jake. "I went to find my dad, and do you know where he was?"

I shook my head, not even wanting to guess.

"Screwing some babe in their room. In her bed. While his fucking wife died in a shit room below him."

He was watching me again. Waiting for my reaction.

"That's…" I ran out of words.

"Crappy," he said just as I said, "Awful."

"You know what's worse?" he asked.

"What could be worse?" It was my turn to swallow hard because the scene he'd set was already pretty messed up.

"When I tried to tell him, he got so pissed that I was interrupting his blow job that he threw a whole bottle of scotch at me."

I tugged at his arm and rubbed my fingers along his tattoos so that I wouldn't cry for this man who I'd just discovered I loved and who I didn't want to suffer.

"There had always been a lot of sex at the mansion. It was everywhere. You couldn't escape it. It had always seemed normal to me, even when it was my dad with someone not my mom. Then, when I found my dad screwing some nineteen-year-old while his wife died alone…shit. It just opened my eyes to how fucked up it all was."

I gulped, trying to imagine a sweet, laughing fifteen-year-old Derek having to see that. Having to watch his mom kill herself so she wouldn't suffer while his dad moved on to sex with a round of girls young enough to be his sister.

"I wanted to kill him," Derek told me honestly and openly. No regret laced his voice.

"Who could blame you?"

"No, Little Bird, I seriously thought about it. I'd even picked up one of the shards of glass that were on the floor next to me. I was seriously going to walk over and slice his throat."

He was still watching me. Still waiting for me to fly. I wouldn't. I couldn't.

"What made you stop?"

"Hugo. I guess the nurse had gone to get him after finding my mom. He'd come to find my dad like I had. He forced me to drop the glass, hauled my ass out of the room, and called Dylan."

I didn't believe that Derek would have killed his father. I didn't believe that with any of the 206 bones in my body, but I did believe that he thought he would have. I could see where his guilt came from. How he was asking for forgiveness as much as trying to forgive. They were double-wrapped cords just like his words on his wrist, hard to tell where it started and ended.

"Dylan got me the hell out of there, moved me in with him, and I never went back."

The deep hug that they shared when we arrived made sense. They weren't just brothers. They were survivors. I was a survivor too. A different kind of survivor, but I guessed that was what had called my soul to Derek's or the other way around. Somehow, we'd found each other.

I continued to run my fingers over his tattoos. It was his sanity. I understood now why he didn't want to give his dad, or his past, any time or energy or space. It was painful. And ugly. But I wondered if, by simply closing the door to it, it would ever really go away. Just like I knew that my ignoring the guilt I felt over Jake, or the hurt I felt over Hayden, as I'd been doing over the last couple weeks, wouldn't make them go away either.

I also knew that Derek didn't want to open the door and face the demons yet. I wasn't going to be able to force him to. He had to do it when he was ready. Just like I'd have to face all of mine when the time came. But at least we'd told each other our stories, and that had to be at least a step in the right direction. Closer to the doors, instead of farther away.

"You're pretty incredible," I said, and even though I meant it with all my heart, I said it in a sassy, teasing tone so that I could draw him away from the darkness.

It worked, because he grinned his impish grin at me. "I know."

"You're also an egotistical moron."

He smiled wider, but then his eyes grew dark and stormy again.

"And now, Miss Mia, I want to get back to that question you asked."

"Which one?"

"The one where you asked how many people I'd had sex with."

I shook my head. "I don't want to know."

"I'm going to tell you anyway. Are you ready?" he asked as he watched me.

I wasn't ready. Probably would never be ready.

"Four. Including you."

I stared at him. My number in my head had been a lot more than that.

"Four?" I swallowed.

He grinned at me.

"After the crap I saw, I wanted to make sure that when I made love, it was just that. Making love. To people I cared about."

"Four?" I asked again, in shock.

He laughed at me.

"You're such a Lothario!" I teased, trying to help lighten his load because I knew that was what he wanted. To move away from this conversation, and his mom, and the mansion, and what had happened there.

"Did you just use your big words with me again, Miss Mia?"

Then he was tickling me. And I was trying to escape, and in the process, I slammed my elbow into his nose, making his eyes instantly water as he exclaimed, "Fuck!" and I exclaimed, "I'm sorry!"

He froze with the smirk still on his face. "What did you just say?"

I pulled away from him.

"That obviously doesn't count. That was a legitimate I'm sorry."

"No. Never again."

He grabbed me and had me over his shoulder and out the door before I could blink. I banged on his back and squirmed, trying to escape, but he held me tight like a cowboy holds his calf. At the pool, he tossed me in, clothes and all.

I came up sputtering. He was laughing. Hard. Back to the Derek that had attracted me to begin with. Back to the smart-aleck, gorgeous BB. My heart flipped; happy that I'd been able to take him away from that scary place in his past.

"Oh my God, I can't believe you did that," I gasped.

He took off his shoes and dove in after me.

He swam toward me, and I went to swim away, but he caught my blouse that was billowing out behind me and dragged me toward him.

264

"I think we should shed these wet clothes, don't you?"

Good Girl Mia balked. "No way! We're in your brother's backyard."

"It's dark."

"It is not. It's barely dusk."

He was already tugging my top over my head, and I either went along or lost a nose in the process. I tried to comfort myself in the fact that my bra was basically the same as a bikini top.

I reached down and pulled off my wedges that were swelling up because corkboard and water don't agree. I tossed them poolside and then reached for his t-shirt. He pulled it off, and it hit the cement with a wet slap. Then he was tugging at my jeans, and I laughed as I got spun upside down while he tugged the clinging material off of my legs.

I came up sputtering again, and then he was kissing me, tongue tangling with mine, hands encasing themselves around my waist and drawing me up tight to him where I wrapped my legs around his middle. Our hands and lips and tongues finding this comforting path that we'd discovered together.

After a long time, he carried me to the steps, out of the pool, and back to the guesthouse where we quickly shed the rest of our wet clothes and found our way to the bed that had become my favorite place in this whole house because it was the place where we came together. Where all my senses came to life, and where he was the only one. Where we were just… one.

Chapter Fifteen

The City

SAVE MYSELF

"I gave you all my energy,
And I took away your pain.
Cause human beings are destined,
To radiate or drain."

-Ed Sheeran

The next day, we had to leave for San Francisco where Derek's next show was scheduled and where we would attend Harry Winston's wedding. My heart cried out in a different way because we agreed to leave Jane the Kitten with Maggie and her nanny. Derek said we'd come back for her, or have her sent to us, but I nearly cried because I didn't want her to think we were abandoning her.

He tugged at my hair, curling it to my lips, caressing them. "She's happy here. We'll be back."

Somehow, in my bones, I knew I wouldn't be back, because this wasn't my home. This wasn't my reality. In truth, I often wondered if it was really Derek's reality either. There was nothing in the guesthouse that said Derek beyond his instruments. It seemed more like a place he hung his hat while he visited the brother and niece he loved.

I kissed my little furball and made Maggie promise to be careful with her. Betty took pity on me, getting my phone number and promising to text pictures every day.

In addition to leaving Jane the Kitten, we were also leaving the Camaro. We were flying to San Francisco so that we could attend the wedding later that day, because Indian weddings are long events. Hours long. The guys in the band were driving up in the "tour bus" to join us for the gig the next day. After that, we were going to rent a car to drive out to the California Caverns while Rob and Trista drove the motor home north to Oregon.

We had another show and one more caving trip planned near the Oregon coast, and then that was it. I tried not to think about that as I left Dylan's mansion.

All of those things, the kitten, the Camaro, my trip ending, were combining in my heart such that I was an emotional basket case as Keith picked us up and dropped us at the airport. It was hard for me to wear my mask with Derek, maybe because he saw it for what it was, a front, just like I could see that sometimes his happy face was a front. By the time Keith left us, I was crying.

I'd cried more with Derek in two weeks than I had with any person in my whole life. He entwined his long fingers in mine as we headed through security. I pulled myself together, and when we got to the other side, the tears weren't flowing, but my emotions still felt raw.

The flight to San Francisco was short, and my mind was still a twirl of feelings and thoughts as we landed.

We got our rental and headed toward the city. Derek was more comfortable here than he had been in the other places we'd been, probably because he'd played here many times. He didn't even need the Google Map lady.

"Tell me about this Harry guy," Derek said after we'd checked into the hotel. He was trying to distract me from my thoughts as I hung clothes.

"Harry was my first best friend."

"So why wasn't he your first kiss?"

"Because, moron, he was my best friend, not my boyfriend."

"I don't see how any guy could be around you and not want to kiss you," Derek said, pulling me onto his lap.

He had me captured, hair twirled up to my lips again before I could protest.

"We were, like, seven years old. We both liked books and not football. We were friends until eighth grade when he moved to California," I said with an eye-roll that earned me a quick kiss.

"Okay. But I may still have to kill him."

"May I remind you, he's getting *married*!"

"Maybe he secretly wants you to be the person to stand up in the crowd and protest the wedding."

I laughed. Derek tickled me, adding to my laughter, and I ended up on my back on the bed, with him lying up beside me, hand swirling under my t-shirt, across my belly button.

"I don't find it funny that I'm going to become a serial killer trying to keep the guys away from you." He smirked.

"He's a traditional Indian! Getting married to the woman he's been engaged to his whole life!"

"You aren't making this any better. An arranged marriage? You know he really is hoping you'll protest, right?"

His hand crept up from my belly button to the wire of my bra, caressing through the satin. My whole body turned to a quivering mass as it did every single time he touched me. I wasn't sure I'd ever get used to it. Or not love it.

"You don't know Harry."

"Obviously."

"He is all about tradition and family. He would as soon call off the wedding as he would commit hari-kari."

"I'd be happy to help him with that."

My concentration on his words began to fade as his fingers caressed my breasts and my body took over for my mind.

"So, what are you wearing to this very traditional Indian wedding?" he asked me while I fought to maintain a brain cell.

"What do you mean?"

"Wearing. You do plan on wearing clothes, Little Bird, correct?"

"Yes… yes." His words faded as his fingers continued doing things to me that made me want to forget the whole world.

"The green dress," I said, meaning the very same green dress he had seen me in at the fundraiser.

Then he disappeared, standing by the bedside, magical hands far, far away from my body. "Oh no," he said.

"What?"

"I am not taking you to an Indian wedding in that plain-Jane dress."

My body was coursing with desire, and he was talking dresses. And standing away from me. I wasn't following.

I knelt on the bed and moved toward him till I could rest my hands on his shoulders. "I thought you said I looked beautiful in that dress. Was that a line?"

"No. You did. You do look beautiful in that dress. That wasn't a line. Although, needing you to drive the Camaro…that was a line." He winked.

I stared because even though I'd suspected it, I hadn't expected him to ever admit it. "What?"

"I had to have a better reason for you to come with me than the fact that I wanted to seduce you in my hotel room."

"You lied!" I couldn't be mad. I'd known. But I could pretend to pout, hoping it would get his fingers back on my skin.

"Of course!" he said.

"You're terrible." I pulled at his fingers, kissing them.

"But irresistible."

"That's it! I'm not taking you to the wedding tonight."

"You will, but not in that green dress. It's not at all acceptable for a traditional Indian wedding," he said.

"How would you know?" I asked just as he grabbed my hand and pulled me from the bed. I stumbled, and he caught me. A familiar move that I should expect by now, but continued to catch me off guard.

"I have been to many traditional Indian weddings."

"You have not!"

He grinned at me. "Okay, one. But I can tell you this: everyone was in bright colors. Had you told me this was a traditional Indian wedding, I would have brought my best paisley. But now we must go shopping."

"You're insane!"

I tried to bring him back to the bed. I tried to kiss him and touch him, but he just wagged his finger at me and dragged me with him from the room.

There was a shopping mall nearby. Plus, a Macy's that took up a whole block. I wasn't used to that. I was used to local, suburban malls. We ended up at the Macy's, and it was hot and overwhelming.

Derek kept bringing me dresses. Dress after dress. Half of which I refused to even try on. The other half were entirely inappropriate. I told him he needed assistance from a woman, and eventually one of the salesladies took pity on him and helped out.

I finally slipped into a fuchsia and teal patterned dress that covered my bra straps, showed off my waist, and flared out to mid-thigh, and I knew that this dress was it. It was bright and vibrant just like I felt like I was when I was with Derek.

I left the dressing room and barely saw Derek's wide-eyed smile before he had me in his arms and was kissing me.

"This. Is. The. One," he said as my heart plunged down to the pit of my stomach and back.

"Go change. I'll meet you at the register. I have to get a new shirt." He smiled his huge grin. I reached out and touched his cleft, which made him smile more.

"Go." H said again as he pushed me toward the dressing room.

When I met him at the register, he had a bright green and blue paisley shirt waiting there. I tried to pay, but he wouldn't let me.

"Shoes," he said. "And jewelry."

"No," I said, but he was smiling and pulling me toward the escalator, and I knew there was no stopping him, like there was no stopping Cam when she was on a roll. So I let him lead me to the shoe department, and from there, to the jewelry department where I absolutely refused to let him buy me anything real.

"I swear to God, if you try to buy me anything with a karat or sterling symbol, I'm really not going to let you come with me."

"Sassy. Miss Mia is being sassy." He grinned.

His grin was infectious.

I love you, I thought, even though I couldn't say it out loud. Not when we were going to have to say good-bye. Not when it would just hurt us both.

We picked out some floral necklace that I knew I'd never wear again, but that he insisted would fit right in at an Indian wedding.

When he was satisfied that I was going to be appropriately attired, he led me back to the hotel where we ordered room service and took a shower together. All soap and skin and hands. But no words. Our words were quiet today, as if we both needed to keep them inside for a while longer.

After, he helped me dress and then watched as I did my hair and put on my makeup. He watched as if it was the most fascinating thing he'd seen.

"You're weird," I told him.

"Me?"

"Only guy in the room."

"You're beautiful. Everything you do is beautiful. There's nothing wrong with me wanting to watch a beautiful woman get ready."

"Okay. How about creepy and stalker-like?"

"That would only be if I was doing it through a pair of binoculars."

I finished my mascara and turned to look at him. He was unbelievably good-looking in his loud shirt, black pants, and dress shoes. I'd never seen him in dress shoes. He looked more business than rocker. It was disorienting and yet still sensual. It made my heart flip in a new way. I wondered, if we were really together for longer than this journey, if my heart would continue to flip like this year after year.

He took my hand and kissed the palm. "Little Bird, you are the most incredible thing I've ever seen."

I flushed with pleasure.

"Are you sure we have to go?" he asked with a knowing smile.

"Yes! And I don't want to be late."

We made our way down to the lobby, fingers hooked together in a way that seemed to be our new normal, and then out to the taxi line. The taxi dropped us at the gardens where the wedding was taking place.

We entered a glorious world of lights and color.

Mr. and Mrs. Winston saw me and greeted me with pleasure, smiling when I congratulated them on the wedding. Once the ceremony started, I was floored to find Harry arriving on a white horse decorated in colors and flowers. The guests were invited to dance around him as drums beat. Then, the bride and her family came out to greet the groom. His bride was beautiful. Dark, silky hair, with beautiful kohl-decorated eyes, and henna over almost every visible space. Harry and his bride, Haleema, exchanged ornate floral garlands while smiling deeply at each other. There was no way you would think their marriage was arranged. There was love in those eyes.

Then, the priest, Harry, Haleema, and her parents sat beneath a tapestry while the bride's parents gave her away. Her mom sobbed quietly. Tears of happiness and loss. It made my heart swell up. Harry and Haleema joined hands before Harry applied a red powder to the center of her forehead and tied a black beaded necklace around her neck.

The whole audience cheered as if they were at a sporting event. Loudly and happily.

We moved from there to the reception. The food was an amazing mix of spicy and sweet, and rich and savory. Both Derek and I found a whole plate of things to sample that we'd never had before.

"You have to try this," he said, and before I could object, he had placed the sweetest honey-and-nut-scented pastry in my mouth.

"Wow," I said after swallowing. The pastry reminded me of not only the scent of him but of how he made me feel, full of buttery, honey sweetness.

"You can say that again," he smiled. Then he leaned forward and brushed the powdered sugar from my lips with his long fingers, caressing as he traced the shape of them. My stomach dropped happily.

"Mia!" Harry's happy voice interrupted us. I stood and hugged my friend. He was no longer the tiny Indian boy that I'd grown up, with or the gangly teen I'd visited several times after they'd moved, but instead was tall and handsome in his beaded jacket.

"Harry," I said as I held him tight, "I'm so happy for you."

"Thank you!" he said as his bride came up and stuck her hand in his. "Mia, this is Haleema. Haleema, Mia."

"Mia!" She reached over and hugged me tight. "It is good to meet you after so long. Harry speaks of you often."

Derek squeezed my hand as if to say I told you so, and I tried hard not to eye-roll him.

"I speak of Harry often, too. He's always been a good friend."

"We are honored that you could join us," Haleema said with a sweet smile.

"Thank you for inviting me. Us," I said, returning her smile.

"Who is this, Mia?" Harry asked, eye-balling Derek.

"This is Derek. Derek, my friend Harry." I realized I hadn't said he was my boyfriend, and hoped Derek hadn't noticed.

Derek and Harry shook hands. Serious. The smile gone as they assessed each other in that way that men tend to do when they are both being protective and possessive.

"She's pretty special. You need to treat her right," Harry said, not letting go of Derek's hand.

"You're right. And I will."

"Oh Harry, stop being so ridiculous," Haleema said with a laugh that said she wasn't jealous in the least.

"Sorry we can't stay longer. Call me soon, so we can catch up, okay? Have fun," Harry said and then took off into the crowd where he was greeted with happy smiles everywhere he went.

Music started up, and all of a sudden everyone was cheering and dancing. "Come on," Derek said, grabbing my hand and leading me into the thick of things where we laughed at our failed attempts to learn the Indian dances even as those around us encouraged us to continue to try.

Eventually, the traditional music was replaced with standard wedding fare. Derek wrapped me into his arms as the music turned slow.

"I like weddings," he said with a smile.

"You're probably the only twenty-something male who does."

"Wait. You don't know how old I am?" He laughed.

I blushed. "It hasn't exactly come up in conversation."

"I thought you were the Google mastermind."

"You're on Google?"

"My own Wikipedia page and everything. You'll find it says I'm twenty-five."

My feet stopped. "That's crazy."

He pulled my hand back up to his heart. "Ouch."

"Not because you're twenty-five, moron, but because you have your own Wikipedia page and yet you're here with me."

"Little Bird, there's nowhere else I'd rather be."

He kissed me, and people around us whistled and hooted.

"Let's go home," he said.

Even though it was only a hotel room, I knew that for tonight, while he was there with me, it would be home. And that thought shook me to the core again because what would happen when I was home in Tennessee and missing my other home?

"Let me use the ladies' room before we head back." I said so I could collect myself.

In the dim lighting of the bathroom, I looked at the girl in the mirror who was supposed to be me in a bright dress that I never would have picked out without him. With my straight hair, and makeup, and a smile that Good Girl Mia wouldn't recognize. Whatever happened, it was good to see this New Mia emerge from her cocoon.

As I exited the bathroom, my phone buzzed. I glanced at Derek waiting across the lobby for me with a smile and then looked down at the phone.

Hayden.

I sank to the nearest chair.

Why in all that was holy was Hayden texting me now?

"Little Bird?" Derek was immediately at my side.

I waved him off. "I'm okay. Just surprised."

"Who is it?"

I showed him the phone. Hayden's name scrolled across the top and the words that read, "Hey Mia, thinking of you."

Derek glowered at the words. I started to type back, and he looked floored. "You're going to respond to the asshole?"

"I can't just ignore it."

"The hell you can't."

He looked pissed. And he was right. I stared at the phone. It wasn't like I really wanted to text Hayden. It was just a bad habit built over four years of dropping everything the minute he crooked a finger.

Derek saw my waffling and a range of emotions crossed his face that I wasn't sure I could read. He grabbed the phone from me.

"If you answer at all, tell him to leave you the fuck alone."

He stuffed my phone in his pocket, caught my hand in his, and led me out to the taxi line. We were both silent. I felt guilty for the first time that day because I knew that I'd hurt Derek. Like I hadn't wanted to. Like I was afraid of being hurt again myself.

The truth was, that when I looked at my emotions for Hayden, there weren't any there. They'd been left somewhere along the road as we drove from Oklahoma to

California. The emotion I did feel was anger at myself for not seeing Hayden and the whole thing for what it was sooner. It had all been so wrong.

Yet, I also couldn't help but want, ever so slightly, to shove it in Hayden's face that he couldn't have me anymore. Was that wanting revenge? Or was it closure?

In the taxi, the silence continued, and I couldn't stand it. I pushed Derek's shoulder. "Hey," I said.

He smiled at me, but it didn't reach his eyes. He was thoughtful.

"You're being a moron."

"Am I?"

"Yes," I said, and I grabbed his wrist, the one tattooed with forgiveness and sanity, and I rubbed my finger over it. I took a deep breath, and took a plunge that I was afraid to take but was the only way that I knew how to reassure him. "You said I was your girlfriend. That makes you my boyfriend, right?"

This caused his face to light up with that smile that continued to stop my heart. "I like it when you say it like that," he responded.

I put my finger on his cleft. He growled and bit my finger. My stomach melted. I rested my head on his shoulder to stop myself from devouring him in the taxi.

The quiet settled over us once more.

"You still want to know what he wants." Derek said it as a statement not a question.

I shrugged.

"Why would you want to give him any more time or energy or space?" he asked.

I struggled to find the right words. Words that would reassure him that I didn't want Hayden. That the only man that could shake my world now was him, and that, truthfully, he shook my world more than Hayden had ever been able to, because Hayden hadn't known the real Mia. He'd barely acknowledged her existence. But it also felt like my past needed a door not only shut but obliviated before I could stop giving it energy.

"I think I just want him to know that he can't have me anymore."

He took this in.

"Sometimes, before you can shut the door, you have to tell the person to fuck off," I told him. His eyes widened at my swear word because I didn't use them often. They became more powerful that way. When you used them sparsely, they actually had meaning.

I didn't know if Derek would understand what I was saying, because Derek had never told his dad to take a flying leap. Instead, he'd tried to seal the door even as the blood and puss still oozed through. Derek looked like he was reading my mind, because instead of being angry at the thought of me texting Hayden, he handed over the phone.

"Tell him your boyfriend has forbidden you from texting any exes," he said with a grim smile.

"He really wasn't an ex."

"But you slept with him."

I nodded, and this made his smile disappear again.

"To be honest, that doesn't seem like you," he said.

He was right. It didn't seem like even the old me. It didn't seem like any version of me. To be fair to my old self, I hadn't known that he was going to dump me when we got back to campus.

"When I went to UTK, I was trying to escape my brother and… well, just all of it."

"I get that."

"And I found Hayden. He was golden, and dynamic, and smart. He sucked me in. He had this idea of starting a co-ed business fraternity, and we made it happen. I did the footwork behind the scenes, and he was our face to the world. We worked well together. We spent so much time together that I thought maybe it was more."

"But?"

"But he found Marcie, who was much more like him. They were a power couple. Both from wealthy, powerful families. I was just the invisible girl from nowhere who, like always, helped from the shadows."

"Little Bird, you are not invisible. You're fuckin' anything but. You are so beautiful that it stops my heart."

I stared at him. He'd said those words before. Or similar, and I was collecting them in my heart and soul. They were slowly taking the place of that torn up note that I'd carried around with me for so long.

"Derek."

"Hmm."

"I…" I chickened out. I was good at chickening out with him. I just couldn't say it. I wanted to say it. I wanted him to know I loved him. I wanted him to know that he had shown me that what I'd felt for Hayden was just infatuation and not love. A little girl chasing after what she thought was a dream. But it wasn't fair to say those words. Not when we'd be leaving each other to go back to our realities so soon.

"You're such a moron," I said instead.

He kissed me, and I forgot all about Hayden, and my past, and the people who had made me feel invisible. Instead, I felt alive, and seen and like I mattered.

♫ ♫ ♫

The next day, Derek left early for the venue with the band, and I went out to the mall nearby to try to pick up some eye-liner in hopes that I could imitate Haleema's lovely kohl from the wedding. I also needed a new pair of jeans because the pair I'd bought in Oklahoma were pretty messed up after their dip in Dylan's pool.

Then, because the guilt always hit me when I was alone, I spent the afternoon texting Cam, and my mama, and even Wynn. I checked in on my Instagram feed and the pictures I'd been posting along my journey with Derek. Not many of them had Derek in them. There were quite a few of Jane the Kitten that made me ache. There were pictures of the caves, and Dylan's pool, and Seth's art. There were a couple of the band. The last was of the lobby of our current hotel, where I'd posted something sarcastic about how many people it must take to keep the marble sparkling.

I tried not to let myself scroll back farther than this trip. I didn't want to run into the picture of Jake and Cam that would cause me to hyperventilate with grief and guilt. I was ignoring it, and I knew that I was ignoring it, but I just had a couple more days to ignore it before I would be faced with it every day looking at Mama's sad eyes.

While I was scrolling, I got an Instagram message. I clicked over to it. It was from Hayden.

HAYDEN: Hey Mia, looks like you are in SF. I'm here too putting together a business deal. Let's hook up.

Hayden was in San Francisco? How ridiculous was that? Old Mia would have loved to meet up with him. Old Mia would have read too much into it and thought he had flown all the way to the West Coast to find her. She would have fixated on it and twisted it all up, but instead, I didn't.

A part of me still wanted to let him know that his hold over me had gone the way of the dodos so that I could securely slam that ugly door on that depressing chapter of my life, but I didn't. Instead, I ignored the message because I knew that it would hurt Derek if I didn't. And I didn't want to hurt him any more than I already would when I went home and he continued touring.

As it neared the time to go to the club and meet Derek, I got dressed in my new jeans, a different blousy tank, and my polka dot sandals I'd worn to the wedding. I played around with the kohl eyeliner I'd picked up earlier. When I looked in the mirror, I liked what I saw. The eye-liner made my mosaic eyes—Jake's eyes—stand out in a different way, and the green in my top reflected the greens in the pattern shining there.

I was running later than I'd planned because I'd taken so long with the new makeup, but it was worth it. I wanted to see Derek's expression when he took me in. I knew he'd like it too, and that made me tingle all over. I texted Derek that I was on my way so he wouldn't worry. His response of, "About fucking time," made my heart beat like the wings of a little bird. The little bird that he claimed was me.

When I left the elevators and started toward the lobby doors, I heard my name and froze.

I turned slowly, shock spreading through my veins.

There was Hayden. Normal, perfect, golden boy Hayden in his typical uniform of dress slacks and a button-down shirt that he had tailor made for him even though it was easy enough to buy one at the mall. His Rolex flashed when he pushed a hand through his tawny hair as he got up from the stool he'd been perched on at the hotel bar. There was a smile on his face that made me think, for the very first time, of the sleazy car salesmen we avoided like the plague at our dealership.

It was then that I realized it. I'd fallen for a sleazy car salesman! That made me smile at myself because I knew better. Hadn't my daddy warned me off of just this kind of person my whole life?

I realized my mistake instantly because Hayden thought the smile was for him as he made his way toward me. The whole time, he was taking in the entirety of me in my twenty-something outfit with my straightened hair and kohl eyes. His smile widened at the New Mia.

"Wow," he said as he leaned in to kiss me, but I turned my face so he got a cheek. "You look fabulous."

I was still stunned. I didn't know why he was here, or how he'd found me. Had he found me? Had he come here for me? To this hotel? Or would he say it was just my crazy imagination? It didn't seem like my imagination, and it didn't quite seem like a coincidence either.

"How?" I puzzled, my astonishment evident.

He laughed. The laugh that used to draw my eyes and hold them. I realized now that, instead of sounding confident, his laugh actually sounded fake. Haughty. There was another laugh that I loved now. One that was always honest and real. Not this hollowed out falseness that was the golden boy's in front of me. I wanted to thunk Old Mia's head for falling for this.

"I hope you don't mind. I saw that you were here, so I thought I'd see if you wanted to have dinner."

"You saw that I was here?"

"Your Instagram post."

It hit me then. I had posted the hotel lobby.

"So you just decided to show up? Like some stalker?"

He chuckled. He didn't think I was serious. But I was.

"You didn't respond to my text." His tone scolded me as his eyes raked my body again.

"What do you want, Hayden?" I asked, crossing my arms over my chest which, unfortunately, just dragged his eyes to my size E's. I rolled my eyes inwardly.

"Come have a drink with me." He grabbed my hand and pulled me toward the bar, but I dug my heels in and pulled away. He turned to me with a frown.

"I have plans."

He took me in again. "I can see that." His smile was so slimy. Almost as bad as Derek's dad. Holy macaroni, how had I thought I loved this man?

"I can't be late," I told him.

As if Derek could sense my thoughts and discomfort over the few blocks that separated us, my phone buzzed with a text.

DEREK: You almost here?

ME: Still at hotel. Hayden showed up.

DEREK: What the fuck?

ME: Getting rid of him.

No response from Derek. I put my phone in my back pocket and looked up at Hayden.

"You look different. Good. But different," he said with that same squalid smile that I couldn't believe I hadn't seen before.

"I am different," I said.

He seemed perplexed by my attitude. This really wasn't his fault. I'd always caved to Hayden. I'd always done whatever he wanted and dropped any plans to be with him.

Somewhere inside of me, a lightbulb went on. I saw it so clearly. My shrink from long ago probably would have nailed it in two seconds if I'd continued to see her. I realized now that I'd never trusted myself to be anything more than someone's sidekick. I'd wanted to be out of Jake's and Cam's shadows, but I'd run right into someone else's. I'd never been willing to stand in the sun on my own. I guess I hadn't believed that I could be anything more than invisible. But not anymore. Now, I wanted to be seen. Especially by one man.

"Come on, one drink? You can be a little late," he said with that knowing smile that had always won him everything he wanted.

"No, I really can't."

"Jesus, Mia, don't make things difficult. Have a drink with me. I have a job proposal for you."

He grabbed my elbow and tried to steer me toward the bar again. I pulled away one more time. "Stop pulling on me."

I said it louder than I meant, and I realized we were starting to draw eyes.

"You're making a scene," Hayden said with a hiss because he hated that kind of attention almost as much as Good Girl Mia did.

Hayden looked around us and shoved his hands in his pockets. He looked like Dylan Waters a bit. They were both men who were used to getting their own way and didn't like it when anyone upset their perfect vision of the world.

Regardless, he seemed to sense that I wasn't ready to tag after him yet, so he tried a different tactic.

"I'd rather talk about this over a drink—or dinner—but I have this great opportunity at my company that I wanted to offer you." He meant his dad's company. It wasn't his, but he always acted like he was CEO when, in fact, he was just a director on the way to becoming a V.P.

I just waited. I wondered if he expected me to say yes already. Probably because I would've in the past. I would have jumped at the opportunity to be near him.

"Do we really have to do this standing in the lobby?" The irritation in his voice was becoming more and more evident.

"I didn't ask you to come find me."

He waited as if I'd beg him for the information, and when I didn't, he continued.

"It's director of advertising. We can give you an easy six-figure salary with bonuses and stock on top." He smiled again. The smile that usually closed his deals without a handshake or a contract to back then up.

"I have a job."

"Sure. But this could give you way more money and exposure than running your dad's dealership."

"I like running the dealership."

That was the truth. I liked running the dealership, just like I liked baking, and reading, and spending time with my family. I liked simple things that others thought were boring, but to me, just meant that I was home.

I could tell that Hayden didn't believe my response. Which was mostly my fault because, in all the four years that Hayden and I had been friends and I'd drooled after him, he'd never seen the real Mia. The Mia that loved all these simple things that to him meant nothing.

"But it's a car dealership," he said with shock.

His response brought out sassy New Mia. Mia who got angry.

"That my family owns. That I'll own when my dad turns it over to me in September. It'll be my company. I'll be in charge," I said, trying to rub in the fact that he wouldn't be in charge of his dad's company for a long time, if ever.

He hadn't expected this. That Mia Phillips would own a company at twenty-two.

"I've missed you, Mia," he said, changing tactics one more time. This just made me more puzzled than ever.

He smiled at what he perceived to be my hesitation and reached his hand out to touch my bare arm. In the past, this would have made me so happy. I would have thought it a tender move. That he was offering me something. Instead, I was disgusted. I took a step back.

"How's Marcie?" I asked.

This made him grimace. "Making wedding plans."

"You're getting married?" I asked with my own surprise.

He shook his head. "I haven't proposed, no."

Then I just laughed because I couldn't help it. Wasn't that so typically Hayden? Overwhelmed and unprepared and wanting to be the big shot while everyone else did the work. Now, it was catching him in the pants because he was going to be roped into a marriage he didn't want. One he'd never wanted.

My laughter made him growl. "I don't think there's anything to laugh about, Mia."

"So just tell her you don't want to get married."

"It's not that simple."

"Isn't it?"

"No."

Right then, I realized that I was wasting my breath. That I'd already not only shut this door but had gone a good way toward obliviating it, and that now I was just giving Hayden way more energy and time and space than he deserved. He had never truly earned any of my time and energy and space, and, besides, I had a sexy musician that I loved waiting for me.

"I have to go." I stepped around him toward the exit.

"You're leaving?" His voice was full of shock again.

I turned back. "Yes, Hayden, I'm leaving."

Before I could register it, he'd closed the distance and pushed his lips against mine in a kiss that was wet, and slobbery, and nothing like the demanding passion of Derek's. It made me gag. Full gag reflex, and I pulled back and slapped him.

"What the fuck?" he snarled.

"What part of 'I'm leaving' made you think I wanted you to kiss me?" I stormed at him.

"You've always—"

"Wanted you to kiss me? Yes. That was true. In the past. But this might surprise the bejesus out of you, Hayden, but I have a boyfriend, and a career, and a life that I love way more than I ever loved you."

He just stared, knuckles pressed against his red cheek.

I felt just a tinge of guilt. It wasn't his fault. I had done this. I'd followed him around and come running whenever he snapped. I hadn't ever done anything that would make him think that I'd tell him no. He'd come searching for me in hopes of getting laid or maybe of getting someone to do his dirty work like I'd done all the hard work in our fraternity. And Hayden wasn't used to being told no.

"Good luck, Hayden, with the company, and Marcie, and the wedding. I'd appreciate it if you didn't contact me any more. It upsets my boyfriend."

I turned and walked out. I didn't look back. I didn't care what he looked like. I felt proud of myself because I'd made another huge step forward today. I was leaving behind my old skin and turning into this new version of Mia that I actually liked. It was the first time I'd liked myself in a really long time. If ever.

Lyrics streamed through my head, and I realized that, once again, the great philosopher, Ed Sheeran, was right. That you had to first save yourself before you spent time and energy on others. That you had to love yourself in order to be loved. You had to stop blaming the world. Stop blaming golden boys. Stop blaming a dead brother. Stop blaming the guilt. Stop blaming your conscious. Just be who you are and let everything else fall into place.

Chapter Sixteen

Love

HOW WOULD YOU FEEL?
"I'll be taking my time,
Spending my life,
Falling deeper in love with you."
-Ed Sheeran

As I exited the lobby, my heart was soaring. Not because I had put Hayden in his place, but because I was going to see Derek. Because I was going to get to feel his fingers tangled with mine. Because I'd get to stand next to him while he twirled my hair up to my lips and caressed them with fingers callused from playing the guitar. That I'd feel wanted and beautiful.

I'd get to be with the man I loved. Nothing else mattered. Not time. Not space. Not miles. Not realities. Just the love we had for each other. Hope filled me completely, in a wave so strong that I couldn't push it aside. I didn't want to.

The fog had settled in early tonight. It was hard to see very far in front of me as I went to get into the taxi line, but then I heard my name again. This time, it was from lips that I loved to kiss, and when I turned, there was Derek, appearing through the fog like he had just apparated there.

"Derek." I flew to him. Little Bird flying to the eagle.

He held me up tight against him where I belonged as if I was part of his chest. Where I simply belonged.

"What are you doing here?" I asked as I took in the scent that I loved. That lemony guitar oil and muskiness that was so completely Derek.

"Where is the asshole?" Derek asked.

I looked up. "You came because of Hayden?"

"Asshole shows up at the hotel unasked. Of course I did!"

I smiled probably the largest smile of my lifetime because I'd never had anyone go all jealous over me. I'd never had anyone care that much. I buried my head into his chest again because I was afraid that if I didn't, I'd lose it. Tears of happiness, instead of pain and guilt. But I didn't want to cry. I didn't want to ruin my kohl and this moment.

Right then, filled with happiness and closure and love, I let it all burst out of me. "I love you," I said into his chest. It was quiet, but I knew he heard it because I felt his arms tighten around me, drawing me even closer.

"Thank God!" he said with equal parts relief and teasing in his tone.

I looked up again to smile at his gorgeous face. His face that was smiling back at me, cleft stretching in that way that had quickly become my whole world.

"This would be the time for you to say it back."

"No time, Little Bird, no time. George is going to kill me because we are going to be so fucking late."

"Holy macaroni! Your show!"

He chuckled. "Don't worry. Lonnie's driving. He's like an Indy race car driver. Or maybe more like those guys from *The Fast and the Furious*. We'll be there in no time."

"Lonnie's with you?"

Derek nodded as he kissed my temple.

"He wouldn't let me come alone. He was afraid I'd go all serial killer."

Derek pulled me by my hand back into the fog where we found the SUV with Lonnie behind the wheel, grinning like the madman I knew him to be. Derek dragged me onto his lap in the passenger seat, and we strapped ourselves into the seat belt in a completely unsafe way that would have had the old me screaming safety rules.

Lonnie spun out into the street, causing people to slam on brakes and honk all around us. I gasped. "Maybe I should drive."

"I've got this," Lonnie said, still with his crazy smirk. Then he turned serious. "Did you beat the shit out of lover boy?"

"Of course not," I responded, slightly offended.

Lonnie laughed hard. "Not you, sweet cheeks, I was talking to my man."

"I didn't even see the bastard. Phillips had already left him in the dust."

"Good for you." He reached his hand out for me to high five, making the car careen wildly.

"Just drive, you big idiot," I said with a smile.

"Hey, I have my own nickname now?"

I eye-rolled him. "If you want idiot to be your nickname, more power to you."

"You call him moron and then sleep with him, so idiot can't be that bad."

Before, I would have flushed a thousand shades of red at the reference to me sleeping with Derek, but the new, sassy me just smiled. Even though Derek hadn't said "I love you" back. Even though he had said there was no time for I love you.

We were twenty minutes late when we pulled up out front of the venue. There was a line waiting to get in that wrapped around the block and reminded me again that this man I was with was going to be singing himself into fame and fortune. The bouncers started to chew us out, but then saw Derek. He tossed one of the overgrown Wreck-It Ralphs the keys and asked them to park it for us, as we flew through the doors toward the stage.

Derek hadn't let me go, and I pulled hard once we hit the steps. "Where should I sit?" I asked.

He just ignored my tug and my words and pulled me up with him. He held my fingers tightly with his as he grabbed the mic from the MC, and I continued to pull in the opposite direction.

"Hello, San Francisco!" he hollered into the mic, and the crowd cheered crazily while eyeing me like I was a fly that flew into their iced tea. "I'm sorry we're late, but I had to save my lady from a monster."

The world erupted in laughter, applause, and whistles.

"And I'm afraid I owe you all another apology. You see, I'm going to kick off our show with a song that doesn't belong to us."

The crowd quieted down, as intrigued as I was nervous.

"You see, my lady—my Little Bird here—she's an Ed Sheeran fan." The audience was a mix of groans and whistles because Derek's music and Ed's music were not the same. Both good, but in very different ways. And I was surprised that he remembered that I liked Ed Sheeran so much.

He grinned at me, that gorgeous BB grin that made my insides and heart and soul turn to puddles every single time.

He turned back to the audience and waved for them to quiet. "I know. I know. But I went and got permission from our man Ed so that I could sing this one song for her."

His guitar was pressed into his hands by Lonnie, and he had to let me go, and I looked for an escape route for the second time this evening.

"Don't you dare," he said into the mic, but it was directed at me.

Then he broke into "How Would You Feel." And I couldn't go anywhere even if I'd wanted to. I was frozen to the spot as he sang one of my top three Ed songs that would now be my favorite forever. Because how would I feel when he told me he loved me like it was something he just had to do? How would I feel if we really spent our life falling deeper in love? How did I feel after I'd just told him I loved him, and now he was telling me that too? How did I feel? Well…I felt like my life had just begun.

♫ ♫ ♫

"Rise and shine, Little Bird," Derek spoke quietly in my ear, his breath tickling my neck and sending goose bumps of pleasure down my body.

But holy Twizzlers, even with the temptation of him, it was too early. It had to be before five a.m. We'd barely fallen asleep three hours ago.

"It's an almost three-hour journey out to the caverns." He laughed at me as I groaned and turned my head away. He grabbed my foot, tickled it, and pulled me to the edge of the bed before I could stop him.

He caught me in his arms, setting my feet on the ground as he always did. "I take it all back. I hate you," I said, but I was already smiling, and he was too.

Rob and Trista left as we did, taking the bus up to Oregon while the rest of us drove out to the California foothills. Derek let Lonnie drive, which I thought was a mistake after the misadventures last night, but I also loved it because it meant I got to ride in the back seat, snuggled up next to Derek, where I was able to snooze again for most of the journey.

The boys' voices, teasing and ribbing each other, washed over me as I slept. It felt comfortable. Like I'd always been a part of this group of overgrown adolescents. Like I was where I belonged. How many times had I felt that way in the past two weeks? More than I ever had at UTK with Hayden, that's for sure.

But this wasn't really where I belonged either. That thought pulled me from my sleep. Because I would eventually need to go home. To my family. To the dealership. I had told Derek I loved him. And he'd sung it back. Yet, we still hadn't talked about our realities. We still hadn't talked about if there was any way to really make this work.

We pulled into the caverns, and Derek kissed me on the temple as if sensing I'd gone somewhere again. I just smiled and went to get my gear.

Mitch, as always, went to check us in. We were going on the "Middle Earth" tour, which was so incredibly appropriate for a booklover like me. Harry Winston and I had read *The Hobbit* and *The Lord of the Rings* series in sixth grade. Our favorite arguments had been over the advantages of dwarf versus elf.

Middle Earth and I were one. I told Derek that, and he laughed. Then he pretended to be Aragorn, trying to swing me onto the SUV bumper like he was swinging me onto his horse, which just made me laugh and tell him that he was no moody Aragorn. He pretended to be offended, huffing off to Mitch and Owen, leaving me with Lonnie.

Lonnie and I checked our packs. "You're good for him," he said seriously.

I looked up at him in surprise. I didn't think I'd ever seen Lonnie serious. Even onstage.

"He's only had a couple of girlfriends, you know."

I nodded. His dad and the PlayBabe Mansion had left their mark on him in all things relationship.

"But you make him happier than I've ever seen him. He seems…I don't know…whole."

I flushed a thousand shades because Derek made me feel whole as well. Like I'd finally found the other half of my cookie that God had sent down to Earth for me.

"Don't hurt him, or I'll have to go all serial killer on you," he said with a teasing tone, but I knew he meant every word.

"I love him."

"That doesn't mean you won't hurt him."

Wasn't that the truth? Because hadn't I just been thinking about our lives, and our paths, and how they didn't cross naturally? Look at what had happened with Jake and Cam, or a million other people who once loved each other and then slowly tore each other apart.

"I can only promise to try not to," I told Lonnie.

It was Lonnie's turn to nod, and then Derek was back with his playful grin.

"No, no, no. Whatever Lonnie is trying to convince you of, do not do it. Walk away, Miss Mia. Walk away."

I grinned and grabbed his hand in mine. An action that I could do now, when two weeks ago, it would have been impossible. My heart soared at it. At the ability to do it, as much as the fact that it was Derek's hand that I'd grabbed. I leaned over and kissed him on the lips. Another huge step forward.

"Are you offering better?" I whispered, our lips still touching.

"Do you want Lonnie to be my first kill? Because he and I go a long way back. High school back."

I laughed and kissed him again until the boys groaned and hollered for us to get a room or get a move on.

Derek flipped them all off, but then pulled me toward them so we could meet up with our guide. None of the boys had been on this tour. We were definitely going to get dirty, and there would be more rock climbing than I'd done up until this point, but I was excited.

And holy Cheetos was it worth it!

The dirt, the climbs, the scraped hands were completely worth it, because that world that Derek had introduced me to was always perfect in its silence. Then again, everything about Derek was perfect to me. Even the shadowy part of himself that he kept hidden from everyone else but me.

Everything was perfect, until it wasn't.

We were heading back out, climbing a last set of rope ladders, when my foot missed the rung. I'd already moved my hand in expectation of the next step, and so, instead of moving up, I found myself falling and panicking. Falling backwards, trying to stop myself, and failing. Hitting all sorts of body parts and my side with my single kidney against outcroppings of rock as I fell.

All I could think was, "Mama!" as I fell with terror welling up inside me with every rock and outcropping that I hit.

I fell a long ways. Not straight. I'd broken the direct route with my body against the natural edges. When I finally hit the ground, my body screamed at me. My insides screamed at me. My skin screamed at me. My lungs screamed for air as the breath was knocked out of them.

Then, I realized Derek was screaming too. "Mia!"

It took Owen hardly any time to reach me because he'd been the caboose again. Derek had to climb down from the ladder he'd just traversed.

"Mia?" Owen said as concern filtered across his face in the green light.

I tried to nod, tried desperately to get oxygen into my depleted lungs while everything hurt. Hurt so badly. But I couldn't respond. He could see that my eyes were open, and that seemed to relieve him some. When the air finally rushed back into me, I gasped at the pain that came with it. Waves of nausea and guilt overwhelming me almost as much as the pain.

"Don't move," Owen said.

I wanted to cry because I'd screwed everything up. For Mama. For me. For the boy that was scampering down toward me.

Then Derek was there, taking Owen's place and grabbing my hand in a way that made me wince, and him say, "Shit!"

He looked me over, trying to assess the damage. But my hands and face were all that was visible in our spelunking gear. And even that visible skin was scraped. I could feel my cheek swelling where I'd hit it on some outcrop.

"Little Bird," he choked.

"I'm okay," I croaked out as my lungs still tried to regain the air they had lost, and my remorse swarmed me again in waves so hard that I knew I would drown.

The guide from the caverns finally joined us, concern etched on his face as well. "Anything broken?"

"Can you try to move?" Derek asked gently.

I tried to nod, but it hurt more than a killing curse. I put my hand in Derek's, and he eased me to a sitting position. Pain scrambled its way across my back and my innards. My side with my solo kidney was wailing, causing my panic to increase until it filled as much of me as the guilt did.

"Does your neck hurt at all?" the guide asked.

"No," I whispered out, but I was holding it steady like I was the rest of my body. I was afraid to move even an inch more than I had to.

"Can you stand?"

Derek lifted me. I didn't do any of the work, but when he put his arms around my waist, I couldn't help the whimper of pain that escaped me.

"Where does it hurt?" he asked, staring into my eyes as he put me on my own feet. Feet that were fine. My left elbow hurt like the dickens. And my insides…my insides were still hollering bloody murder. God. Mama. What would Mama say? Her sad eyes filled my vision, making it hard to breathe. Hard to talk. Hard to answer Derek.

"Inside," I said quietly, my eyes meeting his and swelling with tears that I would not shed in front of these men.

"Shit," he said again. Because he understood. He understood my one kidney. He understood that I shouldn't be doing anything that would damage it. Yet, I had. I'd been on a stupid caving adventure, instead of tucked up safe at home like a possum in its nest.

"We need to get her to a hospital. What's the easiest way out of here?"

"Easiest or quickest?" the guide asked.

Derek looked at me.

"Quickest," I said through teeth clenched against the pain.

"Then that's back up the ladder," the guide said.

I looked back at the ladder that I'd just fallen from. It wasn't the longest one I'd done, but in the shape I was in, I doubted my ability to do it. The thought of trying it again was enough to increase the nausea that I was fighting.

"Do you think you could hold on to me if I carried you on my back?" Derek asked.

I had to think about it. Would it be better to be jostled around on his back, or attempt it at my own slow pace? I didn't know, but I couldn't start up on my own and then halfway, decide for him to carry me. I needed to make the decision now, on the ground.

"I think it'll be less painful if I do it on my own," I said between slow aching breaths.

"Owen, you go first, I'm gonna go right behind her," Derek said.

Owen nodded and went to the ladder, taking my pack with him. That would help. I'd only have me to deal with. Owen started up, I grabbed the ladder, and my elbow burst with pain again. Could I do it one-handed?

"Look, you take the first step. I'm going to try to share each step with you. That way I can hold you up as best as I can," Derek said.

We proceeded up at an excruciatingly slow pace. Me trying to grab with one hand, Derek trying to balance us both against the movements of the rope. Pain worked through me in ways that made my head whirl so that I had to stop, forehead on the cave wall, several times before I could continue.

I just concentrated on the pain and the steps so that I wouldn't have to think about how I'd probably screwed everyone's lives up one more time.

At the top, Owen reached back to grab my good hand as he and Derek maneuvered me onto the ledge of the cave. I sighed with a momentary sense of relief that we'd made it, but when I sat down, my insides burst into such agony that I shot back up.

"You can't sit?" Derek asked, alarm trolling through his voice in a way that made me want to cry again.

I just shook my head, afraid if I spoke, I wouldn't be able to hold back the tears and words that were ripping through me.

The guide, who'd come up behind Derek and me, took charge again. "It's only ten more minutes. All straight walking. I've radioed ahead, and they're going to have an ATV at the exit for us. It'll probably hurt like hell on the trail, but it'll get you to the vehicles as fast as possible."

I nodded. I was getting to be an expert at nodding without pain. I just had to do it slowly and stiffly.

We made our way in silence, Lonnie and Mitch having observed from the top of the ladder. No one really said anything. Derek was the only one who truly understood the magnitude of my fall.

True to what the guide had promised, the ATV was waiting at the cave entrance with another guy and a first aid kit. "Do we need to call for a helicopter?" the new guy asked.

"Mia?" Derek asked.

"No. Just get me to a hospital."

Derek and Lonnie tried to shield me from the jolts as the ATV drove over the beat-up terrain until we got to the cavern's store and parking lot.

Derek jumped into the back area of the SUV, put a seat down, and then helped lift me in so that I could lie flat because sitting in the ATV had pretty much taken everything out of me. Lonnie drove, Mitch was in the passenger seat, and Owen was in the one seat left standing in the middle. Silence. Like in the caves, but this was anything but peaceful.

Google Maps directed them to a hospital in San Andreas. It was the longest ride of my life. But Derek was there, teasing me about keeping them on their toes, and trying to lighten my mood as fear and anger washed over me.

My fear wasn't for me; it was fear for Mama. Mama needed me more than I needed any blasphemous adventure. While we drove, I had time to hate myself all over. To hate this new Mia who'd selfishly gone on this trip with a stupid boy and risked everything for a few moments of happiness. For an escape I hadn't deserved. I'd known I hadn't deserved it.

And now look what had happened.

I'd promised myself that I wouldn't let anything hurt Mama any more, especially nothing that I did. And now there was a good chance that I'd do more than just hurt her. There was a chance that I'd completely devastate her. The remorse hit me again, feeling almost as raw as the pain on my insides. Guilt because I knew if anything happened to me, Mama would never forgive Daddy for telling me to go. Guilt because I should have stayed home.

I wanted to cry. But I didn't. I wanted to scream as the SUV hit curves and turns. But I didn't. Instead, I listened as the man who had taken my heart tried to keep me sane in the midst of my self-condemnation.

The hospital ER was blessedly empty. When I explained what had happened to the intake nurse, and that I was afraid I'd hurt my one good kidney, she reacted with appropriate speed.

I was in my own little curtained area before I had a chance to hesitate. The doctor examined me, ordered tests, and had me pee in a cup all while Derek hovered close by. The doctor ordered an x-ray for my elbow, had an ice pack applied to my cheek, and told me he'd be back with results.

"Tell me," Derek said quietly, grabbing my hand as I lay on the gurney on my good side, staring at him.

"What?"

"How bad can it be?"

He wasn't being sarcastic. He wanted to know. What was the worst-case scenario? I wasn't sure I was willing to tell him that. I was angry. At me. At him. At the world that didn't play fair.

"Little Bird," he demanded.

"If it's damaged, they can do surgery," I said. I didn't have to say that it was my kidney. He knew.

"What the fuck were we thinking?" He put his head down on our hands. Self-loathing radiated off of him in waves so big that it could have been its own radio station.

That softened my heart a little because he was hating himself as much as I was hating myself. My anger toward him melted because it wasn't his fault. I'd known the possible consequences and ignored it for a good time with a bad boy. This was all on me. Even through the anger and self-battery, I still loved him. All of him. Stormy eyes, and messed up past, and all his beautiful words.

"Stop," I croaked out.

"You should have explained how dangerous this was for you," he said, kissing my fingers, but not looking up at me.

I think he was angry too. At me. At himself.

I didn't know what to say to him, because it was true. I should have told him. But even more, I shouldn't have come at all. And if I said that, it would hurt him. And I'd just promised Lonnie that I would try not to.

"I'm not letting you do this any more, Little Bird," he said with a command to his voice and furrowed eyebrows.

That hit me in the gut in a new way, even in the midst of the fury and blame. Because the thought of no more undergrounds with Derek, the thought of having no more peace and quiet and unseen beauty with the man I loved guiding me through, that was almost as hard to take as the guilt. It was yet another new and painful way to be torn apart.

Thankfully, I didn't have to argue with him or myself, because the doctor came back in.

"You have blood in your urine," he said bluntly. My heart dropped, causing a wave of nausea that Derek saw as I felt all the color leave my face.

"What does that mean?" Derek asked.

"She's stable, no other organs damaged that we can tell. I think it's going to heal fine, if she rests. I want to admit her and watch her carefully over the next twenty-four hours to make sure the bleeding doesn't worsen, and that her blood pressure stabilizes."

"Okay," Derek nodded.

"If it doesn't stabilize, we can do a minimally invasive technique called angiographic embolization. That's where the surgeon goes through the large blood vessels in the groin to reach the arteries of the kidney and stops any bleeding." The doctor looked from Derek to me. "But I don't think you're going to need that. I think you're going to be fine after some rest."

Relief hit me as hard as the nausea. I was going to be okay. He thought I was going to be okay. It didn't make me hate myself less, but it at least eased the panic and guilt at the thought of having to tell Mama that I'd damaged my one good kidney.

The doctor continued, "You also have a small fracture to your elbow. It's clean, and I think it'll mend with just a splint. Someone will bring that up and get you into it. You'll want to have another x-ray done in a few days just to make sure it hasn't moved. In that case, you might need surgery on that as well."

He waited for us to ask questions, and when we didn't, he continued.

"I've prescribed some meds for pain and blood pressure. We'll keep an eye out for any stomach swelling or sign of more internal bleeding tonight. They're going to move you up to a room. I'm on call until ten o'clock tonight, and I'll come by before I sign out."

With a few more dos and don'ts, he was gone.

Derek found my bag and reached for my phone.

"What are you doing?" I asked.

"Calling your mom to let her know what happened and that you're okay."

I reached for the phone and groaned as I did so, pain invading me. "Don't you dare!"

He looked up, surprised. "What?"

"I am not going to worry Mama. My God. If she knew...." and I choked on the regret and hatred and sorrow that filled me again.

"Mia, this isn't a joke," Derek said sternly.

"I know! But if everything is okay by tomorrow, then she doesn't need to worry. She doesn't need to frantically look for a flight and almost kill herself to get here," I said furiously. I wasn't mad at him, really. I was still livid with myself.

"She's your mom," he said.

I couldn't hold it anymore; I started crying. "I can't do that to her. I can't," I said as I let the anxiety, and responsibility, and worry of everything that had happened wash over me in all its entirety.

Derek wrapped me in his arms and held me tight against his chest, and I let him because, no matter what I said about knowing I shouldn't have come, I still loved this man who knew me like no one else in the world. And when I felt his own tears hit my arm, I crumbled into sobs, and he gave.

"Okay," he said quietly.

He held me while we both cried tears of guilt, and anger, and pain.

# Chapter Seventeen

Returning Home

ALL OF THE STARS
"And I know these scars will bleed,
But both of our hearts believe
All of these stars will guide us home."
-Ed Sheeran

They moved me to a regular hospital room. There was no one in the bed next to me, so the boys took over that half, fighting for control of the TV remote, and making so much noise that Derek shooed them out to get food. They left and came back with burgers and fries. I wasn't hungry. I was far from it.

After several more hours of the guys clowning around, and seeing that it wasn't doing anything to make me smile, Derek told them to go find a hotel room for the night. I told Derek to go too, but he wouldn't, and I didn't have the energy to fight him.

The pain meds made me feel loopy, like everything was dreamlike. Eventually, I fell asleep. But it wasn't a good sleep. The beeping of the machines, the quiet voices, and Derek's echolocation as he focused all his energy on me kept bringing me out of disturbed dreams. The final one was a dream where Mama was having to attend my funeral, but then it was Jake's funeral, then Cam's, and finally the baby's. My heart was pounding so furiously when I woke that I knew I wasn't going back to sleep anytime soon.

I glanced toward Derek's chair. He was asleep. He looked so tired poured into a too small armchair. Even tired, he was gorgeous as always. I loved him. God help me, I did.

But I also realized that I couldn't do this. I had to go home. I didn't have a choice.

I just didn't know how I was going to tell him that without hurting him. I didn't know how to make him see that our real worlds had finally caught up to us.

He opened his eyes as if he sensed me pulling away from him. His dark eyes stormy in the twilight of the hospital room. "Little Bird?"

"I'm okay, just a bad dream."

He scooted his chair so that he could take my hand in his like he had earlier in the ER. "Have I told you today that I love you?"

"Hey, moron, you haven't told me you loved me at all," I said quietly, as close to teasing as I was going to get at that moment.

He looked up at me with a small grin. "Sure, I did. I told you in front of several hundred people last night."

I reached my index finger to play in his cleft, and he bit it. "No, you sang my favorite song about someone loving someone, but you never said, 'Mia, I love you.'"

He grinned more, which broke me in a whole new way because I was going to walk away from him. I'd thought at the beginning of all this that there was a chance that I'd be left more broken than before, and it wasn't that I wasn't going to be broken when I left him — God, I was — but it was even worse knowing that I was going to break his heart along with mine.

He grabbed my fingers and pressed his lips to my palm. If I wasn't so full of drugs, and tiredness, and worry, that probably would have made me feel things that weren't appropriate in a hospital room and would have made me doubt my new resolve.

He looked up at me, and his smile went away so that there was only serious Derek left. "Little Bird, I love you so goddamn much that I don't know if I'll ever be the same again."

His stormy eyes flashed, and my eyes filled with tears at his beautiful words. Words that I knew I didn't have a right to have. Words that told me how much I was really going to hurt him. But it was a choice between him and Mama. And I couldn't choose him. Not now. Maybe never.

Tears fell again before I could stop them. Because I'd never really been loved by a boy, and now I was going to break us both.

"I didn't think that would make you cry," he said.

"I've never been loved before," I told him quietly, a half-truth in so many ways. I'd been loved. By my family. And Cam and her family. And Wynn. But I'd never been loved by a boy. Wholly and completely in a way that made the world stop the way Derek made my world stop.

"That makes me want to bust something. Or someone. Or maybe go back to my serial killer ways," he said, kissing my palm again.

My eyes started to droop again, medicine kicking in once more. "Hey, moron," I said through shut eyes.

"Yea?"

"I love you too."

Because that was the full truth.

♩ ♩ ♩

The boys showed up as early as visiting hours would let them, and Derek left to shower and change while they entertained me. Which really meant they argued over the free bed and the TV remote again while I supervised like a teacher in a playroom.

I wanted a shower so bad that I itched everywhere, but the hospital said no. I was still hooked up to IVs and monitors.

They retook the same tests that we'd done the day before, and a different doctor came in to give me the results just as Derek returned. This doctor was female and very pretty, so the guys were drooling over her. We had to kick them out to get any privacy. So they decided to go check out of the hotel and get lunch.

Once they were gone, she turned to me with a smile. She'd been entertained by our shenanigans. If I wasn't in regret mode, I probably would have been too.

"Your levels look good. The blood is all but gone from your urine. This was probably just a good scare, but I think we should keep you another twenty-four hours just to make sure," she said.

She checked a few more things, asked if we had more questions, and when we shook our heads, she left.

More of my anxiety started to wash away, along with the dread of having to tell Mama what happened. Even with the relief, it didn't change my mind. I had to go home. Derek needed to finish his tour, and we would have to let reality hit us.

"You need to go. You have to be in Oregon," I told him.

"We can fly out of Sacramento tomorrow morning and be there well in time to get the venue set up. I'm not leaving you."

"Derek—"

"Don't argue with me, Little Bird. It's already done."

I was going to argue, and he knew it, but we were stopped by my phone ringing.

It was Mama, and my heart fell. I hoped Derek hadn't texted her in the middle of the night. I looked at him, ready to scold.

"Mama!" I said, trying not to sound groggy.

"Mia?"

"Yes."

"You sound funny," she said. I bonked my good hand against my forehead because mamas could always tell.

"Just tired," I told her.

"I wanted to let you know Cam went into labor." I realized she sounded really tired too.

"I thought they were trying to get her through a couple more weeks!"

Mama chuckled quietly. "Well, you know our Cam. She does everything on her own timeline and even more so if you tell her she can't."

And wasn't that the truth.

"Is she okay?"

Quiet.

"Mama?

"We think so. Blake says everything's good. But we're all leaving now to head up there."

Suddenly, I not only needed to be home, I wanted to be home. I wanted to be home with my mama, and daddy, and the woman who was my sister like no other soul in the universe. I wanted to be there when she had the baby that should have been Jake's but wasn't. I wanted to be with the people who loved me first. Who still loved me even though my stupid kidney screwed up all of their lives.

"I'm coming home," I told her. Derek's head shifted suddenly in my direction, shaking in opposition.

"I don't know what the flights are like. I'm going to drive up to Sacramento now. I'll let you know as soon as I get something."

"You don't have to come home, Mia, it's okay," Mama said, but I could hear the undertone in her voice. She wanted me there as much as I wanted to be there. This was Cam. Jake's Cam. It was like the baby belonged to all of us.

"I'm coming. Kiss Cam for me. Tell her I'll be there soon, and keep me posted, okay?"

"Will do. And baby girl?"

"Yes?"

"Be safe."

I choked back my default "always" because I hadn't been safe, and soon she would see it. I'd have to tell her. And she'd be as mad as a chicken with a fox in the henhouse that I hadn't told her. But I couldn't feel guilty about that one thing. Because I hadn't told her for a good reason. I'd done it so she wouldn't make herself sick before we knew I'd be okay.

We hung up, and I pushed the nurse's button as I tried to stand. Derek was all over me.

"What the hell are you doing?"

"I'm going home. Cam's having the baby."

"You're hurt. You're supposed to stay another night. People have babies all the time," he said, frowning as he tried to stop me from removing the IV.

I turned to meet his glare with one of my own. "You know this isn't just anyone. This is Cam."

We stared at each other, neither giving in, until the nurse came in.

"I'm going to have to check out," I told her with a weak smile.

"Um. Did the doctor discharge you?"

"No, but she's going to have to. I have to get to Tennessee."

The nurse looked at me like I was crazy and went scrambling away to find the doctor.

Derek took my good hand as I tried to pull on the clean clothes he'd piled for me on the nearby table.

"Little Bird, the doctor wants you to stay."

"She said I'm looking good. It's just precautionary. And I'll be at a hospital."

"But you're going to spend hours at an airport and in an airplane." He was frustrated with me, maybe even angry.

"I know," I said quietly.

"Then I'm coming with you."

I didn't have a chance to respond, because the nurse came in and started to disconnect me from the IVs and machines. It was good I couldn't respond, because he wouldn't be happy when I said he couldn't come with me. He needed to finish his tour. I needed to go back to my reality, and he needed to go back to his.

The doctor showed up and gave me a whole spiel about the risks I was taking and handed me a bunch of waivers to sign.

Then, we headed out to the lobby. Derek's fingers found mine as we waited for the guys to come back from getting lunch.

"I don't want you to come," I said, looking down at our fingers.

"What?"

"You have a show tomorrow."

"So? I'll cancel it. It was the last one on this tour anyhow."

"That isn't fair to you, or the guys, or your fans. You're just building a fan base. If you cancel now, you'll lose street cred."

"What makes you think I give a rat's ass about any of those people more than you?"

"I didn't say you did. I just said it isn't fair."

"Life isn't fair."

That reminded me of what Seth Carmen used to tell Cam when they dated for that brief time back when Jake was being stupid. Words that were true. Life didn't play fair. But sometimes, it also surprised you with the gifts it gave you. Like Derek.

"I'll be fine. I don't want you to come."

"You don't want me to come?" He was hurt. A million shades of hurt.

"I don't mean it like that," I said, trying to take the bite out of my words. "I just… We had to go back to our reality eventually, right?"

"What?"

He pulled me into his arms, and I let myself be pulled because it was easier to bury my head into his chest than to watch his face while I said all of this to him.

"What did you think would happen at the end of this three-week adventure?" my voice was muffled.

He squeezed tight and it hurt, but I let it because the physical hurt matched the one in my heart.

"I don't know. We hadn't gotten that far," he said.

"Derek. I live in Tennessee and run a car dealership. You live in L.A. and travel the world with a band."

"I know that."

I risked looking up at him, and his gray eyes stormed at me. It broke my heart because I definitely didn't want to walk away from this. From him. From the man that thought I was beautiful and anything but invisible.

"I'm just going back to reality," I told him.

"I'm not willing to let reality end us," he stormed.

I looked away again, adding those beautiful words to the collection of Derek's lines in my head. When I didn't respond, he pulled my chin up so that I was forced to see his eyes and the pain there.

"I love you," he said.

I nodded.

"Don't give up yet," he said forcibly.

I didn't have to answer, because the guys showed up, shocked to see us in the lobby, but I knew the conversation wasn't done either. We quickly filled the guys in on what was going on and took off for Sacramento. I was on my phone, trying to find a flight back. Something that wouldn't take me five layovers to get there.

"Buy two," Derek said quietly as he saw me ready to check out on the airline's website.

I shook my head in the negative.

"Little Bird," he said with a plea that I ignored.

He wasn't happy about it, but he also didn't fight me. I didn't know what to think of any of that, except that at the moment, I knew it was the right thing. He had to finish his tour. I had to go home.

Reality sucked. Life wasn't fair. People died who should live. What else was there to say?

♩ ♩ ♩

The terrible California traffic delayed us, and we barely made it before my flight. I hoped security would be light or someone would be able to get me through with my bandaged body. I took my little bag without the books, less to carry when I could barely stand. Derek could send me the rest later.

He went with me to the ticket counter and up to the security line while the guys circled the airport in the rental.

"I don't want you to go," he said quietly.

"I know, moron, but it was gonna happen at some point," I repeated my logic from before.

"I should be coming with you." I could hear the doubt in his voice.

"Stop. I would just feel guilty that yet another person didn't get to live out their dreams because of me."

"What if you are my dream?"

God. What could you say to that? I started to move away, but he pulled me back, crushing me, sore arm and all.

"I'm not letting you go for good," he said, deep emotion running through his voice.

I still didn't answer, because I couldn't. I could hope that there was some version of reality where we would find each other again. But this wasn't a Doctor Who rerun. We didn't get a choice about the realities that were ours.

So instead, I took in the scent of him so that I could remember it when I replayed his words, and his looks, and his touch back in my head at night.

"Little Bird, I mean it. We'll figure it out."

"Okay." My voice cracked because the truth was, I wanted to believe it.

"Text me when you board. Text me when you land. Call me when you find out about the baby," he said, making plans for us even though we wouldn't be together.

That got to me. That he so desperately wanted to continue this when we both knew that it was an impossible puzzle. One that couldn't be put together any time soon.

"Okay," I said again through tears that wouldn't fall yet. Time for that later, when I was alone.

"Go, you'll miss the flight," he said. Then he kissed me like that first time. Slow, and reverent, and yet full of passion.

I tore myself away from him, limped my way through security, and found my way to my gate. Mama texted that they were at the hospital and that Cam and the baby were being stubborn, and that they may have to do a C-section.

I cursed myself again for not being there. For being on this joyride across the country with a sexy musician. For being away at all. But a piece of me, the piece I had thought I left in Derek's back pocket, whispered that I was lying to myself. That I hadn't been away at all, that I'd really been home.

As Ed played in my playlist, I let myself have a tiny bit of hope that he was right, and that after Derek's and my horizons had met and our scars had bled into one another, that the stars would guide us to a place where we could be together once more.

♫ ♫ ♫

I texted Derek like I told him I would as I was ready to take off. I tried to sleep on the plane, but my elbow and insides were aching painfully. At first I didn't want to take any pain meds that would make me groggy for when I arrived, but it was such a long flight that I was finally forced to take something or sit screaming in a cabin full of people.

When I arrived, the meds had made me as addlebrained as I'd known they would. It was really late. I texted Derek first and then Mama. I didn't stop to think about that. That I'd put him first. Mama said Daddy was at the airport, waiting to pick me up, which I hadn't expected.

I made my way out just as Daddy pulled up to the arrivals terminal. He jumped out of his truck when he saw me and was halfway to hugging me when he took in my splinted arm and the ugly bruise that had taken over my face. I had hardly glanced at myself in the mirror because it was scary even to me.

"What the fuck, baby girl?"

"I love you too, Daddy," I said with a tired smile, and I hugged him with my good arm. "Come on, old man, I'll tell you all about it on the way."

And I did. Well, at least I told him a lot. I told him about caving and falling from the ladder, and how everything was okay with my kidney. I told him that I'd recheck everything while I was at the hospital with Cam.

He was serious-faced.

"Your mama's never going to forgive me," he said quietly.

"I'm the one that went."

He nodded, and I could tell he was trying not to cry. I squeezed his arm reassuringly. "It's gonna be okay, Daddy." I slid easily back into my Good Girl Mia skin, making sure everyone else was going to be okay.

I wanted to cry because somewhere out there was a boy who wanted to make sure I was okay more than anyone else in the world, and we were no longer together.

It was almost as if none of the last few weeks had happened. If I didn't have my splinted arm and bruises to remind me, I might have thought it had all been a dream. A really sexy dream in a romance novel. Except I couldn't see the happily ever after for this one.

Faster than I had expected, the hospital lights greeted us. We texted Mama to ask where they were, and she said Cam had come out of surgery and that her and her new baby boy were just fine. They had taken them to a room in the maternity ward.

All I could think was that Cam had had a boy, and what that would have meant to Jake.

We made our way up to the maternity ward. Mama was waiting in the hall, and as soon as she saw me, she put a hand to her mouth in shock. She dropped everything and ran to me. "Mia?"

"I'm okay, Mama. I promise. Just a little scare."

"Is… are…" She couldn't ask, and I saw the fear flash in her eyes and felt the guilt overwhelm me again because I was causing her anxiety when she didn't deserve it.

"Everything's okay."

She hugged me so tight that it hurt, but I didn't make a peep because I was afraid I'd undo the relief I'd seen take over her face in that instant before her arms had surrounded me.

"You should have called me," she told me fiercely into my hair.

"I've already told her that," Daddy said. Which he had. He'd chewed me out about not letting them know. It didn't change what had happened. And I knew I'd do it all the same even if I had to do it over again.

"You had enough to worry about," I told her with a smile.

Mama looked me in the eyes. "Mia, don't do that."

"Don't do what?"

"Make light of it. I know I worry too much. It isn't your fault. It isn't anyone's fault. I'm working on it." She smiled weakly and got all teary-eyed.

"Stop or Cam will never let you in to see the baby. You know she hates tears," I chided her.

She smiled, a watery one, but still a smile. Daddy took her hand, and she held on to my good one, and we made it into the room.

Blake was there, smiling so big that I thought he'd lose his whole body inside it. And his parents were there, and his grandparents, and Cam's parents. Wynn was in her nurse's garb. The room was already crowded with people, but Cam lit up when she saw us.

"Better late than never, kiddo," she quipped. Her smile was a tired smile, but a Cam smile. A smile that Jake had loved, and it twisted my heart because he should have been there. He should have been there to see the dark-haired bundle that she was holding up against her chest. The tiny, blue-blanketed body that should have been his.

I had to carefully hold back my own tears because Cam would kick me out as easily as she'd kick Mama out if she caught me crying. I eased my way over to her, and Blake's face went from smile to shock as he took me in, bruises, splint, and all.

"I'm going to kill him," he said, frowning.

"He already tried to commit hari-kari himself," I said with a smile.

"How dare you walk in here and upstage my labor of love with all of that," Cam said, laughing at me and my ugly, broken appearance.

"Someone's gotta keep you in your place," I said, and I hugged her and kissed the little bundle on its tiny, smooth cheek. Then I whispered to her, "You've got a baby."

"I know. Shocker. It just hit me out of the blue. Had no idea it was coming."

"Everything good?" I asked her.

"Everything's perfect," she said, and she squeezed my hand.

Everyone jostled to hold the baby, and I snuck out to the hall and out to the terrace where I called Derek like I said I would.

"Hey," I said when he answered.

"Little Bird," he said, and my heart jumped at his voice like I was sure it would always do. "How are you?"

I couldn't help loving how he asked how I was first before he asked about Cam or anyone else. He asked about me. Because Derek put me first. It was hard to fathom anyone putting me first.

"I'm good. Tired, but good."

"Have you had anyone check your urine values yet?"

"So sexy when you talk to me that way," I teased.

"Mia!"

"I will. I just left Cam's room."

"How is she? The baby?"

"They're both good. Beautiful. Strong. Happy."

"The baby is happy?" he teased.

"Well, I'm sure it will be. Blake had a smile so big I thought he'd break the windows with it. What baby wouldn't be happy to be a part of that?"

"Our baby," he said back quickly.

I stopped my pace around the terrace. "Wh-what?"

"Our baby. Our baby will only be happy to be a part of us."

Silence, because my brain wouldn't function. How could it? I was a sucker for words. Words like that. But these words were double-edged because they were insanely sweet and yet also painful. Because they talked about a future, when we didn't even know how we were going to get to tomorrow.

"I don't know what to say to any of that."

He chuckled on the other end. "Don't say anything. Don't ruin my image of you all sweaty, holding up a little bundle with my cleft chin."

"Who says it'll have a cleft?"

"Genetics."

"Then screw that. No baby for you."

"You love my cleft."

I did. I loved the way it stretched when he smiled. I loved the way it felt when I touched it. I loved how it led to my finger being in his mouth when I allowed myself to touch it.

My heart flooded with hope at the same time that my brain reminded me that I would just have to squash it again later.

"I have to go," he said, but he sounded like he regretted it.

"Okay. I'll try to call tomorrow."

"Okay."

When I hung up, I missed him already. I missed his arm around me. I missed his smile. And I knew that, tonight, I'd miss his body tucked up against mine like we were the last two pieces in his eagle puzzle. Pieces that didn't make sense and yet belonged.

When I went back, we all said goodnight and promised to see each other in the morning, and I got in the cab of the truck with Mama and Daddy and we drove to a hotel. Somewhere along the way, I fell asleep, and woke up on Mama's shoulder like I had fallen asleep a million times when I was a little kid.

She smiled at me. I squeezed her hand.

♩ ♩ ♩

My phone was ringing. Except that I was pretty sure it wasn't my phone. It was Derek's. Derek had "Little Bird" as a ringtone, not me. I slammed the home button.

It started singing again.

Mornings. Have I mentioned I hate them? Even more so now that I was waking up by myself, still in a hotel room, but one miles away from the sexy BB that I loved.

"What?" I groused into the phone.

"Miss Mia. Up and at 'em," Derek laughed.

My heart leaped at his voice. God help me.

"Did you change my ringtone?" I growled.

"Now you'll know it's me calling." And what could you say to that?

"What time is it?" I asked, trying to let my grouchiness wash away in his voice.

"It's seven here, so it has to be nine there," he said.

"What?"

I sat up, grimacing at the pain, and looked at the bedside clock, and sure enough, it was nine o'clock. My whole body groaned at me, agony radiating through every part.

"Did you have your labs taken?"

Nope, I hadn't. "Yep," I told him.

"Liar," he said, but he wasn't mad. I loved that he could read through my lies and call me on it as no one ever did.

"I was tired and forgot. I'll have it done today, I promise."

"Okay."

"You're not mad?"

"Pissed as hell, but nothing I can do about it. If I was there, you wouldn't have forgotten. Can only be mad at myself for letting you talk me out of going with you."

"What time do you get to the venue?"

"Later."

"That's specific."

"I know," and then he added, "whatchya wearin'?"

His sexy tone made me go to mush even though I knew he'd changed the subject on purpose.

"Clothes."

"Sassy pants. Miss Mia the Sassy Pants. I'm kicking myself for ever letting her out of her box."

"You didn't let her out."

"Sure, I did."

"Conceited, schmuck."

"Yep." I heard someone in the background talking to him. "I have to go, but I wanted to hear your voice."

Which just thrilled me as he always did. My hopeful heart was saying that we'd be okay. My Good Girl Mia, Doubting Thomas, was saying that this would fade in time.

"We're going back to the hospital today to see Cam and the baby, but then I think we'll go home."

"I figured."

"I'll call when I can."

"Okay."

Silence.

"Little Bird?"

"Hmm?"

Silence.

"See you soon."

"Okay. Bye."

When we hung up, I tried not to dwell on the fact that neither of us had said, "I love you." I tried not to dwell on the fact that we had thousands of miles between us and no plan to see each other past Derek's promise that it would happen.

♫ ♫ ♫

I called my doctor at home, and he made arrangements for the Nashville hospital to rerun all my labs. He said he'd call with the results. He also told me I should probably be more careful with the sports I picked. Even though I'd found that to be true, I couldn't help but smile because no one had ever said anything like that to me in my entire life.

When we got to the hospital, Mama and Daddy took off to the maternity ward, and I headed off to the lab.

When I'd finished being poked and prodded, I went up to see Cam. When I got to her room, it was just Cam and the baby. She waved me in. "Hey, kiddo," she said.

"Hey back," I said. "Where is everyone?"

"Went to get coffee, which just means they needed to talk about me behind my back as usual."

She held out the little bundle, and I took him, sitting next to Cam on the bed, looking at the sleeping red-faced baby. I wondered what differences would have been in his tiny features if he'd been Jake's.

"Do you think you and Jake would have had a baby?" I breathed out and glanced from the sleeping face to her own.

Cam shrugged. "I don't know." But she was thinking about it. I could tell. "I'm not sure there was ever room for anyone else in our lives. When Jake and I were together, there wasn't anything else. Does that make sense?"

It did. Because if you had seen them together, you would understand. They were completely absorbed in each other. They were one being. It was why it had been so hard on her when he'd died.

"Plus, he was really concerned about passing the diabetes on. When we were younger, he used to say he was never getting married or having kids because he wouldn't do that to another human being." She was sad, and it made me kick myself as I always did when I made her sad.

We just let it settle in between us. Jake, and the baby, and our love for each other and my dead brother.

"He'd be proud as shit of you," she said with a smile and a laugh that lightened my heart.

"How do you figure?" I asked.

She waved at my splint and beat-up face. "Livin' the daring life. He worried you'd never step outside of your books."

"He did not! He didn't even think about me."

"He did, goofball. All the time. And I think he would want to ask Derek to step outside and prove himself."

"I think Derek could handle it."

Cam laughed. "Quite the man, is he?"

I flushed. "You're awful."

"Do you love him?"

"More than words."

"That's a lot coming from the book girl."

"Yep."

"So what's going to happen now?"

My turn to shrug. Because I didn't know. He had a life that he belonged to in a mansion in L.A., even if it didn't seem to fit him. I had a life that fit me here, but was now missing a chunk of what would make me whole. He had a band, a tour schedule, fans. I had a car dealership and a family I couldn't leave.

"He's got a fan club," I said with a laugh, changing the subject.

"No way."

"Yep. And they're sexy and very, very forward."

"Good thing he has his own sexy, then," she quipped back.

Blake came bounding into the room with that positive energy that was so Blake and took the baby from my arms without even asking. I guessed that was okay since it was his baby after all. He kissed me on the cheek and then grinned at all of us.

"Did you tell her?" Blake asked.

Cam shook her head.

"Tell me what?"

"We've finally agreed on a name." He smiled again his big, goofy Blake smile.

"You agreed with yourself," Cam grumbled.

"Mia, meet Mayson Carter Abbott," he said proudly.

I swallowed hard. Carter after Cam's dad. Carter was Jake's middle name too. It was a family tradition… family. Jake should be here.

"That's lovely," I said, trying hard to hold back my tears.

"Don't you dare cry, or I will too," Cam said.

I didn't believe it. Cam didn't cry, she just punched things. I guess that wasn't true; she had cried for a long time over my brother.

People filtered back into the room, and I lost myself in the feeling of being with family. It was a place I belonged. But difficult, because I knew another place I also belonged now.

The doctor called to let me know all my labs looked good. I felt relieved and wanted to tell someone. So, I texted Derek. He didn't respond, but I just figured he was busy practicing.

Eventually, Mama and Daddy said we better head out. It was two hours home from Nashville. I hugged Cam, and kissed the baby, and promised I'd be up to see them soon. Blake made me promise to tell him when he could kick Derek in the arse personally. I told him I had no knowledge of any opportunities that would present themselves.

In the truck on the way home, I was quiet. I was so tired. I closed my eyes and tried to get comfortable.

Mama squeezed my hand. "Mia?"

"Hmm?"

"How was the trip?"

I opened my eyes and could see so many questions in hers. "It was really good." I smiled.

"So?"

I shrugged. "I wish I knew."

"Do you love him?"

Cam had asked the same thing just hours before. I couldn't quite give Mama my same response, so I just nodded.

"Does he love you?"

"Yes."

No one said how ridiculous that was when it had barely been a couple weeks. No one complained about loving someone I hardly knew. Probably because we all knew from heartbreaking experience that life was short, and you had to take what came your way and be grateful for it.

Be grateful for it, I told myself. That I had loved and been loved back. No matter what happened from here, I would always have that.

There was silence for a while as we were absorbed in our own thoughts.

"You know, you don't need to run the dealership. Carter and I would be perfectly fine with selling it," Daddy said, and I looked at him in surprise. I'd never heard anyone mention this before.

"Scott," Mama hushed.

"I want her to know. There's no reason to stay and run the dealership if where you really need to be is somewhere else," Daddy said.

I could tell this had been a discussion while I was gone. One that Mama had not been happy about. She didn't want me somewhere else. She'd had a hard enough time letting me go to college, even knowing that the plan was for me to come home for forever when it was done. She'd had an even harder time letting me go on a spelunking escapade with a gorgeous musician, even though that one was only for three weeks. Somehow, I think she had known that the three weeks would change me more than the four years. And it had.

The truth was I still wanted to work at the dealership. Nothing had changed that. I liked all the things about it, but I loved most that I was carrying on something that Daddy and Cam's daddy had started. I liked traditions almost as much as my friend Harry.

I just didn't know how that was going to also allow me to be with the crazy man who had stolen my heart. Because I couldn't—wouldn't—ask him to give up his life, and I knew him well enough to know that he couldn't— wouldn't—ask me to give up mine. So, what that left was an impossible love that would probably fade away into nothing as time and the miles wore at us.

"I want to run the dealership," I said. "If you both still trust me to do it."

"Baby girl," Daddy choked, "we wouldn't trust anyone else."

But I wondered, as I always wondered, if he would have trusted Jake more.

"You know Jake never wanted to run it, right?" Daddy asked, and for a moment I thought I'd spoken aloud, but I hadn't. Daddy just knew me. Like Mama knew me. Like I now had a boy who knew me.

"No," I responded. "I didn't know that."

Daddy shook his head. "He was all football, that boy. If he wasn't playing it, he would have been coaching it."

I guess I had known that. He had wanted to go into coaching before the kidney gave out. Before I'd given him mine. And before mine had failed him. Guilt and sorrow overwhelmed me as it always did. Maybe harder because I'd been ignoring it for two weeks. The door that I'd forced shut, bursting at its seams to be opened.

And it did burst. It erupted in such a volatile way that before I could stop myself, I croaked out, "I'm so sorry," and, to my utter horror, started to cry. I tried to hold them back, but the tears just wouldn't stop. I was sobbing.

"What on earth do you have to be sorry for?" Mama squeezed my hand. Then she was crying too just because I was, and she didn't even know why.

"I'm so sorry my kidney didn't work," I said so quietly I wasn't sure they heard. But they did.

Mama wrapped her arm around me and held my head against her shoulder like it had been the night before. "Oh, my baby girl, please don't say that. It wasn't your fault. It wasn't... Jake. God, he was almost as bad as Cam in doing things his own way."

We were both crying.

"Damn, you two, knock it off or I'll run us off the road," Daddy said, choking up himself but trying to tease us out of our tears.

And just like that, I didn't know why I had been carrying this guilt around with me for so long. Because really, I hadn't done anything but try to give my dying brother a chance at life. It hadn't worked, but I'd still given everything that I could. It hadn't been enough. But it was all I could have done.

Chapter Eighteen

Together

THINKING OUT LOUD
"Baby we found love right where we are."
-Ed Sheeran

When we got home, it was late, and we just ate cereal and went to bed. We were all exhausted. I texted Derek, asked how the gig had gone, but was so tired that I fell asleep before I heard his answer.

The next day, I had nothing to pull me from my bed and hatred of mornings, so I found myself sleeping the day away. Mama came to check on me multiple times, but I just told her I was resting the way the doctor wanted me to. She let me.

I texted Derek several times and got only a couple quick, short answers in return. He said the show had gone well, and they were finishing their caving ventures without me. I knew that he would be on his way back to L.A. the next day, with the band in the motor home they liked to call a tour bus. I tried not to wonder what would happen when he returned to the guesthouse, and to Jane the Kitten, and the Camaro because I didn't even know if I should hope for anything. Or if I should just start trying to get over him, even though my heart felt like it never would. Like the hold

Derek had on it was more than anyone had ever had on it in my entire life.

Good Girl Mia had gone quiet again after my confession in the cab of the truck the night before. I didn't know if I'd banned her from my life, or if she was just keeping herself on a shelf in my mind's closet, but I was glad that she was easing her hold on me once more.

I was hoping I could find some ground between old, guilty Mia and new, sassy Mia. A place where I could just be me and not have to think so much about what else I could've, should've, would've done if I had to do things over again.

Finally, in the late afternoon, I joined Mama in the kitchen to help with dinner like I always had. Somehow, tonight it felt more peaceful than it had since Jake had died. Not like it used to, but it felt right. I had told Mama on the night of the fundraiser that everything would be okay. I guess I finally believed my own words. At least for my family.

For me and Derek? Who knew? I'd loved him. He'd loved me. If nothing else, it was a happy memory that I'd still have with me when I was old and gray.

Even though I'd rested most of the day, my sore body begged for sleep. I hadn't had much rest on my venture with Derek, and I flushed happily thinking of all the ways we'd kept each other awake, even before the Wooly Bison. So, after dinner, I headed up to the shower and stared in the mirror at the green and purple bruise on my cheek. It felt like this new scar somehow fit this version of Mia. It would fade, and what was left was going to be better than what was there before.

I pulled on a worn pair of yoga pants and an old t-shirt that had been too embarrassing to take with me on my trip with Derek. I missed my new clothes. I missed my new guy. I missed my new kitten. I missed us.

ME: Goodnight, moron, hope the guys are keeping the bus on the road. Meds are making me sleepy. I'll talk to you in the morning.

No response.

I tried to stay awake, waiting for the response that I hoped would come eventually. I was trying to have faith. I was trying not to give up as Derek had begged me not to, but it was all still a mystery to me how any of it would work out. It was a relief when I was pulled under into a dreamless, medicine-induced sleep.

♫ ♫ ♫

The next day, I went with Daddy to the dealership. We talked through some changes, and I met with Joe in the parts department to see that he'd straightened the mess out there all on his own.

It was good and bad not to be needed.

Daddy sent me home at midday, saying I still needed to rest. I did, but I also felt like he knew I was having trouble focusing on the work. I still had a lot to resolve in my world before I could concentrate again on everything the business needed of me.

I felt like I'd grown tremendously in a short amount of time. I'd closed the door on Hayden. I'd come to terms with my responsibility for Jake. But I'd also fallen in love when I knew I shouldn't.

When I got home, I turned on the TV, and the news was talking about the death of Hugo Brantly and how Hugo's son was going to be taking over the business and the mansion. Ben Brantly planned on cleaning house and making the place over into something of a higher class. It hit me that Derek's dad would probably no longer have a boss or a place to live. I wondered what that meant for Derek and his family. I wondered if Derek would go to the funeral.

I texted him, but I didn't get a response until late, when I'd already curled up in bed.

DEREK: I'm so sorry. It's been crazy here. I miss you.

ME: Are you okay?

DEREK: Better than I have been in a long time.

This, of course, made me both happy and sad. Was he better without me? I didn't think so. I didn't think that was what he meant.

ME: Are you going to the funeral?

DEREK: Yes, it's on Friday.

ME: I'm sorry.

DEREK: Honestly, I'm good. I just miss you.

Then, he sent me a picture of him and Jane the Kitten cuddled up in the bed that didn't seem like him, especially without me in it too.

ME: You're such a tease.

DEREK: Damn right. Keep you wanting me.

ME: I don't think I'll ever stop.

DEREK: Thank God.

ME: Goodnight.

DEREK: Night Little Bird.

Then he was gone, and I only had a picture to stare at of both the kitten and the man I loved. We hadn't said we loved each other again. I didn't know why. Maybe because we'd barely said it to each other in person before our magical bubble world had imploded into real life.

♪ ♪ ♪

The next couple days went by in a blur. Derek and I texted and talked when we could, but we were back to leading our regular lives, and our regular lives were far apart in more than just distance. On Friday, Derek texted me after the funeral to tell me that it was over, and it had been shit, but he was glad he'd gone. He said he had a few things to take care of and that it might be hard to get hold of him for the next couple days, but that he hoped to see me soon.

I just didn't know how to respond to any of that.

♪ ♪ ♪

Almost two days later, he'd been right. I'd only gotten a few one-line texts from him. Even though he'd told me that was going to happen, I had to wonder if this was the beginning of the end. I loved him. He loved me. But as we all know, love is just not enough sometimes.

So, I concentrated on reading my textbooks and working at the dealership, and just continuing the life that I'd led before it all. When I'd known I was a mess.

I didn't feel like as much of a mess anymore because Derek, and my adventure with Derek, had helped heal the wounds inside me some. They were now just that scar that I'd been hoping for, instead of the scab that was ready to break open.

But loving Derek and not having Derek… That was going to leave a new wound. Cam had once told me that living without Jake was like living without a limb. Like suddenly, your right arm was gone. I think I finally understood. She was still living a life without a body part. I was going to be missing two from now on: the one I gave to my brother and the one Derek took.

The sun was barely filtering in my windows Sunday morning when I opened my eyes. I felt like something had woken me, but I didn't know what. I looked at my phone, thinking maybe it had been that, but there was no text and no missed calls.

I took my grumpy, morning-hating body down to the kitchen and made coffee. Then, I decided I needed to bake. I hadn't baked in so long that it felt like a skill that had gone rusty.

I turned on my Ed playlist on the phone, letting his love songs and life lessons wash over me as I went to work on the apple spice muffins that were a family favorite.

Mama came down, ready for our lazy Sunday, in jeans and a plaid shirt. She looked so country, and so like home, and so like Mama that it squeezed my heart with

343

homesickness even though I was already home. She hugged me gently.

"Can I help?" she asked as she eyed me struggling with my one good hand and a barely-there one.

I shook my head. I needed to keep busy. She kissed my forehead, grabbed her own coffee, and headed to the granite bar to sit. I loved that bar. So many stories of our lives started there. The most important one being how Jake had rescued Cam from falling from the treehouse when he was seven and she was four, even though there was no way for him to see the treehouse from where he'd been sitting. That had been the first of many ways that Jake and Cam had saved each other miraculously.

Over the last couple days, the thought of Jake and Cam hadn't overwhelmed me with guilt. Instead, I was beginning to feel happy that they'd had those moments together. I was also happy that Cam now had her little baby and the joyful guy who loved her with all her broken parts. Like I thought that there was a guy who now loved all my broken parts.

The last set of muffins was in the oven, and I was cleaning when the doorbell rang. Mama looked up at me. It was still early. Daddy, no more of a morning person than I was, was still sleeping.

Mama put down the iPad that she'd been reading on and went to the door. I kept cleaning. Salespeople were pretty much the only ones who rang the doorbell, and they were about to get an earful from my mama about Sunday mornings and respect.

So I was surprised when Mama's voice rang out with laughter, "Baby girl, I think it's for you."

I threw down the dish towel and headed toward the door. Then I stopped dead in the hallway.

There was Derek. My sexy BB was smiling at me in that cleft-stretching way that made me turn to melted goo. In his arms was Jane the Kitten, and out the door behind him, I could see the Camaro.

My heart leaped into my throat as if it might become its own entity, and yet I was also frozen, like I hadn't been by the sight of him in so long. I was shocked and confused and happy.

Then, my body took over, and I flew to his arms. Little Bird coming home. I was hugging him, and he was hugging me, and Jane was protesting with a loud mew. And he was kissing me, even with Mama standing behind us, and Jane clawing to get down.

I'd been missing my heart all week, and here it was again. In this man. For the first time since I came back to Tennessee, I felt truly and honestly home. No longer homesick. I was in the place I loved, with the man I loved, with the people I loved.

He pulled back and smiled again. "Miss Mia, did you miss me?"

"God, yes!" I said and pulled his fingers into mine as I went to shut the door, but then Lonnie appeared on the steps, smiling in his happy lumberjack way.

"Phillips!" he said and reached in to hug me.

"How are you both here?" I asked incredulously.

"Drove straight from L.A. after the funeral," Lonnie said.

I looked at Derek in surprise.

"Wh-what?"

"Shit, I just spent thirty hours in a car with this smelly beast, and the girl I love asks me why I did it?" Derek laughed.

"Moron!"

The timer on the oven went off, and Mama said she'd grab it as I led the boys into the kitchen. We put Jane down, and she immediately followed Mama to where the food smells were coming from.

Mama took the muffins out and then bent to pick up the little furball. "Poor tailless kitty! What did these meanies decide to name you?"

"That is Jane," Derek said with all his charm. "Jane Austen, but your daughter refuses to call her that. She's just Jane the Kitten to her."

"Jane Austen, hmm? I kind of like that," Mama said, and I rolled my eyes, which earned me a quick peck from Derek.

I debated rolling them repeatedly to ensure several more kisses, but with Lonnie and Mama present, I wasn't sure—even with Good Girl Mia gone—I could be that outrageously open about my love for this man whose hand I still held tightly in my own.

"And who's your friend?" Mama asked, referring to our tall lumberjack.

It was funny that Mama didn't know him. I felt like I'd spent a year of my life with the band. "This is Lonnie. Lonnie, this is my mama, Marina."

"Mama!" Lonnie said and squished her in a hug that made her yelp.

"Unhand my woman, you maniac," Daddy's teasing voice said from behind us all.

I jumped and turned as Daddy entered the kitchen.

Daddy stuck his hand out for Derek's. "Good to see you again."

Derek shook his hand. "I'm surprised your wife let me in the house after seeing Mia the way she is."

"She's okay. I'm sure that has a lot to do with how you took care of her after it all," Daddy said. I was surprised that he and Mama weren't shooting daggers at him.

"Lonnie, why don't you help me take these muffins and coffee out to the patio? It's a beautiful morning for August," Mama said, and they soon were all headed out to the backyard.

Derek sat on the barstool and drew me so that I was half on his lap in between his legs. "I missed you," he said and kissed me properly. It hit me all the way to the depths of my toes and back like it had each and every time and probably always would.

"I missed you too," I said, pulling back and smiling. "But seriously, George must be going berserk."

"Have I forgotten to mention? I fired George."

"What?"

Derek shrugged. "He doesn't want what I want. Wants the band to be more commercial, less authentic."

"Wow."

"And Rob quit."

I stared, mouth open.

"He said he couldn't stand being away from Trista anymore. I can't blame him; I kind of understand where he's coming from," Derek said, and this time, his smile was full of unspoken promises.

"What are you going to do?" I asked, still snug and happy tucked up against him.

"Well, did you notice that house around the corner that's for sale?"

He was talking about Jake's old girlfriend, Brittney's house. Or at least her parents' house. They had retired to Florida, and the house had been left empty and on the market most of the summer.

"Yes…" I said hesitantly.

"I've already placed a call to the realtor."

"How did you do that?"

"From the driveway when we pulled up. It's a sign from God, you know?"

"You're a moron."

"You keep saying that, but soon I'll be a house-owning moron. And I'm going to need someone to help me keep house. Jane the Kitten demands a mother."

"I'm not moving in with you. And you're not seriously buying that house. You have to go back to L.A., fix your band, make more music, and put out your bonus album. You know, be the sexy musician you are."

"Sexy musician, huh?"

I eye-rolled him and got a quick kiss.

"I'm hiring an agent in Nashville. Blake is already working on getting us into a studio there to finish the album. I'm sure he'll have a drummer connection for me too. Mitch and Owen have already agreed that we can record here. Lonnie's decided he's moving with me, so we might have company for a couple weeks till he gets his own place."

I was stunned at his words again. Unsure how to respond as was so often the case with him. Finally, I breathed out, "Are you really saying that you're going to come live here?"

"Little Bird, you're here."

"Yes."

"So, wherever you are, that's where I'll be."

"But you have a life and family in L.A."

"I have a brother and a niece in L.A. That's it."

"You love them."

"Yes, but they aren't my whole world. You…you're my whole world."

Words. Words that embedded into my soul, but I still shook my head.

"Derek, I can't…"

"You can."

"You don't even know what I was going to say," I fussed.

"You were going to say that you couldn't let me give up everything to come live in some backwater with a girl who wears pantsuits and runs a car dealership."

I flushed.

"I guess I don't wear pantsuits anymore," I said with a grimace.

"Thank God!" He smirked. "Although it would have been fun to rid you of them every time you tried to wear them."

Eye-roll. Kiss.

"Derek, be serious."

"I am very, very serious. I love everything about Tennessee, remember? Sweet tea, porch swings, and especially one beautiful woman."

I started to protest again, but he put his fingers on my lips to silence me. "Besides, as of this morning, I don't even have a place to live in L.A."

"Why's that?" I asked, breathless.

"Dad's moving into the guesthouse, and even though he and I had a heart-to-heart, I sure as hell am not living with him."

"You and your dad talked?"

"Sort of. It was a start at least. Someone showed me that shoving a door closed and trying to forget it was there every time you walked past it wasn't quite the same as not giving it energy or time or space."

My heart filled to overflowing. That he thought that I could have shown him anything after everything he'd shown me. I smiled at him, and he smiled back. His eyes were summer storm clouds as he watched me process everything he was telling me.

"You've had a really big week," I told him.

He nodded.

Even being this revised Mia that I was, there was a thought that flirted at the back of my head near the closet where Good Girl Mia was hiding. But instead of keeping it inside like I would have in my past, I just said it. "What if you regret it?"

"Your man, philosopher Ed, is quite right. When all the fans are gone, and no one remembers my name, and you're seventy, and I've lost all my hair, the only thing that will matter is that I can fall in love with you all over again every day. That's the only thing I'd regret. Not being able to do that."

"You realize how insane you sound after knowing me for only three weeks," I said, trying for sassy Mia even though my heart was beating like it was its own percussion section.

"Mysterious ways, right? I kind of like that Ed song. He wrote it about us."

"He doesn't even know us."

"Every word. Us."

"Moron—" He cut me off with a kiss. A kiss that told me to shut up. A kiss that told me just to hang on to this moment with this gorgeous BB who had somehow found a way to love me in the same way that I loved him. This man who was trying to make our stars align in a way that would become a new reality for both of us.

"Little Bird, Miss Mia, will you come stay and play house with me forever?"

My heart stopped. Painful air trying to get back in my lungs like I'd taken my drop in the cave all over again. Even though he was serious, and I wanted to scream, "*YES!*" I didn't.

"I'll think about it," I teased back instead.

"Sassy. Miss Mia being full of sass." He grinned. "I'm going to have to force your hand by telling your parents you've agreed to marry me."

"I didn't agree to marry you. You didn't even ask me that."

"You're right. I didn't. But I will. Soon."

"No one will believe you're serious if you do."

"I think they will," he said, and he looked out the windows to where my mama was looking at us through the sliding glass doors as she sat talking to Lonnie and Daddy. She looked happy. And God, it had been a long time since I'd seen Mama really happy.

"Believe me, someday in the not too distant future, you are going to be Mrs. Mia Waters," he said, twining his fingers through mine and pulling me with him toward the slider.

"Who says I'm gonna be Mia Waters?"

"No cleft-chinned babies, and now you won't take my name? You really are going to be the death of me."

"But it'll be a good death."

We paused at the door. He kissed me again, regardless of the fact that my parents and his goofy friend were probably watching us. It made my entire body melt into the typical gooey puddle that his every touch and kiss did.

"I love you, Little Bird."

"I love you too, moron."

And then we went out the door to face my parents, his best friend, and our possible future.

Do you feel sad to leave these characters behind? I soooo miss them that occasionally I do random things to give me a few more minutes with them. For example, you can see how Mia and Derek are doing in the future when you download the *EPIC bonus epilogue* for the entire *My Life as An Album series* for FREE when you sign up for my newsletter:

https://BookHip.com/WZVAFM

Are you enjoying the *My Life as an Album series*? I really, really hope so. Do you think you might want more? You can get the entire *4 book box set* with over 2100 pages of southern charm on Amazon (and FREE in Kindle Unlimited): https://amzn.to/3aEHEgS

Annnddd, guess what? With the ebook box set, you get an exclusive short from Blake to Cam entitled *THIS LIFE WITH CAM*. I was so flippin' excited to write this little story in Blake's perspective.

Want to read more about the broken, trash artist Seth and the love he's hoping will come back to him? Do you want to see how he redeems himself?

You get his HEA story in *MY LIFE AS A ROCK ALBUM* which is available now as part of the box set or by itself on Amazon (and Free in Kindle Unlimited):

OR just keep reading here for the first few chapters.

My Life as a Rock Album
Chapter One
Letter One

ALWAYS

"When you say your prayers,
Try to understand,
I've made mistakes,
I'm just a man."
-Bon Jovi, Ingram, & Stanfill

Dear Bella,

I watched you walk away today. You went through security without looking back. I wanted to bust something. I wanted a drink. I wanted you.

You went away because I'm an asshole. I know you say that isn't it. But if that wasn't at least partially true, you'd still be here, or I'd be there with you…we wouldn't be a country apart. Reality is, I can't keep anything good in my life for long.

I almost bought a ticket and followed you through security. When I got to the ticket counter, your beautiful face flashed through my mind. It wasn't your adoring face that I saw. It was your pissed one. Because I knew that if I followed you now, it would only look like I was trying to possess you again. As if I didn't trust you to love me and go. As if I didn't trust you to eventually come home.

I realized the truth standing there. I don't trust you'll come back. Because there is still a messed up part of me that is too used to being tossed away. It's a piece of me that I thought I'd thrown out like the garbage it was a long time ago.

But I should know better than anyone how garbage can come back to life. Don't I weld fragmented pieces together every day? And this garbage, this jagged, bitter piece inside me needs to be mended together so when you come back, as you say you will, you'll find someone soldered together with gold instead of cheap ass glue.

So that you can have someone who deserves you.

I can't let you go completely though, Bella. So, instead of crossing the line you told me not to cross by flying across this godforsaken country, or beating your family into a pulp trying to get your new number, I'm just going to write to you. I don't know if you'll even read the letters. And if you do, I can't promise they'll be pretty. But hopefully my words will be good enough for you to understand something important. To understand that where I belong is next to you and where you belong is next to me, and that's all that matters. None of the other things that you worry about are important. Just us.

Bon Jovi isn't someone that you'd expect me to listen to. But his words sometimes feel like the story of our life. So today I'll use his words to convey to you what I mean. "I will love you forever and always." When you think of our memories, both the loving ones you cherish as well as the ones that made you want to say goodbye, I hope you'll be able to forgive me for making the mistakes I've made as the man I am becomes the man you deserve.

I'll just leave you with one more thought. It's something I wrote when I was a screwed up kid with a screwed up life. Because it's that dumbass kid who's making it difficult to just let you walk away without a fight. Without fighting to keep that wish that finally came true from disappearing all together.

I ache,

I can't cry.

I hurt,

I can't let go.

I wish,

I can't obtain.

- Seth Carmen

Chapter Two
PJ After Letter One

Blind Love
"No one said this would be easy,
But no one said it'd be this hard."
-Bon Jovi

Pj opens the letter from Seth with trepidation. Just his greeting, Dear Bella, makes tears well and her stomach turn. He'd rarely called her PJ. He'd always called her beautiful. His Bella. It makes her ache.

She'd moved almost three thousand miles away from him on purpose. It wasn't just to attend grad school. Although that was what she told him and everyone else in her life.

She'd walked away because she'd been drowning.

She'd been lost in a wave of Seth.

She'd been lost in her own past and her own mistakes.

She'd moved to New York so she could breathe.

And she is doing all of that, breathing and living and going to school. She's even going out some with Haley and Mina. She's enjoying her life and her classes.

It's why she's waited two days before opening his letter. She was unsure about how much of the intensity that was Seth would pour from its pages. She hadn't given him her new number for that reason. Because she'd known he couldn't resist calling and demanding that she answer, and she'd known she couldn't resist answering and being pulled back in.

So, as a compromise, she'd given him her address instead. She'd assumed that a letter would be safer. That she could read a letter and set it aside without feeling the need to respond. And if she was being honest, she hadn't thought he'd write. Seth was always a man of few words and letters seemed like more words than he was capable of.

She hadn't counted on his need for her to counter his lack of communication skills.

As soon as she reads the letter, it brings her back to him and everything that happened in the crazy three and a half months they were together. Just as she knew it would.

What she hadn't expected was to be filled with longing. Longing to wrap her arms around his muscled torso. Longing to reassure the man with the broken kid inside of him that she did in fact still love him. Had loved him from the beginning even though she hadn't been good at showing it. Longing to feel beautiful, adored, and safe as she always did when she was with him.

But…that longing. All of those feelings. They're exactly why she left. There's more to her than longing. There's more to her than being Seth's whole world.

She needs to do this for her. She needs to do this for him. She needs to do this for them.

She puts his letter in a box she hasn't unpacked because there's no room to do so in the crammed apartment. Then she shuts the door and leaves the stinky walk-up she shares with her friends. She catches the subway, hoping that today will be the day that she feels like she's caught up to herself again. Hoping she'll catch up to the girl that's been missing since she was thirteen.

Chapter Three
Letter Two

BED OF ROSES

"I want to lay you down on a bed of roses.
For tonight I'll sleep on a bed of nails."
-Bon Jovi

Dear Bella,

I tried to start this letter a thousand times now. There's a damn room full of balled up paper to prove it. The truth is, I didn't know what to write. Should I try to tell you that I see where we went wrong? That I see where I went wrong? Or should I just beg you to come home?

Part of our problem was that there was so much going on in this thick skull of mine that I couldn't express. Things embedded into me from my past that caused me to react the way I did. But it's also why I loved you the way I did. The way I do. So, I can't believe it's all bad.

But I don't want to write to you about my messed up past. So, the next best thing is to start at the beginning of us. To try to tell you now the things I should have told you then.

When I met you, I was sleeping on a bed of nails. A bed of my own making. Even though I thought I was living in the now and making my life into something my abuela would have been proud of, I was really living as if I didn't deserve anything more. Living as if solitude and art was enough.

The first time I saw you, I thought you were her. That's the reality. I understand you hate that, but I can't stop it from being true. Even though it wasn't true for more than a few seconds, in that moment, she is what I saw when I saw you. I did a double take and my heart stopped, forgetting to pump blood. Forgetting to send air through my lungs while I locked my gaze on a mess of chestnut curls.

359

I was standing with Locke and Dylan Waters who were in in deep discussion about me. About my art. It became a droning in my ear that receded into the background once I'd seen her…you…and suddenly I couldn't shake my body out of its frozen position enough to listen or care. I was stuck in a sudden flight to Tennessee thinking, How is she here?

Locke is the only manager who will put up with my bad attitude, but even he narrowed his eyes at me when I didn't respond to Dylan's question. For one second, I thought he'd snap his fingers in my face, and you know that would have ended with him up against a wall, and me without a manager.

I stepped around Locke to try to see her again, you again. But she was gone, and my brain went into panic mode. My breath was aching to get out of me and yet I still couldn't exhale.

Then I caught another glimpse of a purple dress. Cam had always liked purple. I turned cold eyes to Locke and tossed out, "Text me later."

Before he could think to try to stop me, I strode away with a single-minded purpose. Find her. Find Cam.

When I turned the corner around the waterfall mountain that I'd created when I was a dumbass kid in Tennessee, I caught her staring up at the peacock at the top. It was a bird in flight, and I'd always imagined her as a bird. You couldn't keep Cam down.

My breath finally returned in sharp, jagged movements as if my heart had been removed and then shoved back into my chest. I imagined the surprise that would be in her gray eyes when I eased up next to her. I was sure that it would be followed quickly by her shit-eating grin.

"Ms. Swayne?" I said, hoping I sounded as badass as she used to believe I was. But I was really scared shitless, so I couldn't look down yet. I was worried I'd see the pity that had been in her eyes the last time I'd seen her. When she was wrapped protectively in a muscled arm that hadn't belonged to me.

So, when the voice that returned mine was a breathless volley, it shattered all my hopes into a million pieces. Like I'd once shattered a gilded cage with a glass bird inside it which was supposed to be her.

"Pardon me?"

It was your voice. And even at the time, in the middle of my tortured disappointment, I registered how sweet it was. It was light and melodic, but it wasn't the gravely, energetic one I heard in my dreams.

I looked down at you with what my abuela used to call my devil eyes. I know it. You know it. When I did, I still caught some Cam in you. You weren't a doppelgänger, but something like a wavy reflection. Your eyes weren't gray, but shimmered with a hint of silvery mica that meant they would change colors with what you wore. That they'd change like the sky changed at sunset.

I realized then, as I hadn't from the brief glimpse of you, that there wasn't any way that you were tall enough to be Cam. Cam almost met me eye to eye when we were together, and even though I'd continued to grow once I'd left her, you were way too small. You barely reached my shoulder. At least a foot shorter than my six-two.

You've always accused me of being frustratingly vague when I speak. It's so I won't be brutally cruel instead. At that moment, with the disappointment radiating off of me because you weren't what I had lost and thought I needed, I could only curse and storm away. I'm sorry now that I hurt you.

It took me all of five strides to be staring down at the liquor table. I could feel the thirst. Before that day, it had been a long time since I'd actively had to stop myself from pouring a drink. It had been five and a half years since I'd stopped. And there'd only been one time I'd slipped since then. Only one before you. But seeing you and not her…that letdown…it was enough to make me thirstier than I'd been since my mom died.

When you tapped my arm, I continued to be the bastard I'd always been and ignored you because I was battling for control. Battling to come back from the edge of that loss of Cam all over again.

"Look, jackass, you mind telling me what that was all about?" that combination of your melodious voice and your harsh words dragged my attention away from the alcohol and my loss.

And in those few seconds, you changed my life.

I looked down at you and was caught in a whole different way. A way that had nothing to do with Cam and everything to do with you. You looked close to my age, but also looked way more innocent. Like life hadn't squashed you yet. I know that's not true now, but at the time, that first impression was of angelic goodness.

Yet, even under that sweetness, I could sense you holding yourself together with something stronger. Like you were more steel than sugar. You were so many contradictions rolled into one that I couldn't keep my eyes from devouring you.

Your face was all fine bones and heart shapes, but your body seemed all lean muscle. Your huge anime eyes were flashing at me with a bit of lightning instead of halos while your thick, curly hair had a life of its own that you hadn't bothered to control even though everything else about you screamed self-control. There were hints of Cam in you, it was what had drawn me, but from that moment on, I swear to my abuela's God, Bella, you never reminded me of her again.

As my eyes continued to take you in, you seemed to get more and more irate. And that's what did it. I couldn't help but smile at you then. My very best smile. The smile I reserved for getting what I wanted. A smile I hadn't used in so long it almost tore my cheeks apart to use it. But it got the reaction I needed because the lightning in those enormous eyes swallowed by dark lashes faded just a little.

I wanted to smooth out those ruffles of you a hint more, so I drawled in my Southern accent that I'd never fully acquired in my short stay in Tennessee, "Sorry, darlin', thought you were someone else."

But you, this tiny, fairylike creature in front of me, were not taking my apology or my sexy smile. You put your hand on your hip, daring me to try again. And you continued to flip my entire world as you cast your spell. I'm not sure what you used—Pixie dust, magic, you name it—but I was gone.

"I heard you were an arrogant jerk, who was more likely to try to get my dress off than talk to me, but being an asshole can be a story too, right?"

Your boldness made me chuckle. Your outraged tone and the sassy jut of your hip in that flirty dress were still full of contradictions. You made my head spin with new images of jewels and stone and ceramic.

You didn't seem to appreciate my laugh and I tried to tame it. When you turned to flounce away, I couldn't let you. Not yet, so I took two steps and caught your arm.

"Wait," I said, trying hard not to grin, which only made you angrier, or perhaps it was my hand on your elbow. Your face turned as pink as your shoes as you jerked your arm from me.

"Mr. Carmen, I'd advise you to stop while you're ahead."

"Shit. If this is ahead, I might as well go all in." I pulled you to me and kissed your full lips. The moment our mouths touched, desire hit me like a wave onto a cliff.

You stiffened with shock before you relaxed into me, and you astonished me yet again by darting a tongue that tasted like bubblegum against my lips. I graciously responded by opening my mouth and engaging in some tongue tangling of my own. Just as you'd hit me in the pit of my belly with a craving no one else could quench, you shoved me and backed away with a strength that continued to rock my world.

I staggered and reached for you at the same time. But you escaped.

"Tell Locke he won't be happy with my post." And you stormed away into the night.

As the gallery door clanged shut behind you, all I thought in succession was: Damn, I don't even know her name and Shit, Locke does, and he'll be pissed.

As I turned back to the table of booze and food, I no longer had any desire to drink from the sparkling glasses. Instead, I wanted a pack of Bubblicious.

♫ ♫ ♫

I dreamt of bubblegum that night and woke up with the smell in my nose and the taste on my tongue. It reminded me of my mom and the packs of Bubblicious she used to sneak to me when my shit-for-brains dad didn't know. It reminded me of the taste of you.

The sun was barely chasing away the light fog layer when I left the house for a run on the beach. I was dripping sweat when I got back because I'd pressed myself to go farther than normal in an attempt to push you from my senses.

You never asked me why I run. Maybe you just inherently understood that it was a way for me to burn off my excess anger and restlessness. It was my shrink from back when I was at LaGuardia High in New York that told me I needed to find something physical to get me off the alcohol and anger train I'd been on for most of my life. That's when boxing at John's with Mac and running had become my thing.

We haven't talked about Mac much. Or my shrink. Or my social worker, Marisella, who helped me get where I am now. But I don't want to talk about them at this moment either. Maybe later. In another letter. Right now, I just want to tell you about how you had already changed everything in my life with one conversation and one kiss.

As I headed up the steps from the sand, my cell phone rang and I inwardly groaned. Only one person called me regularly—Locke. Even Mac didn't call; he'd just text. Even now, after you, I only have six numbers on my phone. What does that say about a person, Bella? Nothing good. But I guess six is better than the three that were there before you.

"What?" I groused.

"Seth!" Locke's tone was both exasperated and exhausted.

I sat down on the steps as the waves crashed against the misty shoreline. "It went well last night," I said snarkily, knowing Locke didn't feel the same way.

"You would, asshole!" Locke barked.

In that moment, I lost track of the salty air and the tang of seaweed. Instead, I was surrounded once more with the sweet taste of you. You had already buried yourself into my senses.

Impatient with my silence, Locke continued his lecture. "You blew off Dylan Waters. Hollywood's A-list director and producer. Do you know how many doors he could open for you? And to top it off, you insulted and assaulted PJ? After I begged her to come write a fluff article about you in her OC blog because you need all the softening you can get."

I snickered, as images of your full lips and chestnut hair filled my mind. The best thing was I hadn't even had to ask for your name, Locke had just handed it over: PJ.

"Do. Not. Chuckle." Locke warned.

"Next time, warn me which fairies in purple dresses you don't want me to kiss."

Locke puffed air into the phone. "I've told her you'll apologize."

"She kissed me back," I said.

"That's not what it says in her blog."

"Of course it doesn't," I said with a grin. A grin I was still trying to reacquaint myself with after years of not using it. "You've set something up for me to see her then?"

And if I was thirteen instead of almost twenty-five years old, I might have crossed my fingers.

"I'm not a pimp, Seth. It isn't a date."

"Okay."

"Ten o'clock. The Green Room. And I better not hear about anything happening more than a brilliant apology."

"I promise. I'll keep my hands and lips to myself."

Locke slammed the phone down in response while my heart pounded furiously in anticipation. In happiness. Both feelings I'd come to forget in recent years.

Three hours later, I walked into The Green Room. Locke knew about my eating habits which was why he picked that restaurant—completely organic, locally sourced. At least eating right is a healthy addiction instead of a life-ending one. But I'm learning that addiction is still addiction no matter if it's healthy or not.

I had a tiny gift bag in my hand, so small it could fit a ring box in it. What would you say now if I brought you a bag that small? At the time, I didn't think about it being jewelry-sized. Now I think about it all the time. I want to give you another bag like that, and I'm still hoping that one day you'll let me.

I sought you out at the tables tucked into a room full of palm trees and beach umbrellas. When I found you, there was no Cam in you anymore. Not an ounce. You were this brilliant, shimmery vision that I couldn't get out of my head.

You had your hair pulled up into that loose bun you always wear. Your thick lashes were almost visible from the door as you looked down at the menu in front of you. You were wearing a royal blue top that sat just off your tan, toned shoulders and accented just how lean you were. It did things to me, Bella, things that made me think I needed a trip to the bathroom before sitting down next to you. But you looked up just then with eyes that had turned the color of your top, and I was drawn to you instead.

I put my hand up as the hostess tried to stop me from seating myself, and I saw your mouth tighten at my movement. The young girl huffed at me, but I just continued to the table where you sat.

Easing into the booth, I put the bag on the seat, and my feet tangled up with yours underneath the table. It wasn't intentional. You probably don't believe that now when I can't stop touching you. But the interaction made me tingle and tense in ways I hadn't felt in a long time. Sensing it too, you pulled your legs away. I was disappointed, but not put off.

"Are you always surly and rude?" you asked with a glance at the hostess I'd offended.

I shrugged. As you can attest, I am pretty much always a rude bastard.

"I'm not sure why I'm here then. Seems what I wrote is correct." You were trying to be tough, but even then, when I didn't know you, I could tell you were more nervous than anything else. It was in the way your hands twisted the cloth napkin in your lap. I stretched out a little more, elbows behind me on the back of the booth, and eyed you slowly again. I wanted to see your reaction.

You looked away with a flush on your cheeks that I found adorable. But I wasn't sure if it was in embarrassment at my assessment or in embarrassment at your own thoughts. Either way, it was a turn on. Most girls nowadays don't get embarrassed over shit.

"Locke said I was to apologize," I told you as I picked up the menu, looked it over, and tossed it aside. I was trying to be nonchalant, when really what I wanted to do was slide over to your side of the booth and determine if you still tasted the same as you had last night.

"So, you don't truly want to apologize, but you're being told you should. For your career?" Your eyes flashed angrily.

I grinned. "Nah. I just don't believe in apologizing for a helluva good kiss."

You looked down and turned an even deeper shade of pink which made me long to run my fingers over your cheeks. You were almost a red, white, and blue flag with your red face, blue top, and tight white skirt that ended mid-thigh, showing off a pair of gorgeous legs.

"You make an assumption that it was good," you snapped.

"Your tongue was in my mouth of its own accord," I teased.

My humor turned to panic when you drew in a sharp breath, threw your twisted napkin on the table, and stood. You had your hand on your hip again as you stared down at me. Well, it was really across because you're so tiny. Fucking adorable. Fucking feisty Tinker Bell chiming at me.

"This was a waste of time. I'm done doing Locke favors."

You turned to walk away, but I needed you to stay more than I'd ever needed anything in my life. I wasn't sure if I should tick you off more or grovel to make this happen. One thing was sure, I wasn't thrilled at the idea of you doing any kind of favors for Locke.

"So this was a favor. For Locke."

I leaned forward, bolting my hands on the table so that I wouldn't physically drag you back. Thank God my innuendo stilled you before I did something I would have regretted.

"Don't make it sound like that." You crossed your arms over your chest as if to protect yourself from my stare. But Bella, you'll never be able to escape my stare. Shit. See. Right there. I can recognize it when I do it, but I can't promise I'll ever really be able to stop.

"They were your words," I prodded at you because pissing you off had at least gotten you to stay.

"God. It's not like that...." You were blushing again at my innuendo. Your pink cheeks killed me all over again.

"Damn you're beautiful when you blush." It just escaped. I hadn't meant to say anything. You turned to go again. I thought maybe you were uncomfortable with my compliment but now that I know you better, I know you were running. From me.

"I apologize," I said and my words halted you once more. "I apologize for calling you beautiful. I apologize for seeing a beautiful woman and kissing her. I apologize for thinking you were someone else and getting my heart trampled all over again."

The confession surprised me as much as you. But it succeeded in making you turn back to me instead of walking away. You stared and I held my breath. Unsure if you'd fly away or come back to roost.

"So...you were kissing me because I reminded you of someone else?"

At least I'd piqued your interest, and I knew instantly it would be a good thing. But I'm also not stupid. I understand women don't want to be compared to other women. You can say all you want about what happened later, but even my dumbass brain got it.

"Yes and no."

"You're frustratingly vague, Mr. Carmen." It was the first time you told me that, but it wouldn't be the last.

"It's Seth. Mr. Carmen is my shit-for-brains father. And I'm not trying to be vague, I'm trying to apologize. It isn't something I'm very good at."

"Because you're a cocky bastard."

"Well, yes. Most of the time."

"And you try to get women to sleep with you with a cheesy Southern accent."

"Now, to be fair darlin', the accent is partially earned." I let the Southern drawl out in all its glory.

"You're from the Bronx!" Your eyes flashed and somehow I wasn't surprised that you knew this about me. You seemed like the kind of person who did their homework before an assignment. And I'd been just that: an assignment.

"Some of the time," I said, shrugging.

But I had succeeded in getting you to sit down, so my body relaxed slightly.

The waitress came over, smiling in a way which said she'd be happy to give me a lap dance if I winked at her, but believe it or not, I didn't register it then. I didn't register it until you told me you'd noticed. She took our order and left.

"So." You waved at the waitress. "Is that why you think you can be such a jerk?"

"Sorry?"

"Because women usually throw themselves at you?" You seemed offended on behalf of the entire female race, and I grinned again. I liked that I'd made you jealous. You were. Don't deny it. Just remember what you did later, when the check came.

"Don't grin at me that way," you said, brushing an invisible speck from your skirt. "I'm not most women."

I chuckled and leaned toward you. "But I did get tongue."

You chose to ignore me, but I saw the truth of how you felt in your smooth cheeks that I ached to touch. But I also knew you wouldn't react well if I did. Most likely, you'd bolt like the fillies on Abuelo's ranch used to when I got near them.

To prevent you from running, I took up the little bag I'd brought with me and put it on your placemat. "It's not a bribe. I don't want a retraction. To be honest, I didn't even read what you wrote, but it's increased traffic on my site, so think of this as a thank you gift instead."

You looked as exasperated as Locke had sounded when he called back later and told me that hits on our site were up. He'd still insisted that I apologize with a tone that I didn't quite understand. At that time, I didn't care. I'd just wanted to see you again. If doing what Locke asked was the way to do that, it suited me just fine.

You stared at me and the bag.

"Go ahead. Open it," I prompted as my stomach clenched, hoping you'd like it.

You seemed torn between wanting to throw the bag at me and wanting to see what was in it. Lucky for me, your natural curiosity won out. You pulled out the metal and glass dewdrop ornament that I'd made. Inside was a tiny jewel encrusted fairy. I couldn't keep my lips from twitching in satisfaction when I heard your intake of breath.

"You are talented," you whispered, rubbing the dewy shape gently.

"Yes I am."

You squinted your eyes at me like you wanted to call me on my bullshit, but the food showed up and prevented you from saying something you couldn't take back.

I dug into my omelet with gusto, and I was relieved to see you had ordered real food and not half-assed chick scraps that a lot of women order.

We ate in a silence that somehow wasn't awkward when it should have been when we hardly knew each other. Instead, it felt… expectant. Did you feel it too?

When the bill came, it had the waitress's number written on it with a heart. I didn't pay attention to it, but I definitely didn't bother to hide it as I reached into my wallet. I certainly wasn't going to call her. Once upon a time, maybe I would have. I usually liked women who went after what they wanted. But at that moment, I only had one kind of woman in my head, and she was sitting across from me.

Do you remember what you did? You grabbed the receipt and pulled out your purple pen with that big flower stuck on it. Yet another perplexing paradox because when was the last time you saw a grown woman with a flower pen? You grabbed the receipt, not to argue over paying, but to furiously scribble on it.

I put down the cash and picked up the bill. You had written, If you hadn't flirted with my boyfriend, your tip would have been better.

I couldn't help but laugh. It was a huge, spontaneous laugh that I hadn't let out in so long, that it startled me as much as it startled you. It caused you to scramble out of the booth, but this time I scrambled out with you. When I looked down at your tiny frame, all I thought was, Strength. Not to be underestimated, followed by, Shit, I hope I don't break her.

"So, girlfriend, where to next?" I smirked at you, pleased to see that crazy, beautiful color stain your cheeks again. It was all I could do to not pull your full lips right up to me and kiss you once more.

"I'm going to work," you said, turning to float out the door. I followed, eyes drawn to your perfect little butt in your tight skirt.

Outside, you turned to me, sliding on your sunglasses in the shattering Southern California sunshine. My panic was reasserting itself. I know you didn't see it because I'd been trained early in my life not to show emotion. Emotion was a weakness exploited by my dad. And I guess by my mom too, just in a different way.

"It was a pleasure not being apologized to, Mr. Carmen." You stuck your hand out.

There was no way in hell I was letting you slip away. Not then. Just like I'm trying to not let you slip away now. "It's Seth. Would you like to see my studio?"

I breathed it out before I thought it through. I never had anyone to my place. Only Locke and Becca had ever set foot in it. And you know Becca is just there to clean and mother me. I'd never had another woman there. At the school studios, I'd had to deal with people invading my thoughts and space. At my home, I didn't want any of those fucking complications. But I'd made the offer to you and meant it with every fiber in my being. When you hesitated, I knew I had a chance.

"I'm not changing my story," you said, as if to prove you had the upper hand.

"Okay."

"I'm not writing anything else about you."

"Okay."

"I can't do it now."

"Okay."

You squinted your eyes at me like you were just dying to berate me once more.

"You're very frustrating," you said for not the first time.

"I've heard that before," I teased you.

"I am interested in your studio. How you do what you do. That's it."

It was more than that, we both knew it, but I let it slide. "Give me your phone, I'll put in my details and you can show up when you want," I said, trying to sound nonchalant. Trying not to pick you up and carry you over to my motorcycle and take you home.

You handed me your phone. I typed in my address and my personal cell number which, again, I never did. I know you thought different. You believed I had a long line of women, but that wasn't me. It hadn't been me since Tennessee.

"What if I show up while you're...busy?" You couldn't meet my eyes. This made me realize you were thinking about all the ways I might be busy and that made me hopeful. I gave you my best unused grin.

"Contrary to popular belief, I rarely entertain at home." My words that were meant to reassure, backfired and made you more uncomfortable.

"Your studio is at your house?" you gulped.

I nodded. But it made me think that maybe, just maybe, I was having as much of an impact on you as you were on me.

Our hands brushed accidentally as I gave you back your phone. Your skin was smooth and soft against mine that was calloused from working with metal and glass and wood for so many years. That smooth feeling, along with your sweet scent and your strength and your tininess, hit me all at once. The urge to capture all of it in textures of silk and steel overtook me. My mind twirled with more imagery. I'd been on imagery overload since I'd seen you last night.

You stared down at where my hand touched yours as if the touch had jarred you too. You started to walk away. I was still panicking.

"I have to warn you," I called out and gave you another smile when you looked back over your shoulder. "If you don't call, I will be hunting you down."

You raised an eyebrow at me but just walked away. I don't think you realized how serious I was. I wasn't letting you walk away for long.

Maybe you liked that about me at first. My all-consuming focus. But I don't know when to back off, and so it forced a wedge between us that I couldn't remove even with love. Even now, I can't remove the wedge, but I can't let go either.

All I can say is that I'm learning. A big cat changing its stripes. After all, you're getting a letter instead of me on your doorstep. I know now, just as I could tell then, that you weren't one to be claimed. You were too goddamn independent. But you also need to understand, Bella, that possession, it's a mutual thing. Because you own me as well. Every fucking piece of me, and I won't ever be the same until you're back home.

Keep reading

My Life as a Rock Album

(my life as an album series vol. III)

http://bit.ly/MLAARAamz

EEK! I'm so excited to announce that **this holiday**, I'm releasing a collection of short stories based on the children from the original cast of the album series: MY LIFE AS A HOLIDAY ALBUM. Everyone might be smiling at the start of the holiday, but the secrets that have come home with them might just ruin the entire season for them all! Will they be able to keep them hidden, or will they be exposed with a bang that isn't at all the New Year's Eve fireworks that are planned? It's available on Amazon at special pre-order price that'll last until it releases on December 7th, 2020.

https://amzn.to/330h3bm

Second Message from the Author

Thanks again for reading my story. At the beginning of the book, if you even saw it, I told you I didn't want to fill your head with my social media sites, accolades, and other books because I wanted you to read the story and then decide how you felt about me and my words. I hope that you loved Mia and Derek's journey. I hope their strength and resiliency along with my mix of songs and story burned a memory into your soul that you will think of every time you hear one of these songs from now on.

We talk about music, books, and just what it takes to get us through this crazy thing called life a lot in my Facebook reader's group, LJ's Music & Stories. If you do nothing else with the links here, I hope you join that group. I hope that we can help *YOU* through your life in some small way.

I know that there are thousands (really millions) of books for you to choose from, so I am honored that you chose to spend a portion of your life with one of my book babies. If you liked it, I'd be honored if you took another moment (or two) to write a review on Amazon, Goodreads, or BookBub, but even more than that, I hope you enjoyed it enough to tell a friend about it.

I truly hope to hear from you!

Love Your New Friend,

LJ EVANS

♫ *where music & stories collide* ♫

 About the Book

Thank you for reading my book! As I said in my "Message From the Author," I hope you enjoyed reading it and would consider writing a review. Thank you from the bottom of my heart for doing this extra step.

About the medical topics in this book, I want to humbly apologize in advance to the doctors of the world and those living with one kidney. I know that my book is not completely accurate in all of its depictions of what can happen in these cases, but I beg pardon in that the book was written as a work of fiction intended to entertain and touch the spirit, and not necessarily depict reality.

Regarding the PlayBabe Mansion and Hugo Brantly, some may feel that this is a slight at Hugh Hefner. But it was not my intention to do so. Instead, I intended it to be a much more twisted fictional world than Hugh's ever was, and as such, has been created for the purposes of this story only.

One final note: spelunking (caving) is an adventurous sport. All of the caves mentioned here are real caverns that you can visit and traverse. I have added to their complexity in some cases, all in the hopes of making this novel more interesting.

Thank you for your understanding.

Acknowledgements

The list of people who have helped me with this novel is certainly not small, and I hope that I do not forget.

Thank you to my husband for not only understanding my need to write, even though it takes up so much of our lives, but also for being my number one fan and cheering section. To my daughter, who has started down her own creative path and yet always has time to help me with mine. I can only say I want your adventures to be bigger and better than any I have had. My big sister is the reason these books are out in the world, because she pushed and shoved until I had the courage to make it happen. Love you, Bug. Thank you to my parents who never told me that writing was a waste of time, but instead told me that creating a world that others could see was a gift.

I am grateful for all my beta readers who made this story better in ways I couldn't always see. Thank you to Megan McKeever, who I found through Reedsy and who helped me shape this story into something that my readers deserved. To Autumn Gantz at WordSmith Publicity, your help in launching this book out into the world has helped me in so many unexpected ways. To Jenn Lockwood…I can only say THANK GOD you found me!

Thank you to my author friends who have helped me improve my writing and guided me through this publishing world, especially Kelsey Kingsley, Katy Ames, Lauren Helms, and all the ladies of Romancing the Manuscript. Finally, thank you to Ed Sheeran for writing the beautiful words in the beautiful songs that inspired me.

 About the Author

Award winning author, LJ Evans, lives in the California Central Valley with her husband, daughter, and the terrors called cats. She's been writing, almost as a compulsion, since she was a little girl and will often pull the car over to write when a song lyric strikes her. While she currently spends her days teaching 1st grade in a local public school, she spends her free time reading and writing, as well as binge-watching original shows like *The Crown, Victoria, Veronica Mars,* and *Stranger Things.*

If you ask her the one thing she won't do, it's pretty much anything that involves dirt—sports, gardening, or otherwise. But she loves to write about all of those things, and her first published heroine was pretty much involved with dirt on a daily basis, which is exactly why LJ loves fiction novels—the characters can be everything you're not and still make their way into your heart.

Her debut novel, *MY LIFE AS A COUNTRY ALBUM,* was the Independent Author Network's 2017 YA Book of the Year. For more information about books by LJ, check out any of these sites:

Website: https://www.ljevansbooks.com/

Bookbub: http://bit.ly/LJEvansBB

Amazon: http://bit.ly/LJEvans

Goodreads: http://bit.ly/LJEonGRs

Facebook: https://facebook.com/ljevansbooks

Instagram: https://instagram.com/ljevansbooks

Pinterest: https://pinterest.com/ljevansbooks

Twitter: https://twitter.com/ljevansbooks

 Books by Lj

My Life as an Album Series

My Life as a Country Album — April 2017

My Life as a Pop Album — January 2018

My Life as a Rock Album — June 2018

My Life as a Mixtape — November 2018

My Life as an Album Series Box Set – March 2020

My Life as a Holiday Album – December 2020

Standalone - Anchor Novels

Guarded Dreams — Eli & Ava, May 2019

Forged by Sacrifice — Mac & Georgie, October 2019

Avenged by Love — Truck & Jersey, April 2020

Damaged Desires — Dani & Nash, October 2020

Branded by Love — Brady O'Neil, coming in 2021

Unmasked Dreams — Violet & Dawson, coming in 2021

Coming in Some Dream World When L J Has Enough Time

Untitled, magical realism — contemporary romance

Down on 4th – Historical Fiction

Untitled, Ezra and Elara duet —urban fantasy

Made in the USA
Las Vegas, NV
25 October 2020

10240298R30229